MOTHER OCEAN
FATHER NATION

MOTHER OCEAN FATHER NATION

a novel

NISHANT BATSHA

ecco
An Imprint of HarperCollinsPublishers

Thank you to: Jamie Carr, Sara Birmingham, and the Ecco team; Ryaan Ahmed, Fatima Al Shamsi, Samuel Daly, Emily Hamilton, Kate Hawley, Lydia Kiesling, Stephen Narain, Joyce Carol Oates, Kanishk Tharoor, Rosie Welsh, the Paul & Daisy Soros Fellowship, the Headlands Center for the Arts, and the Prelinger Library. —N.B.

HarperCollins books may be purchased for educational, business, or sales promotional use. For information, please email the Special Markets Department at SPsales@harpercollins.com.

Ecco® and HarperCollins® are trademarks of HarperCollins Publishers.

FIRST EDITION

Design by Angela Boutin
Illustrations by Vivian Rowe

Library of Congress Cataloging-in-Publication Data has been applied for.

ISBN 978-0-06-321178-0

22 23 24 25 26 LSC 10 9 8 7 6 5 4 3 2 1

For Emily

PART ONE

1

"IT IS ANNOUNCED with sadness that Ram Maharaj was burnt alive last night," the broadcast began. Bhumi looked at the red digits on her clock radio with a sense of dread. The South Pacific University had set a curfew earlier that day, and now Bhumi felt paralyzed by the evening's emptiness. A few hours ago she had tried to find Aarti, but she wasn't in her dorm room, so Bhumi had gone back to lying on her bed, finding patterns in the foam of her drop ceiling. And now, at seven in the evening, a bell sounded three times on FM 93.6, Radio Zindagi.

Radio Zindagi was the background hum of daily life for the island's Indian community. Growing up, Bhumi's weekday evenings were organized by the seven o'clock bells, and looking back, it was one of the few things they did together as a family. Bhumi; her brother, Jaipal; and their parents gathered around to listen to the radio announcer, elegant in his use of pure Hindi (as opposed to the patois of the street). He would begin the program by announcing, "Dukh ke saath suchit kiya jata hai ki . . ." *It is announced with sadness that . . .* Then he would list the quotidian deaths of Indians throughout the country: farmers, schoolteachers, and politicians alike were featured when they passed on. After every name and summary of a life and family left behind, Bhumi saw her parents nod their heads, as if, on this small island, they knew each and every person the announcer mentioned.

Brevity was the single rule of broadcast. The announcements tended to focus on the sum total of a life's accomplishments: He was a good husband, she a dutiful mother. Loved by all. Survived by so-and-so.

For the past few days, instead of reading out the obituaries, the announcer had been talking about the missing: the ones the government said had been arrested yet couldn't be found in any jail. It was a jarring change, but everything had all gone to shit in the past couple weeks. Bhumi had arrived on the South Pacific University campus in August 1983 and now, at the end of her second year, it had all begun to fall apart.

Tonight, the announcer didn't even list the names of the missing.

"Ram Maharaj was killed when one woman and three men—all native—emerged from their late-night Bible reading and went to his store on Hamilton Street. He was burnt alive!"

The group of native Christians had been looking to make a point about who this country belonged to, the announcer explained. After the General had seized power, the leaders of various churches had put out a joint statement in the newspaper appealing for peace and empathy.

While the leaders said one thing, their parishioners wanted something else: to restore godliness by cleansing the country of vulagi. *Foreigners.* The first thing to do was to destroy vulagi businesses.

Bhumi shuddered at this and, for the first time, felt a fear for her family. She was cut off from them: the university was a four-hour bus ride from Sugar City.

Witnesses reported that the prayer group had brought supplies. First, they lit their scrap wood wrapped in a kerosene-soaked rag.

Then, they threw their stones through the shop's front window, shattering its panes into long knives. In silent unison, they threw their torches through the broken window.

The torches had, by a grotesque chance, landed adjacent to three tin drums of coconut oil. The heat of the flames had caused one of the drums to explode, leaving its accelerant smeared across the shop floor.

From there, it took only a few minutes for the entire shop to surrender to the flames. As it did, they dropped to their knees, clasped their hands together, bowed their heads, and prayed.

Unbeknownst to the four, the shop's owner had decided to buck the rules and stay in his store overnight. He had heard rumors of looting during the curfew and thought he could shoo off any criminals if he slept near the back of his store, cricket bat in hand.

"Where was the fire engine?" the announcer pleaded. "Some say it took its time to get there, that they knew it was an Indian in trouble, and this did not merit haste. Some others say that it arrived in time to save Ram Maharaj, but the firemen simply joined the crowd and watched him die."

In her mind's eye, Bhumi could hear it, smell it, taste the sour odor of burning hair as the man staggered out the door. The announcer said that his cries were so loud, they masked the rumble of the burning building behind him. He whimpered and shrieked and fell to the ground, where he writhed until he didn't.

"They are not satisfied with taking the government!" The announcer's exclamation was so loud it crackled in her radio's speakers. "Sisters and brothers! Leave if you can. Our fathers and grandmothers left their homes to come here. Now, it's our time."

Bhumi felt a shiver grow from her shoulders to her spine. She raced into the dorm's empty common room. The women's dormitory for scholarship recipients housed only four students, and Bhumi rarely ever saw the other three. In a far corner of that spartan space was a black rotary phone placed next to an old corduroy chair she'd often sunk into between classes.

That was before.

For the past year, Bhumi had been swept up into the wave of activity on campus surrounding the lead-up to the national election. Students held debates, the youth parties leafleted, and finally, in April, a left-leaning Labor government led by a handful of Indians won the election. Most of them were young, too, only a few years out of university themselves. It was Bhumi's first election, and when Aarti joined the Labor Party's campus wing, Bhumi listened to her arguments with rapt attention. "We can join together, native and Indian, and build this country better," Aarti had earnestly told Bhumi. Bhumi felt a sense of infectious possibility: she cast her ballot down the party line.

Almost immediately after the ballots were counted and the results were certified, the protests started.

One week after the election, two thousand native-borns had gathered in the streets of downtown Vilimaji—just across the street from the Parliament building—to protest that the Indian minority, numbering about 10 percent of the country, had gained too much power in the government. The protestors scrawled phrases onto cardboard signs: "We Hate This Vulagi Government" and "Left Party Worst in World." The remaining signless protestors thrust their fists balled tight in the air. The protest was only a half-hour walk from campus, yet Bhumi dared not get close. Growing up, Bhumi had heard cautionary tales from family and friends about how the natives could get jungli—*wild*. This was one of those times. It was safest to keep a distance. She, along with the handful of other women in her scholarship-program dormitory, watched the news report on the television in the common room in silence. She could make out more signs in the crowd: "Our God, Our Land," "Vulagi go home to India."

The country had been us-versus-them since the Empire brought the Indians to till the island's cane fields. In a fit of benevolent paternalism, the Empire had sought to protect the old ways of native society, and in doing so, forced them to stay in their villages under the power of their chiefs. The colony needed to make money, so the Empire took tens of thousands of Indians and moved them here, to labor in sugar fields. In time, they were considered to have enough of a work ethic to be placed right in the middle of a clear hierarchy: White, Indian, Native.

Kept separate, the natives saw the Indians as permanent foreigners. The only time the two groups truly interacted was in the marketplace, where Indians seemed to own it all. Bhumi herself had no interest in India, even though she spoke Hindi and was called Indian. Most of her Indian countrymen had never seen the place their ancestors had left a hundred years ago. If Bhumi was to leave, it was going to be for shores that offered her a measure of opportunity: a country with a respectable graduate program in botanical biology—the dream.

In the post-election chaos came one claiming he alone could bring peace back to the island. He, beholden to no one, could stop the protests and find a solution amenable to all. Bhumi had never heard of the General—without any wars or real foes to speak of, armies in a country as small as hers were made available for parades, national pride, and not much else. At first he showed up to the protests, making grand speeches to rapt audiences of native-borns. Perhaps it was the old colonial mentality: when someone with a gun and a uniform began to talk, the country stopped to listen. Then he took a few meetings with the Indians who controlled the businesses across the island. And finally, he had a meeting with the prime minister.

Then came the day he appeared on television. He arrived in the Parliament building with four men behind him, jet-black semiautomatic rifles slung from their shoulders, index fingers just inches away from the triggers.

For Bhumi, politics had always been distant: men in the capital argued, and potbellied fathers in Sugar City repeated these arguments over drinks. At university, it was Aarti's interest, and Bhumi loved the way her friend leaned into political conversations with a look of focus, a fast-paced clip to her words. But as the General explained his takeover—he kept calling it a transition to peace—Bhumi felt a true sense of the powerlessness that came with the political. For the first time, this country felt like a strange place to her. She, and the rest of her people, were being singled out for who they were. She hoped the General knew what to do to make things right again.

This sense of being off balance remained as she settled into the worn cushion and dialed home, all the way across the island in Sugar City.

"JAIPAL!" SHE EXCLAIMED. HER NERVOUS ENERGY SENT HER FOOT tapping, and she drew a finger along the scar on her neck. "How is work? Did the hotel have to shut down because of the curfew?" she asked.

"The hotel is still open, but last night there were only five tourists by eleven. Five! They told me to close early." Bhumi could feel the lazy saunter of her brother's voice working itself into the frenzied pace of worry.

"They're thinking of closing the gift shop," Jaipal went on.

"Hey," Bhumi said. "Remember, the sea turtle is out there, somewhere . . ." Perhaps what had always reassured her as a child could be turned back onto him.

"You forgot. The chickens came first." She could hear him slowing down again.

"And finally there's the man selling coconuts."

"And if they're all there, we're good."

Bhumi laughed. She couldn't remember the last time they had snuck down to the water and seen all three signs, but the memories of those comforting moments were the frayed twine that bound them close, and what she could use to bring him back.

"How's Papa and the shop?" Bhumi asked.

"It's probably fine, Papa too. No curfew here. They'll kill us in the capital. They probably won't kill us over here, in front of the goras," he said, a macabre joke. He cleared his throat and began again. "Listen, the campus is safe, right? You're not running a shop, don't worry. Remember what the General said: 'The transition to peace is not anti-Indian.' He'll bring it all back. They're saying he might call new elections soon. Those people went jungli, and they killed that guy. It was a one-time thing. It won't happen again."

Bhumi wanted to believe her brother, but the country's newfound peace had been filled with arrests of opposition political leaders and trade unionists.

"Ma wants to talk to you," Jaipal said. "Just stay away from everything, okay? Just stay on campus until this all ends."

Bhumi rolled her eyes at her brother's worry. She hated being told what to do, even if the command was made of hopes and best wishes. "I'll be fine, Jaipal," she muttered. She heard the muffled sounds of a receiver being handed over.

"Beti? Is everything all right? Are you okay?" her mother asked in rapid-fire succession. "You know, yesterday, I saw one of the jungli kill a snake on the side of the road. Who can kill a snake? A dead snake only brings misfortune."

"Ma, I don't believe in that," Bhumi said, her patience already running thin with her mother's nearly infinite supply of superstitions.

"You should take this seriously," her mother said. "Our beliefs will keep you safe from them. Have you thought about leaving?"

"Maybe after exams finish in a month. I wanted to stay to work with a professor in his lab. If that is canceled, I'll come back to Sugar City."

Bhumi could hear her mother take a deep breath. In the silence that followed, the call filled with static and the low murmur of a conversation from crossed wires somewhere in the distance.

"You'll be safer away from here. It's been so long since I've seen you. What can this country offer someone like you? This is your chance: America? Australia? I want you to be safe, beti. I want to see your success." She paused, letting out a small cough. "My mother—your Nani—had to leave India to come here. It's written in your blood—you can leave too."

"Come on, Ma," Bhumi said, shaking off the gravity of her mother's warning. "I have two years left for my studies. And there's you and Jaipal," she said, purposefully omitting her father. "I can't leave you behind."

"God willing, this won't get worse. Just promise me you will think about it?"

Bhumi let out a long sigh. "Okay, Ma. Aarti said that her papa says this will all get better soon. Just a little bit of time and we'll be back to normal."

"I hope he's right. Jeeti raho, beti. Stay safe."

2

JAIPAL WAS ALREADY ten minutes late, and it would take another fifteen minutes to get to the hotel—he breathed a sigh of relief when he saw one lone taxi operating at the taxi stand up the road from home. Portia couldn't be mad, he reasoned to himself, not on a day like today. Not after what had happened with the greengrocer in the capital. Plus, she was always the one who let slip dates and times ("I'm not here to remember what time it is," she would snap).

For now, everything seemed to be normal on this side of the island. All that happened in the capital may as well have been in another world. His sister's world. He hoped she took his advice and was staying put.

As far as he knew, the bar at the hotel was still going to be open later that night. He hadn't heard anything otherwise from management.

Salim leaned out his window and waved at Jaipal from the taxi stand. Salim's younger brother, Maqbool, had been one of Jaipal's close friends back in school.

"Going to the hotel?" Salim asked as Jaipal settled into the backseat.

"Same as always," Jaipal said.

The taxi first cut through downtown Sugar City. From the window, he watched the storefronts pass by on Queen's Street: Brij's Books, Shiv's Travel Agency, Red Fort Restaurant. Above the stores were apartments. From below, all he could see were small balconies. Sometimes, he could catch sight of a bit of a man or woman: a head, a neck, a wisp of smoke floating upward from the red-hot glow of a cigarette.

Onward and north, toward the airport, the city began to thin out, only to be replaced by fields of green sugarcane, still young and looking like thick leaves of elephant grass. They passed the airport, which had the feel of a bunker: a long concrete building fronted by acres and acres of empty blacktop for parking.

"You think the goras will leave?" Salim asked from the front seat.

"I'm not smart enough to predict shit like that. The guys who own the hotels, they supported the General," Jaipal said, pointing outside. "They're as loaded as the rich gora families in Australia."

They had reached the island's resort belt. There were four large beachfront hotels, each of them five or so stories tall and facing the water, their glass windows gleaming with the setting sun. In between these multinational chains were smaller hotels and resorts, each owned by the same Indian families who owned everything else.

Because the Indians were right in the middle of the Empire's racial pyramid, they had been given a chance to make some petty cash: small shops here and there. The moment the Empire left, the families who had a knack for business married into one another, and the rich were born. They were like an octopus: one arm in real estate, another in hotels, another in supermarkets, another in the buses.

"These rich-ass Indians didn't want to pay the higher taxes and shit that the Labor people were talking about," Jaipal continued, "but they probably wouldn't say yes to the General if he would fuck them over. What do you think?"

"That's a good point. And yeah, nobody is setting goras on fire. They just relax at the hotels. For them, everything feels the same here in Sugar City. It's not like the government is stupid enough to let anything happen to them," Salim said. Sugar City had the country's only international airport and was near all the country's tourist resorts. It seemed like the General wanted to at least try to keep the violence of the coup from white eyes.

"Back in their home," Salim continued, "they don't have a General either. They don't have someone saying, 'This is a takeover. Ladies and gentlemen, this is a takeover and a transition to peace.'" Salim imitated the General's bass voice.

Jaipal laughed for real this time at Salim's uncanny impersonation. He had had no idea who the General was before the protests began, but now he was everywhere and everything, a voice that played on repeat in everyone's mind.

"I've heard the soldiers are trying to get free rides in the taxis," Salim continued. "I'll never give those chutiyas a ride." He winked at Jaipal in the rearview mirror.

"What are you saying?" Jaipal asked, staring back at Salim. "You don't know what can happen if you make them angry. Promise me you won't do anything stupid."

"Okay, okay, okay," Salim said, taking his hands off the wheel to lift them in mock defeat. "You sound like a gora. Scared of the madarchods out there. Maqbool's scared too. He's trying to find a way for us to stay good if things get worse, you know?" He let out a little chuckle and met Jaipal's eyes through the mirror.

"Maqbool will be Maqbool, you know him. Always looking for some new way to make money," Jaipal said.

Salim clicked his tongue. "He's right, you know? Make some money just in case. I already took three gora families to the airport today."

"Maybe some will leave. Not all of them. Some of them like it here, eh? They don't want to go," Jaipal said.

"They might like your drinks, Jaipal, but I don't think they'll stay just because you make them so nice!" Salim said with a hearty laugh.

Jaipal smiled at the joke, but the reference to staying and going shot right through to what he had been fixated upon before he had got into the taxi.

The taxi turned left into one of those smaller hotels, the Ambassador. After a year and a half of working there, Jaipal could see the place for what it was: an illusion. The owners spent their money on landscaping, exterior paint, and advertising campaigns in travel magazines across Australia. It was like his father. The man could make polite small talk with those who came by his store, yet anyone who spent more than fifteen minutes with him recognized that he was made up of drafty windows, expired canned goods, and broken tiles.

He checked his watch. Nearly an hour after he was supposed to meet Portia. An hour and a half before his shift began.

"See you later, Salim," Jaipal said as the taxi dropped him off behind the main building: three gleaming white floors with windows facing the azure Pacific. The sun had dipped itself below the horizon. The west was still bathed in a thin orange light, while the east was slowly fading from a bruised blue into night. The goras were probably making their way from the beach to the bar right now. It was May, right on the cusp of winter, when the temperature dropped enough for coughs and blocked noses: more appropriate weather for a long-sleeved shirt. Still, tourist money lived year-round in cold places, and this country was a forever-summer vacation. High season at the hotel.

He avoided walking into the building and went straight to the beachfront bures, thatch-roofed cottages rented out as vacation rentals.

Bure number four: situated down a paved pathway to the left of the main building, furthest away from the hotel amenities so that no noise of the children playing in the pool, none of the bass from the bar's music, and none of the chitter-chatter from the restaurant could bother the resident.

Jaipal knocked. No one answered. He knocked again. Before long, he was swaying up and down on the balls of his feet.

After a few long minutes, a familiar voice yelled up from the path. "How long have you been waiting?" she asked.

"Not that long," Jaipal said. He turned and watched her walk down, fumbling through her small canvas purse for her key.

She leaned in for a kiss. Her lips tasted faintly of salt, as if she had been walking up and down the beach, taking a pause every now and then to swim. Thinking, she called it. Figuring out her ideas. It's what she was here for—to get her novel finished and sent to her editor, though mostly he saw her put that off for her poetry.

"My God, Jay," she started again. She was talking fast now, the words pouring out of her like shots of liquor: the bar, the televisions, the news, everything that had happened to the greengrocer. She pulled out a half-filled bottle of gin and a quarter-empty plastic bottle of tonic from the minifridge and began to pour. She handed him a paper cup. He took a sip and winced. If he ever mixed a drink this generous, management would fire him on the spot for wasting the alcohol. They knew that it didn't matter if he watered down the drinks—the goras all acted drunk regardless.

"I'm sorry I'm late," Jaipal said.

"Late for what? Your shift doesn't start for hours, does it?"

"Starts at half nine, same as always."

"How can you even think about work?" To Jaipal, she sounded strangely free of fear. Almost excited, already forming this into a story she could tell her friends back home.

"Did you hear the actual broadcast on the radio?" she started again. "We were talking about it at the bar. A radio broadcast for obituaries! Telling everyone that a greengrocer was burnt alive! You couldn't even make this up if you tried. It's better than most fiction!"

It was easy to hear what she was saying: *We* talked, and it seemed like this *we* was talking fast and talking together. This *we* nodded to one another. This *we* thought of how this couldn't happen back at home.

"It's fine," Jaipal lied as she slipped out of her jeans. "All that stuff is happening in the capital. What's going on here? Nothing, as always. The government won't let anything happen to where all the tourists are." He put his hand on the back of her thigh, her skin feeling warm to the touch. He pulled lightly, enough to encourage her to sit next to him.

He leaned in for a kiss. He closed his eyes and the world receded to its proper place.

"You believe that?" she asked, pulling away.

"Of course," he said, taking off his black-polo work shirt. She ran her fingers along the line of his shoulder blade, and he shivered from the coldness of her hands.

"Well, I believe you then," she said. She ran her hand over his crotch and he couldn't help but let out a little grunt of appreciation. He kneeled on the ground in front of the bed and began to kiss her, starting from the knees and working upward, knowing exactly where to stop.

The moon hung low outside the window, casting the room in the same alabaster light falling upon the Pacific. He closed his eyes again and the sound of the sea was a soft whisper of appreciation.

His hands sank into the softness of the mattress. He felt a bead of sweat slide down his neck, forming a trail down his back. Jay, Jay, Jay, he heard. She wrapped her arms around him and drew him close enough that he could smell the sea in her hair. He was a bird in flight, skimming the water, until finally—stillness. He turned over and lay on his back.

She lit a cigarette and took a drag before handing it over to him. The anxiety crept, even in the repose that came in the after.

His nerves began anew with one remaining question. "Did anyone say they were leaving?"

"Some of them are checking out early, taking the next flight out."

He leaned over to kiss her forehead, her nose, her chin, wanting his lips to touch it all, before she, like everyone else before her, was lost to him. He took another drag.

"Are you leaving?"

"No. Of course not."

Jaipal breathed a sigh of relief. "I've got to get to my shift. See you soon?"

"Sure," she said with a wink. "Maybe I'll even come back to the bar. Come tomorrow? I need more from you."

He leaned in for another kiss. He never meant to love any of the strangers he met here, but today he was scared. He wanted to make her promise, right then and there, that their everyday habit would never cease. Such promises weren't his to ask for.

3

JAIPAL'S SHIFT AT the hotel bar passed with a dreary boredom punctuated by only two mai tais, four piña coladas, and a single rum and Coca-Cola. Salim's prediction was coming true: the goras were going to leave. No one wanted to waste time at the bar anymore.

The outdoor dance floor should have been crowded with guests, and the canopy area that shielded the bar from the elements should have been overflowing with partiers from other hotels. It should have been a night of control: managing the queue with a nod and a flash of his eyes to the one he wanted to serve next. A night when he rolled his eyes at the rude (manners never came along on vacation) and called the bouncer to tame the rowdy. Instead, the breeze wandered straight through the dance floor. The air felt dry without the usual humid mass of dancers.

"I can't believe it, Qantas is fleecing us, you'd think they'd treat us better," said one of the few sunburned men around the bar, all white stubble and thinning hair. He leaned his forehead forward into the palm of his hand, his elbows propped up.

"Not like this fucking country's falling apart," another replied.

"I mean, I love it here, but it's a goddamn banana republic," said the third. "No offense, Jay." ("Jaipal" had been too difficult for them—his name tag simply read "Jay.")

Jaipal flashed an obsequious smile. Over time, their pleasures had become his script, one memorized from performance night after night. The direction was simple: their problems ended where the bar began.

"You're not leaving yet," Jaipal said, with a playful banter. "Why not have another drink?"

The three let out a hoglike whoop and smacked their hands against the sticky wood of the bar. For the first few weeks on the job, Jaipal had apprenticed in the day, working his way up to shadowing another bartender at night. Since then, he had settled into the muscle memory of mixing a mai tai. He had learned that he could mirror what the garrulous and sunburned man wanted to see, reflect the giddiness of the university student on holiday, entertain the tipsy foreigner on the other side of the counter. He could size each of them up with a glance, watch the way they moved their hands as they waited (deep into pockets, running them through their hair, drumming fingers). He could measure them as quickly and efficiently as a shot poured in a glass, and as soon as he did, he could down them in one go. And they loved it, seeing themselves in another, buying a drink from the big smiling brown man at the bar, someone they seemed to love in a way that they could never quite put a finger on, but Jaipal knew. They loved him in the same way they loved the idea of themselves.

"Jay, you've got your priorities in the right order," the first one yelled. It wasn't enough this time. None of them ordered another drink.

His shift usually ended at midnight. Tonight, the bar had completely emptied out by eleven. Management had sent the DJ home around ten thirty but still made Jaipal stand watch behind the bar, in case a lone guest came down for a drink. He spent the last half hour of his shift cleaning and stacking chairs while he listened to the playlist repeating itself on Radio Zindagi.

When he left the hotel, there were no taxis idling near the front driveway, where there typically sat a line five or six deep. The night air had become stifling, and the streetscape was darkened, like all the streetlights had been put on a dimmer. He could barely see out to the main road. Jaipal doubled back to the rear of the hotel and went straight through the back door to the room behind the front desk.

"No taxis, Ali?" he asked the clerk.

"Haven't seen one yet, Jaipal," Ali said with a yawn.

Jaipal asked to use the phone, and the clerk gave a lackadaisical nod in reply. He called the number for Raj's taxis—or whatever the company was called now. The line dialed, dialed, kept on ringing, until finally the connection dropped with a wordless click.

Jaipal put down the receiver and shrugged at Ali. "I tried earlier, for a guest who wanted to go to the airport. Same thing," Ali said. "You could try Kishore's taxis."

Jaipal felt a vague feeling of guilt and betrayal in doing so. His family had always supported Raj's company. The dispatcher on the other end of the line said a taxi would arrive at the hotel within five minutes.

"Be careful," the dispatcher added.

"Me? Why?"

The dispatcher on the other end of the line paused—Jaipal could imagine him looking over his shoulder. "You'll hear," was all he said before hanging up.

On the way home to Newtown, a fashionable middle-class neighborhood two miles south of central Sugar City, the silence in the car was amplified by the fact that the driver had turned the radio off. Jaipal kept his eyes trained out the window the entire time, scanning the exterior lights of the homes off the road, each one of them an island afloat in a pool of darkness.

When he finally arrived at his own home, the night's stillness had been replaced with a blanketing humidity that left a thin layer of sweat all over him. It seemed like everything was in hiding—there were no animal sounds, not even the oom-oom-oom from the frogmouths, but Jaipal could hear the electric buzz coming from the streetlamps.

Jaipal's house sat high upon four whitewashed concrete pillars to prevent the rains from flooding in. Underneath the house were a few white plastic chairs and a table where his father would read the paper, sip his glasses of whiskey, and nurse whatever grievance he held for the day. His mother never spent much time down there—her territory was the front balcony. While humming some tune from Radio Zindagi, she would hang the laundry and put out into a sunbeam a large canning jar to make sun pickle.

The house sat behind a checkered-iron gate, painted black every six months to fight the continued encroachment of rust. The gate was framed by the delicate white and sunrise-yellow flowers of a frangipani and the droopy leaves of a banana tree. There too was a ten-foot-tall coconut palm planted to the right of the stairs. It had the habit of dropping a green coconut as someone sat outside, a signal, perhaps, that it wanted to join in the conversations, whispers, and shouts that were passed between the people of its house.

The Morris Minor was missing, taken somewhere by his father. Around when his sister was born, his father had managed to procure the car from a white family who left at the first sign of the island's independence—a time when most people in the country couldn't afford to buy a car. The Minor's green color was one of lawns, prestige, and status—their pride.

Jaipal felt a few drops begin to fall, cold on his face. A single light illuminated the room behind the balcony's doors. Coming home sometimes meant a quiet and darkened house, fingers feeling for the correct key on his keychain, fumbling to find the lock in the door. More often these days, coming home meant his mother sitting up at the dinner table with a magazine, her eyes scanning the words on the page in a blank way that Jaipal recognized: something inside of her had been made broken yet again.

He walked to the dinner table to kiss his mother on the top of her head.

"Did you hear?" she asked as his lips left her hair, soft and smelling faintly of coconut oil, her voice cracking underneath some invisible burden.

"No," Jaipal said, stifling a yawn. "Something with Papa?"

The rain began to tap against the window, an uninvited guest.

"No, not that," she replied, turning her body in the chair. "They killed Salim."

"What?" he asked, feeling like he had been slapped awake. "That couldn't have happened. I saw him just before my shift." The rain was coming down hard now, a constant thrumming that shot from the sky straight into his head.

"He had two soldiers in his car. They shot him and left him on the side of the road, maybe three, four kilometers from the airport. They say they're not letting the news talk about it. Poor Maqbool," she said, her voice quivering with sadness. "And Nazeema! She lost her husband so young, now this. How can this happen here, in our city?" His mother looked stooped over, the weight of the news bearing down on her shoulders, curving her body in exhaustion.

He grabbed the chair next to his mother and slumped into it, his fingers trembling. "I just saw him," he muttered. It was an infection. The greengrocer in the capital, and now Salim in his taxi. The General made promises like any another kaamchor liar, Jaipal thought, using the derogatory nickname Indians often used for the native-borns. *Lazy*. Nothing good was going to come from this transition to peace. Jaipal felt like a fool for believing it.

Jaipal and Salim had never been that close. Only Jaipal's trips in the backseat connected them now. He still thought of Salim mainly as Maqbool's older brother, cooler by dint of his age. Jaipal and Maqbool had been friends since primary school: he was the son of a widowed mother who took night shifts at the cannery, far enough in social status and religion from Jaipal's family to ensure that the two would have never crossed paths outside of school. Jaipal had been surprised when his father was fine with letting a Muslim into their home.

"I don't care what they call themselves. To me, they're all still Hindu," he had barked when Jaipal once asked about this curious fact. "Some cousins Catholic, some uncles Hindu, Nazeema a Muslim. They're poor, Jaipal, they're just chasing whatever God might give them some money. Lose one of her boys and I bet I'll see her at the Buddhist temple down the road," he had said with a laugh.

Maqbool had sat in the back of class with Jaipal—one of the kids looking out the window, cracking jokes, running through the litany of excuses for homework never turned in. Jaipal lived in the shadow of Maqbool's larger-than-life personality, and when they were younger, before Maqbool got caught up in his own ventures, they were inseparable, with Jaipal not more than a few steps behind him. Salim had been a kind of schoolyard insurance: someone to look after them, and someone they hung off of to try to seem older and more popular.

Jaipal's mother handed him a mug of chai. When he wrapped his hands around the ceramic, fingers linked through the handle, he felt none of its warmth seeping into his fingers. He thought of Salim's posturing during their last taxi ride. He could imagine his mouthing off at the soldiers, acting the tough guy, and then all at once it was too late. Jaipal had warned him. His warning had been small talk from the backseat, conversation quickly forgotten. Jaipal's head began to throb.

"I'm worried," his mother said. "I saw bats outside the kitchen window. They want to come into our house and bring their misfortune into our lives."

He looked at her and felt like he could scream. The whole world turned on superstitions for her—a bat in the house could only mean death or a departure. She was right to be worried, though. He wanted to tell her that he was scared: What did a death on this side of the island mean for the goras? What did it mean for the rest of them?

"Bhumi needs to leave," his mother said, switching back from superstition to reality.

Anxiety trembled out of his mother's comment, bringing the life back into him: his hands stung hot, red, raw. He took them off the mug and rubbed them against the coarse fabric of his trousers.

"She'll keep herself safe," he said. "She always has her head buried in a book. Nothing safer than that, right?" Jaipal didn't know whether to believe that anymore. "Do you know if she's coming home soon?"

"Home? She needs someplace better than what this can give her. She needs—" His mother cut herself off midsentence.

"I know you didn't want to tell me, and that's fine, and I know it's a secret, but . . ." Jaipal paused.

"What do you know?" she asked, the forced blankness of her face telegraphing her worry. Jaipal could always tell when she was keeping her emotions at bay.

"I know about your plans for Bhumi. I heard you speaking on the phone. I don't think Papa knows," he added to reassure her.

"Oh, my son," she said, reaching out to place her hand on his. "I never have to worry about you, do I?"

He had always been the boy waiting for his mother, waiting for the ruffle of his hair and the words that could sweep over it all: Everything is all right. Don't you worry, don't you worry. And yet, growing older in this house meant learning that the one whose love he sought was filled with so many emotional hollows needing to be filled. He was the one left to take care of her.

"She's so clever. That's my ma in her," his mother continued. "Her good-for-nothing father's side gives her nothing but trouble. She never realizes when she needs help. You always seem to know what to do," she added.

"I do?"

"You've always been so strong, figuring everything out on your own. When you left the store, you found your new job in a week? Less? It's not easy. You always had your little routines as a child: waking yourself up, taking the bus to school, taking the bus to the shop—once you had a habit, you went along."

A gust of wind rattled at the windows. Perhaps this was what family was: a brief coming together, a sharing of stories that left him feeling like a stranger in his own life, dazed at the memories presented back to him.

THE NEXT DAY, HE LEFT FOR THE HOTEL AROUND NOON. A FEW fronds and broken branches lined the footpath from the night's storm.

As he walked, he wondered what Salim had looked like as he died. Jaipal had gone his entire life without thinking about death: never once had he wondered what it looked like to bleed out or what it felt like to drown in the waiting sea. Death was now becoming the chatter and the noise of daily life.

Taking a taxi felt like a bet he didn't want to take. All the soldiers had come from the country's poorest families, and Jaipal knew that they wanted to take from the Indians what they thought belonged to them: money, goods, a life. He trudged to one of the places the soldiers had left behind in their newfound wealth: the bus stop.

The bus route followed the long way up to the hotel, passing right in front of the City and Colony Sugar Refinery before it continued on its way to the airport, and from there onward to the hotels.

When he was a child in primary school, Jaipal would leave his friends behind to board a bus the color of a raw guava to go to his father's shop. Being in transit had given him a small cocoon of freedom. In this space, he learned how to settle inside the overheard conversations of others, leaving himself and entering into something anew. The lives of strangers were the hammer, and he the sheet of metal transformed again and again.

"My wife said they've raised the price of milk. She needs more money," a tired-looking man said, rubbing his hands one over the other.

"You know what my wife does?" replied the man's seatmate, his eyes squinting out the window. "She mixes the milk with some water. She thinks I don't notice. I let her do it. Saves money."

The workers, all in their matching uniforms of baby-blue jumpsuits, disembarked in front of the refinery, windowless, big, gray, and square, with a smokestack that pierced the sky. The City and Colony Sugar Refinery's rhythm defined the seasons in Sugar City. In August and September, it belched out brown smoke as thick as syrup. Flecks of this smoke coated everything downwind (all the hotels were kept upwind), and all that was left out long enough was blessed by its soot. The smoke even changed the smell of the city. As cane was transformed to sugar, every corner of the city was haunted with the odor of burning caramel.

Outside of the main sugar-production season, the refinery distilled case upon case of Resolution Rum. On a day when the wind blew in gently off the ocean, the city smelled like his father, like an old alcoholic left out to dry in the sun.

When he finally pulled the bell chain in front of the Ambassador, he saw the bellhop Ali waiting at the stop on the opposite side of the road. Ali called to him, waving his arms to get his attention. Jaipal waved back, only to be told that the bar was closed and that he should go to the front desk.

Inside at the desk sat the heavyset Arjun, whose round and bearded face flecked with gray was always a delight to those checking into the hotel.

"Ah, Jaipal!" he said with his typical bombast.

"Ali told me the bar is closed?"

Arjun dithered with his answer as he pulled out an envelope from under the counter. He straightened his back a bit, and the light plumpness of his cheeks seemed to replace itself with the dull gravity of formality. "Management told me that given what's happening, they're closing it until, you know, things get a little calmer."

"Are they firing me? I know that sometimes I pour my drinks a little too nicely, but I wouldn't think that they would—"

"No, no, no," Arjun said, cutting him off. "Not at all. They said everyone is on a, what did they say . . ." He looked down at the table, his eyes searching for the word. "That's it! They called it a hiatus."

"A hiatus?"

"A temporary leave of absence, I believe."

"Arjun, am I being fired?"

"We all are, Jaipal," he sighed. "They made me give everyone the news. Who knows how long they'll keep me here. There aren't any goras checking in. They'll probably tell me the same tomorrow. Here's your final pay." Jaipal took the envelope from Arjun's hand, the few bills feeling light in his hand. "Everything is in God's hands now."

Jaipal left the hotel lobby with a nervous feeling like he was somehow watching himself wash away, trash floating on the river Majivu and into the sea. It felt like that time his father had kicked him out of the shop. To be fired conjured up all the firings that came before.

He reached bure number four and knocked, feeling nervous. The evil eye could only invite more trouble. His mother had taught him that.

"Come in!" Portia yelled.

When he opened the door, it was on the floor: a suitcase empty and wide open, clothes thrown in piles all around it. He swallowed, hard. He took a step inside and opened the minifridge. It had already been emptied.

"Wait," she said, holding up a finger. She was sitting in front of the open window at her small glass-topped rattan table, hunched over a yellow pad of paper like a letter C slumped in a chair. "Imagine you're leaving. What does the island look like from an airplane?"

"I've never been in an airplane," he said.

She twisted around in her chair and stared at him with a deeply confused look on her face. She spun her pen through her fingers. "Really? You seem so worldly. You seem like you've traveled everywhere."

"You know me, I'm just some dumb nothing," he muttered.

"I hate it when you do that. Put yourself down. You know you don't need to do that. Now, tell me, what does the island look like from an airplane?"

He closed his eyes while still standing in the open doorway, the heat of the day borne upon his back. The women and men he'd been with at the hotel had all had given him different pleasures. Most of them were built of physical desire. Portia was too. She had also shown him the pleasure of giving voice to the things that danced in his head. If he could focus on the image, the words could come together like a cobweb woven in the corner of an empty room.

Without opening his eyes, he said to her, "The airport is near the coast, and we're such a small country. Even if the plane turned and cut straight across, it probably wouldn't take more than a minute. It's like skipping a rock. The rock kisses the water, once, twice, then sinks. The seconds between those kisses. That's how big the country is. That's how much you'd see of it."

He opened his eyes and Portia was furiously scribbling down what he had said. "That's bloody brilliant. You're a genius, Jay. You should have been a poet."

He turned, finally, to close the door, and felt the same warm pat-on-the-back pride he felt every time she said that. His sister must have lived on feelings like this; it was probably what drove her to keep on with her studies, all the way to Vilimaji.

He could hear her steps behind him. The door was shut, but he didn't turn around, not yet. He felt her arms wrap around him. "I'm sorry," she said quietly.

"When are you leaving?" he asked with resignation.

"Tonight," she said. "They killed that poor man just a few kilometers down the road. The hotel is basically closing down. It just doesn't feel safe anymore."

The emotions of the day were getting all mixed up, leaving a heavy, sludgy feeling like all the colors mixed together into the one he lived: brown. He felt a snap of resentment yet didn't have the energy to argue that the poor man had a name, Salim, and he wasn't a reason to leave the country but a friend.

The first time he had seen Portia, she had smiled at him from across the bar, her teeth as white as pearls. "I never like these resort bars," she said in her posh British accent, her cheeks and forehead reddened from a day in the sun. He leaned into the conversation with an ample-wattage smile framed by the dimples in his cheeks, his top teeth set slightly askew from their light crowding. "I don't either," he said to her, "but they all tip so well." He winked, holding her gaze for three beats of a moment, before he made eye contact with the next customer.

He watched her walk out of the bar after that drink. She didn't even leave a tip. He shook his head and rolled his eyes, and mostly forgot about her until she came back right at closing, and stayed as he cleaned the bar.

She stood right at the edge of the bar's thatch awning, and he felt her eyes following his every mundane movement: from wiping down the counter to locking up the liquor. He was an old hand at this now and knew better than to make small talk—the more he kept from the strangers he wanted, the more likely it was they would hang on for another minute. She was no different. When he finished his work, he walked right up to her and it was all one movement: the kiss was immediate and unspoken, its feeling like fingers drifting down a spine.

That first night, he stayed for a while, lying in her bed, smoking cigarettes, drinking gin. Some of them liked to talk. She was one of them. She was a writer from London, and she now taught at the ANU in Canberra, and she was on sabbatical. He had no idea what that was, and she explained that it was time off from teaching where she had to keep working and finish her novel.

"I see," he said. She was a neither-this-neither-that. Many of them were like that. Separated from their spouse but not divorced. Ready to quit their job but not going to do it yet. Confessed that this was the first time they had done something like this, but their mouths told a different story.

He told her that he didn't read much. Reading had always been like fishing through his pockets for a key. Even though he had hundreds of them, not a single one ever fit into the lock.

"That's beautiful," she told him. She said she could tell that he had a natural way with words, with images, that he had a talent that could blossom if it were ever nurtured. The most frequent question she asked him was "Can I use that?" "Of course," he would reply, confused that someone could own something as flimsy as words.

In every one of his encounters with Portia (or with the others), he flew away from his own body, his own smallness of self, without ever having to leave his hometown. It took nothing to become someone, something—they had their stories, and he closed his eyes and imagined what it meant to study at Cambridge or what the streets of Canberra or Sydney looked like.

They were all lovers without a future, and none of them took interest in his past. They preferred to tell stories, versions of themselves that they were sure sounded glamorous to this bartender. Jaipal could recognize the tone of voice. He knew that they were the ones who needed convincing of their own importance.

He finally turned around from the door to face her.

"I—" He stopped himself. I what? Need you? Love you?—he didn't. And yet, he cursed what he was: a vacation hookup. She had brought him into this room, but it was always her who was going to leave it behind. He had been doing this for almost two years now, and he had spent two long months with her. He said nothing now. He felt porous, liquid, like he was rotting.

For the first time, there was none of the tenderness they had shared as lovers. With women, he tended toward slow pleasure: all rhythm and movement, none of the gaping hunger he felt with men. Today, it was an attempt to control, to keep her underneath him, even if it reduced all that was between them to simple movement: friction, back and forth, silence until everything finally built up and released—a small gasp for air, and a sense of returning to something smaller than before.

As he put on his trousers, he saw that his little white envelope from Arjun had fallen out of the pocket, meager bills peeking out from underneath the flap. He bent over to pick it up and crumpled it into his hand. He walked over to her, framing her in his mind for the last time. In one sweep of his eyes, he took in all the details: the whiteness of her breasts against the tan of her chest and arms, the mole on her right shoulder, the soft roll of the side of her belly when she leaned to one side. He kissed her, one last time.

"I promise I'll write," she said. "Be safe."

"You too," was all he said.

He left the bure and shoved the bills back into his pocket. His last paycheck, one of the few keepsakes left for him from his time at the hotel.

4

BHUMI WALKED TO her nine A.M. O-chem lecture, the morning sun barely breaking through the low clouds that dotted the sky like a moth-eaten quilt. Something felt missing from the day, but she couldn't quite place what it was, a feeling of déjà rêvé that pulled at her like an invisible leash.

The building that housed the biology and chemistry departments was brand-new, with a soaring metal roof that seemed to want to take flight. As Bhumi approached, she could see that something was wrong: all the students seemed to be milling about the quad near the front door. The occasional student would walk up to the door, pull on the handles, and walk away. Others were running, yelling, looking like they were running to safety. "It's happening!" one exclaimed over and over again in a panicked voice.

"No classes. It's all closed. Everything's canceled," a passing student said to her. She didn't even stop to turn around or speak to Bhumi.

"You'd think they would tell us," Bhumi said to herself in disbelief. "You'd think they would care." And it finally occurred to her what had been missing that morning: there had been no staff or professors walking about the campus. The campus lacked the air of adult supervision, giving the university the barren feeling that came with the end of the academic year.

When she returned to her dorm, Aarti was there, reading a bulletin tacked askew to the front door.

"What does it say?" Bhumi asked.

"'All classes canceled until further notice and students must remain on campus.'"

"This can't be good."

"It's fine. I think. We'll be fine." She was biting her nails with a far-off look in her eyes. A feeling sank right out of Bhumi: it was getting worse. Whatever had happened with the greengrocer was spreading.

THE NEXT FEW DAYS LACKED THE MOTIONS SHE HAD BUILT INTO HER university life: getting to class, meetings, office hours. Four times a day, she took a walk around campus and she thought she saw, out of the corner of her eye, students pulling their curtains ever-so-slightly aside to try to see if the outside world was as barren and boring as the inside.

A lifetime of hiding from her father and plotting the future with her mother had created deep pools of energy in Bhumi that needed an outlet. Whenever she sat, her left leg would bounce up and down on the ball of her foot. Normally, in the hours spent studying in the library with Aarti or working in the lab, this action served as both a tic as well as a much-needed kinetic release for all the potential energy stored inside of her. From the day the General had taken over, the news had seemed to get worse by the day, and now she was quarantined on campus. She had to get out. She had to blow off some steam.

Going into the city to take a break was nearly impossible: bulky men in combat fatigues with M16 rifles were stationed at all major intersections. To look more official, each checkpoint featured hastily nailed-together guard posts painted camo green.

In the half-formed gossip that spread around campus, Bhumi heard that the checkpoints did not contain a single Indian soldier. Those Indians who had managed to make their way into the military's ranks had been reassigned to what the newspapers said were training exercises in the island's mountainous interior. Rumors were beginning to spread that this wasn't a training exercise at all.

Vilimaji—a city with a skyscraper that loomed over the central business district, with a stock exchange, with a UN regional agency, with white people calling themselves expats rather than migrants— was growing accustomed to the rhythm of a curfew. For twelve hours, sundown to sunup, no one was to leave their home. In practice, "no one" was defined very particularly: Natives seemed to be able to keep their freedom of movement. Indians had to abide.

As the days passed, her walks provided less and less relief. One night, Bhumi did not hear the bell ringing thrice on the radio. The announcer wasn't there anymore. The military had taken over Radio Zindagi, and there was nothing left to distract her except for the same seven Bollywood songs on repeat. Every minute spent in her dormitory felt like being forced to listen to a leaky faucet drip into a basin filled with water. She needed something, anything, to do.

As if on cue, Aarti came through her open door.

AARTI AND BHUMI HAD BEEN RANDOMLY-ASSIGNED LAB PARTNERS IN their first-year biology course. Bhumi hated being paired off with other students, knowing full well that she was the one who would conduct the experiment with enough precision to merit a verifiable result, and that she too would write the lab report in mellifluous detail from hypothesis through conclusion. She had to share her top marks with another who sat back as she took control over and over again.

Her college social life was a hodgepodge of acquaintances she would eat with in the dining hall, the same few to go dancing with, and boys who fumbled their way through a hookup. There had been no one who struck Bhumi as fundamentally different from the Indians she had lived with in Sugar City. And yet, there had been one she had watched from afar.

It was hard to ignore Aarti's presence—she was always a radiant center of attention, ready to tell some story that everyone, even the professor, would laugh at, or otherwise listen to with rapt attention. Here was someone entirely new. Bhumi had benefited from the accoutrements of a comfortable middle-class life, but she had never before seen the ways in which the children of the rich and the powerful floated with comfort and ease through the world.

She felt a pang of nervousness cross her gut when she was assigned to work with Aarti.

She was pleased that Aarti Kumar lived up to the idea of the person she had observed. "Are you going to be a biologist?" Aarti asked after the professor paired them off. "We've had two exams. Your name is always at the top of the results list." Bhumi was surprised to hear this. She had assumed that quietly working hard at the task at hand rendered her more or less invisible to others.

"Something with botany," Bhumi replied, gently correcting her. "You need biology to understand botany."

"Why botany?" Aarti pressed on.

Bhumi paused before she answered. She wanted to come up with something that could impress someone who seemed so eloquent.

"Did you know trees outnumber people by four hundred twenty-two to one?" Bhumi asked. Aarti cocked her head to one side in interest. Bhumi felt a deep sense of pleasure at hitting the right note at the right time. "We're just a tiny speck among all this life. I want to learn from them too."

Bhumi stopped there, thinking that one bon mot was enough, but Aarti didn't say anything and seemed to be waiting for Bhumi to say more.

"Botany was never something we studied in school, you know? There was a Carnegie Library back in Sugar City. When I was younger, I would find these books and do experiments, like, what branches could I graft together? I once went around the goras at the beach to get some kelp to see how much salt it needed to survive." Bhumi let out a satisfied smile, reveling in the company of happy memories.

When she was a child, she'd spent hours in the driveway. In the evening, she waited for the cane toads to emerge so she could run a finger along their slimy backs. In the day, she explored the dirt: the weeds that were constantly emerging out of the remnants of other weeds, the flowers that bloomed, the waxy leaves of the banana tree. She dug through the slippery and loamy top layer of the soil, through the wriggling worms and rolled-up roly-polys so eager to return to the cool darkness from which they came.

"I love meeting someone that's so passionate," Aarti said enthusiastically, breaking the mumbled murmur of the class. She lowered her voice again. "I assumed that your parents forced you to study this. You know: good girl, study hard, science BA, get ready for shadi-shuda wedding bullshit. You always look so, I don't know. Serious?"

"That's my face," Bhumi said with a shrug of her shoulders. "I think people find it weird. They're always looking at me and telling me to smile, and when I look at them, they get so angry. They say the most fucked-up things."

"Whenever I hear a man say that garbage on the street, I tell them that I'll crush their balls with my fist."

Bhumi let out a laugh so loud that most of the lab section turned to see what had happened.

"How does that work out for you?" Bhumi said. Aarti responded with a smirk. "Anyway, what do you study?"

"Political science," Aarti said. "I love knowing how everything in a country works. There's nothing better than looking at a government and saying: I know that. Who knows, maybe they'll let me into Parliament," she said with a little raise of her eyebrows.

Bhumi believed her—there was something so captivating about Aarti's personality that at that moment, she thought that Aarti could easily become prime minister if she wanted. And even now, after two years of being inseparable, watching Aarti stride confidently into the dorm room, Bhumi earnestly wished that Aarti were in the General's place.

Aarti moved with the swagger that came to her when she was in a good mood. "We're going out tonight," she said.

Bhumi turned to talk to her. She was dressed in high-waisted blue jeans and a form-fitting black shirt covered in gold sequins, light reflected back to Bhumi. Aarti's hair was jet-black, save for one yellow-white stripe along the right side of her head that she'd bleached after seeing a picture of Indira Gandhi in a news magazine. "She was a fucking imperialist, but what a great look," Aarti had told Bhumi when she revealed her new style.

"What about the checkpoints?" Bhumi asked. "I don't want to end up like that fucking shop owner. We're locked in." She gritted her teeth in frustration.

"Listen, we're going to go out with a friend of mine and a couple of friends of his," Aarti said as she sat down on Bhumi's bed.

"Who?" Bhumi asked. It was the one thing she hated about Aarti's involvement in the political side of campus. Factions joined together and broke up with such regularity that Bhumi could never keep track of who was friend and who was foe.

"I drank with them last night and they're cool with the madar-chods at the checkpoints. You can't go alone. In a group, it's fine."

"Do I know these friends?" Bhumi asked as she closed her textbook. It was clear that this new friend had nothing to do with politics:

Aarti had some new boyfriend or hookup. Bhumi felt a mild annoyance at being left out of this piece of information. "Are they Indian or native?"

"You know I don't divide people like that," Aarti said, rolling her eyes again.

Bhumi twisted around in her chair. "You should. Haven't you heard the news? Our people are getting lit on fire in the street! Who knows what else is happening?"

"Fine, fine, we don't have to go out," Aarti said, holding up her hands and widening her eyes in mock deference. "Tsch, 'our people.' Didn't know you spoke like that too," she added with a mutter.

A song from *Amar Akbar Anthony* began to play on the radio and filled the spaces in their conversation. It was the tenth time Bhumi had heard the song that day. Aarti's snide comment, along with the thought of listening to the voice of Amitabh Bachchan crying out in love one more time, caused every muscle in her neck and arms to tense.

"And how did these friends of yours get through the checkpoints?"

"Baksheesh," Aarti said, shrugging. Bribes had emerged as a somewhat reliable way for Indians to get around the curfew. Natives could walk right through. Indians had to pay up.

"Not surprising," she said, a small knot of fear forming in her stomach. She thought of Ram Maharaj, of the unlucky, of burning flesh. "What about us?"

"We don't have to go," Aarti said. "Listen. Papa doesn't like me talking about him, but if we need it, there's always him."

It was true. Aarti's father had been a career civil servant and, before the coup, had risen to become assistant to the undersecretary of home affairs. The long title simply meant that he handled all internal security services while some MP took the credit for his work. It was still impressive: he was one of the few Indians who had risen in the government's ranks well before the election. Recognizing a bureaucrat's knowledge, the General had kept him in the role and even had gone so far as to mention him to a newspaper. Bhumi remembered see-ing it on the front page: "If only all Indians were like Jitendra Kumar."

Bhumi leaned back in her chair and looked up at her ceiling. There was a brown water stain that, if she squinted her eyes, looked like a mynah.

She exhaled, long and slow, before snapping forward to slap her hand down on the off button of her radio. "They've been playing this song all day."

"I can't stand it either," Aarti replied.

Outside, crickets could be heard chirping alongside the guttural voices of the cane toads. From the hallway came the sound of a toilet flushing. "So," she began, nodding, feeling the muscles in the back of her neck relax ever so slightly. "What would we have to do?"

"All we have to do is look down the entire time. Someone else deals with the baksheesh—you know, twenty-five dollars."

"Twenty-five?"

"You've got to pay to play," Aarti said, sounding like an echo of what someone else must have told her when she balked at the price.

"Each way?"

"Maybe we can get a two-for-one discount, eh?"

Bhumi rolled her eyes and laughed. "Set." Fifty dollars was worth it, if it meant a night away from boredom. All she wanted to do was to move her legs, to breathe in the cool night air—anything but lie down and stare at the cracks on her plaster wall branching out from her A6-sized map of the world. "Fine, let's go," she finally said.

"Set!" Aarti exclaimed, clapping her hands together.

"So, where are we going exactly?" she asked as she changed into an outfit for going out: acid-washed jeans, a black V-neck T-shirt, and a brown leather vest covered with fringe. She took off her glasses and cleaned a smudge off their thick lenses with the bottom of her shirt. Years of study in low lighting had rendered her vision without them more or less useless.

Bhumi drew her long black hair back into a ponytail. Everything about her was angular: her small nose, her thin lips, the scar that ran up and down on the left side of her neck. If she had learned strength of purpose from her mother, she had taken her father's skinny and stretched-thin figure.

"Oh, you know, the regular."

"The regular" could only mean Irish O'Reilly. Despite the fact that there was no longer an Irishman to be found in the entire country, Irish O'Reilly was the go-to watering hole for the students at SPU. The place wore its Irish pride on its sleeve. Bright green plastic cutouts of four-leaf clovers hung from fishing wire on either side of the bar, each caked with at least two or three years of puffy gray dust. The bar was Irish in only one other way: its special was a whiskey and cola. It didn't seem to bother anyone that both the whiskey (Jack Daniel's) and the cola (Coca-Cola) were American.

They left Bhumi's dormitory, cutting across a small field of grass wet from a recent cloudburst. Bhumi had memorized the flora after she arrived on campus: surrounding her dorm was a green lawn dotted with slender maba and vuga trees with delicate red inflorescences that looked like hairy caterpillars hanging from its branches. They walked between the cane toads bouncing about, until they finally reached the asphalt pathway that led toward the campus pedestrian gate.

There were two checkpoints between them and Irish O'Reilly: one at the pedestrian gate and another just up the street from the bar. First they had to meet their group, who were already waiting for them where the grass met pavement. They all looked vaguely familiar to Bhumi—she must have seen them in class or at Irish O'Reilly at least once.

"Are you going to tell me how you know them?" Bhumi whispered to Aarti, still annoyed that Aarti hadn't dished any of this gossip yet.

"Student Communist Union," Aarti replied at full volume, causing the three men and two women—all native—awaiting them to turn their heads. Two of them were smoking and exhaled, cigarette smoke backlit by the orange of a streetlamp.

"You're a communist now?" Bhumi asked, leaning into her friend with a whisper.

"You're not?" Aarti said, still at full volume. The cigarette smokers chuckled and exchanged knowing glances.

"Hello, love," one of the smokers said. Aarti walked up to him and in one movement they greeted each other in a dance that seemed well practiced: she stood on her toes, he placed his hand on the small of her back, and then, leaning into each other, the two kissed. Though this wasn't Aarti's first native hookup, Bhumi still had to swallow her surprise—before college, she had never once seen an interracial couple.

He looked like a paper cutout of a university revolutionary. His thin legs fit snugly into a pair of black drainpipes. His white T-shirt had faded into gray from being washed too many times with his black jeans. He wore his hair out in a mess of tightly-woven curls and let his beard grow rough and scraggly. She had seen him before, when Aarti dragged her to some event. Aarti had probably decided that it was time to get Bhumi's approval or disapproval. All Bhumi could remember about him was that he was the one who, in the debates at the student union, said that voting was bourgeois pointlessness. Aarti introduced them. His name was David.

"Nice to meet the young botanist," David said, raising his hand for a wave. "Aarti talks about you all the time. 'The smartest person I've met,' she says. Intellectuals are overrated, but did you know that agriculture was the focus of Lenin's first five-year plan?" He paused to take a drag of his cigarette. "You could have been part of the Lenin Academy of Ag Science. You're important to the revolution, you know."

Before Bhumi could decide whether to thank him or be offended, one of the women in the group cut him off in a loud whisper: "Let's go already!"

"All right, all right. So, little botanist," David said. He was about a half foot taller than her and cocked his head down to speak to her, exhaling smoke into her face as he did. "Stick to the middle of the group and always look down when we go through a checkpoint. Never give a pig a reason to oink oink." He paused to let the others in the group laugh but it seemed like they'd heard the joke far too many times. "If there are too many oinks, we have Aarti's daddy." He turned to Aarti.

"Shut up, David," Aarti hissed, punching him in the arm.

David grimaced and rubbed the spot that had been punched. He turned back to Bhumi. "All right, give me the money you brought," he said. "Do you have any extra, just in case? Pigs are always hungry." He used his thumb to push back the end of his nose and began to sniff loudly.

Bhumi turned to Aarti. They hadn't talked about extra. "Don't worry about it, love, I've got it." Aarti patted her friend's forearm. "Just buy me a drink?" Aarti handed David a few extra bills from a closed palm. Bhumi strained to catch a glimpse of their denomination.

"All right, all right, ladies, we've got our filthy money. Good? Now, they might say some nasty words. They won't touch you though. They're cowards, all of them. When the real revolution comes they'll be the first to go." He moved his index finger across his neck.

Soon, they were near the first checkpoint. Instead of the usual portly security guard who tended to fall asleep at his post at the pedestrian gate, there were now three soldiers in fatigues, each holding the same rifle she had seen in the television broadcast when the General had taken over. All three, with eyes unshifting, stood in a triangle formation and stared down the group.

The group walked slowly toward the soldiers, hands at their sides, each foot dropping in unison. At about ten yards away, they stopped. Bhumi's heart seemed like it would burst out of her chest. She looked down at the pavement, unable to muster the nerve to watch what was happening. It felt like when the air was charged with one of her father's moods and she had to tiptoe around her own house. He had been her first checkpoint, and his moods had been the law.

From the sound of footsteps, it seemed like David was approaching the commanding officer. Bhumi, with her head still down, shifted her eyes up to take a quick glance at what was happening.

The flat-faced and jackbooted officer slung his rifle over his shoulder and held out his right hand. Without speaking, David reached into his back pocket and placed the first payment onto the officer's open palm. He nodded as he counted his money, then put it in his back pocket and motioned to his soldiers with his fist. They moved aside, opening a narrow path between them.

As they turned left from campus, they began to walk along an uphill street. The road would have normally been filled with the exhaust of buses and taxis, the chatter of students walking here and there, and perhaps even the sounds of a tent revival in the distance. Tonight, it was only them, though every so often, Bhumi could have sworn that she saw furtive silhouettes in the distance.

On their left was the campus, shielded from the road by a barbed-wire fence. On their right were gated houses—split-level homes for the middle classes. Glancing at these houses, Bhumi thought of the balcony filled with her terra-cotta pots and felt a pang of homesickness in her stomach. She wondered if the stress of the coup was eating away at her father, whether it was winding him up like a spring ready to launch at her brother or poor mother. She had not seen much of them since she left for SPU, though she called her mother once a week so they could catch up on all the mundane details of each other's lives.

The only sounds from the group were the occasional strike and burst of a match being lit and the stamp underfoot of a cigarette reaching its conclusion. Again, in the distance, another checkpoint. Bhumi felt less anxiety this time and watched the happenings with her head held up. The group went through the motions once more: David as the emissary and the commanding officer as the recipient. This time, one of the soldiers behind the leader raised a flashlight above his head and shined the beam upon each face in the group, causing them to squint at the sudden brightness. When the beam hit Aarti and Bhumi's faces, he tapped his leader on the shoulder.

The leader neither turned around nor began to count the money in his palm. All he said was, "Double for them."

A nod, more money into the palm. Another fist, another parting.

"Indian whores," an underling soldier hissed as they passed through the checkpoint. His words felt like a knife sliding into Bhumi's scar. She reflexively lifted her hand up to soothe the pain. Everyone heard what the leader said. No one said a thing.

In a few moments, they reached Irish O'Reilly. It had been a month since they had been there and Bhumi couldn't help but smile at the return of a routine. Rumor had it that the owner paid off the top brass in the military so that he could so brazenly stay open during the curfew. The bar itself was nondescript: two darkened windows flanking a door. At the entrance was a bouncer who must have weighed at least twenty-five stone. He nodded at David and let them in. A wave of music and a cloud of cigarette smoke washed over them.

David Bowie called out from a jukebox tucked into a back corner.

"I hate this shit," David said.

Bhumi felt her breath loosen, and even though the air was thick with sweat and spilled beer, it all still smelled like freedom. Aarti led Bhumi between the small round tables filled with students leaning their chairs back and drinking bottles of Island Bitter. As they made their way to the bar, Bhumi noticed that they were the only two Indians in the place. Even so, each step seemed to move to the beat of the music. She let out a sigh of relief.

"Two specials," Bhumi said to the bartender, leaving her bills on the counter. They sipped their Jack Daniel's and Coca-Cola and smiled, taking in the first breaths of a free night.

"This isn't bad, eh? If you close your eyes you can pretend that there are no madarchods outside with guns," Bhumi said.

"Let's dance," Aarti said, her mind already free from soldiers and checkpoints.

The evening took on a sweet sense of mild intoxication—a feeling of floating outside of time and anxiety. The rigid organization of the military hour—eighteen, nineteen, twenty hundred hours—gave way to an evening marshaled only by a drink, a dance, a cigarette. Bhumi somehow passed the night without any man imposing his gamy body in between her and her friend. The two were shoulders and hips and arms and legs and bodies, all swaying. Bhumi felt an air enter her lungs and a sense of normalcy that did not heed the barrel of a gun.

That night felt like a flower blooming, Bhumi thought, but the only plant that came to mind was the *Amorphophallus titanum*—the corpse flower. After a growth period of up to seven years, the plant's spathe opened for a single night, using the smells of decomposition to attract its pollinators of choice: all the insects that emerged under the cover of darkness to feast upon rotting flesh.

As she tried to brush off the image, Aarti leaned in. "Want to smoke outside?" she asked, pointing toward the door. "I need some air."

"Meet you outside in a second," Bhumi said. "Going to the toilet."

As Bhumi waded through the crowd to the back of Irish O'Reilly, David, who was sitting at the bar, caught her eye and smiled. On her way back, she felt a light touch upon the shoulder. It was so soft that it could have been accidental, but still enough to bring her forward motion to a halt.

"Where are you going, botanist?" David asked. He was sitting on a bar stool and smiled again, a warm and generous smile, as his eyes moved up and down her body. He made no attempt to hide it.

She did not run away from this attention. The past few weeks had been so stifling, so shut up with fear and anxiety, that a passing flirtation—even if it was from her friend's boyfriend—seemed like an invitation to relax. The semester had been a brutal one: five lectures, two with lab sections. She had been seeing someone earlier in the year, some boy she had met in her organic chemistry lab, but he never seemed to understand why she would choose the library over their brief (and mostly unsatisfying) liaisons late at night. She hadn't heard from him in two months.

"The emblem of your revolution should be a tree," Bhumi said playfully.

"Our revolution," David corrected. "Why a tree? The hammer and sickle work fine."

"They make their own food as sugar. And then they make the air for us to breathe. They make and give. Equally."

"Tell me more?" David asked.

"Plants are the only living things that can take two ingredients—water and carbon dioxide—and turn them into sugar and oxygen. Without those two things, we all die. Trees—"

David cut her off. "So, they don't just own our means of production, but our very life!" he exclaimed. Bhumi rolled her eyes. He didn't seem to get it and she didn't want to push it. His high-pitched laugh faded as he reached out to touch Bhumi—this time on her thigh.

It was another small touch, enough to cause her to begin to back away. As much as touch felt good, slowed her thoughts, and made her body feel warm, it also reminded her who David was—and of her best friend.

"I promised Aarti I would join her outside for a cigarette."

"Wait, I'll come with you," David said. He pulled out a pack of Winstons and handed her a cigarette, which she put in her back pocket. Bhumi led the way out, feeling a new sense of annoyance at

David's continued want for her attention—surely he wouldn't be so stupid as to continue his flirtation in Aarti's presence.

Outside, Bhumi looked left and right under the bar's narrow awning.

"She's not out here."

David shrugged. "She must be back inside."

Something felt wrong about Aarti's absence. She should have been outside talking to the bouncer, asking him about his family on the other side of the island. When she opened the door to return inside, David looked visibly annoyed. Bhumi ignored his petulance.

She waded through the humid mass of students to get to the dance floor. Bhumi scanned each dancing body and sidestepped through groups—ignoring annoyed glances—to get herself to the bar, where she looked up and down its sticky wooden length.

She lightly pushed against the backs of others so that she could get to the toilet. "Aarti?" she called to the closed stalls.

She rushed back to the tables near the front door and, having had no luck, finally scampered back outside to check those casually milling about, oblivious to the checkpoint up the road.

"She's not in there. She's not out here."

"Are you sure?" David asked, sighing his response through an exhale of smoke. "You probably just missed her." He stamped his cigarette out underfoot.

The evening was giving way to panic. The night's stillness began to feel suffocating. The ground was wet from rain and the sky was still clouded over, giving the night a damp and muggy feeling. Bhumi's eyes traveled along the uphill curve of the street, moving between the darkness set off from the streetlamps' feathered islands of light. Almost immediately she felt an electric tingle along the back of her neck.

In the distance, she could see an outline. She was sure it was Aarti—the light from the checkpoint caught upon her sequins. In front of Aarti, not more than a breath's distance away, was a soldier, pointing his finger into her shoulder and leaning in to tell her something.

She didn't think twice. She ran, as fast as she could, toward her friend.

"Where are you going?" David yelled out.

"Aarti—checkpoint," Bhumi said, staccato words between breaths. She focused her eyes upon her friend, pushing out of her mind the stories she had heard about what happened to the unlucky at these stops.

When Aarti saw Bhumi cross into view, a sudden twisted-mouthed look of abject terror crossed her face. She saw the soldier take a step back to pull from his belt a small pistol. Slowly, methodically, he pointed it at Aarti, and then up to the clouds, the hammer cocked back, the finger applying just enough pressure on the trigger. The other hand on Aarti's shoulder.

Bam.

The birds in the nearby trees startled into wakefulness and cried out in flight. Bhumi could see their shadowed outlines swooping up and down in big rope-swing arcs before they settled back down into darkened branches.

Every neuron in Bhumi's body was thrown into reverse. She stopped cold only a few meters away from the checkpoint, feeling the blood drain from each muscle and down into her legs. David had caught up to her, and, for a moment, the only sound was the mismatched beat of their heavy breathing. Bhumi thought she would vomit but felt only the bitter taste and burning in the back of her throat.

Bhumi could see Aarti staring at her, shaking her head back and forth, silently mouthing the word no. It was a small gesture, almost imperceptible. Aarti looked disappointed, as if Bhumi's quickness to action was exactly the wrong thing at the wrong time. And from this, Bhumi felt a strange feeling of guilt rise from somewhere within her, a feeling that told her she had mistakenly taken a turn, opened the wrong door, stumbled in upon the one thing she should have never seen.

After the soldier reholstered his gun, he took both hands and brought them together in a thunderstrike-loud clap.

Bhumi's attention startled into focus. He was not one of the soldiers who had been at the checkpoint before. He was someone new, some sort of higher officer. He was a short and stout man with a blood-red beret atop his head.

He finally turned to look at Bhumi and David. He let out a long sigh and shook his head in disappointment.

"And what the fuck did you two think you were going to do?"

5

"WELL, WELL, WELL," the officer said in a deep and commanding voice. His faintly bored look made it seem like this was a task he saw as beneath him. "It's the little communist."

He walked, with his hands folded behind him, to David. "You know what I hate about this university of ours?" He waited for an answer, but David gritted his teeth and did not look from the ground toward the man in front of him. His hands were balled into fists.

"You don't think we know all of Aarti's friends?" the officer said with a smug look on his face. "Her father stole the idea from the Soviets: trust, but verify."

David still said nothing.

The officer frowned. "All the same, you students, no respect for elders, busying yourself in your stupid little clubs and—" He paused to inhale. "Your interests," he said with a smile and a shake of the head, inwardly laughing at an inside joke.

Without warning, the officer unfolded his hands and punched

David in the stomach. David let out a wheeze from the shock of the blow and fell to his knees, his arms wrapped around himself in pain.

Bhumi saw that Aarti was silently weeping, causing Bhumi's every muscle to seize and shake as if the temperature had dropped below freezing.

"Our country no longer has any time for your little games, David. It's a new day. Yesterday's shit flushed down the toilet." He pantomimed pressing on a lever.

Bhumi could now hear the beat of Irish O'Reilly's bass in the distance. She could feel her heart against her chest, every pulse echoing in her ears.

The officer stepped in front of Bhumi. She couldn't look up and instead stared down at the shined leather of his black boots.

"I said we know everything about Aarti's friends. I suppose I misspoke. I have no idea who you are," he said to Bhumi. "Do *you* know what I hate about our country's university?"

"No," Bhumi replied in a coarse whisper.

"Good girl! You can speak! Unlike him," he said with a smile and a little clap of his hands. "I hate that it's filled with everything this nation needs less of. It's filled with communists, deviants, leftists. It's one big rat's nest. Now, what do you study?"

"B-botany," Bhumi said, lifting her head to look at him. His face lit up into a smile.

"A scientist! Good for you. We need more of you. I'd expect a scientist to have better friends." He took a step back. "Josefa!" he yelled.

A subordinate, a slight man dressed in camo fatigues, with a baby face that Bhumi immediately wanted to punch, scampered to the officer's side. "Put him in the back of the jeep. He's coming with us," the officer said. "Can't have a communist poisoning our country, can we, little scientist?"

Bhumi forced her face to stay frozen as the subordinate grabbed

David's wrists and cuffed him. Bhumi caught one last look at his face: it was red, puffy, marked by tears and such anguish that Bhumi immediately looked away. She tried to take a deep breath as David was put onto the back bench of the military jeep, but all that came was short hiccups of air. "Back to base," the officer barked.

They watched the jeep drive away. After the rumble of the engine faded into the night, he turned back to Bhumi and demanded her student ID.

Her hands were trembling as the officer snatched the ID from her. "Bhumi Persad," he said, her name drawn out. "I suppose it's a good thing I have no idea who you are. Staying out of trouble. Until tonight." He gave her an exaggerated wink as he placed the ID into one of the pockets in his jacket. He turned and walked toward Aarti, again putting a hand on her shoulder.

"As for you, Ms. Kumar, you have a message to deliver. Take your friend with you. And don't forget what I told you. Tell him every word. Tell him who told you. And remember, tell him how easy this can all be." He lifted his hand off her and placed it in his pocket.

Bhumi and Aarti stared at each other, both frozen.

"What the fuck are you two waiting for? Get out of here, now!"

Without saying a word to each other, they ran.

BHUMI HAD NO IDEA WHERE THEY WERE GOING, AND AARTI KEPT THE pace swift, as if every step were propelled by an invisible current that could carry them to safety. They pressed on, moving quietly and quickly uphill through a neighborhood where the timber-framed Victorian homes loomed as shadowed behemoths. Most of these houses were set behind gates much larger than the one that fronted Bhumi's childhood home.

While she moved forward, Bhumi felt a painful longing for time to work itself backward to Irish O'Reilly, back to the dance floor, back to normalcy, but it was useless. Time had cleaved itself into two. There would be only a before and an after.

The roar of a large vehicle—a bus, or perhaps a lorry engine straining against an incline—broke the silence. Without warning, Aarti dove behind a hedgerow of one of the few houses lacking a gate. Bhumi followed, crouching on her haunches with her friend, their hands sinking into a soft and wet lawn. Bhumi could feel something crawling over her fingers, but she dared not move. The vehicle never passed by: its sound rose and faded off as it took a turn onto another street.

Aarti sat down. Bhumi looked up at the house in front of them: it was a three-story stately building, complete with a turret and latticework on its wraparound porch. Based on the homes and how far they had walked from Irish O'Reilly, her mind's map of the city placed them in Civil Domain, a neighborhood built for the Empire, now meant for high-ranking government officials and members of the island's business elite.

Aarti lit a cigarette between her lips, the match's flame illuminating her face from below. She had a dazed look about her and was moving her lips silently in a conversation that Bhumi wasn't party to. Cut off from her friend, Bhumi could feel the intensity of feeling that had taken her to that hedgerow begin to ebb. She wanted to go back to campus, back to class, back to the life she had had up until tonight.

"Where are we going?" Bhumi finally asked.

"What?" Aarti said, looking up wide-eyed from her reverie. "My ears are still ringing from back there."

"Where are we going?" Bhumi asked again.

Aarti forced a smile, a sad attempt to bring levity to the moment. She wrapped her finger around the white strip in her hair.

"It's like we're going out to get chips in front of Hari's," Aarti said, referring to the late-night fast food down the street from Irish O'Reilly.

Bhumi tried to laugh, but what came out was a hollow sound. She crouched back down and placed a hand on Aarti's knee. As soon as she touched the fabric of her jeans, Aarti seemed to spring to life.

"I'm taking us home. Something happened. I don't want to talk about it. I need to tell Papa."

"Is everything okay, Aarti?"

Aarti stood up and brushed off the bits of mud and grass that stuck to her. "Not now, Bhumi. You don't need to know everything all the time." Aarti began to walk toward the sidewalk.

She followed even though her friend's words stung. "What the fuck, Aarti? Why are you keeping this from me?" Bhumi seethed. "You don't tell me you were fucking David, and now David was just arrested. What the fuck is going on?" It was just like Aarti, Bhumi thought, absorbed with herself and her own needs. She felt the tightness in her neck, her shoulders scrunching together, as she thought about the soldier who took her ID.

"Look," Aarti whispered as she stood up on the other side of the hedgerow. "I'm sorry. I just need to talk to my father. It's important." Her voice sounded plaintive and scared.

There was something about Aarti's face that reminded Bhumi of David's misery. It was that look—more than the checkpoint—that felt like a true reminder that something was happening here that was well beyond her control. She had to move forward, even if the path wasn't exactly clear. She absentmindedly touched her scar, glassy and smoother than the surrounding skin.

"Tell me again the story of how you got your scar," Aarti said as they started moving again. "Just one more time."

"Seriously?"

"Bhumi, tell me."

Almost fifteen years ago, Bhumi had been in the driveway, and the low clouds, thick like mounds of cotton, moved gently with the breeze across the sky. She was rolling a coconut back and forth between her hands, singing some song she had picked up from the radio, mixing up the words, but keeping the tune intact. The song kept close to the music of the garden: the shrill whistle of long-tailed koels from some nearby roof, the lazy buzz of fat bumblebees drinking from the flowers of the frangipani, the sound of the wind rustling through the fronds of the banana and coconut.

"The two puppies that came in through the gate looked like street dogs, you know, that same orange-brown color they all have," Bhumi said. "I wanted to pet them. What did I know? Their mother was just past the gate. She lunged, right for my neck."

"And you fought it?"

"I punched and punched and punched and screamed. Ma saw from the balcony and screamed. The dog was confused at the sounds. Distracted it just for a second. I kicked it, and it ran off."

"And you went to the hospital?"

"In the back of a neighbor's truck. He was a vegetable seller for the big markets. I remember touching my neck and it was slippery and sticky. There was all this blood. All I could focus on was this little red onion rolling around and a feeling like I wanted to take a nap on Ma. She kept telling me to stay awake. Then the hospital gave me all the rabies shots in the stomach, and twelve stitches."

"And your father?"

"He came to the hospital, by the end of the day. Ma's dupatta was stained with a big red-brown spot, like someone had spilled old tomato chutney all over her. She told him that any other child would have died. Papa just turned around and left. He didn't care. I think he wanted me to die so he could replace me with a new kid, another boy."

"It doesn't matter, does it?" Aarti said. They had reached a house made of cream-colored limestone framed by tall eucalyptus trees. Beyond the brick wall topped with a rusty bramble of barbed wire, Bhumi could see that the second-floor windows were brightly lit despite the time of night.

"Your father hated you," Aarti continued. "Mine loved me. And look where we both are now," she said, turning to Bhumi. The sum-mation of the relationship between her and her father made her feel uneasy. Even in the dark, Bhumi could see tears in Aarti's eyes, and she wanted to reach out and comfort her.

Before she could, Aarti walked up to the gate and pressed a buzzer on its side.

"Hello?" a man's voice asked, sounding shaky and broken.

"It's me," Aarti said.

Soon, there was the popping metal sound of a padlock being opened, and the clink-clank of a chain bouncing against the metal slats of the gate. The gate swung open only a few feet, enough for Bhumi and Aarti to slide in.

Aarti's father looked tired, and not just from the hour of the night. His salt-and-pepper hair had been hastily combed to the right and his short-cropped beard was nearly all gray. He had a slight stoop in his back that seemed to have been earned from years of hunching over legislation and correspondence—or perhaps just from stress.

"I don't believe we've met," he said to Bhumi with a polite nod of his head. He reached out his hand.

"Bhumi," she said as she shook it.

"Ah, of course," he said with a gracious air. Even with the context of their meeting, Bhumi felt charmed. He clearly excelled at letting everyone feel that they had his complete respect and attention, even if that attention soon gave way. He turned to Aarti.

"I have a message," she said. Bhumi watched her friend's resolve break: the way her eyes began to look glassy, the grimace that crossed her lips. Aarti fell into her father's embrace. He patted her on the back. "I'm sorry," he whispered.

Bhumi looked on, embarrassed to watch their private moment.

Aarti and her father reached the front door, where Aarti's mother was waiting. She looked at her daughter with such sorrow that again Bhumi thought her heart could break. Aarti fell into her mother's waiting arms, crying. Her mother ran a hand through her hair and whispered something into her ear. Then they disappeared into the house.

Aarti's father invited her in, but Bhumi shook her head. "I should go," she said.

"Go where?" Aarti's father asked. "The checkpoints won't clear till daybreak. Please, come in."

Inside, Aarti and her mother were already gone, out of sight. The front door led into a sitting room where Aarti's father gestured to a small sofa with an open palm. Bhumi could see the bags under his eyes and felt a knowing camaraderie—she knew how politeness could mask great exhaustion.

Bhumi had never been in a rich person's house before and now felt so small.

Aarti was Bhumi's first friend who had a life so unlike her own: holidays abroad, an education that, until college, had never before occurred in a publicly funded classroom. There were the downstream effects too—subscriptions to foreign magazines, opinions about politics near and far, and an ability to feel at ease, striking up a conversation with anyone. Bhumi felt like her life had been a struggle to climb up into the canopy, only to find the comfortable nests of others when she got there.

Her unease sank her further into the sofa's cushions. She had no idea what time it was, guessing it was perhaps two or three in the morning. She leaned back and closed her eyes, and she soon fell into a flimsy and dreamless sleep.

THE SOUNDS OF RAISED VOICES IN ANOTHER ROOM WOKE BHUMI UP. The morning light was streaming through the sitting room's window. She looked down to find herself curled up on the sofa with a soft knit blanket on her. In the other room, what sounded like an hours-long debate was finally ending in a tired and hoarse coda.

"We can't do this. Just go to the General and apologize," Aarti's mother pleaded. "Go back to him. Keep us safe."

"I can't. I won't!" Aarti's father exclaimed. "Even if I bend down and kiss his ring, what's to stop him from killing me tomorrow? Next week? Next year?"

"We can be safe now!"

"There's no more being safe with the General!" Aarti interjected. "He knows everything. Nobody else knew I was going to Irish O'Reilly, and he still sent that lieutenant there." Her voice sounded shaky.

A foggy feeling of dread passed through Bhumi as she sat up. It was an instant reminder of the night that had passed. Her friend was going to leave, and there was nothing she could do but watch, just like she had watched what transpired at the checkpoints, just like she had watched David in the back of the jeep. Something had happened between Bhumi's father and the General, something terrible enough to merit a debasing apology. Bhumi knew Aarti was right. Bhumi had been raised with a tyrant: One apology was never enough. There was always going to be another blowup.

The three entered the sitting room.

Aarti's father cleared his throat. "You're awake." Bhumi gave a small awkward smile in reply.

"Did they take anything from you?" Aarti's father asked. "Your purse, your student identification, anything that would let them know who you are."

Bhumi crossed her arms. "They took my student ID card."

He scrunched his face in worry. "Shit. I don't know what your plans are, Bhumi. You should leave."

"What do you mean?" Bhumi asked.

"Trust me. They will never leave you alone. I know how this works. It's like the fer-de-lance snake that kills in the sugar fields. Leave the country as soon as you can."

Aarti pulled Bhumi off to the side, still within earshot of her parents, but far enough away to have a sidebar. "Don't listen to him," she said with a gentle roll of her eyes. "He just gets nervous."

Bhumi let out an awkward laugh, unsure of how to read the conversation to see if she was in danger. "Should I be nervous?"

Aarti beamed so beatifically that Bhumi knew she was fucked.

"Listen, Bhumi, just remember, don't go back to . . . ," Aarti said, trailing off.

"Don't go back to what?"

"Don't go back to hiding in the library. Going out is good too."

"I don't know if I could ever go out again after last night," Bhumi joked. "Maybe we should just stay in for a while."

"That came out all wrong. What I meant was—" Aarti stopped herself.

Aarti was never one to get tongue-tied. Bhumi felt nervous for her, seeing her like this. She tried to offer an excuse. "You're just tired."

Aarti waved it off with a flick of her wrist. "No, what I mean is that, no matter what happens, you just need to make sure you're still out there, you know? That your light is there for everyone to see."

"Seriously, Aarti, let's just go back to campus," Bhumi said, trying to break the conversation and return to normalcy. She reached out to grab Aarti's hand.

"I can't wait to see you, wherever you'll be," Aarti continued.

"I'll be here, Aarti," Bhumi said, in a voice no louder than a whisper.

"You've done this all on your own, don't forget that either. I'll cheer the loudest when you graduate from your Ph.D., Bhumi."

Aarti's father cleared his throat. "Aarti, we have to get going."

Bhumi felt a sense of foreboding like a riptide: her world was slipping from her grip just as something else was pulling her away. She felt that she should say something—witty, loving, tender, caring—to her friend, but by the time she could put half a thought together, Aarti had shepherded her outside the doorway.

"We're still going to do all the things we planned," she said, not quite believing her own words. "We'll go to Sydney after we graduate. You'll show me the opera building you were talking about."

"The checkpoints should be open now," Aarti replied, still smiling in her far-off way. "Do you have money for a taxi? Let me."

"No, no, it's fine. I got it."

Aarti took one step forward and fell into Bhumi for an embrace that ended as soon as it began.

"I'll see you soon, right? Back at the library for exams?" As Bhumi asked this, she could see Aarti's smile finally breaking.

"Take care of yourself, Bhumi," Aarti said. She shut the door. The lock clicked soon after.

Bhumi turned around and walked into the morning light, the breaking of a new day. She was on her own now.

6

OUTSIDE OF AARTI'S house, it seemed like it was close to eight or nine in the morning, and the light was clear. She reached into her back pocket and pulled out a loose cigarette, the one given to her by David. The cigarette had been crushed and its tobacco fell out of its end in small clumps. Still, she put it in her mouth and lit it. Both Aarti and David were gone. It had all happened so quickly.

With one long drag, she began to move.

She needed to feel freedom in her legs—movement was the only way to think. The last eight hours had made it clear that all the violence that had started with the greengrocer was just a prelude to something worse. The country's crisis had felt surreal until the lieutenant shot off his gun. The power of that shot was total and irrevocable, like a white rot turning xylem and phloem to mush. Unlike the forest, she didn't have to stand still and take it. She could keep moving.

As she pieced together the previous night, she saw herself at the

center of it all. Aarti had asked her to break curfew and she had acqui-
esced. They were supposed to go out for a cigarette, but Bhumi had
dragged her feet. At the time, none of it seemed like it would string
together into a narrative that could possibly end as it had. It was just
five minutes of harmless flirting.

If she had gone outside with Aarti, would the soldier still have
taken her? Would David have stayed on his bar stool, never leaving
Irish O'Reilly, never winding up in the back of a military jeep?

The only person at fault was the General. And yet, she couldn't
shake off an incipient feeling of guilt.

She walked toward the Finance Tower, one of the four large buildings clustered together in the heart of Vilimaji. It was fifteen stories
tall—nearly double the size of the next-tallest building—which made
it a beacon for those needing direction. Heading toward the Finance
Tower always meant going to the city center.

She thought of how vines never grew in straight lines and instead
swept back and forth until they latched on to something. This vine—
something that had to do with a country tearing itself apart—had
caught on to her while it swept back and forth looking for Aarti's
family. She had just happened to be nearby.

At the top of one of the city's many hills, she saw the main coach
terminal at the periphery of the city. It was nothing more than a large
parking lot next to an open-air walkway, with the same corrugated-tin
roof as the city market. Buses the colors of ripe Seville oranges and
key limes were driven by their Indian operators to the terminal, diesel fumes belching out of their tailpipes. Along the walkway, people
jostled as they departed buses and walked to their places of work.

The city was awakening from curfew, and what surprised Bhumi
was not the activity but its normalcy, streets filled with taxis, their
engines rattling like the lungs of an old smoker. From a distance, it
looked as if the past week had never happened. Gone were the checkpoints. Gone was the visible violence meted out on the streets. Still,

something was left hanging in the air: the lack of a breeze or a cloud in the sky made the city feel like it was holding its breath for whatever came next.

Aarti was going to leave the country. Bhumi tried to imagine how Nani must have felt leaving her little village back in India. She could only see it in her mind as a cluster of thatched-roof bures, like the ones along the island's little coastal villages. Over and over throughout her childhood, Bhumi had been told how her grandmother, along with her other ancestors, had been driven out of their country by caste, disease, famine, and poverty. Their desperation made the raw deal given by a wily recruiter—five years of indentured servitude on an island thousands of miles from home—seem like a promising life.

"Ey!" someone yelled from across the street. On the street corner, in front of a taxi stand, was a man in faded khakis and a pastel floral-printed bula shirt. He was seated on the bonnet of a small taxi, a radio next to him.

Bhumi braced herself for whatever he would call out at her.

"Sister!" the driver yelled. "Why aren't you listening to the General's speech?"

She wanted to say that she was tired of listening to this asshole. Instead, she crossed the street when he gestured for her to come listen.

She braced herself for some sort of trick, some lewd catcall. Instead the driver asked her if she was a student at the university. She said yes but still kept her distance, standing just past the Nissan's grill.

"Someone says he's gonna talk about SPU. He's in the Heartland right now," he said, referring to the name of the tin-shack-filled slum in the green floodplain just north of the city. "The speech just started."

Bhumi focused her attention on the radio and heard that voice again: calm, resonant, each syllable as solid as a granite block.

"Do you know why you suffer?" the General asked the crowd. "It's because they do not give jobs to us, the people of this nation. The Indians control the buses, the taxis, the shops, and the banks, and do they share their profits with you? Not even a single cent! The only way for our people to get ahead is to tell the Indians one thing: they must share their profits with the nation. It does not just start with businesses. It starts where? In our education system! In our precious South Pacific University."

The sounds of cheers filled the broadcast, almost sounding like white noise pouring through the tinny speakers of the small battery-powered radio. Bhumi felt her heart drop.

"They take our seats in the university! That's why I'm happy to announce that after today, they will no longer have our university in their hands. I am hereby ordering the university to expel from the student body, the faculty, and the staff, all revolutionary elements, and to invite all native students and teachers in their place! This was our country, and will be once again!"

The driver shut off the radio as the crowd shouted a litany of bloodthirsty chants: "Vulagi go home! Lock them up! Cut them out!" It sounded like the General was trying to quiet the crowd, but he had stoked a fire he could not extinguish.

"I can't listen to this shit," the driver said. "Sister, do you need to get back to campus?"

Bhumi nodded yes. It felt like her eyes weren't able to focus upon anything in front of her.

Twenty-four hours ago, she would have been sure of herself as a decidedly nonrevolutionary element, but Aarti's father's fear about her student ID cast a shadow over her confidence. "SPU Pedestrian Gate," she added.

The driver tapped his hand against the shifter. "When are you leaving here?"

"I don't know," she replied. Even though the current was drifting toward departure, she desperately wanted to believe that she wouldn't be swept up in the tide. She clung on to the smallest hope that her life—whatever remained of it—would be waiting for her at the end of the taxi ride.

"The General wanted power. That's why he took over. And now that he has it, he doesn't want to give it up. And the kaamchor?" he asked. "They make excuses for their own laziness. They could drive a taxi like me, instead they just complain that Indians take their jobs. If he wants to keep his power, he's going to have to listen to them, and, sister, we're fucked if that happens."

Bhumi asked the driver if he was thinking about leaving. He shook his head and gave a quiet no.

"What else can I do?" he said plaintively, pleading with Bhumi—or himself. "I don't have the money to leave, sister. I'll drive this taxi until they take it away from me."

Soon enough they were at the Pedestrian Gate. She noticed that the line of available taxis had thinned out, but there remained a long queue of students—all Indian—waiting on the footpath. "Good luck, sister. All these students? They're probably going to the coach station. I'll take them all back and forth until there's no one left. Maybe I'll take you too."

"Maybe."

"God willing, you'll be safe."

Bhumi handed him his fare. "Thank you," she said, before adding, "brother."

She hustled through campus eyes-down. It seemed like the other students did the same—the atmosphere had the energy of a moving day with none of the joy that accompanied the beginning or end of the academic year, only a feeling of anxiety over what came next.

Halfway through, she burst into a sprint to get back to her dorm, and even from a distance, she could see the note nailed to the front door of her building. She rushed up to it and ripped the paper off the wall.

BY ORDER OF THE CENTRAL SECRETARIAT OF THE
TRANSITIONAL GOVERNMENT, THE FOLLOWING
STUDENTS HAVE BEEN EXPELLED AND MUST
VACATE THIS PROPERTY WITHIN 24 HOURS.

Her eyes scanned down the list, and there it was.

Bhumi Persad.

A white-hot feeling coursed through her, taking her vision in and out of focus. She couldn't believe it, but every time she looked down at the paper, her name remained there, unmoving. Every printed character felt as loud and as violent as the officer's gun. She let the paper fall from her hand, watching what had felt heavy glide down with a feathery lightness.

She stumbled into her dorm and made for the toilet. It was a small room lit by a hanging incandescent bulb. The air never moved despite the small rectangular window near the ceiling on the far wall, leaving the smell of bleach permanently hanging like the light fixture. As soon as she entered the room, her stomach folded over. In one movement, Bhumi kneeled in front of the toilet. She dry-heaved a few times before finally throwing up.

When she finished, she looked in the mirror above the sink basin. Her face had turned ghostly pale, with dark, sunken-in eyes.

Her body began to feel wet from sweat as her heart quickened. She opened her mouth and what came out was an animal howl: a mess of fury and spit.

"What the fuck?" she yelled.

She drew a finger along her scar as the faint logic of a plan began to click into place like so many gears of a great machine. She didn't need to know the reasons for her expulsion, but she needed to know the outline of her departure. She needed a course of action, a way forward. Standing still meant standing in the muck of it all—Aarti's father was right, the fer-de-lance had struck, and now there was only one thing to do.

She walked straight to the dormitory's common room and picked up the phone.

7

THE MINOR WAS parked in front of the house. Jaipal still hadn't told his father about the hotel.

Ah, shit, he thought, toeing a coconut at the bottom of the steps leading to the front door. The recent violence of the coup meant that being an Indian man in the outside world felt like having a target on him. Being inside was no respite: his father was home today, the sounds of some crooning love song by Mohammed Rafi spilling out the open windows.

His father was sitting in the sitting room, staring straight at the record player with a scowl on his face.

"They're not playing the death announcements anymore," his father said without turning to acknowledge Jaipal. His dark skin stretched tight over his sinewy body, and what was left of his receding hair was a thin and unruly combover. "He mixed some jaggery with horseshit, eh? Behenchod probably got himself killed. Now tell me," he said, turning to finally look at Jaipal and smiling a stupid grin made from the pride of a joke, "who announces the death of the death announcer?"

"Where's Ma?" Jaipal asked, looking around the room.

"Out. Spending my money, probably. Women don't have chiefs, they don't listen to no one," he said. "There was another speech this morning. General's closing down the university. Maybe they'll kick your sister out." He didn't stop grinning, but Jaipal could see in those wide-open eyes that his usual self-satisfaction had been swapped for resentment—at the country or his sister, Jaipal wasn't sure. His eyes were always narrow and bloodshot, giving the appearance of a man whose nerves were always about to get the best of him, of someone who could lash out in violence without warning.

Jaipal let out a small sigh and watched him get up from the same sofa they had owned for as long as he could remember, the cushions sagging from where each of them took a seat, day after day. His father had always been a wiry man and age was doing him no favors, rusting him from the inside out until the surface would finally dissolve away, leaving a gaping hole where a man used to be.

There were the banal changes: a little stoop to his step, his hair thinning and mottled with gray. There were the more important ones too: how he wheezed going up the stairs to their home, how he forgot little things (keys, receipts, dates) more often, how his hand rested on his chest from time to time looking like a stop sign against some unknown pain. The heart attack had cut him in half.

A month ago, he had woken up in the middle of the night and complained that his chest was hurting. Jaipal's mother had told him to go back to sleep, that it was a bout of gas. Something about the pain scared his father out of bed. Soon his father was shaking him, telling him to come with him to the A & E. "I've got my liver in my mouth, boy," his father had said. "I don't want to go alone."

That was all his father had said. Jaipal drove him to the hospital. His father, though silent, grabbed at his left arm and coughed, over and over again. The doctors said he'd had a minor heart attack, brought on by high blood pressure. He needed to control his anger, his drinking. He needed to become a new man.

In the kitchen, Jaipal filled a bowl with namkeen. He wasn't hungry, but he wanted to keep some space between him and his father.

"I heard you were fired," his father said, still standing near the floor-to-ceiling mahogany cabinet that contained the family's television; combination record, radio, and tape player; and a set of bookshelf speakers. His finger was hovering near the record player's switch.

"I wasn't fired," Jaipal said, picking at the fried bits of sev in his bowl. The man always had his news.

"The hotel shut down and you're out of a job, right?" His father shut off the radio and in the silence, Jaipal craved the distraction that the noise had brought. "One of my girls told me."

His girls. They weren't women to him. Never had been, never would be. They were a collective; they had no names. He spent more time with them than with Jaipal's mother. They came into his life when he wanted and left after he was done with them for the night. His father paid them, a sale no different from the ones marked by the till's bell and the mechanical snap to open the cash drawer. Beyond a good deal, a shop owner prized consistency in his suppliers. And his girls were consistent: there for him two, three, four, five nights a week.

He watched his father rub the stubble along his chin like he had an idea. "I got a deal for you," his father said. "Your belly ain't full, I see it. Can't be choosy."

A deal. Jaipal's heart sank a little further down. "What do you have?"

"A job. You see what's happening. Ram Maharaj in Vilimaji. And what was that kid's name—Salim? You knew him. I don't want to die before I retire. Men my age have to rest when it's like this. I can't work at the shop anymore."

He hated hearing his father throw around Salim's name like that, but hearing it reminded Jaipal that he hadn't called Maqbool yet with his condolences. What could be the right words to comfort someone who had once meant so much to him? He hadn't seen Maqbool in over a year—the hotel had kept him away.

His father went on about how it was so dangerous out there. "It's like the cane days," he said. "Chickens merry, hawks near."

Jaipal knew where his father was going. He was a man of many traits, and bravery had never been one of them. He even handed Jaipal a compliment: his girls had told him that he handled customers well, that he knew how to deal with people. "Shop's yours. All the money you make from sales? It's yours. We get to keep it in the family."

Jaipal didn't want to go along with another one of his father's deals, but he knew the risks. To deny his father was to invite catastrophe. More important, he was out of a job, and nothing was safe. If he was going to ride this out, he needed something.

Maybe if he said nothing, nothing could come of it. He looked his father in the eye and the two stared at each other, each without blinking, waiting. Jaipal felt a tingle run from his stomach outward through each finger, and he blinked. Weakness.

"Store's yours. Starting now," his father told him before he headed off to celebrate. Jaipal put down his bowl of uneaten namkeen and watched his father shuffle away. As much as he hated his father, he hated himself more for buckling every single time.

His father slammed the door behind him and Jaipal stood still, staring at its dark wood. He turned over all the ways in which a country and a life could fall apart. There were a million ways to die right outside that door—Salim's death had proven this—but his father seemed to float through it all without a scratch.

8

JAIPAL HAD STARTED working at the hotel a year and a half ago. It had been a couple years since he graduated from Sugar City Secondary. Unlike his sister, he had graduated from the B-Form. B-Form kids didn't go to college or university. Most of them went on to the trades. The best of them could become a foreman.

The day after his graduation, his father had woken him up early. "Let's go," he said.

Jaipal, without much idea of what to do with his life, turned what he had done in the hours after school into a full-time job: stocking shelves, working the till, coming to his father's store at dawn to receive the day's produce, idly chatting about the weather with the Coca-Cola truck driver.

When he was younger, working in the shop meant building a tolerance for his father's snapping from behind the counter ("If you whistle one more time, I swear I will slap you across the face"). Even if Jaipal cleared his mind into silence, his father could sometimes accuse him of daydreaming, of sloughing off work. He would slink over to the aisle and box his ears with a blow that left them stinging, red, and warm. There was to be no daydream, no dilly-dally, and surely no delight to be found in the aisles of that shop, only the day-in, day-out tasks his father assigned him.

Those tasks were important. "To keep the money in the family," his father said. "You have to learn." Jaipal's father's father had opened the store. The son of cane farmers, he had a third-grade education and had risen up from selling soft drinks to American soldiers. He'd used his belt to instill in Jaipal's father the value of hard work, the idea that poverty lurked like a thief in the shadows, ready to take what the family had earned.

These lessons were whipped through the generations, and now, Jaipal found the family work was easy, consistent, with the added benefit that as he grew taller and bulkier, his father stopped hitting him across the head as much.

There would be those moments when he was lost in his own thoughts, when the store's daily humdrum faded into background noise and the rhythm of the task (one can out of the crate, one can onto the shelf) slipped the clock's hands swiftly forward.

"Ey, gandoo, come here," his father would call out from behind the counter.

Gandoo. The blood would rush to Jaipal's face, and his ears would start to redden with such heat that he could feel them pulsing at the tips of his earlobes with the beat of the word's echo. The first time he heard it, he thought, Fuck, how does he know? He didn't say anything. He narrowed his eyes and drifted to the till, where his father saw his red ears and Jaipal felt like he had been seen right through to everything he tried to hide.

His father's words were fuel to a fire that raged through him, burning up everything in its path. All he had to show for the pure heat of his feeling was sweaty palms—terrible for restocking glass jars— and eyes downcast to the shop's grimy tile.

He knew his passiveness wasn't merely built out of fear of his father's petty despotism. At that age, desire could feel like poison, a slow suicide playing out over years. Half of this desire he could accept, leaving the other half buried. Given the chance, he could joke with his friends, turn women's bodies into a list of parts: she had a fat ass, her tits were big, you could fuck her if you put a bag over her face. Boys talked among themselves in a way that let him own up to his wants.

Secretly, he wanted the friends who hurled the catcalls. He saw in his mind's eye how he could tear off their crass outer layer of boyhood and plunge straight into the pleasure he could take from them.

He was getting nothing from nobody. He blamed himself. He, who looked nothing like the sylphlike women or the lean and taut men in his family. His broad shoulders connected to a barrel chest. It would have been difficult to see him as part of the family were it not for his eyes like his mother's: almond shaped with soft brown irises and long eyelashes. As a child, his sister had teased him that he should wear kohl. It wouldn't have looked out of place, but rather like a natural accompaniment to eyes as feminine as his.

It was only an accident that he discovered that others could desire him as completely as he wanted them.

After he finished up at Sugar City Secondary, he spent some of his free time after his shifts at the store with Maqbool and a group of old B-Formers. It was the type of friendship that lazily continued on from one phase of life to the next. On nights when he watched television or listened to the radio while his mother cooked dinner, he always felt like she was looking at him askance, wondering why a boy his age should stay quietly at home.

One night, they sat underneath another's house playing a lackadaisical game of rummy. By dint of their jobs—mechanic, shift lead at the cannery, bottling supervisor at the refinery, taxi driver—no one quite expected anything resembling success, and by dint of their age, no one expected them to pay heed to the matchmakers, settle down, and have a family just yet. Without anything better to do, they drank and tried (mostly failed) to chase women.

Maqbool—who now worked as a baggage handler at the airport—suggested that they try something new, that rummy was boring as hell, that they should go to one of the hotel bars.

"The owners never want us at the hotel bars," Cheddi spat back, putting down his cards and taking a sip of his rum and cola. "That's for goras. The bouncer or some shit will kick us out and then we'll be all the way by the fucking airport with nothing to do."

Maqbool, always ready to see his plans to fruition, had a response to the objection. He put his cards down and leaned back in his chair. "My cousin got a new job. Bartends at the Beachcomber now. Pay him and the bouncer a little extra on the side, and it's all good."

Jaipal, forever the little boy following Maqbool, piped up. "Let's try it. This game sucks anyway."

Maqbool laughed. "'Cause you're losing, Jaipal?" Jaipal reddened at the retort, but Maqbool gave him a look of recognition with a little grin like a warm touch on the small of his back.

They piled into Salim's taxi to go to a bar at one of the bigger hotels. It was an indoor bar where the hotel guests crowded around a dance floor while others hung around the counter and sipped their beers. The drinks were egregiously expensive—Jaipal and his friends had only brought enough cash for one each, which they sipped as they huddled together in a booth at the far end of the bar, ogling the women who passed.

Jaipal noticed how two or three of those who walked by, men and women, would look, their eyes scanning him up and down, a smile of recognition about to cross their lips. As soon as they did, the tourists noticed that Jaipal's boisterous friends were all Indians. And so, the onlookers moved on, returning back to themselves. In the moment before they left, Jaipal was able to draw their eyes into his gaze. His mouth felt wet, and he felt the breath, sharp between his teeth. He wanted it again and again and again.

Even without sleep, he felt wired throughout the next day's tasks. The hands of the clock moved in a jagged lurch, five minutes feeling like thirty, the next thirty feeling like ten. And yet, he made it through the day, and in the evening, slipped back home into a shirt with a collar—plain white, not a bula shirt—and a pair of khakis.

The taxi driver asked which hotel. Jaipal chose a smaller one, the Ambassador. It was where some families would rent out the ballroom to sing bhajans around Diwali. He knew it had an outdoor bar: he could slip away and escape into the night at a moment's notice.

That next night, he brought plenty of cash. At eight o'clock, it was still early, and the dance floor was mostly empty.

Jaipal walked up to the bar, trying to grab the bartender's attention. Before he could order a drink, the bartender shook his head to say no. Jaipal quickly slid five bills across the counter, the Empire's queen staring back at him from the lime green of each fiver. The bartender quickly took the pile, looking back and forth to make sure no one saw. He stuffed the money into his back pocket and leaned over the counter.

"Boss doesn't like it when we drink here. If he comes, you leave, okay? Otherwise, don't scare the goras."

Jaipal nodded and asked for an Island Bitter, leaving another five dollars on the counter.

It was so easy.

He turned around and scanned the bar: the woman in front of him was waiting to be found. She had been dancing on her own on the mostly empty dance floor, swaying back and forth to the beat, her saltwater-wavy hair bouncing along. Jaipal thought she looked happy, or at least tipsy, but still nervous enough that she barely moved her feet to the song. She filled her dress, a flimsy thing, thin strapped, printed with yellow and magenta hibiscus. Jaipal could see the lines of her swimsuit underneath the dress's straps, and the sight of these quickened his pulse, as if he were seeing something illicit.

She smiled in a conspiratorial way, inviting Jaipal into whatever plans she had. He smiled back, and soon enough, he was on the dance floor, trying his best to swallow the embarrassment at how his heavy body moved to the beat. He was red-faced with shame, ready to leave, ready to give up the entire plan, until he noticed that her eyes were closed and she was smiling all the same. She sidled up next to him and he could feel the wet warmth of her body through her dress's thin fabric. Everything that could keep him from moving turned off—no sorrow, no shame, only wanting more, wanting to feel that heat underneath the tips of his fingers.

She moved her body in front of his, but he still didn't know the script to follow. She placed his hand on her hip and she radiated the kind of happiness that he later learned could only come from a solo traveler far from home.

She pulled him to one of the big rattan chairs off the dance floor, right next to the firepit.

"My name's Janice," she said. She had an Aussie accent.

"I'm Jaipal." He had never talked to a firangi woman before. Thankfully, the only question she would ask him was whether he needed another drink. From then on, she began to talk. Jaipal listened in, the nods of his head moving to the dull drumbeat of desire.

When she told him her age, he said that he didn't believe that she was forty. She laughed and said that this trip was a personal reward for signing the last papers for her divorce. The heat of pure want swirled within. He put his hand on her knee, and she let it rest there for a moment.

She pointed to his empty bottle and asked if he wanted another. He nodded, watching her hips as she walked to the bar, feeling the wetness of his mouth, the sweat in his palms. Don't talk about yourself, he thought. Let her do whatever.

She brought him his drink and she talked on about her life back in Melbourne: how her ex was looking after her kids (eight and twelve), how he had fucked the babysitter and could he be more of a stereotype? How she was glad she had always taken care of herself, used the StairMaster he had bought her, how she definitely took that in the divorce.

Jaipal nodded and asked a question that always led to a new answer about her. She kept drinking until he had no questions left to ask, she put her hand on his thigh and leaned in, and he kept his eyes shut tight as her tongue reached into his mouth. He opened his eyes and saw hers closed. He was filled with the same feeling as when he saw the straps of her swimsuit—seeing something he shouldn't, but in this case, seeing someone laid bare in front of him: the vulnerability of surrender. He felt her tongue again. He closed his eyes. She was leading him again in a dance he had yet to learn.

She put her hand on his and asked if he wanted to come back to her room. Jaipal swallowed. He tried to imagine how his friends would talk. "Yeah," was all he said, with a goatlike gruffness. He didn't say that this was his first time, but she must have known. She told him exactly what to do—take off my clothes, kiss me here, here, here, pushing his head further and further down. She tasted like how heat felt, how a moan sounded, how it was to have a lifetime of wanting found easily in a woman far from home, right down the street.

When it came time, he was surprised by the warmth inside her, different from the coldness of his hands. He kept his eyes open; this was nothing like the self-erasure that came when he wrestled with his fantasies: longing that jostled with loneliness and hatred (of his body, of his desires, of his father's tyranny, his mother's absence, his sister's way of getting exactly what she wanted). This was pure, blissful nothing, nothing, nothing—then, release.

His mind couldn't hang on to a single thought except for pleasure (his own, hearing her small "oh"s escape like breath). There was no Jaipal. There was no time. There was no place.

He finished. Quickly.

He could tell it was too fast because she immediately laughed. When she told him that it was fucking great, she said it a little too loud and quick. She soon fell asleep next to him, her raspy snores drifting from the blood-red of her painted lips. He stared at the lazy swish of the ceiling fan. Not knowing if his invitation stretched through the night, he put on his clothes (his underwear backward, in the dark), and went home, his heart beating from knowledge, from impatience, from a cocky self-assurance he had never before felt. It was easy! It was too easy.

He didn't need his friends when he had a distraction like this. He had to come back.

When his father saw him at the store the next morning, he said he was assigning Jaipal the night shift for the next two nights. He said it with such a brusque cruelty that Jaipal thought that his father knew exactly what Jaipal had been up to, what he wanted to do with his evenings.

Those two shifts dragged on, but he finally got back to the hotel. He waited at the bar for an hour. She never showed up. She must have gone home, he thought, feeling the disappointment fill him straight through. He had missed his chance.

As he lost his nerve, his eye caught the figure of another standing near the firepit, angular features lit dramatically from below.

Half of his face was in shadow. His hair was blond, almost white enough to reflect the fire back into the night. Young—Jaipal's age? No, a bit older, not by much. His skin was pale white, not a touch of tan or sun-addled rash like everyone else. Still, he wore the same beach outfit as the rest of them: board shorts and a white muscle tee. The goras could show up to the bar in anything. Only Jaipal had to watch what he wore.

The man was staring into the fire, the flames dancing in his big aviator glasses. He looked up. Jaipal never stopped staring. It was the smallest of gestures that said go: the tip of his tongue along his upper lip and then the smallest number of muscles pulled together to smile. The dimple on his cheek caught the shadow from the fire.

Jaipal filled again with that feeling, compelled across the dance floor with a mixture of fear and need and all nerves. His feet were moving, but he didn't feel them touch the ground. The man glanced at Jaipal with a look of seriousness in his eyes, eyes as blue as the sea under the noontime sun. And then the gaze was broken, his eyes checking out Jaipal from head to toe, and back again.

Even with the music, Jaipal could hear his heartbeat: fast and sharp.

This man, what was his name? It didn't matter. He did not need to be asked questions. He did not need drink after drink. There wasn't a dance. There wasn't a touch shared between them. He leaned over and Jaipal could feel his breath hot against his ear. He told Jaipal a room number and ten minutes. Then he turned around and left the bar, never looking back once.

Jaipal finished his drink quickly, leaving eight minutes to wait, to attempt to find someone to talk to. No, he didn't need to talk to anyone—he had found what he wanted. Now he had to feel the nervousness shake inside of him, leaving every finger moving, quivering, his foot tapping two measures ahead of the song's beat. Stuck in anxiety's flittering motions, until it was time to go up into the building, up two flights of stairs so that no one working the hotel would see him in the elevator, down the hallway, three knocks on the door.

"It's unlocked," he heard from inside. The voice, at full volume, was nasal, unlike the staccato whisper he had heard on the dance floor.

He was sitting on the edge of the made bed, already naked, all of him ready and alert. Jaipal stood, frozen, in the doorway.

"Close that, please."

Jaipal turned to close the door and felt himself moving on the autopilot of fantasy. All the things that he had denied himself since the age he knew what desire was, all the things he had thought he would never get to feel, now lying there on the bed, right in front of him. There had been the jeers and taunts and threats from every man he had ever known—gandoo, faggot, fairy. Look at the West: fucking a man could kill you. It was happening all over the world with some sort of disease. Voices, warnings, petty hatreds, all to dissolve with the blood that pulsed with the energy that rose within. He took off everything but was excited, nervous, and fumbling—he left his socks on.

He stopped before the bed. Something inside told him to not let the moment move from underneath him. He stared at the hardness of the lean man's body with the eye of an overseer keeping watch over the cane fields. This man was his now.

Jaipal could see how the ferocity of his gaze softened the man, how his eyes kept darting to avoid Jaipal's stare.

He climbed into the bed and let his trembling hands run over what was now his, desire propelled forward by the trueness of his own needs.

Jaipal craned his neck up to press his lips upon the other, but this time, he let his own tongue lead in the dance. Still, he did not linger, nor did he want to: he took the other's hand and led it downward. He grunted simple commands—yeah, like that, keep going—until he told him to stop.

The man knew what to do. He leaned over and pulled open the top drawer of the nightstand to toss Jaipal a condom and a small bottle. Jaipal put on the condom and squirted out the lube until it was all slick and wet, dripping. He closed his eyes.

Something whispered inside of him: *Take*.

Unlike the night with Janice, he didn't feel like he had been invited into something unknown. No, in that moment, he had no idea where he ended and the other began, a lust so complete that everything else disappeared except for the feeling of pleasure that radiated out from the movement of his hips, the reminder that they were two beings only coming from the rhythm set to a beat of skin meeting skin.

Jaipal was beyond words, grunting some animal command.

He was present in time unmoving, and he was all motion, all heat. This was his.

Being inside, hearing this man's sounds of enjoyment—this was what control felt like. He was more of a man now than he had ever been. The person below him grunted, moaned, but his pleasure was secondary to Jaipal's. As he held the man's hips, Jaipal curled forward like a parenthesis closing upon this stranger, everything coiling, tightening.

His hands dug into the man's sides, and Jaipal began to move faster, until he, the room, the hotel—everything except for the wondrous release of pleasure—seemed to erase itself in a flash of light.

There was no expectation to stay, there was nothing more for him to do. Jaipal dressed and left the room, going back to the bar.

He threw his money onto the bar and demanded a shot of Resolution Rum. He downed the shot in one go, feeling its burning as both respite and release. He left, taking a taxi home.

I didn't even know his name, he thought.

He had imagined these moments again and again, never quite understanding how they would transform when confronted by truth. Reality had been no nerves but all muscle—the blind impulse of passion, especially with the man. No fear, no sense of transgression. It was catch and release again and again, though he was the one who caught, the one who sought release.

The voices of self-hatred grew dimmer as soon as he walked into that hotel. He could have as much as he wanted, and if he was ever denied, there was another to take their place.

HIS FATHER CLICKED HIS TONGUE AND SHOOK HIS HEAD. "YOU REALLY are a gandoo."

He wasn't planning on going to the hotel that night, but even so, he felt a newfound impatience with the shop, as if someone had pulled back a curtain to show him the smallness of this stage and the vastness of the world that surrounded it. And yet, he was still his father's son, still his father's only employee. The world could change, yet those facts remained, kept him working for hours in that small space.

He was about to bend over to grab the entryway rug to beat its dust outside when his father, who had been counting the day's cash behind the till, made Jaipal's heart sink.

Jaipal put down the carpet and turned around, separated from his father by the seafoam-green Formica counter. His eyes scanned the shelves behind the till, feeling the full weight of his father's eyes, their whites crossed with narrow and faint lines of red.

Jaipal felt a lump in his throat and strained to swallow. His father's words hung in the room like a bad smell.

"I was joking before, you know?" his father continued. "I never knew it was true." He pulled out a cigarette from an open pack of Longbeaches on the counter, the cellophane wrapper crinkling as he did. He lit it and then leaned his forearms on the counter to drive his point home.

Jaipal said nothing, knowing it was better to let his father complete his train of thought before trying to interject.

"But you fuck women too?" He shook his head in mock surprise. "I guess I can respect that, you know. You want a little of this, a little of that. Something for everyone." He smiled, revealing his upper teeth, piss yellowed from a lifetime of smoking. He took a drag from his cigarette and blew the smoke into Jaipal's face.

Jaipal breathed in the bitter air. To be seen, especially by him—

what he had never felt before now flooded through him. A gnarled mess of misplaced guilt and shame weighed down his neck. He looked down at his toes and asked him how he knew.

His father let out a small and cruel laugh. "My girls. They work the bars too. And then they talk. This is a little island, Jaipal. News don't lack a carrier here.

"I got my girls, kinda like you. I pay 'em, though. Makes things easier. Cleaner, you know? They leave when I'm done," he said with a conspiratorial look.

Jaipal felt a surge of feeling flood through him. Shame mixed with fear mixed with anger: he had been seen, he had been called out, he had been commented upon by the one person from whom he wanted to hide everything.

When Jaipal didn't respond positively to the invitation to commiseration, his father seethed. "Don't think you're fucking special. A goat don't sire no sheep. You're just like me. Working in my shop. Your girls. Your"—he paused for a moment—"men.

"Anyway," he said, shaking his head, "I don't like gandoos working in my shop."

"You're firing me?" Jaipal asked, the words choking him as they came out.

His father shrugged. "For now. Maybe I'll need you back. You'll learn this someday: Never give an answer when there's no need for a question. It's good to keep your options."

A heavy sense of exhaustion fell like a shroud over Jaipal's eyes and ears. He didn't have the words to say anything more to his father. He made for the door.

"Wait," his father said. "I got a good deal for you."

Jaipal didn't turn around, the bunched carpet at his feet.

"You're still my boy. I won't leave you out in the cold. The same girl that told me about you told me that the Ambassador needs a new bartender." Jaipal could hear his father exhale again, could smell the smoke creeping around him. "All the crabs find their hole. Go, you might like it," his father said.

Jaipal turned his head, keeping his body facing the door. He looked his father in the eye, who, in return, gave him a small self-satisfied nod, pleased that he had solved a problem of his own making. Jaipal's heart again burned with sorrow, hatred, and a miserable sense of powerlessness. He was always to be bound, by blood and by circumstance, to this man.

9

IT WAS TEN in the morning and she had just hung up the phone with Rakesh. Bhumi had heard stories of Rakesh from before the coup as a travel agent not for holidays abroad, but for those who needed a one-way ticket to leave. His name now floated upon the wind like so many flecks of soot from the City and Colony Sugar Refinery. She had scheduled an appointment to see him later today, and the jittery nerves of a new plan kept her foot bouncing up and down. As she opened the door to her room, she looked down and saw two folded pieces of paper that had been stuck under her door.

She unfolded the first. It was a flimsy, onionskin piece of paper. In the center was a simple typewritten message.

You really should have better friends.

She began to shiver. She quickly turned around to shut the door and thought of what Aarti's father had said: *They will never leave you alone.* As she remembered his admonition, her chills seemed to radiate back into her as the pure heat of a surge of anger.

"Goddamn it, I know!" she yelled out to no one.

She gritted her teeth, crumpled the first letter, and threw it into her waste bin. She leaned over to pick up the second folded sheet. At the top was an official letterhead. "FROM THE DESK OF JITENDRA KUMAR, Assistant to the Undersecretary of Home Affairs."

Below the letterhead was handwriting unfamiliar to Bhumi. It was a nearly illegible scrawl: each hurried letter was reduced to a line bent into a curve. The crosses on *t*'s stretched across entire words. Dots for *i*'s were scattered as afterthoughts, sometimes placed after words.

After squinting and looking through the letter three times, Bhumi was finally able to discern what it had to say. It was written in Hindi using the letters of the English alphabet.

Bhumi,

We are leaving. We had already been planning to leave when Aarti was given that message, but this has hastened our departure. I wanted to think that there was another way. I now know this was a lie I told myself.

I can't tell you where we are going. I'm sure you will understand why. I'm sure you're not the first, second, or even the third person to look at this letter (I only now realized I have assumed you can read our language, but it will slow them down). I have heard of your future as well. Once we arrive where we are going, we will try to put you in contact with Aarti.

Like our ancestors, we have to cross the black waters. It's written into our fate. Like them, we don't even have the luxury of a border to sneak over. We go where the ocean's current takes us.

What is left for us to do in a country filled with so much hate? This is a country governed by tribe and belonging. And we belong to the wrong tribe. You will need strength, you will need to move quickly.

Take care of yourself, Bhumi, and prepare yourself for your journey ahead.

JK, KK, AK

As she read the letter, she heard her mother's voice: *It's written in your blood—you can leave too.*

The phrase, and its historical baggage, echoed in a way that dulled her mind and warped her sense of time, as if her mother's words had been some sort of prophecy whispered in her ear before birth, and now came the time to live its true meaning, of blood drained of life.

If she had to leave, she had to answer two questions. What would she carry with her across the ocean? What would she leave behind?

She wanted to take it all. The past weeks had made little sense. There had been an election, and because of that, the Indians were leaving the country. She had wanted an evening away from the coup with the daughter of a high-ranking official. Now Aarti had left in a haze of mystery, and her own departure wasn't far behind.

Bhumi pulled out her suitcase from underneath her bed and put it on her desk. The suitcase was made of brown leather, with a thin coating of dust on the top. It hadn't been used since her move to SPU, since that trip across the island. She took a tissue to wipe the top off before she unlocked the suitcase and unzipped it, propping the top against the window behind her desk.

First came the small things. She pulled from her bookcase a copy of *The Varieties of Pacific Plants with Taxonomic Classification*. Knowing how important the book had been to Bhumi, Aarti had gifted her a copy of it for her birthday the previous year. She had found it buried at the bottom of a mountain of books in a secondhand bookshop in the back alleys of Vilimaji. Before she gave it to Bhumi, Aarti had taken her watercolor set and painted in every single plant and flower, making the pandans purple, the flowers of the Christmas tree green, the small coconuts on the palm pink, and the passion plant a swirl of red, orange, and blue. The watercolors had soaked into the mottled and yellowed pages of the book, giving the colors the effect of looking original to the publication, moving the past from black-and-white to vibrant and hallucinogenic color.

Bhumi turned to the page for the tagimoucia flower and laid the book down spine-up to keep the page. She walked to her desk and slid a rattan-basket side drawer out to retrieve a stack of photographs. She selected a few of them and unceremoniously threw the rest in the waste bin. She put those remaining photographs in the book upon the page with the tagimoucia. Her movements were light and easy. It was easier to let the past take control, to let her mind wander away from all that had happened in the past days.

One photograph was a black-and-white photo of her family taken ten years prior. Her parents were seated in the same plastic chairs that sat underneath the house. She and her brother flanked them on either side. Her hair was in braids, his combed neatly to the side. She struggled to feel any connection with the child with the serious look upon her face. What girl would dream of this future? she asked herself, but let the question be brushed aside before she could try to answer it. She filled the rest of the space with clothing: underwear, jeans, a few shirts, a salwar kameez, and two pairs of chappals.

There was one last thing to pack: her dried cane root and drawing, still in the wooden jewelry box. The box had come with her from Sugar City, where, each August, the smell of burning molasses filled all the streets and alleys. She touched the box slowly, drawing her fingers over the fine wood and the ingrained memory. She wrapped the box in a brown dupatta and nestled it among her clothes before placing a small lock on the suitcase's zipper.

She had acquired the box back when she was eight. When each

school day ended, Jaipal took a bus the color of a raw guava to their father's shop, but Bhumi took a different northbound bus. After a few minutes of travel, she would bounce twice in her seat—a sign that she had crossed the train tracks that led to the City and Colony Sugar Refinery. She reached up as high as she could to pull the string next to the window. The bell trembled out its call next to the driver. This was her stop.

Outside was the Sugar City Carnegie Library, a building that was no more than two stories tall but always looked so grand to her. Its design was a neoclassical gesture to the island's colonial past with its cream-painted limestone, a front-facing colonnade, and a sloped roof of white tiles. Walking through the elegant dark-wood front entryway, she took in her first breaths inside and felt like she did when she was reading a book: the din of the world faded down to nothing. What greeted her was the smell of a library on an island: damp paper, like cardboard left out in the rain.

Bhumi looked to be careful in all things: her hair neatly plaited into two braids, her grass-green uniform without the stains or dribbles common to children's clothing after the lunch hour, her small nose never dripping with snot. She, like most eight-year-olds, was filled with the boundless energy of childhood. Instead of directing this energy outward, she channeled it within herself. How long could she sit still in silence? (Thirty-two minutes.) How many books could she read in an hour? (Three and a half.) How quickly could she finish her brother's homework? (Fifteen minutes.) Bhumi's nerves could overwhelm her from time to time. As with her father, feeling erupted from within her, but unlike him, she was able to silence its progression, like a hand quickly placed down on a struck cymbal.

When Bhumi entered the library, she turned to face the woman who stood guard at the door. This woman greeted every child who passed into her realm.

Ms. Edwards was one of the few remaining white holdovers from the colonial days. With her Peter Pan–collared dresses and gray hair pulled tightly back into a bun, she would routinely snap her fingers to send young boys or girls back outside if they ran in and failed to give a proper greeting. Bhumi had been among Ms. Edwards's elect, issued a library card printed upon heavy royal-blue paper rather than the normal and flimsy manila paper. This special card allowed for up to three books to be checked out at a time for a two-week lending period.

After growing bored of the boundaries of the children's section, she wandered into the Dewey-decimal-organized 500 aisle of the open shelves. Her eyes fell upon 581.4: Anatomy and Morphology of Plants. She picked up *The Varieties of Pacific Plants with Taxonomic Classification*. It was a colonial-era book. Each page featured woodcut drawings of various plants with labels in English and Latin.

As Bhumi flipped through the section on roots, she was awed by the sheer variety in the world. There were the adventitious roots, for example, like those of the sugarcane.

At home, her mother was cooking a fish curry and the pungent smell of fried river fish was slowly sifting through the house.

"Can we go to Ashwin Mama's cane field?" she asked.

"Of course," her mother said before asking, "Why?"

Bhumi had come prepared for such a question and held in her hands a green file folder typically reserved for the storage of schoolwork. From within she drew out a piece of scrap paper with a diagram done in charcoal pencil.

The drawing looked like a trident. The center prong, thick and cylindrical, was labeled PRIMARY SHOOT. The smaller flanking prongs, which jutted out from the bottom of the primary shoot at forty-five-degree angles, were labeled SECONDARY SHOOTS. Emerging from the bottom of the primary shoot were several thin tentacle-like appendages labeled SHOOT ROOTS, and so on, down to little scribbles of sett roots. The entire diagram was titled "Sugarcane Cutting, Adventitious Root."

Her mother took the drawing carefully from Bhumi. It was settled; they were going to go on Saturday. Bhumi loved it when life with her mother was an adventure to be kept from her father. It felt like winning a prize.

That Saturday, Bhumi and her mother left the house around ten in the morning and walked a half mile to a taxi stand. They took a taxi fifteen minutes to the east, out of the city and straight into the ramshackle farms of the country. When they arrived, they saw that the cane was young, no more than two feet high and green like the Minor. It looked nothing like a field of cane, but instead like acres of young elephant grass.

As they reached the field, they saw a man with a wide-brimmed hat and a mustache that was reminiscent of a Bollywood hero. The farmer, one of her mother's older brothers, had been waiting for some time with his hands in the pockets of his linen pants stained with dirt. He, like all the other Indian cane growers, was a tenant farmer on the ancestral lands of native-borns. In her Indian-only primary school, Bhumi had read stories of how recruiters back in India lied to the desperate, making them sign a contract for five years of work (never quite mentioning that they would be laboring on a sugar plantation). If they ever wanted to return home, it would cost them five more years of hellish work. Few ever took the Empire up on the offer, leaving the Indians marooned on the island forever.

Her mother greeted her brother with a simple "Ram Ram" and asked how the cane was growing.

"Same-same, like always. God willing it will continue to grow well, and we'll have a good harvest in a few months. May no strangers look at our fields, may their evil eye never fall upon us."

Her mother nodded.

Her uncle then turned and pointed beyond the dirt road from which they had come to an empty and fenced field. "Look at this, didi," he said, speaking to her mother. "Remember how they took Keshav Bhai's farm? Look at that. Empty. These kaamchor. They could fence it in, even raise a few chickens. They keep it empty."

Neither Bhumi nor her mother said anything in reply. In the silence, Ashwin turned and finally noticed his niece. "Ey, Bhumi!" he yelled, a wide smile crossing his face. Bhumi gave him a "Ram Ram."

"She's so impatient, all she wants to see is the cane root," her mother said. "She likes plants. She gets good marks in science." She beamed with the pride of a protective mother, waiting to be praised for her work.

"Takes after her mother," he said. He turned to Bhumi. "You know, your ma was the only one in the family to pass the entrance exam for high school! She could have done whatever she wanted."

Bhumi listened in a half-hearted way. She grabbed a cane stalk by its lower internode and ran her fingers from the soil up to the first leaf.

"Your nani worked this plant," Ashwin said, bending down on one knee to talk to her. "My fields used to be part of her plantation. She worked right here." Bhumi watched as his eyes moved upward to search the length of the field. Even though her father's family had moved into shopkeeping after their time tending the cane ended, most of her mother's family had stayed in the fields.

In the distance, the chattering of mynahs could be heard as they plodded through the fields. Ashwin clapped his hands together. "So, you want to see cane root?" he asked.

He squatted down, reached out, and grabbed the stalk nearest him, pinching it so close to the base that brown soil rubbed up against his rough fingers. In one quick upward jolt, the stalk was lifted from the ground. It made a small effort to resist such movement: clumps of dirt stuck to its spindly roots from its desire to remain attached to where it came from. Her uncle bent over to pick up his cane knife—close in size and shape to a small machete. One downward movement of the forearm was all it took to sever root from stalk.

She cupped the root system and petted its various stems and shoot roots with her thumb. The presence in her hand of what only a few days before she had studied in a book took her breath away.

When she was finished, she tried to hand it back to her uncle, who steadfastly refused. "It's yours now," he told her.

She dried out the root in the sunshine next to jars of her mother's sun pickle on the balcony. Once it was dry, she asked her mother for something in which to keep it. Her mother gave her a wooden jewelry box. The small box was made of a light ash wood with dovetailed corners, inlaid with rosewood that had been chip-carved with a pattern of four-petaled flowers. When opened, the box revealed a lining of smooth red velvet, soft like an animal's underbelly to the touch.

Bhumi had kept the root safe by putting it into a small plastic bag and placing it into the box with her drawing. Now that box would leave with her. The old earth of a country left behind would follow her, hiding in her shadow for the days yet to come.

10

RAKESH'S OFFICE WAS on the second floor of an arcade off Gordon Street, where small Indian shops were operating with a misplaced normalcy: barbers sweeping hair; roti shops cleaning up after the lunch rush; stalls filling the air with the sweet steam from pots of coffee, tea, and Nestlé Milo. Rakesh sat in a frayed and worn banker's chair behind a cheap desk made of rattan, topped with a scratched and scuffed glass pane. Underneath the glass was a six-month calendar that took up the entirety of the desktop. There were two plastic orange chairs in a corner and not much else in the way of furniture.

He was on the phone as Bhumi walked in but still stood up, holding the receiver to his ear with his shoulder, and mouthed a quick "Ram Ram" before waving his hand for Bhumi to enter and to sit in one of the chairs. He was a squat bald man with a goatee, and as he stood up, he revealed himself to be shorter than Bhumi, with a nose so large it occupied his face like the Finance Tower did the city center.

Bhumi looked around as she sat. On the walls were posters of far-flung locales: the Empire State Building on one, the Taj Mahal on another, Big Ben on a third. Each poster had the name of an airline in the corner. Bhumi had never been in an airplane before.

He put the receiver down upon its black base and twisted his body back to face her. He asked her to remind him of her last name.

"Ah," he said. "Satendraji's daughter. Aao, aao, pull your chair here. It's been many years since I've seen your father. I used to go to Sugar City three times a year," he said, holding up three fingers on his right hand. He wore a fat gold ring on his thumb. "I don't go much anymore. How long has it been since I've been to your father's store? Ten years? More? The last time I saw you was when you were this tall." He reached down and held his hand low to the floor. "You're now at SPU, right? Scholarship? How are your studies? How are you?"

Bhumi stiffened at the thought of small talk. It felt like too important of a time to engage in the balm of minor conversation, even if it made the interaction seem more normal. She shook her head and placed her hands on his desk. "I need a one-way ticket."

In one movement, Rakesh got up to open his door. He poked his head outside before he closed it again, locking the dead bolt in place.

"Not many people want to talk these days, but of course, it's understandable," Rakesh said to Bhumi. "Tell me, what happened?" he added in a whisper that sounded a bit too practiced to indicate actual surprise.

"Does it matter?" Bhumi asked.

"Well . . ." Rakesh paused and scratched the hair on his chin before leaning back in his chair, causing it to tip slightly on its rear legs. "Not to me. From here, I see us all leaving, every day, one after another, each on a different flight. Some people are migrants. We all used to be migrants. Now we're twice-migrants. Our parents and grandparents and great-grandparents left once, now we leave again." He nodded and pursed his lips, reminding Bhumi of a schoolteacher proud of his insight. "No, you don't need to tell me anything. I notice things. You call right after the General's speech. You're a student. Were you expelled? Why? Not everyone was. What did you do? You don't need to tell me anything, but you will have to tell them."

Bhumi asked who *they* were. He demurred, first wanting to know where she wanted to go. When she said New Zealand, he shook his head and told her the story of Ahmed Gounder. He was the brother of the Labor Party's chief counsel—a pretty good reason to leave the country. His request for asylum was rejected at the border. Something to do with a half-baked arrest warrant issued by the country and sent over to New Zealand. This fact enraged Rakesh. "They think we're small-small people from a small-small country," he said.

"We're not big enough to leave for New Zealand," he rambled on. "You see, the first people who left this country were the wealthiest. The doctors and lawyers with big money. The industrialists. The big business owners. They got to go to Britain, to New Zealand, to wherever. You know how they got out so easily?" Rakesh did not wait for Bhumi to answer. "They already had bank accounts in those countries!"

The idea that importance could lead to safety gave Bhumi a sliver of hope. Even though the door was locked, she looked over her shoulder and lowered her voice before she asked if he thought Jitendra Kumar's family had a chance to cross to safety.

Rakesh let out a chortle and began to choke on his own spit. After finally clearing his throat, he replied. "He should have left months ago. You know what happened to him?"

Rakesh paused. Bhumi was hungry for an answer.

"The General made his list. He purged the government of the Indians—except for Jitendra. I guess he likes Jitendra. My opinion? Jitendra knew too much about the security services. Our country may be small, beti, but it does like to spy on its people. I would know.

"Jitendra is a damn fool. Now is not the time for small acts. You know what he did? He, being a man who hates to rock the boat, warned the General that he *might* step down in solidarity with the other Indians. The General is a simple man: you are with him or you are against him. Why confuse him with maybe this and maybe that? And someone with Jitendra's knowledge of national security? You don't make stupid threats. You leave, secretly, and you never come back. A fool! A damned fool."

"I didn't know," Bhumi said, looking down at her hands in her lap, thinking of how Aarti had had to deliver the weight, the punishment, of her father's decision back to him. "I was with Aarti. Some officer gave her a message to send to her father. She never told me what it was."

"An Indian is an Indian and an Indian's life is cheap right now," Rakesh began. "He probably said there was a second chance: apologize, grovel, become a lapdog, never question anything ever again. And if he didn't . . ." Rakesh looked away and gave a helpless shrug.

Bhumi looked past Rakesh, unfocused, toward the wall behind him. "Have you ever thought about America?" Rakesh asked, changing the subject. "You already have a tourist visa to go there."

"What do you mean?" Bhumi asked, confused.

"Your mother called, about a year ago," Rakesh said. "Right when it was becoming clear that the Labor Party was going to put in Indian candidates. Sent in a passport application, paperwork, payment. She said that a girl like you needs to have a plan, just in case. Smart woman, your mother. Everything was approved quickly."

"Of course," Bhumi said, feeling a small bit of panic rise like bile from her stomach. She ran a finger up and down the scar on the side of her neck. She couldn't remember signing any papers. She had never seen her own passport. "Raj Uncle and Farida Aunty left for California," Bhumi said, trying to change the subject. "Raj Uncle owned a taxi company."

"Oh yes, I helped them escape," Rakesh replied. "The soldiers put a big target on his little company. Anyway, they know your parents, right? We have a good lawyer near San Francisco. He can make it easier to get papers, get asylum. America is fine. Country is so big, you can hide anywhere. No one cares about our island," he said, drumming his fingers.

Lawyers, asylum, papers—more process, more steps, more logistics for her to learn. "Yes. Of course. Is San Francisco near where Raj Uncle went?"

"Yes."

The thought of the familiar in the unknown was a comforting bit of assurance. "Tiik hai, accha. Fine. Okay. San Francisco. Leaving when?"

"Tomorrow?" Rakesh replied. "Two seats left."

"So soon?"

"Do you want to wait? The General moves fast."

"Set," Bhumi said as she leaned back in her chair, a heavy sigh escaping from her lips. He had a point. So this is my departure, she thought. Not leaving a little village by ship, but taking a flight from the international airport.

"What you need to know is this. When you get into the country, don't tell them anything. You're going on a tourist visa. When you get there, you will say you are visiting your family for six months. Don't say anything. Only when you get in do you ask for asylum. Like I said, there is a good lawyer. His name is Sumit Mishra. He is handling all the cases near San Francisco for us Indians. Your parents' friend Rajji, he already knows about the lawyer. You will go to the lawyer and you will tell him everything and he will start the asylum process. You will have to prove that you can't come back here."

"I won't come back," Bhumi replied, letting her statement hang in the air like a bad smell in a small space. When she asked him about payment, he said it already had been settled, that her mother had called the day after the broadcast about Ram Maharaj to give him her passport information and prepaid for a ticket anywhere out of the country.

As she unlocked the door and walked out, she almost ran into the person waiting. He was Indian—young, slight, and with skin as dark as a kala jamun. He was shaking and sweating, out of breath. He ran into Rakesh's office without saying a word. Bhumi immediately heard the click of the dead bolt.

As she walked down the stairs back into the arcade, confusion clouded her mind. Her mother seemed to have been miles ahead of her, seeing her departure as a foregone conclusion.

In front of SPU, she watched as two young men with large suitcases scurried past her and threw their bags into the trunk of a taxi. Before Bhumi could recognize who they were, the taxi sped off in the direction of the Finance Tower.

As she cut across the campus, the world around her started to take on the eerie glow of finality. Everything, from the stream that ran through the grounds, to the shack where the guard sat near the gate, to the tendrils of the banyan tree near the road—all of it felt like it was speeding from a present to a past tense.

11

JAIPAL NEEDED A nap. Too much had transpired in the last eighteen hours to merit doing anything else. His father wouldn't notice anymore if he started work late—or maybe he would. He always figured everything out, eyes and ears across the island. It didn't matter: the store was his to manage now, the accounts his own to keep.

The country was collapsing, taking everything with it. And yet the question was the same: did he have to go to work? The time clock didn't care if young men were getting shot, if the hotels were closing up and down the coast.

Jaipal's bedroom hadn't changed much in the past five years. On the wall remained a poster of the 1982 national team that had placed last in the World Cup qualification. On his dresser was a dulled bronze trophy from the year his football team won the local championship. He had lackadaisically played team sports his whole life. His body wasn't built for speed, though perhaps he could outlast another, if given the chance. It was too late when he realized he would have been a beautiful boxer: battered, bloody, but still standing after round after round of pummeling.

From time to time, he thought he should clear out his room, turn it into a place for a man to live. He could go down to the artisan market and buy some tapa to hang in lieu of childhood bits and baubles. There was no point—no one entered his room except for himself, and on a great occasion, his mother or father. He had no one to impress. Or if he did, they weren't at the hotel anymore.

He stripped off all his clothes and climbed into his bed. He had never been able to fall asleep unless he was naked, and naps were no exception. The thinness of his linen sheets fell as light as a kiss upon his side as he curled his body into a small letter c. The feeling of the top sheet brought a wave of homesickness.

This wasn't home, he thought as the drowsiness overcame him. Home was lying beside the bodies of others, feeling them twitch and turn as sleep came over them. With empty arms, he fell asleep imagining her hands running down his chest and soon imagined her hands, his hands, his hands, her hands—each and every one of them holding him, lifting him up, rocking him into a rest needed from a day stretching onward, a day not yet done.

AT FIRST, HE HEARD THE RINGING IN HIS HEAD, THE SOUND CONJURED from the leftover remnants of a dream. The telephone's insistence soon pulled him up and out of his sleep: the shrill sound that rang and rang and rang until the receiver was pulled up with a jostle of hard plastic tapping against itself.

His bedroom was the nearest to the phone that sat on a counter in the kitchen. No matter how hushed the voice, no matter how quick the calls, every word, every laugh, and every whisper carried into his room, slid under his door, went right to his ear, the conversations lifted upon some insistent cross-draft. He always heard it all: the gossip from his mother's friends, every single one of Bhumi's boyfriends, the hoarse laughter of his father's drinking buddies.

He listened in, burying his head underneath his pillow, feeling the cold spot it hid below as a caress against his cheek. His sister's voice was coming through the phone. Even before he could make out her words, he could hear her tone, pitch, and cadence. Something was wrong. He held his breath. His mother began to speak.

He had known of his mother's plan for Bhumi, but none of that prepared him for the shock of a sudden truth: this was what it was coming to.

Even his sister was to be punished for being born in this country. His sister, always perfect, always prepared, always moving through life on a ladder, each step taking her up, up, up, further and further from this family into a world all of her own.

What does the island look like from an airplane? A question whose answer wasn't his to give.

It seemed right for his sister to leave. She had already left; Vilimaji felt like another world. The furthest north he had ever gone was Waidiva with his family, the furthest east was Cevaira to go fishing with his old friends. Bhumi wasn't going to leave much behind: this was a country eating itself. If it cared little for people like the greengrocer or Salim, what would it do to someone with actual talent, with a hope for something better?

He tried to think of Salim, tried to conjure an image of his lifeless body left in a roadside ditch. He instead saw his friend's brother as he once was: smiling, bold when all that was needed was meek quiet, a presence as regular as the daily newspaper. His death had burned a little hollow in his chest, but the thought that his sister could escape was cool relief.

The time when he could protect his sister had ended long ago. When they were kids, they'd had their daily bus ride: he took his to the store, she took hers to the library. When everything pressed upon the seams and it all burst out, together they would leave, sometimes under the blaring step-outside-and-sweat sun of midday, and sometimes, only sometimes, under the light of the moon. He would lead her all the way down to the water to see the chickens, the coconut man, the sea turtle.

And then, something shifted. This life became hers for the taking, his for the fumbling through.

In the sitting room, he saw that the doors to the small balcony were open. His mother's back was turned as she faced out toward the street. He knew where she kept it all: in the television cabinet, tucked behind the TV. Travel documents, money, everything someone would need to leave.

He looked at his watch. The store needs me, but fuck it, he thought, I want to touch them, to see what they're like.

He took out his sister's papers from the cabinet, thumbing through the pages, sorting the envelopes, flipping back and forth the pages of a little red passport that would let her out of the country. Maybe this was what safety felt like: a departure whose weight could be measured in a few papers.

He put it all back in the cabinet and turned to see his mother standing in the kitchen. He hadn't heard her enter, hadn't felt her eyes watching as he flipped the pages.

"I just talked to her. I felt my right foot tickling this morning. I knew she would have to go. She has to. It's getting worse here. And she's . . ." She trailed off. "She needs to have her own future, she has to figure it out. She can't do it here."

"And us?"

"We'll manage on our own."

A gust of air and lick of a flame burst within. "I've got to get going," he said, jaw clenched.

"Today? Where? The hotels are closed, I heard," she said, bewildered.

"They're closed. Papa gave me the shop. He's letting me keep the money."

"The money! What good is money now? Don't believe him. He's scared. He's a coward." She paused, and Jaipal could feel her searching for her words. "Don't go, beta. Who knows what'll happen there? You've heard the stories. You know what's going on. It's not safe."

She hadn't sounded this scared on the phone with his sister. Still, he pressed on. "What will he do if he knows I'm not working there?" he asked, goading her on.

"Both my children, afraid of that man. I've lived with him longer than both of you. What's a slap across the face in comparison to your life?" she exclaimed, her eyes wide. She took a deep breath and shook her head.

His mother was right, but there was something else. With his sister, she was cool, collected—with him, she had no plan, and without one she was wide-eyed and fearful. Jaipal was now filled with the momentum of his own emotion. He searched himself for his voice and dug his hands into his pockets. "If we're going to stay in this country, we need to do something. I need to do something. I've got a little bit of money saved up from the hotel. It's not enough. I need more money."

"Enough for what?"

"Enough to live—or leave. Enough to get out of this country or just enough to say no, so that I don't have to be afraid of him throwing me out of this house when he finds out I'm not working for him."

"Oh, beta."

The words were coming out of him before he knew what they meant. "I don't know how much you'll have saved after paying Rakesh. The plane tickets, the bribes, someone to make all those documents. It's not cheap. It's fine. She needs it. What about me?"

"You know I'm here for you," his mother said. Her voice was hushed, meek. From her faltering resolve came more of his own anger.

"No one is going to Rakesh for me," he spat. "No one is putting me on a plane. I have to look after myself." His anger was misplaced, but the feeling of power over someone else was intoxicating. "I'm going to work," he said as he turned around to walk through the door. His mother said nothing in reply.

As he walked past the gate, he felt a sense of miserableness overcome him. With all that was going on, hurting another came much easier than anything else. Above all that, he felt the wretched sense that there was no winning, no victory that could be declared over anything anymore. There was only the smallness of survival, of making it through the days that turned only upon the cruelty of chance.

HE RAISED THE METAL SHUTTERS THAT CLOSED OFF THE FRONT DOOR and windows. The clink-clank of their raising reminded him of his father. It had been his decision a few years ago to put them in. "I don't trust those neighborhood kids," he had said. "They'll steal my stuff."

It was as if he had predicted that the day would come when the front windows of all the Indian-owned shops would become targets for those who had suffered a lifetime of petty jealousies and poverty. The Indians had become the country's merchants and capitalists, while the natives stayed poor. Now the meek were overtaking the strong.

The shop floor seemed reasonably well stocked, but when he poked his head into the back room, he saw the grim reality his father had left him to deal with. Where there should have been carton upon carton of fresh fruit and vegetables, there were only a few crates. When he counted the boxes of everything else, he found that they still had the essentials: cigarettes, batteries, condoms, soda, and bags of namkeen. Enough to get anyone through a crisis.

In the till there was nothing more than a hundred in small bills.

The store was his, and it was empty. Perhaps this was another one of his father's cruel jokes—to give him a store that had no business. He turned to grab a pack of Marlboros from the shelf. Leaning against the counter, waiting for customers, eyes scanning the aisles, he felt a little sense of awe at how casually he had thrown about his last thought. *This was his now.* This feeling must have been what his father had felt when the store was passed on to him.

The store had provided for the family since the Great War. Back then, the Empire and the Americans purchased one hundred acres in Sugar City for an airstrip—what was now the airport. Then came the white soldiers and an economy that catered to them. Nightclubs were built and stocked with Resolution Rum. The greengrocers multiplied and vied to have bottles of Coca-Cola in their iceboxes. The Indians did great. The natives couldn't hustle for a piece of that Yankee dollar—maybe they tried, but the Empire ruled with a maze of permits and passes, and only the Empire could dole them out. The natives languished. The Indians succeeded.

Jaipal's paternal grandfather took advantage of the situation. He was only a teenager, but even then, he could spot a good opportunity. At first, he bought cases of soft drinks from the stores and sold them one by one just outside the bases. He listened to what those soldiers wanted. And when he had the money, he lied about his age and signed a lease. Lal's Market and Goods stocked not only Coca-Cola but Lucky Strikes, pinup playing cards, and sheet upon sheet of soft banana cake topped with a thick sugary icing.

What was his now is mine.

Everything in this store belonged to him, and when someone entered the store, they would have to trade their hard-earned money for his goods.

A customer came through the door: an Indian woman, no older than his sister. He caught her eye and flashed her a smile in the way he looked at the goras at the hotel: welcoming, ready to please. It was a smile of service, slight deference, a look that said, *Talk to me, I'll listen, and I won't say a word.*

Immediately, she looked down and disappeared into the pre-packaged-food aisle.

He took a drag and laughed to himself. No one fucked the man selling cigarettes.

He stubbed his cigarette out on a glass ashtray under the counter. For a few years, he had held fast to the hope gifted to him by strangers. Their kisses, the strange names of their towns and cities, their need, above all, to be heard. They gave him a reason. His body, always towering and bumbling through a world that seemed two sizes too small, was enough to contain their secret wish to be seen, felt, heard, fucked, desired, loved.

They were gone. All of that was gone. Only the store was his now.

He wondered if any of them thought of him anymore, wondered if they saw his country on the news and thought of the man from the hotel, the one with whom they had shared skin and scars and fears and secrets under the lazy swings of a ceiling fan caked in dust.

The guns in Parliament had shot off a reminder across the island. He had lived a fantasy. He had never been more than fifteen kilometers from the home he had lived in his whole life.

The woman bought four bags of namkeen, three packets of batteries, and a carton of Gold Flake cigarettes. She left the store. Two soldiers walked down Albert Lane. He could only focus on the ways their hands rested around their guns' barrels, fingers wrapped loosely against gunmetal, their palms moving ever so slightly, fingers stroking the power that they slung over their shoulders.

The soldiers stopped across the street from the store and a bolt of fear ran through him, a feeling sudden and severe. The pair were young, all buzz cut and square jaw, razor-thin bodies hungry from a lifetime of want, now craving a slice of glory.

He wished he could lock the door, pull down the metal shutters. He could hear his father's words inside of him. *I don't trust those kids.*

The General had been one of those kids. It was never mentioned anywhere, but everyone knew everyone on an island. He had been raised by his mother and her family, his father leaving the picture early in his life. They lived in the hilly bush, and he was neither of the chiefs nor of money. He had left school early to join the fight against the Empire. Scrawny poor boys made the best bomb throwers.

The soldiers now stared through the glass into the store. They didn't look at Jaipal, but instead right through him, making him feel like he was a huntsman spider emerged from a dark corner to take residence upon a door handle—swat it away, swat it away, kill it quickly.

They soon walked away, and Jaipal felt his stomach turn: relief mixed with fear mixed with the cold sweat of the encounter. Death around the corner.

12

THE SOUND OF rainfall on metal roofs pinged in the distance as the light passed from the brightness of the day to the filtered and blue light of evening clouds. In time, the chatter of woodswallows and the chirps of myzomelas were replaced by the din of katydids and cane toads, with the occasional burry song of a pauraque. She could hear the sounds of cars honking their horns in the bedlam near the edge of campus, of those trying to escape into whatever came next.

This had all been hers. She had gone to university—the first in her family to do so. And not only that, her marks on the University Entrance Exams had been rewarded with a full scholarship. There was a room for her in the women's dormitory, where she did not have to make her bed or clean. No father, no mother, no distractions. All she had to do was study and think.

She stood up, straightening the hem of her kameez. With two hands, she picked up her full suitcase off her bed and walked out of her room, leaving the door open behind her. She had told no one she was leaving and, in truth, had no idea whether, besides Aarti, any of her other friends and acquaintances on campus had already left. After the General's speech on the radio, the only certainty was that things fall apart quickly.

The taxi line stretched from the curb near the taxis through the pedestrian gate and into the SPU campus. As she stood waiting, the drizzle stuck to the road and the cars sounded like they were cutting through small waves. The smell of the damp earth, its scent as musty as that of a sweaty body, filled the air.

As Bhumi reached closer to the front of the line, she saw that none of the taxis were driven by the man she had talked to earlier. She heard his words in her mind: *I'll drive this taxi until they take it away from me.*

Someone yelled out to her, and a tall boy with tawny skin whose biceps seemed to pulse underneath his T-shirt grabbed Bhumi's suitcase and threw it on top of a taxi, causing the car to sink ever so slightly into its suspension. As the rain began to pick up, the gray-haired taxi driver pulled a blue tarpaulin cloth from under the driver's seat and draped it over Bhumi's suitcase before tying it down with his piece of rope.

"Thank you," Bhumi said to both of them. Neither acknowledged that she had spoken a word. Bhumi recognized the boy from Organic Chemistry, the type who used his gleaming smile and dimpled cheeks to ensure the help of others for homework or exams. In this light, he suddenly looked older, his smile now effaced by worry.

The boy took the passenger seat next to the driver. Bhumi was stuck in the middle of the back. She sat between a small woman whose eyes never blinked and a man who smelled distinctly of fried garlic. He kept scratching his stubble, and the sandpaper sound this made grated right into Bhumi's ear. His left leg pressed against Bhumi and rubbed against her as he shook his foot up and down. The man made Bhumi aware of her own tics. She stopped herself from bouncing her leg.

The taxi continued toward the Finance Tower and the number of cars multiplied. The cacophony of smog, car horns, voices, and the pitter-patter of rain made its way through open windows into the taxi. When the car finally stopped, the other passengers burst from the doors, leaving Bhumi sitting alone in the backseat. She sat still for a moment, closing her eyes as she took in a deep breath.

At the station, Bhumi's eyes darted from bus to bus. Unmoving, she was a sandbar breaking up the swirling waters of the sea—people ran and scurried around her to get to where they needed to go. She found her bus: stainless steel with a coral-pink stripe running the length of its midsection. In the center of the stripe someone had written, in hand-painted cursive, "Sugar City Lines."

By the time she got to its door, the line to enter was ten people deep, but the delay from a driver change caused many to give up and head over to a coach that was ready to depart. A rotund Indian driver finally showed up. "Single ticket," she offered.

"No single tickets, only return," he replied, shaking his bald head back and forth, rain glistening atop it. Bhumi looked at him in confusion. "Sister, no one is returning. Can't you see?" He gestured around him. "We come back empty. Return tickets are money so we can get paid and we can go back and forth." He chuckled to himself in a distant and forlorn way.

Bhumi entered the coach, and felt no relief. The inside was filled with mothers trying to quell their own fear as they engaged in the everyday work of looking after their children, fathers running their hands through their hair or patting their bald heads, and children looking wide-eyed and alert from being pulled out of a daily routine. Student couples who would normally have avoided being seen in public for fear of gossip sat with their heads resting upon their lovers'.

Every face had the same haggard look that David's had had when he was arrested.

Bhumi thought she could jump out of the coach and run back to her dorm, back to the lab bench, and back to lab partners who never did any of the work. Reality began to worm its way into her fantasy. She would also be going back to Aarti's absence, back to Rakesh, back to the officer at the checkpoint, and back to the General's country. This realization caused her to sink further down into her seat.

The driver started up the engine and its rumble filled the cabin. Bhumi turned herself around and stared out the window. Outside the city, on the two-lane King's Road, which ringed the island, traffic moved at a slow pace, as each car and bus was headed in the same direction. She had talked to her mother after she had gone to Rakesh's, to tell her of her departure. Her mother had told her that she had had a dream last year: she had seen Bhumi in a fishing boat out in the ocean, and she knew that Bhumi was going to drown. She had called Rakesh the next day. Bhumi was aghast. Her mother placed such importance on her inane superstitions, and to have one come true felt like watching gravity turn off and seeing all that was once solid float into the air.

In time, the bus reached the outskirts of Sugar City, traveling alongside sugarcane fields and train tracks. From her childhood, Bhumi knew the beat of harvest time was measured with the high-pitched whistle of a locomotive carrying open-slatted trailers stacked to the brim with dried stalks ready to be pressed, boiled, and evaporated into sugar.

The tracks soon curved northeast, while the bus went north. Bhumi knew that the tracks would keep going until the homes faded and tin shacks grew like hardscrabble weeds next to open-air sewers, until they finally reached the City and Colony Sugar Refinery.

Soon, she was in Sugar City's center, where the bright lights and the movement of people belied the midnight hour. The bus pulled into the station, and as she exited, her heart skipped as she almost ran into her mother, a statue-still woman with her arms crossed.

"You're home." Her mother's two words sounded disappointed but also filled with the possibility of something new. Around her, the city looked like it did during Ramzan, the stores open at night to cater to the city's Muslims.

"It wasn't supposed to be like this," Bhumi said. She had tried to steel her nerves, to encase her feelings so that this return home—an event she had always imagined would be accompanied by the triumph of accomplishment—wouldn't strip her bare.

Her mother leaned in to draw her into an embrace, but Bhumi didn't let herself fully relax into her mother's arms. She was still too angry to feel anything except impatience for her own departure. She kept her eyes open and stared beyond her mother's shoulders to the passengers exiting the coach.

She pulled away from the hug. At first, she saw the woman she had always known, dressed in a tan cardigan sweater over a salwar kameez. Upon a closer look, however, she was surprised by the changes since she had last seen her. Her mother had always been a distinguished-looking if rather unremarkable woman. She had kept her figure and small curves into her middle age. Her eyes had always been lined with kajal. Gold bangles were always around her wrists, and gold earrings hung from her ears. The red sindoor of marriage lined the part of her hair like a thin wound.

Now it looked like her mother had diminished in some way. Bhumi couldn't remember if she had always been so short or if she had lost some of her height since the last time she saw her. Bhumi had always been a few inches taller than her mother, but it now was as if she towered above her. Her mother looked tired—not from lack of sleep, instead from the deleterious effects of time and circumstance.

"Is the store open?" Bhumi asked.

"Jaipal is there," her mother said. "You think your father would risk his own life to work? All this"—she paused to wave her hand at the crowd around the bus—"is what he'll run away from. He'll make Jaipal work for it." Her mother let out a long sigh.

Bhumi was about to say something—a word of support for her

brother, a word against her father's greed—but she saw her bag being thrown onto the asphalt from the luggage hold. She picked it up and brought it back to her mother.

"You shouldn't lock the suitcase," her mother said, seeing a brass luggage lock the size of a fifty-cent coin placed on the suitcase's two zipper pulls.

"Why?" Bhumi asked, looking away from the bus station toward Queen's Street.

"I heard that the military police at the airport take whatever bags are locked and burn them. Anything they can't see or open is taken. May the evil eye fall upon them."

"I'm surprised," Bhumi said, reaching over and yanking on the lock. It broke with her tug. She handed it to her mother to place in her cardigan. "That they would wait for an excuse. You'd think they would burn everything without asking."

Her mother let out a hollow laugh, sounding nervous. Bhumi could tell that the mere reference to violence had put her on edge.

They set off toward the store and passed a Punjabi restaurant that mainly catered to tourists. As she followed her mother's eyes, Bhumi looked through its window and saw its lonely buffet still steaming in the center of the empty dining room. She craved a home-cooked meal, even something as simple as aloo gobi and roti.

They kept on through Queen's Street, the lights of the stores shining through their windows onto the darkened footpath. Familiar faces took on a withered aspect—everyone looked like lost spirits wandering toward the gates of an unknown hell.

"Are you ready?" her mother asked with a gentleness that reminded her of conversations after her father's anger had ravaged the house. It was a voice Bhumi loved: not of a parent who lorded over her with rules and expectations, but of a co-conspirator ready to share a secret.

"I don't know. It's all happening so fast. I'm not ready to leave."

"No one is."

Bhumi felt no solace in the comparison. "That makes me feel worse."

Her mother drew her close, and Bhumi hung on to her mother's arm, a child looking for protection from the world around her. "You'll find your way," her mother said to her in a quiet voice that made Bhumi feel the hollowness of her own escape.

They turned left onto Albert Lane. It was a road wide enough to fit only one car going one-way, and there it was, two storefronts down the road: Lal's Market and Goods, the same as always.

Through the window, she could see Jaipal working behind the counter, getting a package of AA batteries for a customer, punching a few numbers on the beige mechanical till, and placing the batteries into a plastic bag.

Bhumi hadn't seen her brother since she'd left. When talking to him on the phone (a difficult proposition, for her brother rarely had anything to say on the phone besides curt answers), she would try to coax him to take the coach to Vilimaji. She thought it would be fun to show her big brother around the town, to take him out for a drink, to introduce him to her friends. "Sure, I want to," he would start, before doubling back. "I've got something going on this weekend." He never came. Now he would never see her in Vilimaji, or on the SPU campus.

As soon as Bhumi entered, she was surrounded by a familiar smell, an intoxicating mix of nostalgia and appetite: the pungent aroma of spices from the dry-goods aisle and the green freshness of vegetables. Her stomach let out another growl.

"Welcome home, Bhumi," Jaipal said. He slowly swung the counter upward on its hinge to move into the store's open space. She was surprised how calming it felt to see him. The world outside could subside, if only for a bit.

He placed his hand on her shoulder. "I heard what happened," he said. "I'm sorry." Without missing a beat, he began again: "You leave tomorrow, right? Why don't we worry about tomorrow when tomorrow comes?" He smiled.

Bhumi watched with her brother as their mother took a few silent and slow steps to move forward toward them and drum her fingers upon the counter. She stared for a moment at the cigarettes lining the wall before she turned around.

"Where's Papa?" Bhumi asked, more of a formality than anything.

"Papa stays out late and sometimes comes home drunk," her brother said.

"Okay . . . ," Bhumi said, trailing off. He had always drunk—he had no other hobbies. And anyway, drinking when the country was falling apart felt like a reasonable response.

"The problem," he continued, "is his heart."

"His heart?" Bhumi asked, her face scrunching in confusion.

Her mother chuckled for a moment, and Bhumi turned toward the sound. "A lifetime of anger does nothing good to the heart," she said in a scratchy voice that sounded both rueful and wistful. "He had an incident last month."

"An incident?" Bhumi asked.

"Yes, well . . ." Her mother trailed off again.

"Last month he woke up in the middle of the night," Jaipal said quickly, clearly frustrated with their mother's wandering thoughts. Bhumi felt like he too easily grew annoyed with her meandering emotions, though now wasn't the time to bring it up. "He had some pain in his chest. Papa said he wanted to go to the A & E. They said he'd had a minor heart attack. His blood pressure was too high. He needs to eat better—no samosa, mithai, beer, grog. He needs to control his anger."

Their mother let out another chuckle as she looked out the window onto the street, still awake with activity, and balled the hem of her cardigan into her fist.

"Why didn't anyone tell me?" Bhumi asked.

"We didn't want to worry you or bother you," Jaipal said. "You had your studies. The protests had just started. We thought you had enough to worry about."

"He went to the hospital!" Bhumi yelled, feeling like the shoal that connected her to her family had started to submerge after the arrival of the tide.

"We should go," their mother said. "I need to get Bhumi a meal. She hasn't eaten yet."

Bhumi was hungry, and yet she felt a minor sense of annoyance at her mother's taking her away from the conversation. She wanted to catch up, hear something from her brother: how had the hotel been, who was he spending time with, what was life like outside the suffocating context of the coup? Beyond that, there was the childhood draw toward safety, the idea that perhaps together they could weather the storm that surely would pass. There wasn't enough time now. Everything was a quick shuffle to a goodbye.

"Customers are waiting," Jaipal said with a tired look on his face.

They said their goodbyes, leaving Jaipal to the night.

The taxi dropped Bhumi and her mother at home, and something was bothering Bhumi, an itch deep inside her that could never be scratched. It wasn't her father's condition that bothered her, but rather that a crucial piece of information had been kept from her.

Once they were inside, the smell that greeted Bhumi let her know that she had finally come home. Home was the faint aroma of nag champa emanating from a corner where there was a small cupboard that housed a pantheon of stone statuettes and framed images. She could see dinner waiting for her in the kitchen: roti, chicken liver curry thick with onions and potatoes, and aloo bhindi. She shut the door behind them, put down her suitcase, and walked around the sitting room's rattan chairs and love seat to the dinner table. Years prior, at such an hour, her mother would sit with her here as she studied for her exams.

Her mother opened a stainless steel tin and leafed through a pile of rotis as if they were pages in a magazine. Looking satisfied with their warmth, she put the tin down in front of Bhumi. She then put her hands upon the scuffed and worn stew pot that held the chicken curry.

Bhumi's place had been set hours prior. Her mother grabbed the plate and piled it with thin rotis, curry, and aloo bhindi. As she leaned over, Bhumi smelled her mother's sour breath and winced—she reflexively washed her hands in the sink in the kitchen.

So much of growing up had been an attempt to uproot the past, carefully disentangling her mother's roots from the ones she had grown for herself: her future would be wholly her own. She had tried to rid herself of her mother's infuriating insistence upon superstition. She had cleansed herself of her gestures—the smacking of her lips when she ate, the laugh that was shrill enough to drive her father to anger. At the end of the day, when Bhumi would catch the scent of her mother's breath, sour from a day's worth of housework, Bhumi would run to the bathroom to brush her own teeth to wipe away the remnants of any lingering odor. Where her mother wouldn't (or couldn't) leave the house, Bhumi decided that she would explore all that made up the natural world.

When Bhumi returned to the table, the day's hunger thundered through her: she tore off pieces of roti, using them to scoop up the curry, grab pieces of fried liver and onion, and mash together the aloo and bhindi.

When she finished, she leaned back in the chair and pushed the plate away. She put a hand upon her full stomach, yet the smile so common to finishing a meal did not cross her face. She had only staved off her appetite's gnashing teeth.

"I'm going to go to bed," she announced after her mother took her plate away. The heaviness of sleep weighed down Bhumi's eyes as the effects of the meal and the days wore on her and she walked to the sink to wash her hands of the remnants of food. With a resolution brought on by exhaustion, she left the kitchen, leaving her mother standing alone.

Her childhood bedroom was now devoid of feeling: for all her mother's talk of the past, the house had been scrubbed clean of her existence. Her books had been removed and taken to SPU (where most of them had been left), and there were only a few lonely clothes left in her almirah made of golden-brown dakua makadre. Not a single picture hung from the walls.

This wasn't surprising.

Growing up, her drawings and academic awards had routinely been thrown away. Her father wanted no visual reminder of her life, of her living. Meanwhile, Jaipal's sports memorabilia and mediocre grades were kept on full display. As a teenager, she couldn't help but harbor a hatred for the fact that her brother was allowed to live his life so freely. As she grew older, she stopped holding it against him. Bhumi was trying to sidestep the past held up as a mirror by her mother, although Jaipal's fate was even worse. His father's attention had always been her brother's prison.

She closed the bedroom door and left the light off. In the darkness, she pulled out an extra-large T-shirt from her armoire. She took off her jeans and kameez, unhooked her bra, and slipped the T-shirt on, feeling comfort in the way it draped down from her shoulders. It was the kind of shirt that made her feel like a child wearing the clothing of an adult. The past day had made her feel the same way: that she was some small thing playacting in a world in which she had little or no say.

Without pulling back the sheets, she lay down on the bed, falling into unconsciousness almost immediately.

13

THE LATE-NIGHT RUSH after Jaipal's mother and sister left was unrelenting, and yet, he felt a sense of purpose in helping all those who came in get what they needed before their departure. Many of them bought bags upon bags of snacks, and the remainder of the purchases were for the basics: batteries, condoms, cigarettes, lighters, matches. It didn't matter that his stock of fresh fruits and vegetables had been run down to whatever bits were left in their stainless steel bowls. No one was going to stuff a vegetable in their last-minute suitcase.

Jaipal's legs were filled with a dull throbbing from standing—he had been on his feet for twelve hours at that point. He shifted the weight from left to right, front to back, teetering from heel to toe. He longed to sit, but there was no chair. He tried to lean back against the wooden shelving behind the counter and every time he heard it creak, he would bolt upright, fearful of what his father would say if he found out he had broken a shelf.

He had to remind himself that it was his shop now.

The small digital watch on his wrist read two in the morning. He stared down at the blinking colon in the watch's face that separated the numbers. The blink slowed down, slower, slower, slower still. The door opened. The bell tied against its interior handle jangled: ring ring. Then the sounds of rubber soles against tile, flint and steel shifting with weight. Two men—soldiers. They were in the store now.

"Everybody out!" one yelled. The three customers in the store abandoned their shopping baskets in their aisles and bolted out the door.

Jaipal looked into the soldiers' faces and saw fear and memory made flesh. It was the two men from yesterday—their buzz cuts looked so similar that he wondered if they were twins. In his exhaustion, his mind wandered: what was the possibility, he asked himself, that two twin brothers had joined the army, and they had been placed on the same detail? The more he looked, the more he saw that his tiredness was playing a trick on him, or that he was guilty of their mistake: all Indians looked the same. No, they were different: the one who had yelled was clearly taller than the other. His arms seemed more muscular, their shape stretching the fabric of his fatigues.

The bigger one opened the cold-drinks fridge door and pulled out a glass bottle of Coke, using the bottle opener bolted to the side of the fridge to open it. The bottle's cap fell into the cap collector—a corroded tin of instant coffee on the ground—with a clink. Jaipal watched as he took a long drink from the bottle, the only sound the glug of a quenched thirst. After so many hours of work, the scene had a hazy quality to it, as if Jaipal wasn't sure whether he had fallen asleep.

The soldier let out a satisfied belch and then held out the bottle expectantly, jiggling it back and forth, an invitation for Jaipal to come and finish it.

Jaipal swung the counter up and walked over. He stopped a few paces away and saw that the soldier was no more than a boy, that he hid the soft contours of his face under a scowl and thin, narrowed eyes. For a moment, a rush of desire passed through him like a shiver. He could reach out and grab this boy by the neck, if only to bring his body to his own. He would put his lips upon this boy's, not to love, but to suck the confidence and bravado straight from his snicker.

The gun on his shoulder meant that Jaipal wouldn't dare make a move.

The soldier let go of the bottle and Jaipal watched as it fell straight down to the floor, letting out a high-pitched crack against the store's cold tile. The soda splashed, then oozed out from a nick in the glass, its carbonation bubbling against the floor with a faint hiss.

"Your store is dirty, vulagi fat-ass. You need to clean it up!" the soldier said with a sneer.

Jaipal moved his stare from the floor to the soldier with a wide-eyed look. The soda oozed about like a bloodstain. Jaipal didn't budge. Surely this was some kind of trick.

"What are you, stupid?" The soldier shifted his rifle on his shoulder and pointed, open palmed, down to the floor. "Clean it up!"

Jaipal walked to the back room. He felt his heart beating against his chest, his breath growing shallower, each muscle feeling tight. He grabbed the mop and went to fill its bucket with water from the tap of the large steel basin sink, a rust stain running along its side like a scabbed-over gash.

"Hurry up!" the soldier said from the front of the store. The other soldier let out a laugh. "Fucking piece-of-shit vulagis. We're not going to clean up after you anymore. What do you think the General would think of your dirty fucking store?"

The bucket had a splash of water in it. The rough wood of the mop's handle felt slippery against his grip. Back in the front of the store, the other soldier was now drinking a Fanta and the first had started smoking a cigarette from a pilfered pack, flicking the ash into the liquid on the floor.

Jaipal put the mop to the liquid, knowing full well that without a little soap, he was swirling the sugar around, asking for ants. He swallowed hard.

"I don't want any trouble," he said meekly. "If you want more drinks or cigarettes, please, take them."

"You hear that, Jone?" the bigger soldier said. "He says we can take whatever we want." The soldier walked up to Jaipal, who hunched over, hugging the mop handle close. "We don't need your fucking permission, vulagi." He grabbed Jaipal's chin and he felt the roughness of the soldier's palm against his late-night stubble. The soldier forcibly turned Jaipal's neck back and forth, and he felt a sharp spasm of a crick form in his tense shoulder muscles. "See all this shit? I don't need your fucking permission to take what's mine, do I?"

Jaipal said nothing.

"It's a question. Answer the fucking question!"

He shook his head with a tremble.

The soldier took a step back and, in a flash, punched Jaipal in the stomach.

Jaipal doubled over and fell to the floor, feeling the sticky residue of the soda against his cheek.

"Jone, grab me some fucking cigarettes."

From the ground, Jaipal watched a pair of boots shuffle from an aisle to the counter and back to the door. The door's bell rang as it opened.

"Close the shop and go home. There's a curfew. All stores are closed tomorrow. You'll hear when you can open up again. Follow what we say and you won't have any more trouble."

After the soldiers left, Jaipal rolled onto his back and felt that he was no longer one person, like a soul shaking off a body during a cremation. He saw himself from a distance, saw his body in the washed-out fluorescent light. Small mayflies and beetles buzzed around the blue-white glow of the light's tube.

The body's stomach cried out in pain. The body felt like it could puke. But it didn't move.

Together, both he and the body watched the bugs flying around, thinking that this light was the moon. How don't they know that it's a fucking lightbulb in this stupid shop? Jaipal thought. When that light goes out, they'll stay here, locked in the dark. Some of them will die in that corner. The ones that think they're smart will fly into the window, over and over again, looking again for some other light.

The tile felt sticky and cold against his skin. His business would now be transacted through the currency of fear. He wanted to stay here, get his footing in this country. He hoped he wasn't just another bug looking for the moon. He hoped he wasn't just flying around another light until the end.

14

BHUMI WOKE A few hours later to the sounds of wandering tattlers chirping their ringing birdsong outside her window. The digital clock on the small table read six o'clock in the morning. There were no voices in the house.

As she got up and stretched, she noticed that someone had moved her suitcase into the room while she had slept. After showering in luke-warm water and getting dressed, she placed a hand upon her stomach and thought of the day ahead of her. She felt like she could vomit.

No, she thought. Breathe. She walked out of her room and into the kitchen, where she intended to pour herself a bowl of Weetabix.

As she walked into the kitchen, someone called out from the sitting room.

"There's more news," her father said, his voice gravelly and raw. "I thought it would stay in the capital, and look, it came here. These days, there is always more news."

Her father was slightly unsteady on his feet after a night of drinking. To Bhumi, he looked older, smaller, unkempt in his appearance. His posture was stooped and he seemed like he had lost weight. A two-day beard of white stubble was growing on his gaunt face. His linen pants had an oily splotch near the crotch from food spilled on one of his nights away.

"You know what I'm hearing?" he asked, not pausing to hear an answer. "They want us gone. They want us out of here. They want us dead. The General says we have nothing to worry about. What does he know?" he asked, his words eliding into a messy slurry.

She hadn't seen the man in nearly two years. She wasn't quite surprised to see him like this—angry, drunk, unstable—and yet it still brought forth a wave of pity from deep within her. His political analysis seemed both spot-on and pointless. For the first time that Bhumi could remember, he actually had a reason to get drunk.

For most of her life, their relationship had followed a theme. The men on the island, perhaps like all men, expressed their hatred for women in two ways: ownership and violence. Some men fawned over their daughters, keeping them away from others, showering them with attention and gifts, and holding them as dear as a family dairy cow. Other men, like Bhumi's father, could find no love in their hearts for their girls and berated and beat them for the smallest of slights.

Bhumi muttered in a half-hearted way that everything would be fine.

Her mother appeared in the open French doors that led to the balcony, looking like she had stayed up all night.

"You don't have to worry like us, right? What!" he yelled as he pointed to her mother. "You think I don't know what goes on in my own house? I know." He turned back to Bhumi. "Go! Leave here, you already left two years ago. Leave again."

Jaipal walked into the kitchen, apparently hearing the cacophony. His hair was askew and he looked like he had just woken up.

"Why aren't you at the shop?" her father barked.

"Military closed down all the shops last night," Jaipal said, rubbing the sleep out of his eyes.

"This stupid fucking country!" Bhumi's father cursed. "I bet you just let them close the shop. It's the weakest goat that gets eaten first."

"What do you expect?" Bhumi interjected. "Do you want him to fight the soldiers?"

He lurched toward Bhumi, pointing a finger at her face. "I wasn't talking to you," he seethed.

"Calm down," Bhumi said, "I heard about your heart." She didn't mean to sound sarcastic and dismissive—she really did feel sorry for him—but she had no idea how to show any sense of concern to a man who had given her none.

"What do you know?" he snapped. She saw his anger take control of him: the familiar bulge of the vein in his neck, his jaw clenched into a tight square of muscle and sinew. He would always draw his fingers in and out of a fist, stretching them in preparation for slapping her. Bhumi's anger flared within, but she took a breath and relaxed her shoulders. She didn't have to be like him. She could turn and run— and she wouldn't have to return.

He backed away toward the front door. When he finally reached the doorway, he said in a voice no more than a coarse whisper, "Get out of my house." And then, he was gone.

Bhumi saw her mother smile as she walked from the balcony to close the front door. "That went like how I thought," her mother said.

"Come with me to California," Bhumi said. She felt the lightness of victory with her father and thought, for a moment, that she could win her mother over.

"It's too late for me, beti. You learn this when you're my age. It's like a bird that flies into the house. If it's smart, it finds the window and leaves quickly. If it can't, it flies back and forth, up and down, until it's too tired to do anything. Until it's nothing."

"That only happens when we're not there. If we're home, we're the ones who catch it and take it outside."

"Smart girl," her mother replied. "I will join you. Not today."

Bhumi's mood darkened. As she was about to reply, her brother cut in. "Bhumi, we don't have visas," he said. "There's no place for us to go."

The bureaucratic logic of departure and its paperwork crossed Bhumi's face like a shadow. Her mother walked up to her and wrapped her arm around her. "Come now, let's sit for a while. You're leaving so soon. Let's sit."

Bhumi sat in the love seat and Jaipal settled into one of the chairs. Their mother fetched three cups of chai in bone-china cups.

"Might as well use our nice things," her mother said as she sat down in the love seat next to her daughter.

Bhumi would never see this place again. She hadn't come home much in two years, yet at least she had known that home was there, that it existed for her if she ever needed it. Now she looked around the room to take one last mental picture.

"I need to tell you something about Nani before you go," Bhumi's mother said.

Again came that sickness when Bhumi heard her mother mention her grandmother, the cloying sweetness that fed a nausea deep inside her, as if there were something trying to pick her up from her own path and drop her into some predetermined way.

"At eight she was married to a man twenty years her senior. When she was thirteen, she moved into his house. She was expected to bear him children—even better, a son. For seven years, no children, nothing. A childless woman is inauspicious.

"Finally, her husband's family came up with a plan. They would kill her so he could remarry. They even told her father about what they were doing. They said they would give back part of her dowry."

Jaipal let out a wheeze and shook his head in dismay.

"What did her father say?" Bhumi asked, though she knew the answer to her question.

"He said that he would spare them. He would do it himself."

Bhumi stared down into her cup. All men were the same, Bhumi thought. The gun in their hands, the gun in their trousers.

"He came to visit his son-in-law and daughter. He sat up with his son-in-law all night drinking country liquor. The son-in-law gave him a pistol. My mother wasn't stupid. She knew something was going to happen.

"When he walked into her room, she jumped out and grabbed him by the neck. They fought. The gun went off and the bullet hit the wall. Others in the house began to wake up and yell. The commotion was enough to give her a chance. She ran as fast as she could into the night. Gossip moved fast: the arkathi found her the next day and said she could come here to work the cane. Of course she said yes to whatever he could give her."

Both Bhumi and Jaipal shook their heads. The story had the effect of quieting the conversation down to nothing. Still, they finished their chai in a silence that was as comfortable as an old blanket washed into delicate softness, warming the three of them and keeping them safe.

"We should go," Jaipal said, putting his cup down on the center table. "Everyone's going to the airport. It may take a long time to get there."

Bhumi knew the routine for leaving: first to the cupboard to light two sticks of incense, to fold her hands and place them in front of her heart. The unspoken words upon her lips were a prayer to cross the unknown into safety. When she finished, her mother handed her a bowl filled with yogurt and a piece of rock-hard jaggery—the last meal always to be eaten before a departure. It was a tradition carried over from the peasant villages of Bihar into a new land by their indentured ancestors. Bhumi ate the meal in three spoonfuls and saw tears in her mother's eyes.

"You'll have her strength," her mother said. "She crossed the black waters and so will you."

"Are you coming to the airport?" Bhumi asked.

"I can't watch you go," her mother said, looking down with eyes so full.

Bhumi understood. She drew her mother into an embrace. In that moment, it felt so close to when her mother had held her in the back of the truck as they sped to the hospital. As they broke their embrace, she reached down to touch her mother's feet for a blessing.

Her mother caught her and held her shoulders. "Jeeti raho," she said. *Live long.*

Jaipal reached behind the television and took out a manila folder. "Ma put everything together. I think this is everything. You will need all of this when you get there," he said. Bhumi took the folder and put it in her purse.

Jaipal grabbed the suitcase and walked outside to put it in the back of the Minor. The checkered gate had been opened and their father had already wandered off beyond sight. Bhumi walked down the steps to the car, her mother right behind her.

Bhumi and Jaipal got into the car. There was nothing left to say.

The morning was filled with birds chirping in the distance, the sounds of the diesel engine, and the deep, deep ache of emptiness. She turned around in her seat and watched as the figure of her mother grew smaller and smaller as the car drove away from her home.

And then she was gone, never to return.

15

"LOOK AT ALL these people," Jaipal said. He was nervous, drumming his fingers against the wheel. Around them was a sea of red taillights, and beyond that, bright-green fields of young cane a few months away from harvest. "Looks like it's half the Indians."

"So many people are staying, too," Bhumi said. "What's going to happen to them?"

Jaipal glanced at his sister. He knew she was mostly worried about their mother.

"Who knows?" Jaipal said. "Some people think it's going to get better. Some people think it's going to get worse. For every person here headed to the airport, there's another who thinks, even after he's seen everything that's happened, 'I'll stay another day.'"

"What do you think?" Bhumi asked. "I can never tell what you're thinking."

"I wish I knew," he said. He felt a phantom pain in his stomach where he had been punched. "I think it'll get better. It has to. The

General wants power. And if he wants to stay in power, he needs us, especially the rich Indians. He'll calm down the jungli, he'll get them to stay in line."

Jaipal wanted to reach over and hold his sister's hand, to remind her that she was the smartest among them all, that she was the only one who had a chance, really.

"Last night, before you arrived from Vilimaji," he began, "Ma said that you will figure out your own future. And us? We'll manage."

"She said that?" Bhumi asked.

"Ma always knows how to plan for your future," Jaipal said.

"Sometimes I feel like I don't know anything about her."

"What do you mean?"

"Why do you think she keeps bringing up Nani?" Bhumi let out a small, rueful laugh. "That she died nine months before I was born? That I was born because of her? Do you believe that?"

"It's not that I believe it, eh? It's just that . . ." He trailed off. *To have a family member who compares you to the strength of others is a gift,* he wanted to yell. *All I have is Papa, bringing me close—take what you're given and run!*

"It's what?"

He felt the words swirl within him. "It's like blood. It leaves, goes around the body, and comes back to the heart. It always goes back to where it started. She's our family. She's your blood."

Through the front glass, the sun shined down through the green thickets atop the ridgeline in the east. Along the road outside the car, some of the more enterprising native-born women had set up tables under the shade of cabbage trees thick with clumps of sweet-smelling pink flowers, selling banana cake and soft drinks to those sitting in traffic. Dodging and weaving with quick steps around the stalled cars were Indian women—foreheads speckled with sweat and grime and the hems of their kameezes stained with dust—waving foil-wrapped roti packets in their thin hands to sell.

Bhumi turned to him. "What's the inside of an airplane like?"

He winced at the similarity of her question to what Portia had asked. "I don't know," he said, wishing to change the subject. "I've never been in one."

"You have friends who work at the airport."

"They were all fired. I hope your bags get on the airplane with these new kaamchor guys," he said, rolling his eyes.

"Yeah, me too," Bhumi said quickly. "What did your friends say about the inside of an airplane?"

"They only get to go into the bottom part, where the bags are. They usually say that airplanes are very loud and are filled with beautiful women," he said with a smile. It was true—they were beautiful at the hotel, were probably just as beautiful inside the plane.

Bhumi laughed deeply. "I bet airplanes are like coaches," she began again, looking out the window. "I wonder what the world's like from the clouds?"

What does the island look like from an airplane? A dark look crossed Jaipal's face. "You should let me know."

SOON THEY WERE NEAR THE LOW-SLUNG TERMINAL. ON A NORMAL day, the comings and goings of flights were spaced far enough apart to focus the airport's activity in small bursts, giving the place the feeling of a theater where audiences arrived and departed at precise hours.

Today, the airport was chaos.

Stationary cars stretched from the awnings to the streetside gate into the airport. Every parking space was filled. Most gave up on getting their vehicle into the airport and instead pulled over across the road into an empty acre of red dirt. Someone had knocked down the temporary fencing around a neighboring construction site for an American hotel chain and turned it into a parking lot. Jaipal turned right, honking his horn to make space between the traffic coming from the north. The journey had taken an hour.

"Could've got here faster if we walked," Jaipal said as he turned off the engine.

"The drive back won't be as bad," Bhumi said as she stretched her back like a cat waking up from a nap. The first true pang of sadness hit her: she wouldn't be with him on the drive back home. The realization grabbed her and shook her down, like a mugging in broad daylight. All she was left with was the fear of what came next.

Jaipal pulled Bhumi's suitcase from the Minor.

"They're not letting anyone without a ticket beyond the airport's front doors," he said.

They walked across the street, weaving through the stalled traffic. Among the horns, idling engines, nervous families, and tearful goodbyes, they could see small Indian men running from car to car as families stretched their legs and pulled out their suitcases.

"What are they doing?" Bhumi asked her brother.

"Buying cars. People drive here and forget that they have to get rid of their car. These men buy it in cash and try to sell it later."

"Wow," Bhumi said. A seller scampered by like a roach across a counter when a light was turned on in the middle of the night.

"Look. No kaamchor buying or selling," he said. "One day even these guys will have to sell their cars. That's when the native-borns will come. They will buy the last cars at the cheapest price."

"Until that day, a dollar to be made," Bhumi said.

"Ey! Jaipal!" Maqbool yelled. He looked slight and greasy, darkened from too many days in the sun of the airport's car park. "Selling your car?"

"Not today, Maqbool!" Bhumi knew Jaipal's friend always had a side hustle, and she wasn't surprised to see him in the parking lot.

"Next time!" Maqbool yelled back.

"Maqbool and his projects," Bhumi whispered.

"He's never going to stop," Jaipal said.

They pressed through the current of those headed toward the airport. Each step transformed the departing men, women, and children from citizens into refugees. Of the large crowd, only a few would go through the airport's doors and onward toward escape. The rest would mill around like dying leaves, unsure of whether to float away with the wind or fall into the decomposing morass underfoot.

Several soldiers with fingers itching to pull the trigger on their rifles were guarding the doors into the airport, checking each ticket and shooing away those who weren't supposed to enter.

Jaipal put down Bhumi's suitcase, and as he did, Bhumi looked at her brother. For the first time she felt her hands burning with an electric tingle. A sense of weightlessness filled her stomach.

Bhumi pulled Jaipal into an embrace and whispered in his ear. "I'm scared," she said.

"Me too," he replied. "I couldn't give you much, you know?" he said, voice cracking.

"Jaipal," Bhumi began, feeling tears well in her eyes.

"Remember the bay? Whenever you feel scared, I hope you can think of those three things, like we did as kids. Whenever you don't know what to do, just think of me."

Bhumi was crying now, and so was Jaipal.

"I always wanted to take you to where you would be safe," Jaipal continued. "Now I'm taking you here, and I know you will be."

They held each other, an embrace they hadn't given one another since childhood, quiet sobs shared between them. The silence behind their goodbye was filled with the wails of mothers watching their sons leave, the shrieks of infants handed off to relatives, and the gruff shouts of the soldiers at the doors.

Jaipal broke away from the embrace and placed a hand on her shoulder. Bhumi racked her mind for the right thing to say, but it was like trying to grab a drop of water from a bowl.

"Be safe," Jaipal said before she could think of something. The love for the other could only be expressed as a simple wish for everything that came next.

Bhumi tried to think of something beautiful, and again came the ineloquence that she had felt with Aarti. All that came out of her mouth was a sound made broken by her own sadness: "You too."

BHUMI GRABBED HER SUITCASE AND FISHED HER TICKET AND PASSport out of the folder in the black leather satchel that hung from her shoulder. She walked up to a glass door, where a soldier snatched her documents out of her hands. "Get in!" he yelled. She took one large step into the terminal, far enough to be out of reach of the officer.

The wave of people entering the building caught Bhumi and carried her further into the airport. The last thing she saw before she turned around was Jaipal watching her leave.

Every check-in counter had been closed. Instead, a folding table had been set up in front of the metal detector. Sitting behind this table, flanked by two standing soldiers, was a middle-aged man whose officious sneer, pressed trousers, and Coke-bottle glasses that slid down his nose gave him an air of bureaucratic importance, as if he had just come from a meeting with the General.

When Bhumi reached the front of the line, she passed him her passport and ticket and he took them without looking. There was something about it that reminded Bhumi of the Iblis ka Na'ib—the Devil's Assistant. It was a character that mothers conjured to scold and scare their disobedient children. The Na'ib was a costumed character, complete with a large papier-mâché head with piercing blue eyes and a comical grin, that showed up during Tazia, the carnivalesque festival that had its roots in India as the Shia mourning of Muharram. As the years went on, Tazia became a holiday where all Indians came together to celebrate the abolition of indenture.

During the festival's march to the sea, people would dress up as the Iblis ka Na'ib. Though a second-in-command, he looked like the devil himself with his large blue eyes and a comically enormous head. The Na'ib always carried a large ledger—like the man in front of Bhumi—where he wrote down the names of all the damned souls who passed him by.

The man at the table wrote down Bhumi's name in his brown leather book, adding the words "San Francisco, CA, USA." He then reached into a small gunmetal box and flipped through its dividers inside. He hid whatever he had found in the palm of his left hand.

He handed her passport and ticket back to her. With those, he added a bright yellow tag on an elastic band that, in a large and bold text, read "SFO."

"Tear the bottom off. Tie the top to your bag. Leave your bag in the proper bin over there," the man said without looking up, speaking so fast that each word seemed to hang desperately onto the one that came before. "Check-in is at the boarding gate." He ran his thumb over the card that he still held in his hand. He glanced up and held it out. "I believe this is yours," he said, his locution suddenly as sharp as a glass falling to the ground in a silenced room, his blue eyes cutting straight through Bhumi.

Bhumi took the card: it was her university ID card. She felt like hands had wrapped around her neck and squeezed.

He leaned across the table and pushed his glasses up along the ridge of his nose. In a low voice meant only for the two of them, he said to Bhumi: "The man who gave me this said, 'Good luck.'"

Bhumi said nothing and stood in shock as the line moved forward, pushing her to the right of the metal detector, where there were several labeled luggage bins.

A stout woman was standing to the side with her two children as her husband threw suitcases into the MEL bin. Without saying anything, she walked over, checked the label on Bhumi's suitcase, and tossed it into the SFO bin.

"You're almost there," she said. "You will be home soon." She walked back to her two energetic children, who were, in her absence, trying to climb into the MEL bin.

Bhumi put her purse on the belt for the X-ray. Both she and her purse passed through security without a beep.

She had five hours until her flight. She moved quickly—she was no longer weighed down by her suitcase—and found the nearest toilet. She wanted to cry in the safety of a locked stall. Nothing came out.

She thought of all the things broken, the secret eyes that watched her every step, the tumult that had entered her life without her permission, Aarti's unknown departure, the fact that she had seen her home for the last time, and still nothing came out. She had entombed everything so far down that exhuming it was beyond her capacity.

She stayed still, waiting for something to move from within, even as people walked by and knocked on her stall. She stood until she had no more effort left to give. She stared at herself in the mirror and was surprised by the hardened look on her face, her hands that could not stay still. She splashed some water on her face and the sting of its cold against her skin sent shivers down her arms. Then she waited near the departure board.

Soon, the plane was boarding. A woman asked for her passport and ticket, her high voice thick with a Kiwi accent. Bhumi handed over her documents. She asked if Bhumi had flown before. Bhumi shook her head.

"Seems to be the case for a lot of people today. I've given you a window seat in the nonsmoking section for your first flight. You can take a seat here and we will let you know when boarding begins."

Bhumi took a seat near the gate. "California," she said to herself. The word was bizarre. It reminded her of the English word for gobi. "Cauliflower." *Brassica oleracea.* Cauliflower, California—like a mantra.

It was time to board. Bhumi heard her row called, and she walked

down the Jetway and entered the airplane. She marveled at the order-liness of it all. Each seat was in a row and there was room to put things above each seat. It really was like a coach. A coach in a hollow alumi-num tube.

After everyone was seated, two soldiers entered the aircraft and a suffocating sense of fear swept the cabin. The soldier who walked down Bhumi's aisle was no more than a boy, with a smooth face yet to be touched by the wisps of a beard. He walked slowly, staring into the eyes of each passenger.

The man in the middle seat next to Bhumi began to rock back and forth. A soldier reached their row and stood still. She looked forward at the seat back in front of her.

Finally, she looked up and met his gaze. He looked at her for a mo-ment, turning his head slightly askew in recognition. His eyes quickly shifted away.

"You!" he yelled with a thunderclap of anger to the man in the middle seat. "Come with me." The soldier pulled the man up, flinging his body across the shriveling woman seated in the aisle seat and onto the plane's floor.

The man cried out like a dog that had been shot. The smell of urine filled the cabin.

They left, and the plane began to move.

Bhumi pulled out a brown bag from the seat-back pocket and vomited the bitter emptiness that rose from her stomach. A stewardess came through the aisle with an aerosol can and sprayed a floral mist as she walked. She took the bag from Bhumi's shaking hands.

With a sinking feeling, Bhumi wondered if they had found Aarti and her family. If they had pulled them out of their seats like they did to the man.

As the flight began to push from the gate, the only thing she paid attention to from the cabin crew's explanation of the seat belts and life vests was the cardinal rule: *put on your own mask before helping others.*

Finally, the engines revved and the plane began to barrel down the runway.

The deafening roar of the engine began to dissolve her fears into the recycled air that circulated through the cabin. The plane accelerated, faster and faster, until it left the earth. In that moment, Bhumi felt a lightness rising in her stomach from the plane's taking off.

She swallowed it all and looked out the window. She saw, in a flash, acres of bright green cane field. Then they were over water, pure turquoise blue, not like the black waters she had always heard of—the black waters that her grandmother had crossed, the oceans that cut off people from caste, kith, and kin.

The plane banked east. The country was gone, already out of sight.

She had escaped.

PART TWO

PART TWO

16

IT HAD BEEN five months since he'd said goodbye to his sister, and it felt like every day since had brought some announcement. New rules. Old rules. Rules only half-baked before they were sent out into the world. A sampling: All businesses had to be open Monday through Saturday. Any store that was closed without explicit permission risked what was only described as "punishment." No business could operate past seven P.M., unless that business was involved in the transportation of goods or people, in which case, it could operate until midnight. On certain designated Wednesdays, stores could stay open until midnight if and only if they had received approval to do so. Jaipal wondered why they had chosen Wednesday. Why not Thursday or Saturday?

One morning, before work, his mother came through the front door, probably returning from haggling over the price of meat at the morning market—prices knew only one direction lately. She had a look of motherly condescension; her face irked him, poked at him— she looked too calm. The days had thieved the happiness away from him, leaving him only with worry. He turned away from her to pour himself a cup of the lukewarm chai sitting in a saucepan on the stove.

"I saw two crows outside," she said to him. "You'll be safe now. It confirms it."

Two crows shitting on the car probably meant nothing, Jaipal thought. Still, he wanted to know what she was getting at. "What's going on?" he asked her.

"Mandakini told me that a kaamchor kid tried to loot a store when everything was closed."

Acquaintances and far-flung relatives were becoming more important as the General's government learned that the easiest way to delay elections and stay in power was to scapegoat the Indians. Some local musician had written a steel-pan tune, and he had been invited on the evening television news program to sing it. It was searingly stupid in its simplicity:

> *Rich Indians never work for the poor*
> *Of course us natives will be sore*

Actual news—arrests, business seizures, the escape of the entire class of capitalist Indians, body counts—had no official way to be transmitted anymore, yet its remnants and shadows weren't that hard to find. In primary school, he had once been told a story—it was always easier to remember what he learned from school if it had been told to him as a story—about when Indians had fought the Empire in 1857. They had told one another to take up arms by secretly sending chapattis from house to house. He had imagined his mother opening the door in the middle of the night, only to be silently handed a stack of steaming chapattis.

Jaipal understood now that news needed just three hands: one to make the chapatti, one to take it across the city, and finally, a willing one to receive it—and carry it on to the next.

The store that had been looted was just outside Sugar City, owned by the cousin of the importer-exporter who lived next to them. His mother said that the kid had three bottles of Fanta in his hands when they shot him.

"Who shot him?" Jaipal asked.

"Two soldiers on patrol."

Jaipal's eyes widened. "Two soldiers shot a kaamchor kid over a couple of Fantas?"

"They say he's in the hospital, but someone saw him dead on the sidewalk."

Petty shoplifters were the bane of any shop owner's life. His father, who had watched countless boys in his store try to sneak a Coke, had complained loudly that he would shoot them if he had the chance. His father's bloodlust was a fantasy, an illusion of justice—quick, clean revenge against someone who cost the store hard-earned money.

"They killed him? Man, chicken merry, hawks always near . . . ," he said, trailing off.

"You sound like your father," she said with a pouting look of disapproval. "Mandakini told me that she heard that it's because the soldiers want to protect the storefronts, the goods, the cash boxes. They're saying that everything that's ours will be theirs when we're gone."

Jaipal looked around his house. Everything that was his was his. Ownership implied some sort of longevity: nothing could belong to him if it was going to leave his possession. Maybe everything he owned was in actuality something borrowed.

He shook away the feeling.

"Well, doesn't this mean that I don't have to worry being behind the till?" he asked with a bitter smile. "If you're right, they're going to leave our stores alone so they can take them when we're gone. I still don't believe they're going to get rid of us though. It ain't gonna happen."

"I worry all the time," his mother said in a quiet voice bereft of confidence. "The soldiers won't do anything in the store, but the streets, the taxis?"

He couldn't remember if his mother had always been like this. From a distance, he had known her as a woman full of plots and bluster, particularly with his sister. It was easy to ignore all the stupid superstitions if her plans worked. Now she seemed to be more question than answer.

"Why would they want me, Ma? I'm nobody. And anyway, we need the store," he added in a low voice. Their father had spent more than they had thought. When Jaipal looked at the accounts, he saw how their numbers had dwindled.

These were problems for another moment, some different day. He had to get going.

"Don't worry, Ma," Jaipal said. "I'll be back tonight."

He left the house and was surprised to find the Minor parked in the driveway. Even more surprising was the sight of his father sitting at his table underneath the house. At first Jaipal almost didn't recognize him—he looked as haggard as a beggar. His head was leaning forward with his chin near his chest like he was dozing. When Jaipal walked by, he perked up.

"Take the car," his father croaked. "Key's on the front seat. Cow needs help when there's no cud to chew."

Jaipal gawked at his father. He was thinner, more rags and bones than man.

His father looked up, and Jaipal could see the changes in him, the tremor in his head and neck, as if he were bound to endlessly agree with something. His eyes looked glassed over but still unclean, like a sheen was fogging up the pane. Whatever it was he was fighting, he was losing.

Jaipal tried to look, really look. "Are you . . . ," Jaipal began as he leaned against the coconut tree. "Are you okay?"

"I'm fine," he barked, his evergreen anger a constant.

Jaipal bristled with annoyance. He turned to go to the car.

"Wait," his father said.

"What?" Jaipal asked, turning around, his arms crossed on his chest.

His father took a hard swallow, the tremor in his head still nodding with gentle agreement. "You'll always be my boy," he said. His lips dropped into a grimace.

Jaipal's lips opened to reply, but no sound came out of a mouth made dry by such a comment.

He drove off from his house, every so often glancing back at it in the rearview mirror until he turned the corner and it was out of sight. His father must have been drunk. Yes, that was it. He was probably drunk—that sloppiness, that slide into an emotion, that wasn't him. It had never been him.

Maybe it was a trick.

Throughout the drive lingered a thought, a question, an unease: The fuck was that?

AT THE STORE WAS ANOTHER DAY OF WAITING AND NO ACTION. THERE still weren't any fruit or vegetable deliveries, and the pace of his sales was starting to dry up to a slow trickle. The regulars were gone: office workers coming in for a soda and a snack on a break, the smokers needing their fix, the evening mothers buying what they needed for a night's meal, the nighttime lovers needing a condom, the occasional tourist needing a bottle of water—none of them came anymore. From time to time, someone would wander in with a wide-eyed look on their face. They would browse the shelves, go here and there, buy one thing for every ten that they picked up and studied.

Some of the deliveries had stopped altogether.

The morning walkers didn't come by for their newspapers, because there were no newspapers for the time being: they had been closed, the remaining journalists fired, most of them disappeared. The coup had a strange body count. Everyone knew someone who had died, but the official tally counted few, if any, of them. The math was all off. In regular life, someone was born, and they became a person. When they died, they turned into a corpse, a lifeless body. In this way, every life was balanced. Now people were born and there were no bodies waiting on the other end.

Maqbool showed up near the end of the day, a welcome break from the tedium. Jaipal was surprised to see him—they hadn't seen each other since he saw him at the airport car park. Jaipal had called him a week or so later and they had talked about the different ways the coup had stolen a sibling, a conversation so filled with tenderness that Jaipal thought of it every time he was stuck in the mire of work. He had kept meaning to call again, but the drudgery of his own hustle kept his energy low enough that an evening call was just too much more, something pushed to the next day, and the day after, until months had passed.

"Ey, Jaipal!" Maqbool said as he walked in. His hair was slicked back, each strand coated with pomade. He had a few days' worth of stubble on his face.

"Not selling cars today?" Jaipal asked.

He looked over his shoulder at the door. "Army shut it down. Didn't want us at the airport anymore. We tried moving across the street to the empty parking lot. They kicked us out of there too. Don't worry, I got another thing going. Anyway, did you hear about that kaamchor kid?"

Jaipal nodded his head. Though Maqbool had also been a B-Former, he had a rare and different kind of intelligence. He was always hustling for something, making plans: Finding all the cans on the school campus and hiding them away underneath the bleachers on the field so he could recycle them all for some cash (giving a cut to those who helped him). Collecting discarded pens, notebooks, papers at the end of the year from the trash at all the schools, selling them back to the families who needed them at the start of the next school year—at half off. His brother's death seemed to have amplified this in him. He looked like he was planning five things at once.

Maqbool pulled out a bottle of Coke from the drinks case. He opened it using the can opener on the fridge, its cap falling into the can of coffee underneath with a clink. Jaipal shuddered at the sound.

Maqbool walked up to the counter and put down two coins. They were separated by the counter, but Jaipal could still feel the heat coming off of him through the linen fabric of his long white kurta. A sheen of sweat lined his high forehead, drops forming where his curly hair was swept back. If a woman were this close to Jaipal, others would assume that they were together, whereas men were given a pass.

"The kaamchor kid is gone. Disappeared. They'll kill anyone if it means they can kill more of us. Fucking savages. You know they used to eat people?" Maqbool said, putting the bottle down on the counter, finally taking a step back.

"What the fuck are you talking about?"

"You know. The jungli used to eat people. Before us. Before the Empire."

Jaipal knew what he meant. It was a gory bit of truth used to lure tourists to buy trinkets from the hotel gift shop. They did used to eat people—their shamans and priests and kings did, at least. Now replicas of the special forks they used were sold as trinkets. White people would buy anything.

"You know why they did it?"

"Whenever they won a battle or something, right?"

"Exactly," Maqbool said, pointing his finger at Jaipal. He took a swig of his Coke and put the bottle back down. "Some king or whatever would kill you in some war. It's not enough to kill someone. Bodies have power. You have to make them disappear."

"Why not, I don't know, burn the bodies? You know. Cremate them?" Jaipal asked, wondering about all those older relatives who had been cast off the earth as a handful of dust.

"Fuck. I don't know, eh? You gotta always make the bodies disappear. It's happening again. They're doing it again. It's not just about the government, man. Even if we're weak, even if we're dead, we still have power. They need us all gone. They need us to disappear."

They stood in silence. Jaipal watched as Maqbool finished off his drink, wiping his mouth with the back of his hand. He had forgotten how much he liked listening to his politics, his stories. He was the type of guy who always had an explanation for something.

A song from *Dil Ki Baat* came on Radio Zindagi. Maqbool perked up. "No announcements today, right?" Maqbool asked.

"Not yet," Jaipal said.

Over the past month or two, when the Radio Zindagi broadcast quieted, Jaipal knew that it meant one thing, that the tap-tap tap-tap of a drumbeat came next. And then, the gravity of an announcer's voice: "This is a special bulletin . . ." Then, live to the General. Confident, cool, collected. Cruel. Always cruel with his new rules and announcements.

"Right, 'not yet.' How's business?" Maqbool asked, his hands in his pockets.

"Slow as shit," Jaipal said.

"It's 'cause shit always goes downstream."

Jaipal chuckled and asked what he meant. "No goras means no hotels, no taxis from the airport." As Maqbool listed these things, he uncurled the fingers on one hand, counting them with the other. "Means no beaches, no selling little banana cakes, no taking them snorkeling, no tours into the bush, no one going to restaurants. City and Colony is only half-full because there's no one to drink the rum. No money, Jaipal," he concluded. "It starts with something small, and then most of us don't have a job."

"Fuck," Jaipal said. "I didn't think of that."

"It doesn't have to be like this, eh? I've got this way to make some cash."

Jaipal narrowed his eyes, bracing himself for some bizarre scheme.

"See those?" Maqbool asked, pointing to Jaipal's pack of cigarettes on the counter. "You know how much of those goes to taxes?"

Jaipal poked at the pack. "Too much."

"Look at this." Maqbool pulled a sealed pack out of his pocket. "See something different?"

Jaipal looked closely as Maqbool turned the cigarettes in his hand. "No stamp. How'd you get that?"

"Every tax stamp costs fifty cents. Your distributor pays it, passes the charge on to you. With these packs, you save that money, and you can charge the customer the same amount. Hell, you can even make it 10 cents cheaper for your customers and still make a good profit."

Jaipal nodded, knowing where this was going. Maqbool's plans always needed another person. The kids who carried the cans, the kids who found the notebooks. He glanced at the till. Cigarettes were all that were selling. An extra fifty cents was good money.

"I got something more," Maqbool said. "Cigarettes are small-small money. Ganja. You know, chimbi. Prerolled. Ten dollars a joint."

"So you gonna be a dealer now?" Jaipal asked, shaking his head. He swung the counter up and started to pace the entry area with his hands in his pockets. He stopped near the door and turned around. "Wait, everyone knows you can get a joint for a dollar down the street from that guy next to the grog shop."

"Can you? Last I heard he was arrested. The soldiers got him."

"Then they'll get you. This deal is fucking stupid, Maqbool."

"They're the ones getting me the cigarettes and the ganja."

"What the fuck, Maqbool? Soldiers? You should know better!" Jaipal yelled.

"Me? Know better? I know what they can do," Maqbool seethed. He turned around, fists balled.

"Listen, I didn't mean that," Jaipal said. "I'm sorry. You know what happened to me a few months back? Two soldiers came in and stole shit and one punched me in the stomach. And you're telling me they won't get you?"

"Fuck those guys," Maqbool said, throwing up his hands. "You gotta calm down, eh? I got this under control. Half the soldiers they got in the army now are from way out there in the bush, you know? That's where they grow the chimbi. Now they're in the army, but their mama, their chacha, they're all still growing it back home. The little babies are rolling it up. The soldiers are giving it to people like me to sell. Easy money in the cities."

"How can you work with them?" Jaipal asked with a pleading tone.

"There's nothing left, Jaipal. No business. We have to do what we gotta do to survive. You telling me you don't know that?"

Jaipal shook his head, walking the cleaning supplies to the back of the store. He wanted to believe Maqbool; he wanted to think that there was some way to ride out this shit and get by. "How do you get the cigarettes?" he finally asked.

"The soldiers get them fresh through containers at the port. They give them to me. I don't know any of the details," Maqbool said with an exaggerated shrug of his shoulders.

"Cigarettes and ganja. What do you need me for?"

"A place to sell it. I'll get you the cartons and the joints. You don't have to do anything, just keep it safe back there." He paused and pointed to the storeroom. He pulled a pack of cigarettes out of his back pocket and Jaipal passed him a book of matches. "Keep it safe, eh? Keep it locked."

"And what do I do when they find out I'm selling chimbi and no-tax cigarettes?"

"They'll know. It'll be what will keep you safe. I'll let them know who you are and what you're selling. Don't you trust me?"

Jaipal paused, bit his lip. He looked around the store at the thinned-out aisles, shelves lined with dust. Things were getting harder to find, more expensive. The price of meat had tripled; flour was available only in half-kilo bags. They needed the cash. "How much money are we talking about here?"

"Jaipal, you're too honest. You're too good. Your first questions are about being safe and shit. Trying to convince me I'm wrong. My first question is always: how much do I get paid? I'll do anything if the money's good. They're keeping eighty percent. I take ten and you take ten. Should come out to five hundred a week, net, if business is good. And business will be good. Better, maybe."

Jaipal's eyes widened. Five hundred a week was impossible these days.

"Shit sells good when no one has anything to do. Can't work? Can't do fuck-all except be afraid? It passes the time. If you could get a grog license for this shop I'd connect you to get some no-tax booze. Take a hit, drink some rum. Good life, eh?"

"Are you sure you trust them?"

"There you go again. What do you think? Do *you* think these goondas can be trusted?"

"So why are you asking me to do this shit?"

"You call Rakesh yet? I want him to get me the best fucking visa and plane ticket. I'm flying first-class out of this shithole. If I hear one more dumbfuck kaamchor calling me a vulagi, I'm going to explode. I need the money to get out." He took a long drag of his cigarette. "Don't you?"

Jaipal thought of his mother at home. "Yeah, I need the money."

"So you're good?"

"Yeah, I'm good."

Maqbool walked up to Jaipal to embrace him and stayed in the hug for just a moment too long. Jaipal felt the insistence of his body saying to hold on longer, the lock that tied them together, and his heart began to jump. He didn't say anything.

"I might start taking the glass bottles I find, you know?" Maqbool said. "It's not much, but it's something. Maybe it doesn't matter. The real question is: do we have to pay rent if they're going to take all our shit anyway? Can I have these bottles?"

"Sure, take it, it's yours. I don't need it," Jaipal lied. He, like his father before him, sent the bottles with the distributor to get the glass deposit back.

Maqbool smiled. "Let's meet up tonight. You wanna smoke?"

"Where?"

"I'll meet you at your place. We'll go to the water or some shit." He walked out, whistling the tune of the song they had heard on the radio.

After Maqbool left and Jaipal closed up, he sat in the front seat of the Minor with the window down, a cigarette between his fingers.

Jaipal felt a deep ache of nostalgia for his life from before: to have found that single someone in a crowd, to have felt that little feeling in his stomach that fluttered when he made eye contact, and, finally, to grab on to his hips and be drowned in that pleasure that erased his sense of anything else.

That was all gone now, and the hole that it had left needed to be filled. Maqbool had come in at the right moment. Jaipal had put his hopes in the transition to peace, that there had been a plan for everyone to live and be safe, but if they were shooting kaamchor kids, all bets were off.

Jaipal and his mother needed cash. Money could buy safety now. It could buy bribes, it could buy papers, it could buy anything. To stand still, to simply wait for what would come, was to live in the curl of a question mark.

Jaipal wanted to keep his heart beating, to live to see another day with the help of another. Not just another: a friend returned. Jaipal could not remember if Maqbool had always rolled up his sleeves so he could see his tanned forearms, or whether his curled chest hair had always poked out from underneath a top button unbuttoned on his shirt. He liked it.

Jaipal could have what he needed if he wanted it. This was his to take.

17

WHEN HE RETURNED home that evening, his mother was in the sitting room. He wondered if she had left home at all, and if she had, what chaos had awaited her at the stores and markets. She deserved better. Money was the only way.

"Ma," he said as he sat down across from her.

She continued to stare forward, and he looked at her face in profile: the gray starting to appear at the roots on her temple, the holes in her ears gently stretched from years of earrings. It was clear that she had passed through time, especially in these last few months since Bhumi had left, but to Jaipal, she had lost none of her luminance; she was still the beautiful woman she had always been.

"Was everything okay at the store?"

He wanted to keep what had happened with Maqbool to himself for now. If it all went to shit, it was better that she didn't know what he was doing. Still, he wanted to share the dustings of good news. "I think business might be getting better," Jaipal said. His mother raised an eyebrow. Everyone knew that shops across the island were in disarray.

"Don't do anything stupid, Jaipal," she said, like she knew that business would always be terrible and that the only way into money now was through the black market. "You'll be safe at that shop as long as you don't cross anyone. I want you to come home every night." She had a mother's mixture of hard-nosed sternness and fear, the kind of voice used when she knew that there was no right answer.

"I'll be safe. We can get some money, we can pay the baksheesh to the police if something happens to me. And we can buy some good flour, not the shit they're sending to the store. Get some chickens instead of the eggs we're eating now."

She turned her head away. "Bhumi's gone. I can live with egg curry. I don't want anything to happen to you."

LATER IN THE EVENING, AS HIS MOTHER PREPARED DINNER: THREE LOUD knocks on the door, the sound as sudden as a glass falling off a counter. Jaipal felt the muscles along his shoulders and neck tense at the sound.

"Who is it?" his mother asked him, sounding tense.

"I don't know," Jaipal said. He had thought Maqbool was coming over much later.

"Ey, Jaipal, it's been a long time, what's going on?" Maqbool said after Jaipal opened the door. He had shaved and had the sharp citrusy smell of aftershave on him. He leaned in for a long embrace, the kind he'd have given if they hadn't seen each other in years.

"Maqbool, is that you?" Jaipal's mother asked from the kitchen. "What are you doing here? Is everything all right? Do you need anything?"

"Salaam, Padma Aunty," Maqbool said with a warm smile. "I was taking a walk in the neighborhood and I thought, 'What is Jaipal doing these days?'"

"You were taking a walk? At night? With all the soldiers outside?" Jaipal watched her wince, perhaps remembering what had happened to Salim. She looked like she regretted what she'd said.

Maqbool sauntered over to the sofa as if the place were his own. He sat down and shot a glance at Jaipal. "Just needed to get out of the house, you know? I heard about Bhumi, it's so sad. Still, it's better—what's there for us here anyway?"

Jaipal looked from Maqbool to his mother. Maqbool looked satisfied, like he deliberately was being kind-but-cruel to shut her down. She was staring down at the curry in her pot.

"Maqbool, you going to stay for dinner?" his mother asked, changing the subject.

"Of course. What are you making?"

"Egg curry," she said.

"Wow, Ma can't get any eggs at the main market near the bus station. Says the price there is three times what it used to be. Where do you get yours?"

"Someone up the street has a houseboy who keeps a few chickens," she said in a quiet voice.

"Always good to know someone, eh?" Maqbool said with a wink.

"Does your mother know you won't be eating at home?"

Maqbool grinned. "Yes, she knows. How can I say no to your egg curry, Padma Aunty? Ey, Jaipal," he continued on. "Have you seen my new scooter? Let me show you, let's go outside."

Jaipal opened the door and led the way down the stairs. "What are you doing?" he asked.

"Listen, you start saying 'I'm going to meet Maqbool,' and she hasn't seen me in a year? She'll get suspicious quick. This way, she sees us together. She thinks everything is safe. She doesn't give you a hard time. Check it out, check it out."

"Check what out? And you couldn't let me know you were going to do this?"

"What you don't know isn't going to hurt you, Jaipal, it's gonna keep you safe. Remember that. Now look. You looking at this?" he asked, pointing to his new moped. It looked like all the other mopeds that weaved through the island's streets—gray, with little rearview mirrors that looked like antennas on a bug. Maqbool had attached a large steel lockbox to the back of the scooter, its glossy coat of black reflecting the light from the windows as small filamentous pools of white.

"It's in there," Maqbool said.

"You sure you want to keep it in there, you know, outside? I wouldn't."

"Eh, it's safe in this neighborhood. Anyway, let's go eat some of your ma's curry before it gets cold."

MAQBOOL STAYED FOR DINNER AND A CUP OF CHAI, SIPPING IT SLOWLY as he sat with Jaipal in the sitting room, asking him about the hotel, the store, playing the perfect role in his own story. In their conversation, Jaipal kept glancing from Maqbool to his mother as she placed the leftover curry into old glass jars, as she filled the sink with soapy water. He kept looking for some indication that Maqbool's story would break, that somehow they would be caught. At one point, Maqbool put his hand on Jaipal's knee, just for a second, like he was telling him to stop drawing attention to himself.

Maqbool finished his chai and brought the mug back to the kitchen. "Jaipal and I are going to take a ride on my new scooter. Just to the water and back."

"You two are going out now? Are you sure? It's not safe to leave, you heard about the curfew. I saw a dog barking on the roof of a house today. That can only mean something bad."

"I'm wearing silver," Maqbool said, pulling out a little chain around his neck. "We should be okay."

"Good," she said. "Jaipal never listens to me. Look, he wears silver." She looked at Jaipal. Maqbool laughed. Jaipal felt the red rising in his ears.

"There's someone who lives in the building next to me," Maqbool said. "He's a police officer, eh? He says curfew is for businesses. And anyway, we just need to avoid Queen's Street, avoid the businesses. If we're taking a walk, he says it's no problem."

"Jaipal, are you sure?" his mother asked.

Jaipal had already gotten up to put on his shoes. "We'll go sit near the water, down by Tulivu," he said. "It'll be fine."

"Just don't stay out too late. Stay together. They won't do anything if you two are together," his mother replied, sounding like she was trying to convince herself.

Jaipal had to sit behind Maqbool on the scooter, sandwiched between the warmth of his body and the cold steel of the lockbox. The night was clear, a cool caress set to the song of the katydids singing their chorus with the bass of the cane toads. Jaipal grabbed on to Maqbool's shoulders as he started the engine.

"Tulivu, eh?"

"My sister and I used to go there. It was our secret place."

"Yeah? Tell me about it when we get there. First we gotta get to your store."

The din of the 150 cc engine drowned out any possibility of conversation. Maqbool traveled deftly from side street to side street. They took the Sugar City Back Road, hugging the river Majivu, crossing it on the wooden slat bridge wide enough to fit a single car, bump bump bump, the movement causing his hands to drop down from Maqbool's shoulders just briefly to touch the blades jutting out from behind his shirt. He smelled good—that sweet mixture of aftershave and pomade. They passed the Buddhist temple with its peepal tree sending its branches deep into the earth before they turned onto Albert Lane. Maqbool shut off the lights on his scooter.

The street was silent: so quiet that they could hear the echoes of a caterwaul from a stray in heat somewhere in the city.

Maqbool parked the scooter on the footpath, right in front of the store's front gate. Jaipal looked over his shoulders, squinted into the empty pools of light from the streetlamps along Queen's Street.

"What are you waiting for?" Maqbool asked.

"Making sure no one's around, trying to be safe."

"Be quick," Maqbool said.

"I thought you said they won't bother us," Jaipal whispered quickly.

"I don't wanna test it."

Jaipal rolled up the gate halfway with a sudden thrust of his arms. The noise broke through the night, and a few birds squawked into flight. The caterwaul ceased. He fumbled in his pocket for the key, finding the correct one with his thumb and his finger before he even took them out. Maqbool opened the lockbox on his scooter as Jaipal opened the door.

"Here, take it," Maqbool said. "Quick quick, let's be fast, eh?"

"I heard you," Jaipal said, grabbing a carton of Marlboros, then another, then another. He placed them into the entryway of the store, piled up, looking like any other delivery.

"Here, take this," Maqbool said, handing him a small metal box, like the one he used to carry cash from the store to the bank.

Jaipal pressed his nose to the box. "Can't smell anything," he said.

"Good, that's the point."

"That's it?"

"We're starting small. If things go well, you can start putting it in the back. This should all fit beneath the till."

"So what do I do, stop selling the cigarettes I have here?"

"I mean, sell what you have, but stop buying from your distributor. They front me the cigarettes at cost and expect me to give their eighty percent of the profit after the sale. I don't give them anything for the package of ganja, so they take all the money from sales and give me what's mine.

"You got to keep the paisa straight. On a week where you're making five hundred, you'll be passing through five grand, mostly ganja money. Don't put it in the bank either. Just keep it safe."

The number made Jaipal feel sick. "You sure this isn't going to land me in some shit?" Jaipal thought of the look on the soldiers' faces a few months back, that one that told him he was nothing more than an insect to be killed underfoot.

"Just gonna get you some money." Maqbool smiled. "Let's get outta here."

"Should I grab one out of here for us?" Jaipal asked as he put the small box under the counter.

"Number one rule, Jaipal, never take from their stuff. Never. Promise me. They give it all to me, I do a count, I tell them the numbers, they expect to get cash based on those numbers. Everything has to add up. That's when we're fucked: when they start to notice things aren't adding up. So don't give them anything to notice, eh?"

Jaipal stared at Maqbool for a moment, the softness of his lashes, the way the gray was already starting to reach into the curls of his black hair. An upwelling inside of him—feeling, desire—erased all the questions, save one.

"Well, do you have any?"

Maqbool reached into the pocket of his long kurta and pulled out a joint rolled fat with tobacco and chimbi, its end twisted shut. "Let's get outta here," he said.

They stepped outside. A mosquito buzzed by his ear and he swatted it away. In the distance, Jaipal could hear the sound of a lorry rumbling along Queen's Street. His heart began to beat faster. He locked the door and pulled down the shutters as fast as he could.

"Keep it quiet!" Maqbool snapped in a fierce whisper.

The two hopped on his scooter. Lights off, they followed the path they had taken, until they instead took a right before the Newtown block where Jaipal lived.

Tulivu Bay wasn't a real bay. It had been built out by the Empire and the Americans during the war to launch their boats and ships. They had used dynamite to blast through the land, creating a crescent moon of green that hugged the water. Then they dredged the seafloor, erasing it all.

The result was a patch of nearly still water that lapped along white sand. From the beach, the waves broke ashore at the height of a few coconuts. It was deceptively inviting. What was hidden was the fact that a few meters out, the water dropped off, an underwater cliff. Some of the fishermen said they had taken the bottom down to twenty meters.

There was a small patch of asphalt in front of the sand, and in the corner, a shack made of corrugated sheets of tin, no bigger than Jaipal's kitchen.

"The coconut man," Jaipal said when Maqbool pulled the scooter next to the shack.

"The what?" Maqbool asked.

"Nothing, I'll tell you about it some other time. Like I said, me and my sister used to come here."

"That's nice," Maqbool said. Jaipal both bristled at the coldness of the reply and felt a surge of empathy at what had been so cruelly stolen from him.

They took off their sandals and left them near the scooter, the small rocks of the asphalt poking into the softness on the arches of their feet. To avoid the pain, Jaipal danced on his toes, one jump, then another, until he reached the safety of the sand.

"You can always tell who doesn't have to walk barefoot," Maqbool said, "you can't handle the way the ground cuts your feet."

"Funny," Jaipal said. He had hated this about Maqbool. Everything was about where your people came from. Those from better-off families bore the brunt of Maqbool's sarcasm. Those who weren't could only be heroes or victims.

"No, man, I'm just joking, you shouldn't take it so serious. Come on, let's go sit on the sand."

In the darkness, the beach was deserted, and the sound of the soft lapping made a drone of peaceful white noise. Maqbool pulled out the joint and put it in his mouth, cupping the flame that burst forth from a pack of matches while puffing smoke in and out, until the tip was red-hot, ready for the taking. Maqbool took a breath in, deep, and coughed the smoke all the way out.

"Good shit," he said.

Jaipal took the joint from Maqbool, pinching it between his fingers, breathing in as deep as he could, and holding that breath within him for as long as a prayer. The smoke scratched at his throat as it left him, and he coughed from deep within his chest. He passed the joint back.

"So you came here with your sister?" Maqbool asked in a dream-like way.

"It was a secret, you know," Jaipal said, his tongue and muscles loosened from the hit. "When the shit got too much with Papa, I'd take her here and we'd go swimming. It's the perfect place. You don't have to go against the tide to get past the breakers, you just walk in and dive."

"That's cool," Maqbool said, his voice throaty and raw from the hit. He passed the joint back to Jaipal. "Were you and your sister close?"

"I mean, not like you and Salim. You guys were close."

Maqbool waved off the comment—or maybe he was swatting away a mosquito.

Jaipal went on. "You know how my papa is. I did what I could for her. She's so fucking smart, she had her own life with the libraries and books and shit. I tried to be big brother, you know? Tried to be something for her." Jaipal took another hit, shorter, like a quick jab. "I don't know," he said. "Sometimes, I felt like no one remembered me. There was this time when I was a kid. My sister had just gotten bit by this stray dog, right in the neck."

"What the fuck, right in the neck? Just randomly? Is that how she got that scar?"

"She was playing out in the driveway. Of course my ma took her to the hospital. I was supposed to meet my father at the shop. I get there, and the door is locked. No one there."

He could see himself sitting on the curb in front of the shop and his eyes at the level of the legs of workers walking home, the western sun streaming through Albert Lane. "So I took the bus by myself. I get home. No one was there either. I was yelling for my ma, for my sister—no one. It was fucked."

He remembered lifting the lid on a pot on the stove, peering in at the watery-looking dal, half-cooked and abandoned. Next to the stove was a chunk of dough and a pile of uncooked, rolled-out rotis. A small trail of ants fanned across the dough like moving flecks of black pepper. He had hustled away from the kitchen and into Bhumi's bedroom: her small bed with the purple sheets was made, but the window was open, blowing his sister's curtains in and out like a lost flag.

Maqbool nudged him out of his reverie and asked him to keep going.

"I hid in my closet for a while. I cried. Then someone came into the house."

Maqbool stared closely at Jaipal, his eyes lost in the story.

"Probably some family friend or something. I was scared. Once they left, I got out of the closet. I kept crying."

"That's fucked up, man."

"It's always been like, my mom and Bhumi, super close, like this," he said, lifting up two fingers, their tips lit by the soft light of the moon. Maqbool had put out the joint and was puffing on a cigarette. He offered Jaipal one from his pack.

He took it and looked straight at Maqbool. His fingers tingled with some new feeling. He grabbed the cigarette out of Maqbool's mouth and used its end to light his own, taking a puff and then holding the cigarette between his fingers. He handed the cigarette back to Maqbool.

When Maqbool grabbed the cigarette, he grazed the inside of Jaipal's wrist. It was only inches away from a handshake, but the touch brought fire straight into Jaipal's veins.

It had been quick, fluid: one decisive movement. Cigarettes dropped into the sand, hands running up and down the backs of each other. And Maqbool's mouth, something different for Jaipal—an insistence: he was driving, it was his tongue in charge. Nothing for him to take, everything for him to give.

Maqbool finally pulled away. He was fishing through the sand. "Shouldn't let a good cig go to waste." Jaipal could see the white of his smile, the faint red in his eyes from the chimbi.

"How did you know?"

"You look so cute when you're confused," Maqbool said, laughing. And the sound of his laughter was beautiful, contagious. Jaipal began to laugh, deep, from his belly out into the world. The first time in months he had laughed like that.

It took some time for their laughter to die down. "No, seriously."

"You did a shit job at keeping your hotel stuff a secret."

"Wait, really?"

"I mean, you didn't hide it from anyone who wanted to know. I heard it from someone."

"People gossip? I mean, about me?"

"Everyone talks about everyone, even you, Jay. What the fuck else is there to do on this tiny-ass island?"

Jaipal felt himself tightening up, from muscles to nerves, to his eyes.

"Hey, no, it's fine. No one knows who could cause some shit," Maqbool said, leaning in, kissing his neck, his jaw, his cheek, then again they were locked together. He tasted like chimbi, cigarettes, and ever so faintly, mint.

"No one talks about you," Jaipal said. "I didn't even know you, you know. Not anymore, not since we were kids."

"I keep everything a secret. Everything is for me to know and no one to find out. It's just been me and my mom and my brother, my whole life, just us three. And now it's just me and my mom. All anyone has to know is that I hustle, for both of us. After I get out, I'll send some money so she can get the fuck outta this small backbiting place. You'll see."

Jaipal watched Maqbool draw into himself, one arm wrapped around his shins and the other stretched out to rest his hand upon Jaipal's. Jaipal stretched his legs out and leaned back, balancing most of his weight upon one hand behind him. Everything felt so far away. The sound of the ocean past the breakers filled his ears with a low rumble. He felt himself easing into someone new, something knowable, something comfortable. Maqbool looked like the sea turtle from his memories with Bhumi, he thought—something hardened against everything that could emerge from the deep.

18

IT WAS ALREADY four thirty and Bhumi was going to be late for her Ecology lecture. The mother of the boy she was nannying was supposed to be home by four o'clock, and here she was, pushing it yet again. It had started with her coming home five or ten minutes late, testing Bhumi's patience. When Bhumi said nothing, the lock started clicking at 4:20, 4:25, and now, the woman was a half hour late.

Bhumi was trying to get Amit to stack blocks, but he wanted to throw them ("Want throw! Want throw!" he would shriek). Bhumi hoped the mother wouldn't notice the dents in the drywall. He was still learning how to throw. Sometimes, the blocks would go backward, right into Bhumi's face.

The boy was a little hell creature—hyperactive and loud. He spoke at deafening volumes, and he hit and bit in tantrums that raged and waned without regularity. In short, he was a toddler, and Bhumi was exasperated.

Bhumi heard the snap-swish of brass in the door and the footsteps of the woman as she entered her home, the squeak of comfortable trainers against the tile of the entryway. The woman wasn't much better than her child. She flaunted her Indian appetite for gold (gold chandelier earrings, gold bangles, gold chains) and was the type who, outside the home, spoke with others in tones of forced cheer but preferred the comforts of a scowl with the help.

Farida Aunty had used the grapevine to help Bhumi find this job, just days after Bhumi had arrived to stay with her and Raj Uncle. The job came with a warning: desi Indians like Amit's mother saw them as second-class, useful only as nannies because they knew English and Hindi. Farida said these Indians told them what dishes and cutlery they could use, haggled over hourly wages even though they lived in mansions, and laughed mockingly when Indians from the island hummed a Bollywood song. After her first week on the job, Bhumi knew one thing: She wasn't Indian. Not to this woman. Maybe she was like her grandmother: lost in a foreign land.

Bhumi grabbed her bag and headed for the door, informing the mother about the child's bowel movements, meals, and nap. If she wasn't careful, she could lose an entire unpaid hour: the mother would take another half hour to drink a cup of chai while Bhumi kept chasing after the child.

From the house, she walked double-pace to the BART station, one hand upon the nylon bag she had bought from Goodwill, which, no matter how many times she cleaned it, always smelled faintly of roasted peanuts. It was large enough to carry her lunch and any of the toys she needed to take to the park for the boy, as well as the more important things: her notebooks, her pencil case with three highlighters (green, yellow, pink), pens, pencils, a sharpener, and the pack of Marlboro Lights she always carried now.

She had never smoked that much back home, but here, she couldn't walk from place to place without a cigarette. Her hands needed something to do, and it also kept the hunger at bay—lunches missed from lack of money, or from the fact that there was never enough time. The stress, the intermittent meals, the cigarettes, had shot her digestive system to hell, but it was just another thing gone wrong that would need to be fixed later.

On the train, two stops back to Santa Ursula; from the windows, she could see the golden Mediterranean grasses dormant upon the East Bay hills. At the public library, she had read that the golden hills that defined the California landscape were, in fact, not native. The original grasses had been perennial bunch grasses like the purple needlegrass, with its thin green blades; soft, purple-tinged awn; and roots that could reach six meters into hillside soil. These hardy bunches were perfectly suited to California: green year-round, drought tolerant, and able to withstand fire.

Then came the Spanish and their cattle, Catholicism, and smallpox. They too brought their grasses: filaree, foxtail, and clover. These foreign grasses were well adapted to cattle grazing. They took root and spread, outcompeting the bunch grasses across the state. And since these plants were annuals, they died every summer and left thousands of acres of kindling to catch fire.

It was so strange, Bhumi thought, that this defining feature of the Californian hills was just another empire fucking up another place. Those with power could change a landscape. The rest had to make do with the fires that ravaged and burned.

From the BART station, she took the bus up to the Cal State Santa Ursula campus—a smattering of drab midcentury buildings of poured concrete, a facsimile of the SPU campus, though without the lush lawns or meandering streams—and slipped into her lecture hall.

The professor was a bland white man with a soft, round face and a receding hairline of salt-and-pepper hair, prone to speaking directly to his slides rather than facing his class. Attendance was always sparse. This infuriated Bhumi. Did the students not appreciate what they had? Or know how easily it could be taken away?

Exploitation, the professor was explaining, was an interaction between populations that enhanced the fitness of one and decreased the fitness of another. Predators, he said in a flat drone, could immigrate from other areas to take advantage of oscillations in prey populations. She wrote a little note in the margin: *Am I a parasite or a predator?*

Finally, a reminder: the midterm was in a week. He would be holding extended office hours for any questions.

When the class ended and the murmur of departure rose side by side with the shuffling of papers into backpacks, Bhumi walked down the lecture hall's stairs to the front of the class to ask him if she could sit in on the midterm. The professor couldn't remember her name and when she reminded him, he said, "Of course. Bhumi. My best auditor."

His reminder stung.

SHE HAD LANDED IN SFO IN LATE MAY, ALMOST FIVE MONTHS AGO. After a brief and lazy interrogation from the immigration officer at SFO, Raj Uncle had picked her up from the arrivals hall in the taxi he now drove (Raj now stooped with the hustle of a migrant, and his three boys lacked their former kinetic laughter). The next day, Raj had taken her to an immigration lawyer whose office was in a strip mall sandwiched between a store called Island Cash and Curry—"The center of our community," Raj said—and a discount carpet retailer. She left that appointment owing him $1,000 and went back to the pull-out sofa in Farida and Raj's two-bedroom apartment. After twenty-four hours in America, she already had a debt to pay and a warning that her asylum documentation could take months to be received by the INS, and perhaps up to a decade to be decided.

Farida knew the debt was coming and had already started to find

Bhumi a nannying job. Bhumi inwardly resented how everyone assumed that, as a woman, she knew how to wrangle a child. It had taken time for her to learn how to deal with this child, and not through any inborn feminine understanding. She had used her scientific eye and gradually learned: this was the action that led to a meltdown, this was the way to get him to calm down. Hypothesis, observation, conclusion. And every Friday, at the end of a long day spent corralling the awful child, Bhumi was handed an envelope with six twenty-dollar bills.

Months had passed like this, and still no word from the INS, the same drudgery of home-child-home, interspersed with Farida and Raj's encouraging her to go to the occasional Saturday night at someone's apartment, the women crowded around a kitchen table, the men drinking in a living room, aunties trading lewd jokes about their employers. Bhumi would catch Farida's eyes drifting to her hands, the skin between her index and middle finger yellowed from chain-smoking, a mournful look on her face, like she had failed to step in and be a surrogate mother to Bhumi.

It was only by chance that Bhumi discovered there was a college just up the street. A flyer for adult education had been tucked into the mail: Cal State Santa Ursula. Head down in the hustle, she had missed it, only three miles away.

It was too late to apply, and she couldn't anyway, not while she was still waiting for her papers, the flimsy documents that could prove her worth to be more than that of a young nanny. She wandered around that campus anyway, all the way to its edge, where the footpath—sidewalk, she corrected herself—turned into lookouts over the bay. She could see Santa Ursula below, and beyond, all the way up to Oakland and the Bay Bridge, the long fingers of fog shrouding San Francisco and touching the horizon.

Before her visit she had Xeroxed a few pages from a dog-eared and worn copy of a two-year-old course catalog at the public library.

She hoped the Ecology class still met at the same time and place. It took her a few doors to find the room she was looking for. She quietly took a seat in the back with her pens and highlighters, and talked to the professor after his lecture ended. He stammered through his answer—he was sorry, so sorry, to hear about her situation, she was welcome to sit in.

She came back the next day and tried the same thing on a mycology course called The Fungi of California. From the way he stared at her chest, Bhumi saw the professor was the same type she had encountered back home. He let her audit as well.

These hours were a small victory, and victory felt like rushing from work to campus, then going home to reheat dinner in the microwave at Raj and Farida's. Victory was staying up to review her notes and starting it all over the next day. Victory felt like the giddiness of exhaustion, which was enough to make her forget.

On the dreadful weekends, when there was no work or class, she would go to the public library, and when that grew boring, she would create little projects to keep herself from going mad in the empty time. She entered corner liquor stores to buy a pack, but also to walk up and down the aisles and examine what they held. The Punjabi man behind the counter reminded her of home, and he didn't seem to mind her wandering around. A simple experiment: what was the difference between a Frito and a Dorito? On one day, she purchased both, tasting one and then the other. She preferred a Frito.

"DO YOU THINK I COULD SIT IN ON THE MIDTERM?" BHUMI ASKED THE professor.

The professor shrugged. "Sure. Most students would prefer to *skip* the midterm. If you want to take it, fine by me."

A little shimmer of joy—she was buoyant at the thought of returning to what was familiar.

As she bounded up the steps and out of the lecture hall, a student with thin wire-frame glasses stood in her path. He wore a black T-shirt, some sort of band or musician, the words *Talk Talk Talk* emblazoned on the top.

He cleared his throat nervously and gave a little smile. "I sit behind you in class," he said. "You're always taking awesome notes, like with those highlighters and stuff. I was wondering, do you want to join our study group for the midterm?"

"Sure," Bhumi said, trying to dampen her excitement at being recognized for what she did well. "When do you meet?"

"Awesome! I mean, that's great. We're going to meet tomorrow at the Puzzle, you know where that is? Down in the basement of the student union."

"What time?" Bhumi asked.

"Like around seven. Does that work for you? It might be me and someone else, or it might just be me. I'm still trying to figure it out."

"Seven sounds great."

"I'm Vic, by the way," he said, holding his hand out.

"Vic?" Bhumi asked, puzzled. She had thought he was Indian.

"Yeah, like Victor."

"So your name is Victor?"

"No, it's Vikram. I just go by Vic because people think it's easier."

Bhumi finally shook his hand with a warm smile. "Vikram is a beautiful name. I knew a Vikram back home. My name is Bhumi. I'll see you on Friday?"

"Yeah, great! I like my name too. Anyway, I gotta get to a South Africa divestment meeting. It was nice to finally talk to you, Bhumi."

Bhumi felt an unfamiliar sense of possibility. She wanted to treat herself before she spent the evening studying in the library. In the student union, a two-story building that looked more like a government office back home, she bought herself a little pizza from Pizza Hut and ate it overlooking one of the campus vistas. It was cute how nervous he had been, but there was something beyond that awkwardness. He seemed so relaxed in himself, like an American. She wondered what it would feel like to be from this place. The next day would finally bring something to look forward to, a feeling she hadn't had since the night she went out with Aarti. She watched the sun dissolve itself into the hazy fog.

19

JAIPAL WAS IN the shop, staring out the window, smoking a cigarette as a customer went on and on about how the shit still flowed downstream, and in new ways.

"They're going to take over the sugar refinery," a customer told Jaipal. "They're going to make it government rum."

Jaipal nodded lazily. He passed the customer a joint. Could a stoner be a reliable source of information?

"Think about it," the customer continued, even after Jaipal handed him back his change. "They're taking the abandoned cane farms. Why not just take over the refinery? Integrate it. Give it to the jungli. They'll take what we built."

"That's a good point," Jaipal said. "See you tomorrow, Romesh."

"Tomorrow? I'll see you this evening. I'm so nervous. This is the only thing that helps. I still haven't heard anything from my brother. I don't even know if he's alive. They arrest him, put him in the back of a van, and that's it. I need this."

Jaipal watched as Romesh shuffled out of his store. The cigarettes, but really the chimbi, were keeping Jaipal afloat. When the General's goons decided to take over some business, prices inevitably skyrocketed. He was putting military lackeys in charge of farms, and they had no idea how to handle a harvest, how to manage supply, how to placate demand.

Prices went up: 25 percent on radishes, 50 percent on onions.

The government panicked at a demand collapse due to higher prices, so they lowered them and offset the losses by putting tariffs on food imported from India. Jaipal stopped buying Indian snack food from his distributor. It wasn't worth the 35 percent tariff, not when he had Maqbool's hustle.

Was this all petty revenge? It wasn't the Indians' fault that the Empire had once thought them more capable of handling the island's commerce. Now the natives wanted payback for years of perceived bad deals, years of being left out. The Indians deserved a taste of their own medicine.

To Jaipal, this made no sense—he had seen it with his own eyes. They never wanted to work! The Indians toiled. The kaamchor sat in their villages. And every square inch of soil in the nation belonged to the chiefs and tribes of the natives—it was codified in the country's first constitution. The Indians could till the land, could bring up the tallest buildings, but it all sat upon that which belonged to the other. This wasn't hate or racism. It was the agreed-upon way of things.

If the shop felt hollowed out, things at home had been turned inside out and upside down. His father lived there now. All the time.

Mostly, his father slept. Sometimes, he ate. He confined himself to his bedroom, where he spent most of his time lying in bed. This in itself wasn't too out of the ordinary: it was often his behavior after a bender. Disappear for a few days and come back to sleep it off. Then he would pretend like nothing had happened.

He stayed in bed now. And when he was awake, he had this look in his eyes like there was nothing left to see. Filled with tremors, his head nodding up and down. Something had happened.

"This isn't like him," Jaipal's mother had said to him that morning. "I've never seen him like this before."

"Give him a week, he'll be back to normal," Jaipal replied. There had to be some trick underneath it all, some deal to be found.

"The evil eye is in this house. You think he will be back to the same as before?" She asked this question plaintively, the way someone might haggle with God in a prayer.

Now, at the shop, the familiar drumbeat came on the radio.

What now? He asked himself.

"This is a special bulletin," the announcer said. "This program has been interrupted. The General has announced today that all international travel involving those of Indian descent will halt while the country conducts its first official count of people of Indian origin. No person of Indian origin will be allowed to leave the country without explicit permission.

"Government officials will count each and every person of Indian origin and issue a document to ensure that they are counted. This will ensure adequate representation in the newly formed government. Failure to participate will be punished. Any Indian not present in the country for the census will immediately relinquish his right to citizenship.

"This is a special bulletin," the announcer repeated, going over the same speech once again.

Jaipal couldn't make sense of what he had heard. The announcer repeated it a second time, then a third, and finally, it was repeated in Hindi. They were closing down the airport. No one was going to leave the country. They wanted to know everything about the Indians.

"Fuck, madarchod," Jaipal said, a whisper of fear. His mind shot straight to Maqbool—what would this do to his plan, his savings for

Rakesh? Jaipal wanted to see him, but he couldn't leave. He knew the rules. He didn't have an excuse to leave the till and close down the store.

At least Bhumi had escaped just in time. The image of Salim's body, shot dead in a ditch, stuck to him. He asked himself: What will they do to us? What will it do to me? This country could take anything it wanted, and quickly and efficiently, it could break a people down and flatten them like a cardboard box left on the footpath, all with words spoken over the radio.

20

CAMPUS SEEMED EERILY empty on a Friday night. The sun had yet to set, and the lack of activity reminded Bhumi of the drained energy of the curfew, when every minute was filled with a dreadful possibility, the fear that each breath could have an exhale that would never come. She hustled into the student union, down its stairs, and into the brightness of the artificially lit basement.

The bar had a black-and-white checkerboard-tile floor, and the music was playing at a low-enough volume to keep conversation going. The dance floor was empty and there were only a handful of students in the red vinyl booths.

She saw him sitting in a corner booth, his hair a mess of tight curls, wearing another music T-shirt and thumbing through a copy of a book. His eyebrows were knit into a look of concern, and his eyes would narrow when he was reading, widen when he reached for his pencil to underline a sentence.

"Vikram," Bhumi said with a smile. "What are you reading?"

"*Orientalism* by Edward Said—it's fucking wild. The West, it's just been representing us as this *other,* you know? Exotic. Unknowable. They've been doing it forever. Have you heard of it?"

The book sounded vaguely familiar, something that Aarti would have read and gone on and on about, while Bhumi would have tuned out after a while with little "uh-huh"s and "that's great"s.

"Yeah, I think a friend of mine read it. From back home." There was a small basket of fries in the middle of the table with a dollop of ketchup in the corner, its dredged remains streaked out from dipping. The place smelled too clean and fresh, and was too well lit, to be anything like Irish O'Reilly. Still, when she sat down she felt the floor stick to her shoes little bit like it did back home, and just for a moment, she expected that Aarti would come by and sit right next to her.

"Where's back home?" he asked. "That's a stupid question. I hate it when people ask me that question. Don't answer it if you don't want to." It was clear he was nervous, that he was shooting a look down her sweater as she leaned forward to grab a French fry.

She told him about the island, and he said he hadn't heard of it. "There are Indian people there? That's hella crazy," he rattled on. "I've never heard of that. It's like, growing up, I only knew Indians who were Bihari and from UP. And then I get to college and there are Punjabis and Gujaratis and Tamilians and all of them are different. And then there are Indians from all over? Shit is wild."

He was babbling, and there was something so sweet about it, but talking about the past made her uncomfortable. She was unsure of what she could or should share with him, what he actually wanted to hear. "Should we get started on this study guide?"

"Oh yeah, definitely. I'm just taking this course as a science elective. I'm majoring in anthro. It's cool though. Just not my thing, you know? What are you majoring in?"

"Back home I was a biology major. Here, I'm—what do you call it?—I'm auditing two classes. Until I can apply to university again. By the time I arrived here, it was too late to apply," she added quickly.

"You're auditing and you're taking the midterm, just for fun?"

"It's what I love. And it's better than my job. I work as a nanny for a family in Union City."

"Why'd you move to Santa Ursula?"

"It's complicated," Bhumi said curtly. "Should we work on the study guide?" she asked again, hoping he wouldn't take her reticence about her own story as a sign that she was uninterested in his.

They traded notes on the first question, exchanging ideas, confirming disagreements. She glanced up from the paper to steal a look at the softness of his eyelashes, the stubble forming only above his upper lip. It was as if one satisfied craving led to another. Here, time could go backward, and she could again be the person she had left behind.

"What about you, Vikram?" She wanted to hear more about him. "Here's a question you'll hate: did you move here from India?"

Vikram laughed. "It's cool when you ask it. Yeah, I moved here—I was like two years old. My dad got a job as an engineer at MicroDev, back when the semiconductor industry was really starting to get going. We moved down to Fremont, and I've lived in the Bay ever since. My mom mostly stays home. She teaches kathak dance on the weekends. So I guess I'm from India, but like, I don't even remember much Hindi anymore, you know? This is all I know."

It was fascinating how this country could erase his birthplace. The opposite could happen too. Bhumi saw how those from back home were sticking together. Here, they were just an undifferentiated group of people from the island—no more religion, family name, or class. They all now carried more of the island inside of them than they ever had back home.

"Do you like that? Only knowing California?"

"Fuck. That's a question. I mean, do I like being an American?

Do I like Reagan? Hell no. What can I do? Move to Canada? I'm not sure. Most white people, they're like, 'Where are you *really* from?' They can't imagine me being an American. This is my place, with all of its problems, and it's my place to fight for, or whatever, you know? Man, all this talking is making me thirsty. You want a drink, Bhumi?"

"Budweiser Light," she said with a sense of relief. She had never before had the drink but had seen it advertised on billboards across Santa Ursula. The ads were all filled with women who looked like they were enjoying themselves, heads back in laughter: this Bud's for you too.

He brought back a can of Budweiser Light and a bottle of Corona for himself.

"What about you?" Vikram asked. "Do you feel like you're from here?"

"Here? America? No. Absolutely not," Bhumi said, surprised at the vehemence of her response. "I came here a few months ago. How can I be from here?" Bhumi took a sip of her beer. "I came here seeking asylum and the INS hasn't even told me they received my application. That means I'm from nowhere right now." She hadn't talked to anyone outside her own community about what was going on, and despite that, there was an ease to talking with Vikram.

"It's terrible, Vikram," she continued. "You *have* to be from somewhere. When you're from nowhere, you can't be anything. The family that I nanny for, they think I'm invisible, like I don't matter. They treat me like that. I'm from nowhere and I feel like I'm being erased, like I'm doing work no one can see."

"Fuck, I'm sorry, Bhumi," he said with such an earnestness that Bhumi thought she could hear his heart breaking. "My friends are activists, maybe we can do something—protest the INS building in the city or something, I don't know. We can try?"

Bhumi gave him a warm smile. "Maybe we can finish this study guide?"

The two kept working. Madonna's "Borderline" played from a record behind the bar.

"I've never really been into Madonna, but it's all they play here. More mainstream stuff. Do you like Hüsker Dü or the Jesus and Mary Chain or any of that stuff?"

"I've never really listened to them," Bhumi said.

"Oh, man, you gotta come over to my place. We can listen to my tapes."

The dance floor had slowly filled up as the night passed. Bhumi's leg was bouncing up and down under the table. She wanted to make a move but had no idea how. "How about a dance first?" Bhumi blurted out.

They danced, one song, then another, then one beer, and another, and his body moved close, and she could feel him against her, and before she knew it, they were outside, the night still warm, the feeling within her light.

He leaned in to kiss her. He was tentative, pecking his lips lightly upon hers. She pulled him in, put her tongue into his mouth, let her hand run down his back.

"I live down the block. Do you still wanna listen to those tapes?" he asked.

"Sure," Bhumi said in a breath.

They ambled together down the hill from campus, back to the traffic of Mission Boulevard below. She felt like she could, for a night, pretend, leave behind the drab nine-to-five life, the General, the nagging worry about her mother and brother.

Vikram's roommate was out for the evening. Vikram's room was tidy and spartan in the way men could live: a twin bed with a thin beige blanket, a desk strewn with books and papers, a full hamper of laundry, and nothing on the walls.

They continued to kiss on the bed, and she grabbed his hand and placed it on her breasts over her shirt. She kept leading, kissing him, pushing him down, climbing on top of him. They made out for a few minutes until Bhumi asked if he had a condom. His eyes widened and he pulled out a box from the drawer next to his bed.

She stayed on top. It was clear he was a straightforward lover, not one to insist upon his way of doing things. She grabbed his hand and moved it to her lower back.

"Write me something," Bhumi said in a grunt. He shook his head, confused as to what she was saying. "Use your fingers, write on my back," she commanded. He began to draw his hands along her back, and she shuddered with delight.

She closed her eyes, and he wasn't there anymore. Nothing was there. She wasn't in Santa Ursula. She wasn't in California. This was the true nowhere she sought. She was wanted, she was desired, she could feel.

She ground herself into him so she could feel the pleasure she wanted. She held her breath, one, two, three, and the room burst from black and white into pure color. She cried out. It was only once—and she could feel many more building within her, lining up one after another, but her joy brought him to completion, and soon he was done.

She rolled off of him and he asked if she was okay.

She touched her face. Her cheeks were wet. Her muscles, tightened over months, were finally easing into relief. Her body, given the smallest joy, was letting itself loose, letting her feel all that she had kept from herself.

"It's fine," she said. "It's fucking great, actually."

"You sure?"

"I'm sure." She wanted to enjoy what she had earned, so she let herself relax into him. He fell asleep quickly, and while she stared at the bare wall across from his bed, she couldn't help but think of how she and Aarti would have gossiped about this hookup, how Bhumi would have asked whether *Orientalism* was a good book or not, about whether his activist friends were on the right or the wrong side.

It was too much: a burst of sorrowful longing inside what should have been something joyful. She swallowed hard and closed her eyes and started to count backward from one hundred. She wouldn't let the past break this moment.

ON THE DAY OF THE MIDTERM, SHE STOPPED BY ISLAND CASH AND Curry, nervously hurrying past the lawyer's office. She walked through an aisle filled with bags of snack mixture: sealed polyethylene bags filled with spicy-fried lentils, peanuts, sev, puffed rice, and fried onions. The store's interior, with its aisles for fruit and vegetables, spices, snacks, and refrigerated goods, looked like it had been airlifted from her past in Sugar City.

The back of the store was divided into two. On the right was a counter that looked back into a small kitchen, from which came the delectable savory odors of chicken curry, roti parcels, and biryani. She grabbed two foil-wrapped roti parcels: one for lunch, and one for the train ride to Santa Ursula from work. She liked to go there in the morning to check in on Aarti.

Farida had told her about the lost-and-found system that had developed. Shop owners from back home had scattered to the San Francisco Bay Area, Melbourne, London, Toronto. Their customers from the island wanted to know where so-and-so had ended up—if they were still alive. So, the store owners decided to form a lost-and-found mesh network.

Each store had a posted list of names—the owner, Jagdish, had taped his on top of the counter next to the register. If a customer saw someone they knew on the list and had a phone number for that person, they would give Jagdish the information. He would then forward this information to his phone tree to let them know that the lost person had been found.

When she had asked Jagdish to add Aarti to the list, he had asked her where the network should look. Bhumi had no idea, so she had told him Australia.

The store that morning was already filled with people, the line to the phone in the back stretching to the front door. Bhumi shook her head—all this trouble for a simple rumor.

"Any news on Aarti Kumar?" she asked when she was finally able to get Jagdish's attention. Bhumi's meager question was always a sharp-jab reminder of her exile. She felt a pang of sadness and tried to store it away, crumpling up her emotions like a piece of paper, until they were a small ball that she could shove into some wastebasket deep inside her. She gave Jagdish a half smile.

"Sorry, nothing. Bad news from home, though," he said. Jagdish's bearded face was usually stretched into a constant smile, but today, the crow's-feet by his eyes telegraphed a heavyset weariness.

"The rumors *are* true?" Bhumi asked. Raj and Farida had been talking about this all weekend. It seemed so nonsensical to Bhumi that she thought it was just another scrap of news that had been twisted into something bigger as it had passed from person to person.

"Was finally able to get someone to confirm it last night. No Indians can leave. Those junglis always wanted us dead. Now who knows what the General's going to do to us."

Bhumi's panic was instant. She wanted to try to call home now. Jagdish had set up a phone in the back of the store, but Bhumi had been unlucky. About half of the Indians at Island Cash and Curry couldn't call home: the call quality was so bad it reduced the voices on the other end of the line to a muffle. There seemed to be a randomness to this: some people would have better luck another day. For Bhumi, it never worked, and she had stopped trying, resorting instead to aerograms sent across the sea, each taking weeks to arrive, all of them filled with the kind of bland news meant to hide from the other the truth of their misery.

She didn't have time this morning to see if the lines would finally connect and she could hear their voices, but she still needed to know if they had a plan. She should have been there, with them, on the island, but she was here, taking care of some awful child, taking a midterm for a class that meant nothing.

She could skip the midterm and call them right after her nannying shift. After all, the exam was her own personal extracurricular. But what would Vikram say if she wasn't there? She wanted to see him, wanted to get a drink again, wanted to go back into his messy room, if only to feel a touch that wasn't her own hand in the dark.

THE LECTURE HALL WAS ALREADY FILLED WITH STUDENTS, MOST OF whom she had never before seen. She scanned the hall and found Vikram. "I realized I didn't have your number," she told him, sitting down next to him. "I wanted to see you again."

He wrote down his number on a piece of paper. "Good luck today!" he said with a smile. "I'm sure you'll do great."

"Good luck to you too," Bhumi said. "I'm staying with some family friends right now. Here's their number."

The exam was a breeze, and she was surprised to see that most of the other students were still working on theirs when she finished and checked over her answers twice.

"Let's meet up again," Vikram whispered.

"Friday," Bhumi whispered back.

SHE CAUGHT THE BUS JUST IN TIME, AND AS IT DESCENDED INTO THE orange haze of the flatlands below campus, she felt the dread of returning to a life she had left behind.

While the kitchen took up the right in the back of Island Cash and Curry, the left fit only a folding chair in front of a small wooden table covered with a pink crocheted tablecloth that would not have looked out of place in a grandmother's house. Above the phone was a sign in handwritten block letters:

RECORD THE TIME WHEN YOU START AND STOP
YOUR CALL

DAY RATE: $1.00/minute NIGHT/WEEKEND RATE: $0.50/minute
MINIMUM CHARGE: $1.00

IF SOMEONE IS WAITING, KEEP CALLS TO 10 MINUTES

She sat in the chair and wrote down the time on the pad of paper in front of her. She had already memorized the time difference: three hours behind, the next day.

She picked up the receiver and punched in a familiar number. It rang once in the long American style before pulsing in the international staccato way as the call routed outward through undersea cables.

"Hello?" Jaipal said. The call had connected, even though some static remained. She had tried several times to call home, but this was the first time she had heard his voice in months.

"Hello? Jaipal?" Bhumi said, increasing the volume of her voice.

"Bhumi?" Jaipal asked. "It's connected!" he shouted.

"I heard what happened," Bhumi said, wanting to burst through the pleasantries into the conversation. "Tell me everything, I don't know if the connection will stay."

"The General said no one can leave. Everyone has to stay. They said we can't take the international flights. They're going to count us all, see how many of us are left. They're calling it a Yellow-Card Census. They're going to give us a card when it's done. Listen, Bhumi, they also said . . ." He trailed off.

"What did they say, Jaipal?"

"They said that anyone who left won't be a citizen anymore. You can't come back."

Bhumi felt stunned, as if someone had just pushed her down. The static of silence filled the call, filled her brain, scattered her thoughts.

"Bhumi, are you there?" Jaipal asked.

She had no place to retreat. "Are you okay? How is everything else?" she asked, trying to recover.

"We're fine. Staying home. All Indian-owned businesses have been closed for now. There's no looting yet. We'll see."

"Looting, oh my God," Bhumi said. Her eyes followed the second hand on the clock. She needed more. There wasn't time. The call was eating through her money.

There was nothing else they could say: the call was again fading into whispers of static. Bhumi said goodbye, unsure whether Jaipal could hear her. She wished she could speak with him a little more and get the chance to talk to her mother. She was separated from them not only by an entire ocean but also by a phone system that worked only when it wanted to. Worry and anxiety were left to fester on each side of the call, with no easy way to heal.

Bhumi put the phone down and scribbled the time on the pad before she tore off the paper. A hunched-over man rushed to sit down, and as she walked away, she heard him slam down the receiver and complain that the call wasn't working. "Ey!" someone yelled. "Don't break the phone!"

Bhumi stared straight through her reflection in the door to the chilled shelves holding small tubs of off-brand ice cream. Everything had been cut away from her.

Her eyes fell on a package of vanilla ice cream, which seemed more real to her in that moment than the fate of a country left behind. There was absolutely nothing she could do with the news from home.

She had to soldier on, doing what, she had no idea. She had still heard nothing from the INS about her application. She opened the door, grabbed the ice cream, and continued on to the counter.

At the counter, Jagdish asked her what she thought of what was going on as she rummaged through her purse to pay him. She felt her words rise from a hidden place: that part of her where she kept her dashed hopes.

"The same thing always happens," she said. "Some of us will die. Some of us will suffer. The rest will escape. And we'll find ourselves here or there." She reached over and handed him ten dollars.

He took the cash and scribbled some numbers on a piece of carbon-copy paper. He held the yellow copy of the receipt along with her change and stared at it for a moment. He did not smile. "You're right," he said as he handed both to her.

Bhumi knew what he was going to say next. There was something about the way his eyes glazed over. She was of a people who sifted through pockets looking for talismans to protect them from the evil eye. She believed in science, not superstitions, Bhumi thought as she touched her scar. And yet, these were the only people she had here. She had to navigate both worlds, be something to them now, whereas before she could just try to live her small little life.

"Our fathers and grandfathers left," Jagdish said. "So will we. That country won't survive. But we will. Just like our ancestors."

21

"EY! JAIPAL," HIS father yelled in a hoarse and slurred voice. "Are you listening?" The question lacked any of the jeering that Jaipal was accustomed to hearing from him. It was as if his father truly was wondering if anyone could hear him anymore.

His mother turned to him with a look of surprise. Jaipal could see all the lines of her face clearly, how they all seemed to point toward the tenderness in the sound of his father's voice as a sort of betrayal.

His fantasy of love and togetherness was slipping away—or perhaps it had never been real in the first place. They had never before relied on each other. There was no script for this relationship.

Still, he felt like there had to be some part of him that could bridge this gap between them. Somewhere within him was a child who carried the ghosts of all the children his parents wanted him to be, the child he never was.

"Ey! Jaipal!" his father yelled again, sounding muffled, like feathers had been stuffed into his mouth.

He walked into the room where his father lay. The right side of his father's lips drooped ever so slightly. He saw how he sat himself up using only his left hand, even though he knew his father to be right-handed. His father didn't seem to mind—or notice. He swallowed hard and moved his head up and down.

Jaipal looked around. There wasn't a single bottle in the room and yet there he was, clearly drunk, unable to even speak properly or move.

"Come here," he said to Jaipal.

Jaipal walked to the bed. A faint smell of urine hung in the room. His father opened his mouth and kept moving his jaw, chewing the empty air. Jaipal felt a rush of impatience—*What is it?* he wanted to yell. His hands kept moving: into his pockets, clasped behind his back, on his hips, his thumbnail into his mouth to bite.

Finally, his father seemed to find his words. "They're doing something else." And then, a return to the openmouthed chewing.

"Papa, who? What are they doing?" Jaipal asked.

His father closed his eyes, seeming to doze off for a moment. Then his eyes opened quickly. "They're building something for the people like you. You know."

For the people like me. The phrase made him feel dirty, and the slow and measured pace of his father's speaking was driving him mad. Jaipal's deference built out of fear froze him in the room.

"My girls told me about it. They haven't been there. It's in a hotel. They haven't been there, though."

"Which hotel?" Jaipal interrupted, trying to get his father out of his repeating thoughts.

"The Sunshine. Listen. Listen. Listen. Listen. Listen," he said, repeating himself like a broken toy.

"I'm listening," Jaipal said.

"You can only go around midnight. They're not doing it at any other time, and don't forget. Don't. Forget."

"I won't," Jaipal said.

"Always said, fool-fool dogs bark after midnight," he said with a serene smile.

Jaipal wanted to walk out, leave this unreality behind, but a scrunched look of confusion crossed his father's face. "I haven't told you yet. I don't know what the questions are. There are three answers. A memory, the cane, into the ocean. A memory, the cane, into the ocean. A memory, the cane, into the ocean."

"I got it," Jaipal said. His father was talking nonsense, but there was some hidden logic that he could faintly discern under it all. He didn't want to lose the thread and decided to commit the words to memory. "A memory, the cane, into the ocean," he repeated, the words seeming like the answers to so many riddles.

His father exhaled a long breath and slowly lowered himself back down to his resting position. Jaipal watched as he did this, waiting a moment after his father closed his eyes again.

"We have to take him to see a doctor," Jaipal said as he reentered the sitting room.

"He doesn't want to go, I asked," his mother replied, her answer sounding far-off.

"Then we'll bring one here. I'll call. Something's not right with him."

"IT'S A GOOD THING YOU CALLED ME," THE DOCTOR SAID AS HE LEFT his father's room, "but there's nothing I can do." The doctor lived down the street and was a sparrow of a man, small and short, persistent enough to be heard. He wasn't wearing a white coat but a blue floral bula shirt and slacks, and his stethoscope hung around his neck. He had been his father's doctor for years.

"Nothing at all?" Jaipal asked.

"He's clearly had a stroke, and a major one. Has he been taking his blood thinners?"

"I don't know," Jaipal said. "The pharmacies are only open a few days a week now. He hasn't sent me to get anything."

"I told him to take aspirin every day after his first attack. When did this start?" When Jaipal said that he didn't know, the doctor shot him a confused look, as if this was important information that a son had to know. The doctor turned and, in a louder voice, began speaking to his mother. "Make sure he gets lots of rest and is eating," he said before turning back to Jaipal. "Why don't you come with me outside. We can talk."

Jaipal's mother shot him a confused look. The doctor reached over and patted his mother on the shoulder. "Not to worry, I want to hear a little bit more about how Jaipal is doing."

"Why don't you stay?" his mother asked. "Have a cup of chai?"

"I really must be going," the doctor said.

"Are you sure?"

He picked up a small leather satchel, presumably filled with his doctor's tools.

Jaipal walked him to the door and out down the stairs. They stood by the coconut tree. Jaipal rolled a coconut under his foot, feeling its glossy green outer skin massage his arches.

"Jaipal, I'm going to be honest, I don't know how much longer he has."

"But you said—"

"I know," the doctor said, cutting him off. "I don't want to worry your mother. As his son, you should know. Given what little control he has on the right side of his body, it seems like the stroke was quite large. I can't say any more for certain—I'd need to have some tests done. If you take him to the hospital, they'll probably say the same thing."

Jaipal shook his head. He had no interest in going there.

"It's a damn farce. Last I heard they're not letting us in anyway. The chutiyas aren't letting pregnant women into labor and delivery, saying our doctors wouldn't treat them and that their mothers gave birth at home. So can we."

"Aren't we all the doctors?" Jaipal asked. "Who's working there?"

"I'm glad I don't do rounds there anymore. They're forcing them all to work. Miss a shift and they'll beat some sense into you. Miss two shifts, and"—he lowered his voice—"you're gone. For good. Anyway I'm not sure taking him there will do anything."

"How much longer do you think . . . ?" Jaipal didn't finish the question.

"That, I cannot tell you. It could be a few weeks. It could be a few years, depending. The heart attack was the first blow. This stroke was the second blow. The third blow, whether it's a stroke or a heart attack, it'll be too much."

"Why not tell Ma this?"

"You know women," he said with a strained look. "I prefer to give information like this to husbands and sons." The doctor patted Jaipal on the shoulder with a firm hand. "Good luck, son, you'll need it. We all need it."

Jaipal said nothing in reply, watching him walk down the driveway and out into the street.

"What did he tell you?" his mother asked back in the house, standing near the door that led to the balcony. She had been watching him the whole time.

Jaipal felt the weight of a choice fall upon him. It was him and his mother now: his father incapacitated, his sister gone. The choice was between future and past: to continue on with what it all had been, or to do away with this bullshit—all the anger and secrets and lies. He could stick everything out there in the sun, like they did with the bedbug-infested mattresses at the hotel. Let the bleaching light kill them all, or at least drive the filth back into the earth.

"Papa had another attack. He called it a stroke. Papa might have another one, and if he does, he may not survive it."

"He didn't tell me," she said in a spiteful whisper. She balled up the fabric of her yellow churidar in her fist. "That doctor is a coward. Can't look me in the eye. He finds it easier to hide behind other men."

Jaipal shifted his gaze out the window. The sun was beating down in its late-afternoon intensity, leaving the Minor looking washed out, its top paint weathered with splotches of white and faint streaks of rust from the weather. Jaipal turned back and looked at his mother, and for the first time could feel an inkling of what she felt. He could see the fear and the confusion, the haggard anxiety of one problem after another, the look of weariness that came from the cascade of shit that was her married life.

His mother shook her head. "I should have known something happened to him," she said, finally letting go of her balled-up churidar. "I'm glad," she added.

"For what?"

"I know where he is now."

A soft moan escaped the room where he lay. She attended to all his needs now, and Jaipal could feel the purpose in every step she took.

22

THE MORNING WAS bright with the clear light of summer in late autumn. The day already seemed warm, and Bhumi felt a bit restless. There hadn't been a single drop of rain since she had arrived, and the extended dry weather made her feel like something was being kept from her.

As she walked into the store, Jagdish stood behind the counter in a baby-blue short-sleeved bula shirt covered with pink hibiscus. He tapped his big hairy knuckles against his counter to the beat of some song he hummed under his breath. From the back of the store came the sound of a radio playing the morning news.

She walked around to the counter. "Any news on Aarti Kumar?" she asked.

For the first time, Jagdish's eyes looked full.

Bhumi felt that she was both shrinking and accelerating into some horrid vision, a nightmare that she had never truly expected to arrive.

Jagdish came out from behind the counter, unsure of what to do with himself. He stood in front of Bhumi twisting his fingers together in his hands while he surveyed his store, looking for answers in his aisles.

"There's nothing official," he began, "but I heard this from a friend in Melbourne."

Jagdish cleared his throat. His eyes darted to the floor. He took in a deep breath. "What I heard from Krishan is that the army was taking people the General wanted gone, putting them in helicopters, and flying out over the ocean—"

Bhumi didn't need to hear the rest of what Jagdish had to say. Aarti and her entire family had been disappeared. In his letter to Bhumi, Jitendra Kumar had said that they, like their ancestors, had to cross the black waters. Bhumi knew the stories of the ships. Not everyone survived that crossing. The sea had taken so many lives as it went on in its immortal churning. The journeys of men meant nothing to the black waters. The sea would shrug them off with its monumental and deadly heaves.

She broke off the conversation and ran out the door.

"Bhumiji! Bhumiji!" she heard Jagdish calling from his doorway.

She could barely hear him now. Thoughts began to unravel before she had a chance to put them into words. Something ruptured inside of her, a sweet sickness that was overflowing out of her pores, only to boil off when it reached her skin. The pain of this breaking was enough to propel her into motion.

Aarti was gone. Forever.

She wasn't running but her legs were still moving. To the BART station. She was going to work. No choice. She had to. The money.

She would never see Aarti again.

At the Union City station, the initial concussed feeling of the news gave way to heaving sobs. She braced herself against the wall of the station as she cried, her back turned to all those who walked past her. In that burst of sorrow, everything came to the surface: her grandmother's legacy, which she was doomed to follow; the nation that had never cared for her; the General, who wanted them out; the American government with its byzantine rules; and the cage that all these made.

She pulled out a tissue from her purse to clean up her face. The agony and miseries of the day's news—and the past—were winding through her, around and around and around and around, until she was a tightly coiled spring.

THE BOY WAS SITTING IN THE KITCHEN WHEN BHUMI ARRIVED at the house.

"You're late," the mother remarked, staring right into her puffy and reddened eyes. She hesitated for a second but soon left in a hustle.

Bhumi looked at the boy in his high chair. This child is a waste of time, she thought. Every tendon tightened and her jaw hurt from how much she gritted her teeth. The sickness had boiled off from within her, leaving in its place a hole that filled with the bitter sludge of the present.

She forced herself through the motions. He ran from her at the park. Instead of chasing him down, she sat still on her park bench and let her eyes follow him from the play structure to the adjacent baseball field.

As he reached the ballfield, he turned around to see if he was being chased. Seeing no one, he slowed down until he stopped and found himself both alone and far from the play structure. He fell to the ground and began to wail. Bhumi took her time to reach him, purposefully walking at a saunter. She grabbed him by the arm and took him back to the play area, where the sight of the slide calmed him down enough so that he stopped crying.

Finally came lunch. The boy was taking a bite of his peanut butter and jelly sandwich, running from the table with the sandwich in hand, returning after being coaxed back by Bhumi, taking another bite, and running off. As he ran, the bottom slice of bread fell to the floor. The boy threw the remaining slice at Bhumi, leaving a purple splotch of grape jelly mixed with brown gobs of chunky peanut butter on the bottom hem of her shirt.

Bhumi slammed the thrown piece of bread onto the table, feeling its jelly ooze out from underneath. The boy was standing silently, waiting for her response. With one hand, its palm dotted with sticky purple jelly, she slapped the child across the face.

Here was this child: the job she had never wanted, the journey she had been forced to take, the feeling that the past only strangled the life out of those unlucky enough to hear the echo of migration resound across generations.

He didn't react—not immediately. His eyes widened and his lips began to tremble. It looked like some essential thread in his little life had broken, something that held up all the routines, roles, and rules of his day-to-day.

Finally, he began to cry. It was that kind of helpless silence-building-up-to-a-shout-cry that he made when he felt a true measure of pain. It was a cry that shook him down to his little fingers, that broke the cadence of his breath into gasps of air.

Bhumi stood back and stared at her hand as if it were someone else's. It was every feeling all at once: sorrow felt like fear felt like anger felt like release. There was something real about it. Amid all the denials she had experienced, this feeling was all her own.

She did not try to calm the child. The hand that whipped could do little to soothe. Instead, she stepped back and fell into the kitchen chair.

The child cried until he soiled his diaper. Bhumi eventually changed it and put him down for his nap, where he cried himself to sleep. When he awoke in the late afternoon, he played with his trucks with a glazed-over look.

Bhumi spent most of the day in a recliner in the family's living room. Images swirled around like a living dream: the last moments with Aarti, the coup, the stories of her grandmother. The past was always there; the present owed its existence to it. At the same time, she couldn't be bound by both. Her friend had been killed. Everything was so small compared to that fact. Bhumi didn't want this kind of life anymore.

At the end of the day, after she received her envelope, she turned to the mother.

"This will be my last day," she said plainly.

"What do you mean?"

"I will no longer be working here after today," Bhumi replied, looking the mother straight in the eye.

"But—but," the mother stammered, "what will I do? You can't quit, I need to find someone to take care of him." She pointed to her son.

"I'm sure you can find someone else," Bhumi said. "There are more of us, I'm sure there's another that will work for you."

The mother clicked her tongue and shook her head in dismay. "You're all the same," she hissed.

HER FIRST INCLINATION WAS TO HIDE, TO BURY HERSELF UNDER A mountain of reading, to find silence. She sought out the comfort of a refuge, a place surrounded by green patches of grass, the sagging branches of willow trees, and the conical crowns of dawn redwoods: the public library. She needed to go where no one else knew anything about bodies cast out into the sea, families in Union City without child care. A library had always asked only for her quiet presence and given her everything in return.

When she arrived at the branch of the Santa Ursula Public Library that she used to go to before she started auditing classes, she was surprised at the ferocity of her own energy. She needed desperately to speak to someone. She wished, as she often had when she was a child, that Jaipal could be with her. He had rarely gone with her to the Sugar City Carnegie Library. By the time she was spending most of her days there, he had already been pulled into their father's orbit, made to work the shop after school. She tried to imagine his sitting right across from her, their conversation hushed.

"Why are you here?" he asked pointedly.

"Don't you know what happened today?" she said to him, her fingers drumming on the table in exasperation.

"You don't think shit is happening to me too? I'm back here, working the shop. I used to at least have the hotel. It's not like what you have, but it let me get away from Papa."

"I know, bhaiyya, I know. Our parents, we have to get away from them. I loved being so far away in Vilimaji. And now I'm here," she said, trying to take pride in her resilience. She had left. She had survived.

"Why are you like this?" he hissed, his eyes wide. "I wish Ma loved me like she loves you. She knows you better than you know yourself. She called Rakesh, she got your passport and your visa. And don't you remember what Aarti said? She told you not to go back to the library. You know what she meant. Stop hiding. There's something out there for you."

Jaipal had always sought out love: Hanging on to the hem of their mother's salwar kameez, getting only her cold silence in return. Doing everything their father told him to do—what did he expect from it all? He had always tried to find himself in others. She had known better. But now she needed more.

At a pay phone, Bhumi called Farida and told her that she was going to be staying over at a friend's that night. She took the bus, one that skirted the edge of campus, the apartments where students lived. She didn't know whether she could—or even if she wanted to—trust him, but she needed someone to talk to, and he was there. It was a fleeting and new connection between two bodies, but it was something nonetheless.

"Have you eaten anything? You want some spaghetti?" Vikram

asked as she walked in. He didn't seem surprised to see her, and Bhumi felt like he could see straight through her feeble attempts at hiding her weariness. He was like an aunty—offering food as a way to soothe.

She pulled out a cigarette and lit up, needing to do something with her hands, needing to move the anxiety, the fear, the sorrow, out and into the smoke trailing from the burnt end of a habit. And there he was: lanky and thread-thin, pushing up his glasses as he boiled a pot of water and took out a half-finished jar of red sauce from his fridge.

He kept looking at her, and Bhumi inwardly squirmed. Surely he knew she was hiding something. When her mother had these moments, her father would always ask, "Who did this to you?" more spit than words, and she would tell him what went wrong: some slight from an old friend, some choice words from a shopkeeper. He would defend her. The insults that flew out of his mouth. It was as if in his ownership of her mother, he was the only one who could insult her for doing wrong, and everyone else could fuck off and go to hell.

She could tell that Vikram was giving her a measure of space: the way he seemed to tiptoe around his own kitchen, controlling the sound of his presence to somehow make her feel better or more comfortable. She felt a misplaced sense of nostalgia—if only what was her mother's could be hers for a moment. But there was another truth: her mother had put herself out there every time she needed something, even if it was from a man like her husband.

Vikram didn't have a kitchen table, so they ate side by side in the sinking cushions of his corduroy sofa, the television playing an episode of a show Vikram called *Family Ties*. Bhumi looked into Vikram's face.

"What?" he asked, smiling sheepishly from being stared at. At first, she saw him for his pieces: tousled black hair running down onto his forehead, overdue for a haircut; brown eyes with delicate eyelashes set just above an aquiline nose; his thin lips open just enough to let the air in. She saw lines of worry etched into his forehead and around his eyes. And then, in an instant, she saw him all at once. She put out her cigarette in her bowl, the hiss of red heat against sauce sounding like a faint invitation.

It all came out like a cyclone, wind and sideways rain uprooting trees. She started at the beginning: university, Aarti, that one night at the bar, her own escape, and now, the finality of a friend disappeared. He sat there with a look of pure surprise on his face. This American boy who had only known comfort and ease could not believe how quickly a life could turn around. Even in his surprise, it still felt as if he were reaching into the darkened and closed-off place where she hid herself—if not to bring her to the light, then simply to sit with her.

He placed his hand into hers patiently. "I'm sorry," he said.

She wondered if he felt her flinch. Even if he did, he didn't move, just sat there, the spaghetti getting cold in his lap.

From this brief measure of calm emerged a desire for his hand, clean across her face, the heat from the redness like the spiked pain of impact from hitting the water from above. The past and the present contorted her own sense of pain into the violence, the submission, she had watched in her own home.

On impulse, she moved, trying to take control. Their bowls fell onto the floor with a thud, a trilling clang of the spoon against ceramic. Her mouth pressed against his, but it was a call without a response. She kept trying, and soon he was leading her into his bedroom—finally giving her something to feel. When they were on his twin bed, it was as if he knew only how to make love, and not how to grind her into the small disparate pieces she longed to become. Halfway through, neither satisfied nor humiliated, she began to cry.

"What's wrong?" he asked.

When she said nothing, he shook his head. "That was a dumb question. Everything's wrong. You want to just lie here for a while?

I should probably throw away that spaghetti first. Tim'll probably be pissed if sees that there. I'll be right back."

When he came back, Bhumi had curled herself to face the wall. He wrapped himself around her. The little spoon was a perfect place to feel miserable: safely cocooned in the arms of another, facing nothing but the blankness of a white wall inches from her face.

"I need to get out of here," she said.

"Where?" Vikram asked her.

"Here. Santa Ursula. This is all so fucked," she said, her voice broken by little sobs. "I had something. I need something else."

"I know, I know," he said, and she wondered what he actually knew. "We'll figure it out," Vikram said, his voice filled with so much worry that Bhumi almost felt bad for troubling him. It must have been only a bit of trouble, because he was soon twitching softly, the jagged movement from wakefulness into sleep.

For Bhumi, she fell asleep only when she surrendered to the sublime wretchedness of self-pity, like pressing into a bruise. There was a stupefying effect to giving in to this feeling: the lullaby of the unlucky and the forlorn, the song she never wanted to sing.

23

MAQBOOL SHOWED UP unannounced at Jaipal's. Jaipal had been trying to call Maqbool but couldn't reach him, and now Jaipal's routine
desires were competing with the racing questions raised by all the
changes: he wanted to know how Maqbool felt, what was going on in
his mind, what he was going to do with these new restrictions.

When Jaipal's mother delivered a scant plate of dinner to his father,
Maqbool acted as if he didn't hear the groans of pain that emerged from
the room. Jaipal didn't know whether Maqbool had already heard
from others about his father's health or whether he was just being polite. Still, he was grateful to not have to explain what was going on.

After dinner, Jaipal waited for his announcement, which came, as
expected: "Jaipal and I are going to take a walk. Got a lot to talk about
from the General's speech, eh?"

His mother smiled a weak smile. "Be careful," she said. "The evil
eye sweeps the street after dark," she added after a moment, giving
Jaipal a knowing look.

Outside, Jaipal rolled a coconut under his foot. It was another dry and clear night, sounds floating on the dissipating heat from the day to reach Jaipal as a mixed-up warble of clicks and shrieks.

"How you been?" Jaipal asked.

"You've heard the news. How the fuck do you think I am?" Maqbool said, his voice sounding raw with exasperation.

"I tried calling you. I wanted to make sure you were okay," Jaipal said slowly.

"You see me now," he said, his voice hardened and mean.

"Sorry for caring," Jaipal said, his defenses rising. "Should have known better."

"Let's just go to the bay, okay?"

"Sure, whatever, Maqbool. It's not like we can go anywhere else," Jaipal said, a shot-of-venom reminder for Maqbool to remember that not everything could bend to his whims.

"Said who?"

"Said the fucking General. We're all stuck here." After a moment he added, "At least we have something to sell, at least we can make some money."

"Is that all you can think about? Making money? The money is the first step. We have to be thinking about leaving, Jaipal, not staying to make cash. Come on, let's go."

Jaipal climbed onto Maqbool's scooter, the wind doing nothing to cool the frustration that burned through his face. Maqbool had no idea what he was talking about, and he was being an asshole. And why the fuck was he coming over, Jaipal fumed. He felt like a pawn in one of Maqbool's get-rich plans. Jaipal couldn't bring himself to place his hands on Maqbool's shoulders. He leaned back and gripped the cold steel of the box.

They pulled into the car park, again near the coconut shack. Maqbool pointed to the structure. "Coconut man," he said with a small laugh. In the darkness, Jaipal couldn't see Maqbool's face, couldn't distinguish scorn from smile. He took off his sandals and walked ahead.

Above him, the fronds of the coconut palms rubbed against one another with the sound of a soft rake, a scratch above the din of the waves.

Jaipal stood, facing the ocean—a beast that never slept, its heaving sighs making the beat of the night. He felt Maqbool touch him on the shoulder.

"You mad at me?" Maqbool asked him.

Jaipal narrowed his eyes, and a weary sense fell over him. "What do you want, Maqbool, why are we here?"

"Let's smoke first," he said. Jaipal turned around and saw the chimbi between his lips, Maqbool's face lit from underneath by the fire of a match, the ragged edges of his features thrown into shadow, his darkened eyes pools without light. He passed the joint to Jaipal.

"Come on, sit with me," Maqbool said. "Shit's fucked up, isn't it?"

"They're jealous of us," Jaipal said, his head thrown back. The moon was a farmer's sickle, a tool holding the stars in its curve. "We do the work, they don't do anything." He dug his fingers into the sand. The coarseness tickled the backs of his fingers, and that tickle, made manifest by the chimbi, ran itself up through his arms as a delightful sense of possibility. He closed his eyes and buried his fingers.

Maqbool coughed into a laugh. "Remember, Jaipal, don't smoke your own shit."

Jaipal didn't know why, but the comment landed upon him in a way that let out a flurry of a giggle. After it passed, he turned, curious. "What do you mean?"

"Don't believe what you hear. They're not jealous of us."

"We make so much more money than them."

"This isn't our country, Jaipal. Never was. Never will be."

"We built this country too."

"You sound like some fucking uncle drinking whiskey under someone's house, don't give me that shit," Maqbool said, taking another hit.

"What do you think then?" Jaipal said, feeling his high dry up in the exhaust of Maqbool's cross attitude. Everyone he knew thought it was about time that *a few* Indians were elected to the government.

"We don't belong here," Maqbool said with a bitter air. "We're just some fucked orphan of the Empire, brought here and left behind. We made some money, but you know what really matters? Power. Land. Guns. Our fathers were stupid as shit. They signed that constitution and signed over all the land to the natives, thinking we could just count our money in the corner. They got the land, they got the government. Who said we should rock the boat? Things were fine until that election. We fucked it up. We wanted more. It wasn't ours to take. And now, they're done with us."

"You really think it's that simple?"

"You either have power or you don't."

"And what do you do if you don't have any power?"

"Get the fuck outta there, find someplace where you can get some for yourself."

Jaipal shook his head and took another hit. He shot his hands back into the beach, cupping the sand, looking again for that feeling.

"So, you used to swim here with your sister?" Maqbool asked. The question was filled with a tenderness that stood in stark contrast to the resentful way he talked politics.

"Yes," Jaipal said, keeping his eyes closed. He didn't know what else to say: he wanted to keep his memories safe from the possibility of Maqbool's lash.

"In the night too?"

"It's the best at night, you can't see anything," Jaipal replied, the force of memory breaking through the small and temporary barriers put up between them. "It's like you're not even there, like you're floating through something that's holding on to you but can't touch you. Nothing can touch you."

"That's fucking scary, man. Can't see nothing? Shit."

"Can't see the water, can't see the under the water. It's not always dark. Bhumi found out. If it's pitch-black out, like if there are clouds and no moon, the water glows."

"Glows?"

"She had a word for it. Bio-luma-something. I don't know. There's something in the water. Some little bug or something. It glows in the dark. The water runs blue. Blue like the signs on that one bar on Queen's Street."

"Scary. Weird. I hate it when nature does weird shit like that."

"No, beautiful. I wish all the water could do that."

"And what about the coconut man?"

"What about him?"

"What's the story about him?"

"I'd tell Bhumi that if we saw three things when we came out here to get away from our parents, everything would be okay. First we'd see these chickens on the side of the street. Hens running around, just up the road. There was a rooster too. Then the man selling coconuts. He sold them off a cart in the day, lived in that little shack at night. And there was this turtle here in this bay. If you swim around long enough, he'll pop up, he'll say hi. We always saw the turtle if we were here for a few hours."

"What about now?"

"What do you mean?"

"The chickens, the coconuts, the turtle, what about them now?"

"The chickens, I haven't seen them in a couple of years. Maybe they got old and someone finally killed them. Maybe a mongoose ate them. The man selling coconuts died, remember? The newspaper even did a story up about him. Wasn't it cancer? And the turtle, I don't know. Maybe he's still there. Maybe he's waiting for us right now."

"Right now?"

Jaipal wasn't answering any more of Maqbool's questions. Already he had gotten up and was taking off his jeans, unbuttoning his shirt. "Come on, you know how to swim, right? We won't go far." He stood, naked, a hand out to help Maqbool up.

"You're fucking crazy, man. No, I'm not gonna die."

"You'll be fine. Look, there's no one here. Just us. Come on."

In the light of the moon, Jaipal could see how Maqbool's smile shined silver, his teeth flashing in a trill of a laugh. Maqbool put his hand up and Jaipal could feel his weight pulling him down as he hoisted him up. Maqbool extinguished the joint with two fingers and put it into the pocket of his long kurta before he stripped naked.

"Just hold on to me," Jaipal said.

"This is fucking crazy!" Maqbool yelled, laughing.

Jaipal led him into the water. Hand in hand, they crossed the tide line, where the sand sank like a wet cloth beneath his toes. Then he waded into the water, warm like a soft touch, the salt licking at his skin. "You know how to swim?" he asked Maqbool again, as they crossed the invisible line that took them into the deep. Maqbool was still laughing. The sound of his shrieks echoed throughout the bay, as if the fish were leaping out of the water, only to fall back in as a thunderous applause.

"Let's just go out this far," Jaipal said. They were no more than an arm's length from the underwater cliff, enough distance to lie back, to let the warm water hold them as they floated gently with the tide. He scanned the night and found the Southern Cross, the only constellation he could remember (they had always been Bhumi's to learn and memorize).

"I think I can see it! I think I can see the blue!" Maqbool exclaimed.

"It's not dark enough," Jaipal laughed, letting his ears fall below the waterline, and he could hear the clicks and electric wisps of sound, the animals who took residence in the deep. He imagined it was the chattering of the turtle, the voice that whispered that everything would be okay.

Jaipal floated, and when his ears rose above, he could hear Maqbool splashing along, the sound coming closer, closer still, until it was no longer a sound, becoming a feeling, an embrace, a kiss from him: needy, groping, seeking comfort where there was none. Jaipal guided them back beyond the cliff and toward the shore, and soon his hands were searching along Maqbool's body.

Maqbool let out a soft moan but then pushed Jaipal's hand away. Maqbool walked back to his clothes, dropping himself down upon the sand with a soft thud. "There's always someone watching. You don't know who's watching," Maqbool said.

"Why are you looking over your shoulder?" Jaipal asked. He looked around and couldn't see anything besides the shadowy outlines of the fronds along the beach, and the swaying movement of the overgrown ferns and vines that lined the bay.

"Maybe I am, maybe not. There's a place."

Jaipal thought of what his father had told him, and the chimbi smoke that lingered within him pushed the words right out of his mouth. "The Sunshine? It's real?"

"Who told you?" Maqbool asked, again sounding like someone was just in the distance.

Jaipal shied away from answering, feeling embarrassed at the truth. "No one," he said.

"Bullshit. Tell me, who told you?"

"Papa," Jaipal said, his mouth dry, his cheeks reddened with shame.

"Oh," Maqbool said, sounding calmer. That one word was enough explanation—everyone knew what his father did. "I've been going for a few weeks. The hotel, it's for us, it's safer than here. Do you know the answers?"

Jaipal nodded. "Will you be there?" he asked. He finally walked from the water and he bent over to pick up his clothes. The sand stuck to his feet and bristled against his skin from the inside of his jeans, while his shirt felt stuck to his chest from the salty damp.

"Tomorrow night," Maqbool said. "I'll be there tomorrow."

"Can I come with you?"

"You have to go alone. I'll be there. You'll find me," Maqbool said, brushing the salt off of himself. He pulled on his linen trousers and leaned over. Jaipal met him halfway. The kiss was filled with what Jaipal wanted: the insistency, the tongue at the door, begging to be let in. Maqbool obliged and ran his hands over Jaipal's back, the tips of his fingers dragging along the mixture of salt and sand that stuck to him.

But it was Maqbool who quickly broke away. "Tomorrow," he said. "Should I take you back home now?"

Jaipal felt his heart drop a bit. He wanted simple things above all else, and one of them was the security of some sort of routine with Maqbool. Even that was kept from him, slipping from his hands like cupped water.

There was tomorrow, where something, anything, lay in wait.

THE NEXT DAY, JAIPAL'S FATHER HAD A MOMENT OF FRIGHTFUL lucidity.

"Jaipal!" he called out, repeating his name five times. He had to repeat himself over and over again, as if he were infected with his own thoughts, bound to spew out the same words.

It would do no good to yell that he was coming from another room. His father's cries could go on until Jaipal finally entered. "Have you gone yet? Have you gone yet? Have you go—"

"Not yet, Papa," Jaipal said, not adding any more of his plan for later that night. "It's closed," he lied.

"It never closes. You're lying, like the sna-sna-sna—" his father stammered, terrifyingly present in the moment. And then he was gone again. Jaipal breathed a sigh of relief.

To get to the Sunshine meant he had to take the car—the taxis stopped operating at midnight, so there would be no way to get back. To take the car meant he had to sneak out without waking his mother. This wouldn't have been a problem, except for his mother's insomnia. They were always up together, sitting, saying nothing.

"I'm going out," he said that evening, summoning his resolve.

"Now? Where?" his mother asked, startled into looking up from the dinner table. She had been sitting with a cup of watered-down chai, a new copy of *Filmfare* open in front of her. She was clearly not reading the words. Jaipal didn't know when or where she had picked up the magazine. For all he knew, she was with his father for most of the day when he worked the store.

"Papa mentioned a place to me the other day. He said I had to go at night."

"He's probably just talking nonsense," she said.

"He is, I think. But he's starting to ask about it every time I go into his room."

"So tell him you went!"

"I do, and he knows. I don't know how," Jaipal replied, looking toward the door, wishing to be on the other side.

"There's something you're not telling me," she said in a quiet voice.

"I promise, Ma, I'll be back soon. He's probably confused. I'll leave and then come back."

"Jaipal, you're acting like he used to. He used to do this all the time, saying things like 'I'll be back, give me trust.'"

Her words felt like ice. He was so many things, but never his father. Never, no, the one thing he wasn't. "I'm not," he said quietly, meekly, the voice of a child chastened by his mother, the one who knew where to strike if she had to hurt.

"Go," she said, her paranoia hardening her face into something ugly and contorted. Jaipal couldn't look her in the eye. "Come back quickly."

AT THE SUNSHINE, THE GATE TO LET THE CARS INTO THE PULL-through was closed.

It's not real, he thought. His father had no idea what he was talking about. And Maqbool? A joke. Maybe he was waiting around the corner. Maybe he would tell Jaipal not to believe everything he heard.

Something tugged at him to stay. On a whim, he pulled over across the street from the gate and turned the engine off, staring out the driver's-side window at the darkened hotel. The night was clear, the humidity from an earlier cloudburst rising from the earth. In time, his eyes grew accustomed to the darkness. Where there was once shadow and hazy outline came the figures of a mongoose darting from one corner to another, the thin tendrils of a silk cotton tree moving with the night's gentle breeze.

The shape of a figure moved along the road, pushing open the small pedestrian gate that had been closed but not locked. The person walked toward the front door, and briefly, a flash of a dim light came from within. He stared at that door, unsure of whether what he had seen was just a trick, a dance of colors that eyes beheld when seeing into the dark.

Minutes passed by, and the car grew sticky with the sharp jabs of his breath. Soon, there it was, yet another. Head low, a walk with quick steps, through the gate, and again into the door with that pale yellow light.

There was something there.

This is insanity, he thought. This could be anything. The General didn't force any of the hotels to shut down. The owners all closed their doors voluntarily. It was simple math: no tourists, no hotels. These people could be owners or family or some skeletal staff there to turn on the faucets in each hotel room to make sure everything works.

He exhaled a long breath, letting its steam build up on the window, using his finger to draw a circle where he had seen the light.

Even though Maqbool had told him about the Sunshine, anything associated with his father came with a doubled sense: it was dirty, while also filled with the chance that something could go wrong. He tried to figure out his exits as he got out of the car, calculated how quickly he could run from the door to the gate, from the gate to the Minor. He turned its key in his pocket over and over again, a talisman to protect him from whatever was next.

He passed through the gate and went to the door. The light, so dim from a distance, was enough to cause him to squint and lose focus upon entering.

The Sunshine looked so much like the Ambassador: a tiled entrance with a few rattan chairs along the wall. A front desk with a teakwood top. And a man—someone familiar—behind the desk with a round face and beard flecked with gray.

"Arjun?" Jaipal asked.

"Ah, Jaipal!" he said, sounding like this was any other day back at the Ambassador.

"What are you doing here?"

"I work here, temporarily," he said, drawing out his words in the same way he had told Jaipal that he was being fired. "I could ask what you're doing here, but that would be a lie. I was wondering when I'd see you walk through that door."

"Really?" Jaipal said, walking up to the counter and resting his hands on its surface, cool to the touch.

"Oh, yes. There are the secrets you keep and the secrets you know."

Jaipal felt himself flush with embarrassment. Everyone had been watching him at the hotel. He had always supposed he was lucky, that he somehow was able to hide himself better than most. He should have known.

His face must have betrayed his feelings because Arjun reached out to pat the top of his hand. "We all have them," he said, raising an eyebrow. "Especially here. The number one rule is to keep everything you see a secret." He let out a wide smile and cleared his throat. "Oh, dear me. I've gotten ahead of myself. I have three questions for you. We do this to keep safe from those who shouldn't be here. First: what is the place we came from?'"

Jaipal remembered the three answers his father had given him. "A memory," he said, his mouth dry. The answer seemed to stick upon his tongue.

"Good. Now, why are we here?'"

"The cane."

"Now, last question. When we die, where do our ashes go?'"

"Into the ocean."

"And we'll all be there soon, brother. That's why we've made this. For us. In our life, our pleasures are always taken from us. Hidden from us. We're told it's wrong and dirty. Now there's nothing left. We know what's waiting for us, we know what happened to those who've disappeared. So we come here, to celebrate what we have left: in death, we have life.

"Now, Jaipal, there is one rule above all else: the men you see tonight were never here. The lights are off in the ballroom for a reason. Touch, but never see.

"The owners know a little bit of what we're doing, but we have to pay them to keep anyone else from knowing. To enter costs a small sum, one hundred dollars."

Jaipal pulled out his wallet and handed him the bills, his mouth still feeling sticky from nerves.

"Your father has you working the store, right? It's a pity. You belong behind a bar with us. As the answers go, we were born from a memory, lived with cane as our blood, and now we're off . . ."

"To the ocean," Jaipal said.

"Of course. Now enjoy. That's what this is all for. Enjoy it while you can. The ballroom is up a flight of stairs and down the hall."

His knees felt weak as he climbed the stairs. He knew what was waiting for him in that ballroom, and each step felt light and quick, channeling through him a feverish energy as though each fingertip were filled with an electric arc of nerves.

In the staircase, an echo in his mind. *I didn't even know his name.*

When he entered the ballroom, he found it darkened, the presence of others unseen, but still felt, their movements like a beat kept on a tabla. The smell came to him first: raw, sweaty, human, of pleasure finished and pleasure yet to be found. A loamy smell, of damp mossy earth and callery trees in blossom. The air in the room was like steam so thick he could stick his tongue out and lick it. The sounds: grunts, moans, laughter, of ten, fifteen, maybe even thirty men finding themselves in the throes of another, all when the world outside continued to flow downstream, everything that had piled up into a dam ready to burst.

His breaths grew quick and his palms grew sweaty. When the door closed behind him, he didn't know where to go, so he kept walking into the darkness, and the sounds grew like vines. There it was all around him, but none of it touched him until he reached out to the one who stood alone, face in shadow, body radiating heat. And then there was a hand taking his, and he was pulled in. Soon, his mouth felt the mouth of another (rough, scratchy, lips so soft, a tongue warm, wet, willing).

A familiar feeling now, the lips begging against his lips, the hands taking Jaipal's own and bringing them to what had earlier been denied. "Maqbool?" Jaipal whispered. The only reply a curt shush; silence was the rule, and pleasure too: to find and be found.

There had been a world inside his own country and among his people, a world that existed for no one save the men in this hollowed-out ballroom. He had spent so much time trying to escape, trying to leave himself by going to the hotel, finding all those from without to satisfy the needs he kept within. He hadn't known where to look, to find himself in those who lived around him. They had always been there, and this was for them.

And his body was knowing and willing as he was pulled further in, hands wrapped around him, the pleasure of pressure seeking its release. It was fast. This hand, this body, the whispers (do you like that, do you like that), his answers (yeah, yeah, don't stop, don't stop). His breath fast, then held. Release, quick and easy, everything pent up. Finished. He could now give back, or he could find repose. He saw them, thin outlines off to the side lying supine, each no more than the red-hot glow of a cigarette—clouds of smoke waiting for their bodies to return to the strength needed to go again.

He was slicked wet from exhaustion and took up a place among those lying in wait. He tried to scan for Maqbool's wiry body but couldn't find him in the mass of men who took up the center of the ballroom, and he didn't think he was near either. Someone tapped him on the shoulder.

"Did you bring any to sell here?" a voice asked. He couldn't make out who it was. For all Jaipal knew, he was talking to a ghost hanging in the thick air.

"Sell?"

"You know, what you have at the store," the man said, a voice familiar enough that, if he closed his eyes, he could possibly place him among the men he saw day in and day out.

"I don't have it with me."

"Bring some next time."

"Sure," Jaipal said. Here—a last testament to desire in a country where the next day was an unknown—was also a place like any other:

one where money could be made. Maqbool would be proud. More sold was more money, was more of his chance to finally leave.

If he could ever leave.

If there ever was going to be a chance to leave.

Until then, there was this.

HE CAME BACK THE NEXT NIGHT WITH A SMALL GUNMETAL LOCKBOX in a canvas bag stamped with the Ambassador's logo. It was a bag for the guests to use to carry a beach towel to and from the sand. He had taken it from Portia's bure.

He hadn't noticed the divisions the first time, the way they separated themselves based on what they wanted. That part of the ballroom was strictly for giving, the other for those wanting to take, and still another for those who wished to luxuriate in the feeling of a desire held at bay. Jaipal took the bag off and stashed it upon the ballroom's stage—a platform no more than a knee's height from the ground.

Maqbool seemed to appear out of the humid darkness with a tap on his lower back.

"You brought some chimbi?" he asked. "Smart, we can make a lot of money here. They like it. I like it. To mix that with this. Are you going to leave the bag there?"

"I can't take it with me over there," Jaipal said, gesturing toward the moans and grunts of men. Jaipal felt a lightning flash of annoyance as it dawned upon him what Maqbool had meant. "I'm not here to just sell," he snapped. "This is all for me too."

Maqbool laughed with a nervous sound. "I figured you would get bored. There are no girls here," he said.

Jaipal turned around. He didn't think: he merely felt the anger radiate from his heart to his fingers as a quiver of warmth, tensing the muscles along his arm. He pushed Maqbool, two hands straight to the chest. Even in the shadows, Jaipal could see the half breaths quickly rising and falling.

The anger within had risen and fallen in the same measure, and though he wanted to hurt Maqbool, he still put his hand out to help him up. Maqbool grabbed his hand, and soon Jaipal was on top of him, and the fury of the two bound hands to bodies: pulling at clothes, scratching at the skin, lips pressed against each other—the dance of pleasure against pain. Jaipal was pinned underneath Maqbool, and he gave himself, willingly—even in the hangover of his wrath, he was still hoping to receive the routine comfort he sought.

Maqbool dug his nails into Jaipal, and he felt the pain from his desire. New was this feeling—giving his body to someone else—the invitation to domination, the specter of humiliation from the power of another. When Maqbool finished, quickly, there was no movement toward Jaipal, to give him what he wanted.

Wanting something from Maqbool was wishing into a void.

Across the room Jaipal saw the other bodies, the hands that would give him his own release. He turned around, and in no more than a whisper asked, "What are we, Maqbool?"

Maqbool was lighting up now—he had probably brought his own. Again the deep inhale, again the cough from within. Jaipal waited for a moment longer, unwilling to leave without an answer.

"We're not this. We're going to leave," was all Maqbool said in reply.

24

WHEN BHUMI TURNED and stretched her limbs, contorted from the smallness of the bed, she was surprised to see that Vikram was wide awake, looking at the popcorn ceiling above them. She was used to getting up early to give herself enough time to get to work—although that wouldn't be a problem anymore.

"You said you want to get out of here, right? Let's go somewhere," Vikram said, his voice clear with determination.

"What do you mean?" Bhumi asked, the question creaking out of her morning voice.

"Let's go to Stinson Beach. It's up in Marin. I used to go there as a kid, with my parents. It's a small town on the water. The drive up there is hella nice."

"You know what I meant," Bhumi said.

"I know what you meant," he said. "Maybe you can take the day off? Leaving town, even if it's for a day, it might be good for you,

you know? Like, you don't have to do it if you don't want. I just thought . . ." He trailed off.

"I actually have the day off today," she lied, relenting.

Later, beyond the windshield of Vikram's Honda, the day blazed with sunshine and not a single cloud in the sky. The weather was forecast to be clear at the beach with a high of sixty-five: a taste of summer in the California winter.

The car was on the highway's terrifyingly serpentine route where the road was all blind curve and no guardrail. Vikram slowed the car down, admitting his fear of the steep drops into the ravines abutting the road. Every so often, he pulled into a turnout to let the cars behind him pass.

Bhumi paid little attention to the highway, her eyes drawn toward what was growing next to it. At one of the turnouts, she tapped him on the shoulder and pointed out the window. "Ice plant," she said. "Don't get back on the road yet."

"What?" Vikram said, looking confused.

"They planted it as ground cover for the highways. It helps stop erosion. I've read about it, but I haven't seen it yet. It's from South Africa, I think. Just a second." She opened the door and snapped a leaf off of a nearby ice plant, a thin spine of green with soft red undertones. She scampered back into the car and broke the leaf in half, smearing its juice on her index finger and licking a gingerly lick with the tip of her tongue.

"It's so sour! Want to taste it? It's edible."

"No, thanks," Vikram said. He looked at her with a blank stare of confusion. "Should I be worried? Will you be jumping out of the car again?"

"You're the one who said we should leave town. The plants near the coast are so strange. So wonderful. And they've planted stuff from all over the world. People forget that, how there's all these things from everywhere just growing by the side of the road."

"I never thought about that," Vikram said, looking down to the leaf in her hand. He held his hand out to Bhumi, and she swiped the leaf across the tip of his thumb. He took a lick. "It is sour," he said, shaking his head with an incredulous smile.

He merged back onto the highway. The car soon rounded a blind curve and there it was: a glimpse of the sparkle of the open ocean that, from their distance, looked like both moving water and wrinkled leather. The salty smell of the Pacific filtered through the car as they descended from the cliffside heights into the sleepy town of Stinson Beach. It was a weekday, and the town seemed deserted. A chill from the water wafted strong toward their cheeks as they opened the car doors. At the Stinson Beach Market, they picked up a few supplies: grapes and oranges and two cans of Coke.

"You used to come here a lot?" Bhumi asked as they left the market.

"Once in a while. There were a bunch of families down in Fremont. They were all from the same part of India my parents were from, like the eastern UP or whatever. We'd hang out all the time, like every weekend. And then once a year everyone would pitch in and we'd all pick a place to have a summer picnic, just like, a place to spend the day with all the families."

Bhumi thought of the ways in which the families from the island stuck together, the weekend parties, everyone cramming into an apartment living room. She felt a sense of safety in Vikram's story: even if someone came to this country as a hotshot engineer, the experience was still so terrifying that they had to spend entire weekends with familiar faces.

They walked to the tideline, passing a few yappy dogs that were sprinting from the sand into the undulating waves, swimming into the tide to grab a tennis ball. Gulls flew overhead in circles and squawked before they arced downward to land on the beach and pick through the kelp. There weren't many people: a few couples walking hand in hand, and a few beach joggers running barefoot near the water.

Bhumi watched the larger waves in the distance form out of swells in the water, their moving lumps looking like a great cat moving underneath a sheet. These larger waves crashed and formed smaller and smaller waves, until the water formed a snakelike curve of white foam that lapped at her feet.

"I've never felt like this before," Bhumi said, facing the water. "I've spent so much time in the ocean, in this ocean. And now, I'm scared of the water."

"You don't have to stay here. You can go to Kansas or Iowa or something like that. You can be a thousand miles from the nearest ocean." He said this with such an earnestness that Bhumi didn't know whether she should lash out in anger at his naïveté or embrace him for the fact that he could find some glimmer of hope in this mess.

"I quit my job yesterday," she confessed.

"Is that a good thing or a bad thing?"

"It's a good thing," Bhumi said quickly, before realizing that she had no idea whether it was true. It was a seizure of control where she had had none.

They began to walk again. "It's a good thing," Bhumi repeated to convince herself of the rightness of her decision. "Right?" she asked, turning to Vikram.

He shrugged and stuffed his hands into the pocket of his nylon bomber. "Based on what you told me at the Puzzle? Yeah, I'd say it's a good thing. You said the job made you feel invisible. I would say it's a shitty job if it makes you feel like that. Are you going to get another nannying job?"

It was an innocent question, and in it Bhumi found her anger again. It wasn't *this* nannying job. It was all of them. "You're not listening! Do you know what it's like to have to do the shit she asked? To change filthy diapers on some stupid kid?"

Vikram looked thrown off balance by her burst of anger. "No, I get it. I agree. You shouldn't be doing that," he said, trying to backtrack.

"And you know what the worst part is about it?" Bhumi went on, not giving him an inch. "It's something all you Indians do. You treat us like we're nothing, like we're beneath you, like we're not even Indian. You look at us like we're coolies," she seethed.

Vikram now took his hands out of his pockets to throw them up. "I don't know why you're yelling at me. I never said anything like that. I never did anything like that."

"You're probably thinking it, you all probably think it," Bhumi said, looking out at the ocean.

"That's a little fucking hypocritical, don't you think?"

"What?"

"To say we 'all' are like that. Aren't you doing exactly what they do?"

"What do you know about what we're going through?" Bhumi asked. She didn't realize she was going to say "we" until after it came out of her mouth, as if solidarity could only appear out of a shared sense of misery.

"What do I know? What do I know?" Vikram repeated, the agitation appearing as a tic of his lower jaw moving like he was trying to pop it out of a sliding lock. "Look, what *do* I know? Nothing. Okay? I didn't know anything. I'm learning, I'm trying to listen. Have you ever been down to the Headlands, down to the Nike Missile Site?"

"No?" Bhumi said, confused as to what Vikram was talking about.

"They closed it down like ten years ago or something. Nukes, ready to shoot down other nukes. We're all like, this close," Vikram said, stopping and squeezing his thumb and forefinger together in front of his face, "to just being wiped off the face of the earth. And you know what I think? I think it means something to care, even just a little bit. Care about me, care about you, care about whatever. That's what I know."

They walked on in silence, the white noise of the waves filling in the hollows and rounds of feeling left in the aftermath of their first fight. Bhumi looked down, and she wondered if this was what had drawn Aarti to the student union: passions curled into fists, the thrill of a fight expressed as belief in bettering another. She looked at Vikram and she looked into her memory at David, one in the same.

She remembered how Aarti would maneuver beyond a spat: she would move the conversation on with a question that invited the other to speak. It would bother Bhumi—why couldn't she just apologize for being an ass? Here, Bhumi had no intention of apologizing. A question could possibly soothe him. Bhumi decided to give it a try.

"They want to meet you, Vikram. What do you think?" To say his name, to tell him that there was someone who wanted to meet him, Bhumi was sure no man could resist the twin pull on his ego.

"Who?" Vikram asked.

Bhumi let out a little smile. "Oh, Farida Aunty, Raj Uncle, a bunch of other people. You know, everyone from the island, really."

"They know about me?"

"Of course, why would I keep you secret?"

"I never tell my parents or uncles and aunties about anyone I'm dating. I don't know anyone who does."

"Is this something that all Indians do?" Bhumi asked with a wry smile.

"Yeah," Vikram replied idly. "No wait, I mean no. I mean it's just like, I dunno. I guess with all the emphasis on arranged marriages, no one talks about dating."

"Listen, you're a student at the university, you're cute, and you're from India. You're already a golden boy to them."

"I grew up in Fremont," he said. "You really told them I'm cute?"

"No, I told them you look like an elephant," Bhumi teased with a smirk and roll of her eyes. "It doesn't matter you're from Fremont. If there's one thing these uncles like to talk about, it's India, the old country. Just be prepared for that."

They walked inland and found an empty spot. Vikram dropped the plastic bag and helped Bhumi unfurl the white sheet. They sat next to each other, close enough that they could each feel the heat of the other, but far enough away to let a slice of the salty air cut through the space between them.

Bhumi played with the orange in her hand, passing it back and forth from left to right. She thought of his little smile when he seemed so surprised that she had called him cute. They had seen each other naked, and yet these little intimacies seemed to excite him more. She put her orange down into a little hollow formed by the sheet in the sand. She leaned in, closed her eyes, and kissed him.

Their shadows loomed long against the bunched folds of the sheet, where grains of sand had worked their way into each curve of its surface. Bhumi stretched out her body and laid her head into Vikram's lap, and he played with her hair, and she let out another little laugh. The sound of the ocean filled her ears with a low rumble. Dogs continued to splash in the shallows. The depths seemed to ripple into infinity.

25

THE EVENING FELT cold as the temperature dropped ahead of a storm. Bhumi waited for Vikram outside his apartment. She was still smiling, still feeling the lightness from the morning, when Farida had handed her an official-looking piece of mail with a black typewritten return address in the corner and a plastic window through the front of the envelope. It stated simply that her application for asylum had been received and any further communications or updates to the status of her application would be sent at a later date. With this letter came some sort of recognition. It opened up the possibility of a work permit and official registration for classes, even if there was no way to truly apply to a university for a degree yet. Still, the party they were headed to could be a celebration of this little victory.

They were going to walk the half mile from Vikram's place to Sonali Aunty's apartment for the party. At first Vikram had found the address unbelievable. "I know that building," he had said. "It's a student rathole. Like, I remember going to a party there once, and there was just like, a fucking hole in the front door. Are you sure that's where we're going?"

"I was just there a few weeks ago," Bhumi fumed. "Sonali Aunty and her son live there. They're stuck here without Balram Uncle. He stayed behind to get some money in order, then got locked in when they shut down the border for Indians."

"Oh," Vikram said, chastised. "Sorry, I didn't know." She could have gone on, but he looked embarrassed enough that she didn't push it.

When they walked, they were close enough that they brushed against each other, and the feeling that arose from this brief contact was enough to make them stop for a kiss.

"How's not working working out?" Vikram asked, looking proud of his play on words.

"I need to find a new job," Bhumi said, ignoring the joke. "I hate knowing how much I owe."

"How much you owe? I thought you were staying with that uncle and aunty."

"When I got here, I had to see this lawyer. You need someone to get your papers to the INS. It was expensive. He didn't charge me all at once. I have to make payments to him."

"And if you don't?"

"I don't know, I've heard he'll tell the INS and rescind your status. That's just what I hear. I don't want to find out. I saved something, but it'll run out soon."

"That's fucked up," Vikram said.

They arrived at the building, where the apartments each faced an exterior balcony like a motel. Bhumi could hear music and the whooping from a party.

"Is that where we're going?"

Bhumi laughed and gave him a gentle elbow in the ribs.

"Anything I should know?" Vikram asked. "Anything I should do?"

Bhumi shrugged. "You're fine," she said, giving him a kiss. They passed some kids hanging out in a circle near an idling car. "Hey, Bhumi," Sonali's son yelled. "Your boyfriend?" She rolled her eyes.

"You know them?" Vikram asked, sounding worried. "They're smoking weed in the parking lot."

"They'll be fine."

Bhumi didn't even knock, and inside the apartment, smaller than Raj and Farida's, every light was on, like Diwali, and from a boombox in the sitting room, a tape from *Hero* was playing. Three or four families had Tetrised themselves in the apartment: the wives crammed around the snack table next to the kitchen, the husbands in the family room drinking white rum mixed with RC Cola, the youngest kids shrieking in the apartment's sole bedroom. And all at once, it felt like every eye turned to stare at Vikram.

Bhumi grinned. "I'm going to get some phoulourie," she said.

"Some what?" Vikram asked. It was too late: Raj had ambled over, the drink nearly spilling out of his plastic cup. "Vikram! Vikram! We've heard about you. Come, come. Sit with us."

Farida handed Bhumi a plate of phoulourie and kachourie, topped with a mix of tamarind and fiery mango chutney. She gave Bhumi a knowing smile, enough for Bhumi to feel a little sense of embarrassment at the attention. "He seems nice," Farida said in a little whisper, before she gazed back at all the other aunties, who began to laugh at the comment.

Bhumi took a bite of the phoulourie, the crunch of the perfectly fried brown exterior giving way to the softness of the spiced doughy chew. The mango chutney lit up the inside of her mouth, searing heat and saliva together. She grabbed a two-liter bottle of cola and poured herself a cup, hoping no one would notice the little bit of rum she mixed in with it (though she knew everyone noticed, and knew that the aunties would silently click their tongues).

The uncles were asking Vikram to speak in Hindi. "Pure Hindi," one of them said. "Speak something. It reminds me of the radio. Say something," he pleaded.

Vikram sputtered through a sentence.

Bhumi walked up to save him from himself. She handed him a kachourie and watched him writhe through his bite. "It's so spicy!" he exclaimed.

"What, you don't have any chutney at home?" Samaroo uncle asked him.

"We do," Vikram panted. "Nothing like this."

Raj flashed a toothy smile. "We like it a little spicy where we come from. Ey, Sonali!" he yelled. "Where did you find these peppers? Island Cash and Curry has nothing like this."

"The Mexicans have a grocery down the street, cheaper than Cash and Curry and better peppers!"

"Arey, arey," Narayan uncle interrupted. "The boy is gonna cry, get him a drink!"

Bhumi watched them pour him a rum and cola that was mostly rum and ice. "Drink, boy, drink!" the uncle said.

The cacophony died down, leaving Bhumi and Vikram to settle onto the rough carpet. Bhumi looked around: something was so relaxing about these little parties. She'd never imagined she would be one to be comforted by a weekend night spent with her parents' friends, but there was something about this that was more home than home had ever been. Maybe because the only way gossip could go back to her mother was a two-week aerogram. She felt like she had nothing to hide, nothing to be but herself.

She put her hand on top of Vikram's, and he nodded in disbelief. "If I pulled half this shit at the parties we had growing up . . . ," he muttered.

"We're different," Bhumi said in reply.

"Better," Vikram said with a naive grin. "Way better."

Bhumi could see the question form inside Vikram, that buzzed look of curiosity about where he found himself. He looked to Raj. "So, I don't know how to ask this question: how, or why, did you come here?"

Bhumi slapped Vikram on the shoulder. "Vikram!" she shouted. It seemed like a private question, like asking someone about a dead child.

"No, Bhumi, it's a good question. Not a single person here has asked me that. And if we don't tell our stories, they'll be forgotten, and with them so will we." He took a long drink and began.

"Here, I drive a cab. Back home, I used to run a taxi company. Aftab was one of my best employees. Damn, he was a real follow-the-teacher type. Always ran the meter. Never took fares from riders who tried to haggle away from it.

"This was the early days of the General. We believed what he said, like chickens who never know they are going to be eaten. Aftab took three soldiers on a ride from the bar on Queen's Street, all three drunk off grog, and maybe thinking themselves to be big men.

"They were going to the Standard hotel. It's, eh, not a good hotel. The place where they rent rooms by the hour, you know what I mean?

"The soldiers tell Aftab they wouldn't pay. Aftab, God bless his heart, locked the back doors of his cab. It's what we do in normal times, eh? Get the passenger a little scared. These guys, they take out their guns and bashed the back windows, boom! That's when Aftab radioed back to dispatch to call for help.

"I had to tell his wife. Hardest thing I've ever had to say to anyone, that he had been beat up real bad by three soldiers. I tell her that we'll take care of Aftab, that we'll pay for the hospital, for everything.

"The next day, the three soldiers, they come to my house, sober as the day is light. They drag me, my wife, and my children into the street. They make us sit in the driveway as they shoot up my house. I'll never forget the sound of the bullets hitting and the concrete falling off my house. Bang, bam, bang, bam.

"One of them big-man soldiers turned to me and said, 'Next time, it won't be the house that's filled with bullets.' I call Rakesh." He paused. "Rakesh knew how to get people out of the country fast. We all came here because of Rakesh. Anyway, he works his magic. We were gone by the end of the week. I made sure to divide my company among my drivers. They turned it into a co-op. Good for them."

Bhumi had never heard the full story. To imagine those three young kids watching those soldiers take aim at their home. Bang, bang, bang. (*And what the fuck did you two think you were going to do?* the soldier had asked her when she tried to save Aarti.)

Raj took another drink. "And now I'm here," he said. Vikram nodded. The uncles shook their heads in silence. The aunties quietly laid out the dinner spread of aloo and channa curry, baingan, and chicken thick with onions and topped with a thin layer of grease, all to be eaten with a side of hot kuchela mango pickle. Someone flipped the tape to start up the music again. Slowly, the party came back to life. Even so, something hung over it all now. Bhumi glanced at Vikram, who seemed to have the look of a lost traveler. Every person in that room had been driven out, and here was the only place they could come together again.

By the time they returned to Vikram's apartment, their drinks had been mostly soaked up by soft white rotis, rice, and plenty of curry. Full and mildly buzzed, the two collapsed into bed, and as they lay there, Bhumi realized this was one of the first times they had slept together that lacked any pretense of sex, and this felt tinged with the joy of novel comforts. They lay side by side, nestled into each other, the noise of the party still ringing in Bhumi's ears.

"That's hella crazy," Vikram started. "What Raj said happened to him. What you told me happened to you. Like, I knew that you all had to leave, but I never thought about why you had to, you know?"

"It's a good thing not to have to worry about this, not to have to think about it."

Vikram turned to Bhumi. "I want to think about it. I want to do something about it."

There it was again: that belief, so earnest and American, that he could fix something, that he could swim against the currents of history and power to help someone else.

"Like what?" Bhumi asked.

"I want to introduce you to someone. Professor Lifschitz. She's one of the faculty advisors for the apartheid divestment campaign. She's really great, Bhumi, she just always seems to know something or can figure it out. I think she can really help."

"Help with what?"

"You! I'm pretty sure she knows exactly what to do with you and the lawyer. She can definitely get you a job. Or fuck up that lawyer. One of the two. Maybe both."

Bhumi's first reaction was suspicion. Easy answers seemed unbelievable, and hope felt like too much of a risk, too much of an invitation to disappointment. But she wanted to believe him, wanted to feel the same enthusiasm he did.

"Monday?" Bhumi asked.

"Perfect, Monday, I'll take you to her office hours."

They fell asleep, entwined in that bed, the sorrow and weight of the past slowly drifting off into the night.

26

THE GENERAL'S GOVERNMENT counted the Indians without pomp or circumstance. A native man in a sleeveless white shirt and a sarong came to their house, clipboard in hand. He looked like the Mormon missionaries who walked around Queen's Street in pairs, always on the lookout for new converts. He had a small clip-on badge on his chest, nothing more than a piece of paper in a small plastic shell. "William, Bureau of Statistics and Demography."

Jaipal had answered the door.

"How many residents live here?" he asked. He had an exhausted look to him, like the past few days had given him more work than he had bargained for.

"Three," Jaipal replied.

"And the fourth?" he asked.

"She's gone," Jaipal said, wondering if he should add more.

"Oh, right, I see. Says here," he replied, tapping on his clipboard.

He scribbled down a note. "I'm sure you know the rules regarding her citizenship."

Jaipal nodded.

"Good, good. Take this." He handed Jaipal a small canary-yellow index card. EMERGENCY CENSUS OF RESIDENTS OF INDIAN ORIGIN, it read across the top.

Jaipal took the card, seeing its neat and logical division: a hand-scrawled number three next to the phrase "Persons of Indian Origin/Remain," the number zero next to "Citizens," and the number one next to "Persons of Indian Origin/Renounced Citizenship."

"Is that it?" Jaipal asked.

"Set," the man said, turning around and hustling down the stairs.

He was surprised at the ease and efficiency of the task. There had been talk in the weeks leading up to the census of soldiers, of round-ups, of forced relocations, of disappearances. When it came to pass, it was all bureaucrats and door-to-door visits.

EACH DAY BLED INTO THE NEXT, BOXES IN A WALL CALENDAR TO BE crossed out with a mixture of dread and routine. Monday slipped to Thursday slipped into the General's day of rest. Crisis, Jaipal learned, was filled with as much routine boredom as anxiety.

Jaipal's mother had taken to being his father's caretaker with aplomb. In his father's needs and routines, she found an energy, a reason to go about her day. She doted upon his meals, asked Jaipal to move him to a chair, where she would wash him with a cloth, clean him when he soiled himself.

At the store, most of his money was now coming from the tax-free cigarettes and ganja loosies. When his customers asked why he didn't have their brand, he drummed his fingers on the counter and waved at the cartons, saying, "What do you expect?" The coup was the great excuse, and the customers seemed to believe it, even those who muttered that such-and-such shop had their brand. To that Jaipal could reply, "Do they have my prices?" And the conversation was over.

When he had taken on the job from Maqbool, he had feared that it would be one of control and deception on the part of the soldiers, but he never saw them. They had fit themselves into the supply chain like the vendors for every other product in the store. He never saw the suppliers, just the distributors in their trucks. The face of the soldiers' enterprise was Maqbool. Still, perhaps it was because Maqbool lived with one foot in their world that he was never quite free of danger.

"What happened?" Jaipal asked as he watched Maqbool come in one day with a black eye.

"A couple of soldiers saw me going through the trash looking for bottles. Arrested."

"They arrested you for getting some bottles?"

"Laughed at me, asked what would the General think if he saw me doing that. Fuck this place, man," he said, looking like he was hiding something. Jaipal didn't press him.

Maqbool and the hotel were the only two things lately that made Jaipal feel whole, wanted, desired. He had someone with him now, a new rhythm to a life that hurtled through the unknown whims of a country run by a madman. If he could somehow keep his head above water, there was some joy to be found at the end of the world, and maybe more too if things went back to normal.

It had been at Maqbool's insistence that Jaipal had ordered passports for himself and his mother. When Jaipal had asked about what to do with his father, Maqbool was dismissive in a way Jaipal had never been—"You won't need him," he had said. When Jaipal had finally made enough money through Maqbool's scheme, he sent off their passport applications through Rakesh.

In October, as spring began to creep out of winter's clutches and the rains began to pick up, the General had convened a special conference of Indian leaders (the smattering that were left on the island) to present them with a formal list of Indian malpractices in daily life. The special bulletin on the radio said that they were guilty of price gouging, employment discrimination, collusion, disloyalty, nonintegration, ethnic discrimination, and even "preventing the uplift of native-born life."

His mother followed the news and the rumors closer than he did. She told him that the census had found that a fifth of the country's Indians had left. Everyone knew they were mixing up the numbers, combining those who had departed with those who had been disappeared. They had numbered around 10 percent before this had all begun, out of a total population of seven hundred thousand. A minority, a fraction of the nation that, in the opinion of the majority, controlled all of daily life.

All the while, prices changed constantly with the government's new taxes and tariffs. When Jaipal's Coca-Cola vendor dropped off a case of soft drinks along with the news that the price was going up another 50 percent, Jaipal asked him what was going on. He was native-born, but he worked hard—he wasn't kaamchor like the rest of them, Jaipal thought. He had a sort of streetwise way of seeing the world.

"My distributor is based out of Australia," he said with a grimace. He had just taken a dolly to the storeroom and was wheeling it back to his idling lorry outside. "All this stuff the General is doing, it makes him angry. The General is raising taxes on everything, and his soldiers, they steal, they close down the port, they open it up again. When things are like this, prices only go one way," he said, pointing his thumb up to the ceiling.

The government raised taxes, the distributors raised prices. The store wasn't making any money anymore—the cash was in the black market.

Within weeks, Jaipal received the passports in the mail from Rakesh. His mother seemed pleased that he was providing for the family. He didn't tell her that he hadn't applied for his father, nor did he tell her that he hadn't applied for any visas. He couldn't see the reason—why waste money on a visa when they weren't being let out of the country anyway? The travel restrictions had put a distorted pause upon everything, and in that calm Jaipal felt safe. There was nothing to do except wait, to live each day, to enjoy the nights he had time with Maqbool, to feel fleeting pleasures at the hotel.

JAIPAL WALKED FROM THE STORE TO MAQBOOL'S APARTMENT, EAGER to make it a quick stop and get home, to prove to his mother that he was able to keep a promise and that he would be there for dinner. The summer's rain that had filled the day had eased up completely, and the sunset was filtering through the overcast.

Next to the shoe store was a barred gate painted black, the type of door that was almost imperceptible to passersby. Next to the door was a buzzer, labeled with handwritten names mostly rubbed off over time. Jaipal pressed one where he could still discern the last name: Kabir. The door quickly buzzed back at him with a loud click of a lock.

No one had been in the shop that day, and Jaipal had been staring out the window at the stream of water that rushed down the sides of the road, counting one-two-three between a call of lightning and its response from thunder. When the phone had rung, Jaipal hadn't expected it to be Maqbool, and was even more surprised when Maqbool told him to come to his flat, that he had something important to say. Jaipal called to tell his mother he would be an hour or so late, that he would still be there for dinner and to help with Papa. She had sighed into the phone, the weight of dashed expectations hanging heavy on every word.

A short woman opened the door, her wavy hair streaked with rivulets of gray, a pale yellow dupatta thrown over her shoulder. Her eyes widened a bit, and Jaipal knew that Maqbool hadn't mentioned he was coming over.

"Hi, Kabir Aunty," Jaipal said. She leaned over to give him a hug.

"Jaipal!" she exclaimed. "It's been so long. Maqbool didn't say you were coming." She turned her head. "Ey, Maqbool! Jaipal is here!" Jaipal took a brief look into the narrow hallway and down to the coir mat near the door, its little brown hairs shed all around the scuffed tile of the landing. There wasn't enough room to enter the apartment and take his sandals off. He slipped them off in the hallway.

The apartment's entryway was filled with stacks of old magazines and newspapers, and on top of them balanced a plastic crate filled with bottles. Jaipal had to turn sideways to get past it. The galley kitchen was off the entry, big enough to fit a range top and a small round breakfast table, the surface covered in half-empty glass jars of pickle. The entire apartment smelled like fried fish.

The sitting room fit only a small black-and-white television (whose antennas stuck out almost the width of the wall behind it) and a small rattan love seat with a few throw pillows. The hallway was like a snake that had just eaten an egg, narrow at the entrance, bulbous in the sitting room, narrow once again. Along the hallway was the only closed door in the apartment, and Jaipal was sure that it had been Salim's room. Further down, Maqbool poked his head out a door.

"In here," he said.

Unlike the rest of the apartment, Maqbool's room was surprisingly empty—and clean. There was simply a mattress on the floor—the bed made—and opposite that, an almirah with a hazy kitchen-oil-and-dust sheen to it.

Maqbool was sitting on the lip of his window, biting his nails. He looked up. "Close the door."

Jaipal closed it. "What's going—"

Maqbool cut him off. "I'm leaving."

"Leaving? Where?"

"Tonight. I'm going to London. Sometime in the night. I've saved enough money, finally, I'm gone. I even did namaz at the masjid today. First time I'd been there since I don't know when."

Jaipal laughed. "What the fuck, man? You've never been out of the country, and now you're going to London? And you know what's going on. No one can take a flight out. You gonna be like those boat people? Arrested before they made it past the breakers?"

"I found someone to take me."

"Don't trust those fucking boatmen, Maqbool. Tell me, right now: how are you leaving?"

"I can't tell you. It's not by boat. This is as much as I can tell you. They told me not to say anything."

"Does your ma know?"

"She knows enough."

"So she's just going to wake up tomorrow and hope she hears from you again? What the fuck, Maqbool, how can you do this to her?"

"Listen, we gotta take our chance when we have one, okay? I wanted you to know. I want you to come with me, tonight. We'll go together."

The invitation shocked Jaipal into silence. There was nothing more he wanted than to be with Maqbool in a constant way, not in the darkness of the hotel, but somewhere.

His life wasn't one he could abandon in a heartbeat. "M-my ma," Jaipal stammered. "I'm the one who's getting her money now, I'm the one supporting her. And Bhumi's gone. And Papa is basically gone. It's just me and her. I have to look after her."

"Think about how much money you could send from London. Just come with me," he pleaded. Maqbool turned around to look at the streetlamp right outside his window. "When I was a kid, I used to see this lamp outta the corner of my eye, and I thought it was a trick. I thought the sun came back after it set. The sun was always shining, just in this window."

Jaipal recalled being on the floor of his shop: all the insects dying looking for the light to guide them where they needed to go.

"The sun is shining, Jaipal. Just for this last time, it's shining. Right here." Maqbool tapped on his chest. "Just for me." He turned back around. "Are you coming with me tonight?"

Jaipal knew he couldn't say yes, but he couldn't bring himself to say no either. "What time are you leaving? Meet me at the store. I'll see you before you go."

"Bring six thousand and your bag. Don't make me go alone," he said, his voice cracking. He walked up to Jaipal and kissed him, long and slow, without any of his usual hunger, as forlorn as the first winds of autumn coming in from the south. Jaipal grabbed on to Maqbool's hands, the emotions—the reality—of departure only coming to him now.

Once again, he was cursed to stay behind.

"When you get there, and if you're really not taking a boat," Jaipal said, ignoring what Maqbool had commanded, "call me, write me, just tell me one thing: what does the island look like from an airplane? Promise me, okay, tell me that?" Jaipal's voice was cracking. He felt the first few tears, hot against his face.

"I won't have to tell you nothing," Maqbool said. "You can see it with me."

Jaipal wiped his cheeks with his hand and turned to leave. He passed the kitchen. He was sure that Maqbool's mother saw his reddened eyes, the puffiness in his cheeks. She gave him a motherly half-broken smile in response, as if to say: *There's nothing anyone can do anymore*. Her second son was as lost as her first.

JAIPAL WAS DISTRACTED THROUGHOUT THE DINNER WITH HIS mother. He added up all the loose ends, figured how it could all work: his mother could have the store, all the money he had saved. She could have his father and Bhumi.

He had tried to strike out all the secrets, tried to fill the hole that Bhumi had left in her life, but the habits of parents and children could never die. Relationships like the one they had were formed within the first few years of life. Theirs had set like a broken bone healed incorrectly, a limp as a constant reminder.

It was nearly midnight when he left. He packed light: his passport, a duffel bag with a few days of clothes, an envelope thick with cash. He would see Maqbool and would go with him if he asked one more time. The drive to the store was filled with a joy he had never before known—a sense of possibility, of a new beginning, of something just for the two of them. The sun would be shining, wherever it was they ended up.

At the store, he waited. With every minute that passed after midnight, his heart sank a little more. Maqbool had forgotten, or been so rushed that he couldn't bother to come one last time to take him away. Jaipal cried, little silent tears, his body squeezing out the last bits of something left in him, something yet to be crushed by the wreckage around him. This was a confirmation of his worst fear: that he existed as a mere footnote to the lives of others, that no one could be bothered to notice him when he needed it most.

27

THEY AGREED THAT Vikram should go in first, and Bhumi could wait outside her office. She sat in a fluorescent-lit hallway in a plastic chair in the staid concrete sarcophagus of the sciences building. On her frosted glass door, the professor had put up a sign-in sheet for office hours, ringed by political cartoons deriding Ronald Reagan: the president riding a rocket labeled STAR WARS, the president destroying cities labeled "social welfare programs," and underneath all that, a round green sticker with the words "YES ERA."

Bhumi could hear laughter from inside, the murmur of voices blocked by a closed door. She wondered what she was doing here.

Men had sweet-talked her mother and grandmother into a prison. Her grandmother's own father and husband had betrayed her, had forced her to make an overnight decision upon pain of death. And then came everything else, five years toiling on a plantation. All the pictures Bhumi had seen of her grandmother showed a wrinkled and stooped woman, and she could never tell if the way her back was bent over was from age or from the years spent hunched over picking cane from the earth.

When her grandmother finally left the plantation, she settled down in Sugar City, marrying the first man who didn't ask for a dowry. He was descended from cane farmers and worked the night shift at the City and Colony Sugar Refinery. After getting married, her grandmother never left Sugar City. Her life was defined by her home and hearth: the kitchen, seven children, getting them married, and the cruel, swift transition to dotage.

She had never been educated, never had a chance. A woman's life back then ended right at birth—if a girl was going to be lost to marriage, why send her to school, why do anything?

And all the idiotic superstitions her mother held fast were the product of that woman's mind. When her father was feeling especially cruel, he would belittle her grandmother to her mother's face. "She was useless, and so are you!" her father would roar.

In darkened moments, Bhumi could see herself squirreled away somewhere in Santa Ursula, in an apartment even smaller than Raj and Farida's, rolling out rotis for mouths as hungry and loud as the little boy's, the pain radiating out from the arches of her feet after hours of standing in front of cabinets, worn to nothing from a lifetime of raising children.

To trust a man was to invite disaster. She steeled herself against the possibility of disappointment.

Her hands were slick with sweat, and her leg bounced with worry. After what felt like hours, Vikram emerged with a big, goofy smile.

"All right, she's all yours!" he said.

"What?" Bhumi asked. "Should I go in?"

"Yeah, of course, go in. I need to go pick up a book from the library. I'll meet you there in a half hour or something?" He leaned in and gave her a little kiss on her lips.

Inside the office, seated behind a wide wooden desk, was a professor by the name of Liora Lifschitz. Her desk was stacked with papers, and the steel shelves on the walls were filled with books, old worn copies of academic journals, loose-leaf papers. Blocking some of the shelves was a large chalkboard on wheels with a list of what looked like names divided into two columns, scribbled in barely legible scrawl.

Bhumi hadn't been expecting someone so young. She was a sleek woman, with auburn hair in wavy curls pulled back behind her head. Her small green eyes were set behind a pair of black acetate glasses that seemed so fashionable to Bhumi.

"Hello! Bhumi? Am I pronouncing that right?" she said, getting up from her chair and sticking out her hand. Bhumi was surprised to hear her voice. She had been conditioned by her experience at SPU to associate the title "professor" with the sound of a man's voice.

"Not Bummi. Bhoo-mee," Bhumi replied, shaking her hand.

"Ah, I see. I'm Professor Lifschitz. Sorry for the mess!" she said with a mocking air.

On the desk sat a portrait-sized framed image of a large dog with bangs covering his eyes and thick wooly hair that grew in gentle waves.

"That's Winston. He's my baby," Professor Lifschitz said. She spoke with a confidence that matched her height: four or five inches taller than Bhumi. "He's a Bouvier des Flandres. Six years old. He's usually here, though today my boyfriend is off from work and is looking after him. You don't mind dogs, do you?"

"Oh, they're fine," Bhumi said in a quiet voice as she moved a finger over her scar. There was something that seemed so undeniably cool about this woman—she seemed to be a decade older than her, maybe a little more. And yet: boyfriend, dog, biology professor. Bhumi straightened her back in an effort to impress her.

The professor explained that she had been very interested in what Vikram had to say about her. "You were a nanny for a month or two?" she asked. "And you're sitting in on a few classes here?"

"I'm not a nanny anymore," Bhumi said. "I quit. Taking care of children isn't for me," she added, trying to distance herself from the past, trying to ingratiate herself to this person she had met only moments ago.

"Not surprised at that. No one likes taking care of children," Professor Lifschitz said with a laugh. She leaned back in her chair and crossed one leg over the other. "Remind me," she said. "You also did some coursework in botany at the South Pacific University?" She didn't wait for a reply. "I remember learning a little bit of botanical science in Cell Biology back when I was an undergrad at UCLA. Your future is in science, isn't it?"

"Yes," Bhumi replied with a confidence she hadn't felt in months. She loved hearing of her future from this professor.

"Of course it is. I can't even convince half my students to come to class, and here you are pursuing your education right after you arrived in this country. God, I can only imagine what's going on where you're from. You know, there's lots of things to get involved in on this campus. The fight against apartheid, the fight against Reagan and his goons, it's all related."

Bhumi listened to Professor Lifschitz in a doubled way, hearing her and also hearing Aarti drone on about something or other. Without thinking about it, she said something that Aarti always used to say. "Yes, we have to fight for the third way of the third world."

Professor Lifschitz's face seemed to light up. "Of course! That's what we're fighting for. You understand it completely." She seemed so pleased at Bhumi's comment. "So what kind of botanical science research are you interested in?"

"Well," Bhumi started, feeling her confidence begin to erode from underneath her, "I finished all my required courses, and we could start to take specialized courses in our third year. I was going to register, but everything happened before I could. I'm enjoying this course on ecology, but what I want to do is more bench science—I love being in the lab," Bhumi rambled on.

"You're right on the cusp of specializing. My Ph.D. is in molecular biology, but I did my undergrad in bacteriology. Along the way I became really interested in viruses, particularly bacteriophages in marine life. I'm working on a paper right now, and I'm estimating that bacteriophages are the most abundant entity in marine environments."

Bhumi nodded along, rapt at the description of her research.

"Are there any things in particular that interest you? Genetics? Virology?"

Bhumi was at a loss for words. "I'm not sure. What you described sounds fascinating," Bhumi said.

"Sure," she said in a way that made Bhumi feel deflated. "How about this: tell me a little bit more about what's going on where you're from."

Bhumi mentioned the country's name and Professor Lifschitz shook her head.

"It's a small island in the Pacific." Bhumi imagined the map she used to have on her wall in her dormitory. "Put your finger on Australia on the map and move east and north. There it is."

"I didn't know there were Indians there. Vikram said that you were applying for asylum?" She uncrossed her legs and leaned forward into the conversation, as if this was what she really wanted to talk about with Bhumi.

"Yes. I'm not sure if you have seen the news from such a small place, but it's all I can think about sometimes. There was a coup there. There's been a lot of violence. They say it's only a matter of time before they expel all the Indians from the country. I had to leave," Bhumi said, not knowing what version of her story this woman wanted.

Professor Lifschitz took in a deep breath through her nostrils. "You know, my dad came to this country from Poland. I'm Jewish. My father and his brother, they were the only ones to escape. They stayed in London for a year or two. My dad's brother says to my dad, 'I'm going to stay here.' My dad says to his brother, 'I'm sick and tired of the rain. I'm going to Los Angeles.'" She laughed, and Bhumi saw how she did so with a wide, open mouth, the type who enjoyed the humor of her own jokes. "He heard that it was as sunny as could be. I was born down in SoCal."

Bhumi laughed—perhaps a bit too loud, the self-conscious voice in her head said—and silenced herself, nodding her head with a more demure smile.

"You see," the professor said. She paused for a moment, taking off her glasses and rubbing her eyes with her free hand. She put her glasses back on and cleared her throat. "We—I—have a responsibility to other people in these situations. It's clear you have drive, you have the capability, you just need someone to show you what you can do. Why don't you come into my lab? I can always use someone to, you know, run the autoclave and prepare agar plates. You can stay on campus and keep looking at classes. When can you start to work?" she said with the resolve of a conclusion foregone.

"I'll need a work permit," Bhumi said, surprised, yet feeling a deep sense of resolution and pleasure at the turn of events. "You'll have to fill out some paperwork, I think."

"Whatever. If the paperwork doesn't work out, I can pay you out of my research stipend. What matters is that you're here and you're learning," Professor Lifschitz said as she stood. She held out her hand to Bhumi. "I look forward to seeing you here."

As Bhumi shook her hand, she filled with a newfound sense of direction. She had been ambling around in the dark and now had stumbled upon a door. She had knocked, and to her surprise, she had been let in. It was a meager first step, but it was all hers to take.

That night they were going to celebrate. It had been Vikram's idea—getting dressed up, going to a restaurant. "Something special, you deserve it," he had said.

She hadn't packed going-out clothes when she left and, at this point, didn't have the cash to buy a dress, even from the Goodwill down the street. She tried something she hadn't worn since she was back home: a simple pale blue kameez over jeans. Farida said she looked wonderful, and Bhumi waited by the curb with a warm feeling of confidence, Farida's smile a shawl wrapped around her cold shoulders.

Vikram laughed when he saw her. "You look like a FOB," he said.

And just like that, the warmth left her. "A what?"

"You know, a FOB. 'Fresh off the boat'? It's what we call people who just got here. From India."

"I did just get here. Not from India," Bhumi said, feeling defensive.

"Sorry, I didn't mean it in a bad way. You look nice," he said with a nervous laugh. Bhumi felt an annoyance at her own draw toward anger and harsh judgment. She had been taught, without realizing it, that anger was the only way out of discomfort, that lashing out was the only way to soothe herself.

"I know what you mean," Bhumi said. She hadn't realized she had balled up her hands into fists. She released them: open hands to take out what she had accumulated. She flashed Vikram a smile and let out a little chuckle.

"You sure?" Vikram asked with a little grimace, his eyes narrowed in concern.

"Of course," Bhumi said.

Dinner was at Hunan House, a small sit-down Chinese restaurant with an aquarium filled with darting yellow and blue fish near the entrance, and tables with paper covers on white tablecloth, a little spinner in the middle filled with red-hot chili paste and glass bottles of soy sauce. Vikram ordered the sickly-sweet and bright red deep-fried prawns, and Bhumi a plate of chow mein, hoping it would be like the noodles in the handful of Chinese restaurants from back home, spiced with a tremendous serving of garlic and green chilies, but it was nothing like that. Not in a bad way. Just a confused feeling of taking a bite and expecting one flavor and getting another.

They sat near a corner, next to a big window that looked out onto a parking lot and a Taco Bell drive-through. They watched the dogs and children and spouses and lonely selves in each of those cars, and Bhumi felt an ease doing this with Vikram—the two made an us, and the rest of the world could be a them. When the waiters cleared the plates and they finished their fortune cookies ("A Long Journey Lies Ahead," said Bhumi's, and she rolled her eyes and laughed with Vikram, saying it had gotten it all wrong, that the long journey lay behind), they walked outside, where she slipped her hand into his and gave him a deep kiss.

"Thank you," she said. "For the dinner. For everything."

Vikram drove them back to his place. The sex between them had, until that point, been an affair of she-on-top until she came, switch to he-on-top until he came, and yet there was an undercurrent she wanted, a desire that she had felt the evening she came over after she had quit the nannying job.

"Put your hands around my neck," she told him when he was on top, finally working up the nerve to say so. "Squeeze. Not hard. Just do it." He was baffled. Scared. They had to stop.

"I'll tell you if it's ever too much. I'll tell you to stop. I want this," she said without hesitation. Underneath her desire ran the roots of all the loss and pain of family and a nation. They were things that she wanted to feel given back to her, and now, in the safety of another who could do no harm, it was that she could be hurt tenderly, carefully. She could control what could be given to her, and there was no better pleasure than that.

ON THE DAY BEFORE HER FIRST SHIFT AT THE LAB, SHE TOOK THE BUS to the Southland Mall, to the Emporium, and the first thing she bought was new underwear—something that no one (besides Vikram) would see, and as a result, a purchase that felt like she was truly spending money on herself. She wore it to work—good underwear was invisible confidence, a pep talk to and from herself.

At work, she found her tasks simple and straightforward: agar plate after agar plate waiting for her to prep. She had been given a white coat to wear, and what it protected was not her or her clothes. It was the keratinized shell that could keep safe the dream left dormant.

Inside the lab, the radio was playing softly in the background, KFOG's selection of Prince and Jefferson Airplane. It was a small operation: two postdocs and a Ph.D. candidate, alongside a few undergraduate research assistants. Bhumi found a world that seemed to revolve around the professor's grant applications, research, and direction with an efficiency she had never before seen. This was a single professor at a middle-of-the-road college in a small city in California, and yet, the lab gleamed with new equipment. Nothing at SPU could compare.

At lunch, Professor Lifschitz asked Bhumi to visit her office. When she sat down, Winston put his head between her knees. Bhumi swallowed hard, feeling her heart racing in her chest. She could feel the wetness of his nose soak through the fabric of her jeans. She gingerly placed a hand atop his head, surprised at how soft his fur was.

"Everything seems to be fine in the lab, I hope? I haven't heard about any fires or catastrophes," the professor said with a laugh. "Let's start thinking about next semester. What classes are you considering?" the professor asked. Winston crawled back under the desk to nap with his head tucked between his paws, and even like this, Bhumi felt like Winston was guarding her in some way.

"I'm really becoming more interested in viruses and their connections to botany—maybe I can audit your virology class?" Bhumi asked.

"I'd love that," Professor Lifschitz replied with a welcoming smile. "I think you'll really get a lot out of it." The smile stayed with her for the rest of her day in the professor's lab. She left that day feel-ing like she had won a prize: she had chanced upon someone to guide her through her passions.

When she grabbed some curry powder for Farida at Island Cash and Curry on her way home, her pride and joy bubbled into small talk. She told Jagdish the good news.

"Congratulations!" Jagdish roared. "A real job, working for a professor. You're making us proud."

And from Rekha Aunty, in line behind her, "A professor! What's it like working for him?"

Bhumi grinned and shook her head at the mistake, not being able to imagine Professor Lifschitz as a woman. "It fits into my studies, Aunty. She teaches biology."

"You had a scholarship to SPU and you're making us proud here, beti. You're doing well for everyone."

It seemed so linear to her, but Bhumi knew the work that was in-volved, the difference between the passive accomplishment and the thing that had to be grabbed by her own hands.

When her first paycheck arrived, it surprised her—surely there had been some mistake in the amount she was owed. No, there had been no mistake, only a realization of how little the Indian families paid to take care of their children.

She began to make her payments to the lawyer again and was able to give a little rent to Farida and Raj, in addition to helping out with the bills. "No, no, we can't accept this," Farida said. "You're like a daughter to us now. What's this?" Bhumi insisted that she help those who had given her so much, and Farida finally relented.

28

THE MORNING AFTER Maqbool left, the shutters at the shop were already raised, the door was unlocked. Instinct made him rush to the door, to see if someone had broken in, to check to make sure that everything remained in its right place.

When he crossed the threshold, he saw instead a soldier leaning against the drinks case.

"Right on time," the soldier said, his face still set into a scowl. He was drinking a bottle of Coke, the bottle half-empty, looking like the soldier who had roughed him up before his sister left. "Ey, he's here," he said, yelling across the store. Jaipal could hear the other soldier grunt alongside the swish-crackle from opening a bag of chips.

He downed the rest of his drink and let out a deep belch. He tossed the bottle in his hand and tightened his fingers around its neck. Then he walked three steps to Jaipal and slapped him across the face with the bottle.

Immediately, Jaipal could feel the throbbing pain radiate across his jaw. He doubled over and cradled his face. As he did, the soldier walked up to him and kneed him in the stomach. Jaipal fell to the floor and the soldier stood in front of him.

"Do you know the rules?"

Jaipal rocked back and forth like a monk in prayer, the pain like hot coals searing through his face and stomach.

"You seem a little stupid, so here's the answer: all of this is ours. Did your friend not know?" He turned around. "Didn't we tell his friend?"

The other soldier stood off behind the counter, taking cartons of cigarettes and placing them into a large olive-green canvas bag.

"We did," the other soldier said.

"Fucking stupid," the first soldier said. "Tell him why that's a problem."

"We have one simple rule. Keep the split. We take eighty, you and your friend split the rest. And we count the money. Every time. Now, why did your friend give us seventy last time? How is that fair?"

Jaipal, shaking, sweat on his forehead, the pain reducing to a dull throbbing, shook his head. He kept his eyes focused on the tile beneath him. How could Maqbool be so stupid? He had skimmed off the top at the last minute, hoping in desperation they wouldn't notice before he left.

"We were waiting for him to confess," the soldier said. "Give us back what's ours. Motherfucker kept his mouth shut. Even when we told him that we would shut down that hotel, he thought he could play tough with us."

"We just got back," the first soldier said with a cruel chuckle. "Good for you that you weren't there."

Jaipal tried to swallow hard, but the muscles to swallow didn't work; the spit stayed in his mouth.

"This country hates liars and queers. And now we have less of both," he laughed. "As for you, you're done. We're taking the cigarettes and the chimbi. And whatever cash you had in the till. We took enough back from your friend before we were done with him."

Terror pressed down on Jaipal's chest and he had to fight to take a breath, to get the words out. "Where is he?" he asked, in no more than a coarse whisper.

"You don't need to worry about him anymore."

The soldiers took the goods and left, and in the silence that followed, Jaipal leaned back against the wall and cried. A pressure had fallen upon his chest, holding every muscle down, taking from him every last breath. He stumbled out of the store, gasping for air. There was nothing for him.

He wanted to move, needed to get away—the water, the bay, the roving chickens, the coconut man, the turtle. It was all too far; the store kept him locked into place. Rules were rules: he couldn't close for the day without permission. The tears, hot against his flushed skin, a shiver down his spine, all thoughts obliterated from his mind, except for the shaking fear, like a stray animal beaten in the street.

He paced, back and forth, from the till to the store's entrance. And though his feet moved, they were like the feet of another, and his hands seemed so strange and far away. He sucked in all the smoke he could, but the cigarette had long been finished. All the world seemed to slip forward from his grasp. There was a blunting to his senses: there were no scents, no sounds, nothing to touch—only the binding terror of what had been delivered to him.

A man passed, the hair at the side of his head a stark white, the creases running along his face like rivers from the hills. He made eye contact with Jaipal through the window and quickly looked down and sped away, as if it was too much to bear the feelings of another.

The man's glance grabbed Jaipal and shook him back into the present. Terror still encased him like a coffin, but the tremors began to slow, leaving a feeling like being drunk or mildly concussed.

A breath, deep and slow. And then another. And then another.

(*I take deep breaths,* Portia had told him once. *It always helps.*)

(Another one lost from him.)

A customer, a paunchy young man, always fidgeting with his hands, walked in. He was one of Jaipal's chimbi regulars.

"You got any for me?" his customer asked, looking away, ignoring the wretched look that hung from Jaipal's face.

"Not today," Jaipal said, blinking his eyes, feeling unable to focus on the customer's face. He found it easier to stare just past his head.

"What about tomorrow?"

Jaipal grimaced and shook his head.

"How about cigarettes? You got my pack?"

He pulled a pack of Marlboros from the shelf behind the counter. The customer put down his coins. "It's fifty cents more."

"So you don't have any chimbi and you raised prices on cigarettes?" The man pocketed his coins and left the cigarettes on the counter. "I'll try somewhere else. Bad business, eh?"

Jaipal could feel the beginning of a headache coming on, the feeling of his pulse pounding along his temples. His face still throbbed with the hot tenderness of a bruise. Maqbool was right, you either had power or you didn't. And you couldn't be safe until you escaped. Nothing was guaranteed anymore. Nothing could stop the fear from wrapping its cold hands around Jaipal's neck.

BY THE TIME HE LEFT THE STORE, THE SUN HAD SET, AND THE PURPLE-orange of the sky was fading to blue, onward to black. He had no interest in going home. As he drove, it felt as if he were staying still and it was the city that moved about him, with the edges of things turning feathered and blurred, like there were no definite lines between solid objects, transforming Sugar City into a city of ghosts. When he looked out at the unfolding diorama, he saw the street hawkers, the men standing around with sleepy eyes, waiting for the edges of a cool evening to emerge from the heat of the day, the beggars making their rounds, the faces weathered by the haggard remains of daily life, and the country that woke up every morning hiding from itself the truth: all was crumbling to dust.

He sat himself down close to the bay's waterline, his toes digging into the cold touch of the damp. The sun had given way and the moon was covered by a wash of low clouds. In the small waves that lapped near the shore, Jaipal could see veins of blue luminescence in the water, the light breathing, pulsing with the tide, exhaling the cool breeze that pinched Jaipal's face with the ocean spray.

Neither Maqbool's warm embrace nor his sister's presence. Both always with an idea of what to do, both gone from him. One to be found beyond the dark waters, the other lost to him.

He asked himself: Why hadn't he stopped him from trying to leave? Why hadn't he grabbed him, slapped him, told him how stupid his plan was, that he was sure to get caught, that he was going to leave his mother without both of her sons? Why didn't he tell him of the love he had begun to feel, of the care, of the tenderness, of the desire? Surely even one of those things could have been a bulwark, could have stopped Maqbool from being taken.

He was sobbing again, great heaves to his cries: a wretched sight seen by no one. No comfort to be found. No coconut man, no chickens, and no turtle, only the waves lapping, as they did, forever.

If Jaipal had managed to grab Maqbool and tell him all the things he had to tell him, it would have been of little consequence. If he'd needed some money, why hadn't he just asked Jaipal? He would have fronted him whatever he needed—and more. No, Maqbool's sin had always been pride. He thought he could fix everything himself. And it was this same pride that had dug his own grave. There was nothing Jaipal could have done.

He needed his sister, needed someone who had always been smarter than him, someone who knew how to stretch as far as she could away from family, nation, someone who knew how to find her own. In the silence that hung over the beach, a question: was this what his sister had felt? She had felt the whip and the lash of the country, of those who turn others into rubbish to be burned behind the house. She too was gone from him. He could call the store she used in America, but he would have to leave a message. There was no way to reach her now, when he needed her most.

He knew she would be able to take one look at this situation and render judgment. Maqbool always had his plans, she would tell him. His schemes. They seemed like games to you, but he made the rules for everyone else to follow.

None of that mattered to Jaipal. He would follow whatever Maqbool commanded. He wanted him.

Bhumi would have raised an eyebrow at this. *Was he ever yours to want?*

The imagined conversation fluttered off into silence like a flame snuffed out by a sudden wind.

He began to pace the beach, footprints sinking into footprints as he walked back and forth. Perhaps there was nothing left here anymore. She had taken a flight, he had been taken away. Either way, the result was the same: he was alone.

He had to become her. He had to do what Bhumi had done. He moved with a sense of purpose that tensed the muscles along his jaw— the pain from the bottle causing him to clench his hands, once open and willing, into tightened fists.

Purpose, he learned, was different from desire and its aftermath. If a picture hanging crooked on a wall could feel something once it was righted, that was close to what Jaipal had felt when he returned back home from the hotel, either the Sunshine or the Ambassador.

The hotels had given him the home he had never had: comfort, routine, the knowledge that the other was there and willing and waiting for him. What was fleeting was what took him back, every single night.

He felt a need both raw and fierce: to never see another soldier again, to lose no more friends and lovers, to keep his heart beating, to live to see another day. He was going to take up Maqbool's admonition to leave the country behind, move from the safety of what was known and cross into the safety of where he could find some power, even if it was over his own little life. London, that's where Maqbool was going to go. He had to be a little bit like Bhumi, a little bit like Maqbool: never settle, reach out and steal back what was rightfully his.

Jaipal's life was important too. They had taught him something: he could take what he needed if he wanted it. He would stand up and make a decision—to leave.

AT THE SHOP THE NEXT DAY, JAIPAL PICKED UP THE PHONE, AND after a brief conversation with the operator to find Rakesh's number, he was connected.

"No one's leaving right now," Rakesh said bluntly. "That means none of them are processing many visas. Small-small rush."

"I heard some people are leaving," Jaipal said in a quiet tone.

"No one's leaving," Rakesh said slowly, with each word punctuated with a bit of static, like he was speaking loud enough to spit into the receiver. "Not a single one. I don't do that other coyote shit. Who do you think I am? Someone once told me in East Germany that people who plan this shit are crazier than crazy. He's right."

"No, no, it's not like that. My friend. They arrested him before he was going to leave."

"I'm sorry," he said. Jaipal said nothing in response to the hollowness of those words.

"It's dangerous," Rakesh continued. "Every single person doing that has been caught. We're a fucking small country. It's easy to keep track of every damn one of us. They'll let us go, soon, I think. It's a matter of when. I can feel it. I've got hope."

"I want to go," Jaipal said, before adding, "And my ma too. Can I join my sister?"

"Where is she? My memory is good, but I've planned so many of these a week. Remembering the specifics of one person from months ago—I wish I could have a memory like that."

"She's in California."

"Then no." It was so final, it could have been the click and dial tone of a hung-up call. Jaipal was taken aback by the forcefulness of the answer. Still, he said nothing, hoping for something more.

"It's just that America is giving too much shit. It's hard. Trust me, something good is gonna come down the pipeline with some of the other countries. How about Canada? It's not too far from California. There are a bunch of us near Vancouver. It'll work out. And since you have money, they'll get you a good deal. Trust me."

Trust me. How much of the past few months had been putting blind trust into Maqbool. The cold meanness of a prayer: to put so much in and not to know whether to expect anything in return.

"Mail me your passports, notarized bank statements, anything proving you have money in the bank, and seven thousand dollars, cashier's check only. If the bank statements are not enough, I'll tell you what to send me."

Jaipal winced at the price. "Are you sure they'll get us a visa?" he asked.

"No. There's a chance it goes either way. I can't tell anyone anything is guaranteed anymore. Maybe when your sister left, things were easier. Now? Now, I can't lie like that."

"So you want me to send you seven thousand? And there's a chance nothing happens?"

"Listen, all we have right now is just a little hope. Hope that the

General will turn around and say, 'Just kidding, back to normal.' Or hope that they'll let us leave. Or live in peace. And this? It buys you some hope. Hope that some chutiya at the High Commission will feel some pity and stamp your application. Or maybe he likes the little something extra I give with my papers. Or hope that if anything else happens, you have a backup plan. Hope is all we got."

"You're selling me hope. Seven thousand to hope for the best." Jaipal was incredulous. "I'll send it to you tomorrow. I have to go," Jaipal said before putting down the phone. There was a customer waiting. Another chimbi regular. Another disappointment.

THAT EVENING, AS HIS FATHER SLEPT, HE AND HIS MOTHER SAT around the table after dinner. He had been getting worse lately—breaking out in heavy sweats during the night. She was tearing up his old undershirts and soaking them in ice water to use as compresses for later.

"They arrested Maqbool," Jaipal said, tight-lipped, weary from the day, uninterested in explaining more. He felt himself sliding into his usual secrecy.

"Hai Ram," his mother said, her raised eyebrows showing some measure of shock, her eyes looking deadened from so much bad news. "What happened?"

"I don't know, I found out through a friend," Jaipal said, cradling his face. He could see his mother eyeing the blue and black swollen mess on his face.

"How don't you know?" she said. "And what happened to your face?"

"How can I know why the soldiers do what they do?" Jaipal said, raising his voice. Getting stuck in his lie made him impatient, a child caught doing wrong. He had no interest in being punished. He wanted to tell her what he had done.

His mother looked at him, her eyebrows raised in surprise.

"I talked to Rakesh about us leaving," Jaipal said, trying to keep his cool. "I phoned him today. I'll send him the seven thousand dollars and the passports tomorrow."

"It's bad luck to send money on a Wednesday," his mother said, before realizing how much money he was in fact sending. "Where did you get that money?"

"We need to do this to be safe. The General could close all the businesses again, I don't know. We have to have hope that he'll let us go, or that there's something better. And you should be near Bhumi," he finally added, knowing that this facet would draw her closer to his resolve.

"Where does he want us to go? California? To be near her. That's where we should go."

"No, he said we have a better chance for Canada."

"Canada," his mother said. "I don't know where Canada is."

Jaipal could relate. He had no image to put to the country. He had met those from New Zealand, from Australia, from California, even from as far away as England. In whispered, cigarette-smoke breaths, those from the hotel had told him bits and pieces about the cities they came from, and he'd always imagined his lovers wandering through their daily lives, huddled against themselves in the cold. They always described where they came from as colder than Sugar City, but Jaipal knew that the heat of a day didn't necessarily give the warmth they were looking for. He always drew them close and kissed their foreheads when they told him this fact.

"Will it be close to Bhumi?" she finally asked.

"Rakesh said it wasn't far."

"Close enough to drive?"

"Maybe."

"And what about your papa?"

He narrowed his eyes at her. It hadn't occurred to him to consider his father. "You see how he is." Jaipal saw a half smile flash across her lips—one that seemed as heavy as a fifty-pound bag of rice to be lifted from the back room into the store, one filled with so much of the past's weight that it was less of a look of happiness and more of a curse.

"You're more like him than you think," she said. Words like a hot iron straight through him. "Making a decision and having us all follow it." After a moment she added, "So you'll leave him here?"

"You really want me to answer that? What do you want me to say?"

His mother said nothing. He couldn't help himself—he pushed his chair back with a hard scratch against the tile floor and let out the sharp sound of a grunt. How dare she compare him to that man. He could tell her: His father's drinking wasn't just drinking. His absence with them was presence with another. Jaipal knew all this.

"You know what he did when he was out of the house? You know where he went?"

"Beta. Please," she said, raising a hand to him to stop. She closed her eyes in a grimace and looked away.

"You should know," Jaipal said with an air of benevolence.

She turned back toward him and her eyes flared open with anger. "You don't think I already know? You think he tried to keep it a secret? He never hid what he was doing. Not from me, not from our friends. I don't know who doesn't know."

The anger she shot back in return stunned him into silence. Jaipal looked at his mother and wondered, for the first time, what she knew of him, the knowledge she kept hidden away.

"You're asking if we'll leave without him. If we have to, that's what we'll do. How can I tell you what it feels like to be bound by marriage? To feel like I'm leaving him behind, when he left me years ago, when he left me every night? I'll keep him now, and I'll keep him until he leaves me for the last time."

Jaipal swallowed around the lump of embarrassment and shame

in his throat. Oh, he knew what it meant to be left behind. Of course he did.

Jaipal wanted to reach out his hand through the gap between them and touch all that she felt, to claim it as something they shared. He wanted to clear the silence. He took a deep breath and walked to the stove to offer a cup of chai. His mother reached for her cup and swirled around whatever was left in it. She nodded in silent agreement.

In the kitchen, he boiled a tea bag along with water, milk, sugar, and a few cardamom pods. A vague sense of guilt lingered. He had spent his life watching and trying to grasp the lives of others, but it seemed that this ability ended at his home's wrought-iron gate. He saw his mother only as his mother, knew nothing of who she was. All he could clearly think of was what he'd wanted from her for all these years: he had a deep yearning to be seen, and not at all in the way his father saw him.

He walked a mug over to his mother and sat down with his own. "We'll see," he said. "Rakesh said we're just hoping. We'll see if anything comes of this."

"Hope," she replied in a quiet voice. She let out a small laugh and shook her head before taking a slurp of her tea.

There was nothing left to say about it. They had to wait for Rakesh's answer. Departure could be his to have. Though his mother had thrown into question the issue of her and his father, the air still felt conspiratorial: there was a plan, a destination, and even though it had come out all wrong, it was just him and his mother now—no one else to come between them.

HE HAD BEEN KEEPING TO HIS LONELY ROUTINE AT THE STORE FOR A few weeks. There was still no news from Rakesh, no word from the Canadians. Phone calls made to the High Commission or to his office were left unreturned or with vague assurances of good news being around the corner.

The store was nothing more than a half-empty vending machine: chips and soda, assorted snacks. His cigarette and chimbi customers had simply gone on to the next, looking for their cheap fix elsewhere. He thought of Maqbool and, to a lesser extent, the life that preceded him. He saw it all as a dream in such vivid color that he swore he never could have truly lived it.

Strangely, the store was filled with ants. Every day there would be a new column coming in from the doorway, fanning into a scattershot array. And every day, for the better part of an hour, he would clean them up.

He dipped his mop and killed a few hundred of them, dipped the mop again and killed a few hundred more. Perhaps it was his proximity to death and departure, but he wondered if this was how God felt. The remaining ants scattered, sending themselves over the tile scuffed from years of soles. The floor must have seemed like an endless plain to them: somewhere, there must have been a chance for escape. There was none. Power could never be wielded without consequence: to clean was to kill. He picked up his mop and drowned the twitching stragglers attached to the mop's braided head by washing them away in a bucket of bleach water.

After the mop came the bristle broom. With the front door opened a crack, he swept the rest out of the store. As he swept, some more ants were crushed under his foot, while others were flung onto the footpath. Yes, this was exactly what God felt like: He, in his immense power, couldn't keep track of the tallies of the living and the dead.

Jaipal laughed at the thought, a rueful sound breaking the silence of an empty store. This was what the General felt, too: a gun, a speech, a death, and thousands scattered across the face of the earth.

As a kid, when his grades were slipping, he had been forced to go with his sister to the Carnegie Library. He sat at the table as she looked over the sheets, his hands fidgeting. She did his homework for him. For three weeks, top marks on everything. It took her no more than fifteen minutes of whispered dictation. And then, he would leave at fifteen minutes to four, when rugby gave way to football on the nearby pitch. He was mediocre at homework and mediocre at being a keeper, but at least there was the camaraderie of the field. His sister would stay, content with the quiet. She had read every book she could get her hands on. She browsed the shelves, always another book to check out. He never even had a library card.

Maybe if he had tried harder, the words would have come together. Maybe if he had sat with her, some of her would have rubbed off on him: the hard work, the late nights, the top marks. If he had done all that, his reward would have been the same fate as his sister's. He would unceremoniously have been dumped from university and sent off.

When the floor was cleaned and the ants drowned or swept away, all he felt was fear. Fear that the sliver of freedom he had once felt at the hotels had been taken from him forever—to have felt the possibilities of desire, only to have lost it.

Nothing whispered anymore, it all resounded, clear as a bell rung three times: leave, leave, leave. The door had been opened, ever so briefly, only to allow Bhumi to squeeze past. In a blink of an eye, it had shut in front of him. Maqbool had tried to find his own escape, and was lost forever. Jaipal would try to break that door open. For him, and for his mother. He had to.

29

IT WAS CLOSE to noon on February 10, and Jaipal was eating lunch at the counter, a foil-wrapped roti parcel of aloo and matar that his mother had made that morning. There had been so many special bulletins, so many angry tirades and calm reassurances, so many meaningless announcements and rule-filled proclamations, that he barely registered the shift on the radio from music to the General.

"A few months ago, we conducted the Yellow-Card Census. There are fifty-two thousand Indians left in this country. They were brought here, and we had no say in the decision. They came to this country as vulagi, brought to till the cane planted by the Empire. And they did. Then they left the cane fields, and they became merchants and taxi drivers, they bought buses and shops. Have they shared their bounty with the rest of us? No!

"For too long we have let our own country slip from our hands. I returned our government back to our people. And now, I give you one promise: this nation will be forever for its native sons and daughters.

"Many years ago, the Indians came here to plant the sugar. Our people have told me, in one clear voice: The sugar has been planted. The Indians must leave.

"All Indians must depart by the the first of April. There will be no exceptions. Their greedy mouths have drunk the milk of our nation, but their hands have never fed the cow. I will be ordering the high commissioners from all the nations of the Commonwealth to immediately come to Government House. This is their problem now."

"What the fuck?" Jaipal said out loud. He waited for the broadcast to repeat all over again. And when it did, he listened closely to the words that came from the radio. April first. Everyone must leave.

He swallowed hard and looked outside. Home. He had to go home.

The soldiers were out in full force, patrolling the streets in pairs. There wasn't a cloud in the sky, and Jaipal had kept the front door open for some air. On Queen's Street, a truck passed by slowly. From its mounted bullhorn, an announcement came clearly through the open door.

"All shops must remain open until the allotted time for closure. Today's closing time is seventeen hundred hours. Failure to adhere to this requirement will result in a fine, jail time, or both."

He was stuck at the shop for another five hours. Small gnats were circling in front of the till. Nothing else had come through the door that day, and there probably weren't going to be any more after that announcement. He could feel the panic rise up through the city like heat waves from the asphalt.

His initial disbelief was giving way. It was happening.

Jaipal felt his heart flutter in his chest and the sweat slick his palms. He could already imagine giving up the shop. He could already imagine leaving it behind forever. He could taste it, the freedom that could be his.

He picked up the phone and dialed Rakesh's number, a number memorized from his previous calls. He heard the tone of a busy signal before the call dropped. He tried the Canadian High Commission. Same thing. He tried to call home, and the phone rang and rang.

He had four more hours left.

The other side of hope was a cruel truth, leaving a metallic taste in his mouth like blood: Maqbool had only been a month away from departure. His arrest, disappearance, and in all likelihood, death (as with the others, there was no body) would have never happened had he put away his incessant need to be in charge of his own life with some crazy idea. His life had been snuffed out because he refused to wait in line, wouldn't let anyone tell him what to do.

And if he had waited, Jaipal would have taken his hand in his. They could have left together. Where they found new land, the sun would be shining—not the light framed by a window, not the glow from a streetlamp, and not the pinholes of light in a hotel ballroom. Together, they would have had what they wanted. Maqbool had never been patient. To bend the world to his own will was to always risk the pain of recoil, of it all going back toward him.

Jaipal knew that everyone was now coming to grips with this new world. Everyone he knew had been born on the island and most of them had thought they would die on the island. Here came the General, saying that none of them had the right to live in a country that they had called home.

The hours passed, slowly. He watched the gnats circle, he watched the soldiers march. The sun took its transit toward the sea. A few people came into his store. They said nothing. Cigarettes, they said. Two packs. Didn't care about the cost. It was that kind of day—smoke 'em if you got 'em. Jaipal smoked one after another. The gnats, the soldiers, the sun.

Maqbool was gone. And so was every single one of the men and women he had met at the Ambassador. They'd all had return tickets. It was so simple for them to leave, a quick blink of an eye from an airplane. When they arrived at home, they would hear familiar accents and then they would walk into their homes or their little apartments, the air so stale from windows shut for days or weeks upon end.

It was different for the Indians. Jaipal would leave this country, and on the other end would be some unknown home that he would have to make as he went along. His life had been one long vacation that he wasn't aware of, until now. Home had been out there, waiting for this day, waiting for the moment he would leave to find it.

The hollow of his heart, where there lay all the misspent love for Maqbool, Portia, and the others, echoed with a new feeling: a resolution. Yes, yes, he thought, none of this was his home anymore.

It felt right, somehow. Home had never felt like home for Jaipal. It was an empty shell, where fragments of feelings crashed into a heaviness defined by his father's anger. His sister had sidestepped that anger, somehow using his mother and her own wits to carve a life for herself. Jaipal thought with resentment that it was easy to stand up tall when there was someone to help you up, when there was no one trying to keep you down.

A country could never be a home. It was a place. Draw a border around wherever he felt desired again, and call that place home. And it would be.

By the end of the day his throat felt raw from the cigarettes he had smoked. Before he left, the shrill ringing of the rotary phone sounded behind the counter.

"He's getting worse," his mother said.

"Ma? Are you okay? I called earlier. No one picked up."

"It's your father. We were listening to the radio together. I didn't think he was awake. He heard everything, Jaipal. Come home soon."

He rushed home after work. "Ey! Jaipal!" his father called out from bed when Jaipal walked in, his voice sounding as hoarse as that of a beggar.

Jaipal entered the room, lit only by a small bedside table lamp, its dim orange light casting most of his father into shadow. His father's eyes seemed clear, glassy, but not, for once, from drink. They were searching, already looking upon the life that awaited him at the end of the one he had lived.

His lips were dry and he kept trying to lick them to begin to speak, and it was obvious that this brought no satisfaction. Jaipal grabbed the glass of water from the nightstand and tried to bring it to his father's lips.

"No, no," he said, raising a thin and shaking hand to shoo him off. "Promise me you'll never leave this country."

"What?" Jaipal asked. The request made no sense.

When he and Bhumi had been children, every Sunday, his father had gone from room to room before dawn to force everyone awake, his fist pounding on their doors. His father would drive the family north to the little port town of Waidiva on the bumpy gravel road that ringed the island. Waidiva had the country's only marina, where the monthly dues meant that only foreigners used it to dock their sailboats and yachts on their jaunts around the South Pacific.

His father's only extravagance for the family: Sunday lunch at the yacht club. Even as a child, Jaipal saw how he would look to the foreigners there. It was a look of a man born in a colony, of someone who wanted to imagine himself as something more than a brown man on a small island.

"I see the weather is quite hot in Melbourne!" his father would say to a white foreigner whose life on the water was evidenced by his red and leathery skin. "Oh, is it?" the gora would respond in a surprised and hesitant way. "Haven't been there in months." These white people came to the island to be charmed by the beaches and the natives. Indians were a curiosity, but really just an annoyance to be shooed off.

"They're going to try to make you leave," Jaipal's father said now, his voice like a rickety axle on a bicycle. "Don't leave."

"We don't have a choice."

"Then come back. This will all pass and you can come home," he said, the hoarseness rattling around in his throat like a dying engine. "No better fish than the ones in your stream."

Jaipal shook his head in disbelief. "All you ever wanted to do was leave the country. Don't you remember?"

"Goddamn it, Jaipal, you never listened to me. Listen to me now, you think it's easy?" His father's whole body was shaking now, and his eyes, still glassy, looked wild and wide. They searched for something beyond Jaipal.

"My father's father, he was the one who came here," his father said. "He was happy once, some stupid happy fuck in some little village in India. Then he came here and tasted what being poor could be like. He fought for us, made the store. Do you know how to fight for yourself?"

"Fight who?"

"You're my boy. I loved you always. I never kicked you out of my house. Not even when I learned about your life. Stay here. You'll forget about me and your family if you leave. And you can be something here. They'll break you over there. I'm not being cruel, boy, I'm being honest. You're not strong like your grandfather. That's why I worked. You can keep the money from our family. Stay here. Promise me," he said, seeming out of breath from his speech.

Jaipal saw the energy drain from his face as his eyes shut. For the first time, Jaipal thought, he could raise a hand to his father, and it would break him forever.

Nothing had to keep on. Everything could stop.

"I promise," he said, feeling the lie flow out of him. There would be no argument and no violence. It would be a final conversation on Jaipal's terms: the dead and the dying deserved to hear whatever they wanted.

Now his legs were moving, taking him backward, out of the room.

His father grew smaller, weaker, eyes closed, body nothing more than a collection of dust. Jaipal stood on the threshold of the room, half of him in and half out, a precipice teetering perfectly between past and present.

His eyes focused upon the look on his father's face. Jaipal saw the stillness of it all, like the coolness of a Formica counter in an empty shop. Defeat. His father let out a moan, a low animal sound that Jaipal had never before heard, yet he knew meant one thing: he had already passed away from this life, and it was a matter of hours now. He took one last step out of the room.

That night, his father died in his sleep.

30

THE MORNING IT all fell apart, Raj and Farida were arguing in the kitchen. Bhumi couldn't believe what they were saying: the General was going to kick out every single Indian from the island. Raj thought it was nonsense, but Farida thought it was true, and Bhumi wondered, why would the General do something so stupid? She found herself on Raj's side.

There was one way to settle the argument. She left for the corner store and bought a copy of the *Mercury News*. Page G10, a small block in the middle of the international section. And Bhumi could hear the General's voice loud and clear in the quote featured in the article: "All Indians must depart by the first of April. There will be no exceptions. Their greedy mouths have drunk the milk of our nation, but their hands have never fed the cow. I will be ordering the high commissioners from all the nations of the Commonwealth to immediately come to Government House. This is their problem now."

It had all happened a few days ago, the rumors stalking the fringes of the community until more and more confirmed reports brought its cold reality to the center. Raj mentioned that Island Cash and Curry was going to host some announcement later that day.

In the interim, Bhumi took to walking up and down Mission Boulevard, stopping only to buy another pack of Marlboro Lights. She walked until the arches of her feet throbbed in her worn-down trainers. She didn't want to tell Vikram anything—not yet. Not until she knew what it all meant.

She made her way to Island Cash and Curry around noon and found a curious setup outside the store's entrance. The table and telephone from inside the store had been brought outside. The phone was off the hook and placed next to a microphone hooked into a receiver. On the ground sat a pair of worn bookshelf speakers with their cones peeking through torn fabric. A crowd of what looked like fifty people had formed a half circle around it.

Bhumi tapped the shoulder of a woman on the outside of the circle to ask what was going on. The woman was one of the nannies Bhumi saw on the train, but she struggled to remember her name. The woman told her that some Canadian minister was going to make a speech. Jagdish had arranged for someone in Vancouver to hold his phone next to the radio speaker as the minister spoke. They were all gathering to listen to the call.

The whispers in the crowd crested and faded like a sine wave. Then the sound of a man clearing his throat came through the speakers, and everyone hushed.

"I've just spoken with my colleagues in Wellington, Canberra, and London," the man began. He sounded as serious as a grimace and had a voice like a newsreader's: confident, with each syllable enunciated clearly and slowly. "It is clear what is occurring in the South Pacific has the potential to be nothing less than a human-rights crisis. After prolonged discussion with the ambassador, it is becoming clear that the military government will move forward with the expulsion of the island's remaining Indian citizens.

"That small island nation is part of what we call the Commonwealth. This is not simply a sporting association or a name. It's a shared history that binds and connects our nations to one another. What was once the relation of city and colony is now a shared destiny of equals. We will do what we must.

"We are prepared to offer an honorable place in Canadian life for all the expelled Indians willing to come to Canada to work here and build industrious lives. We have reserved twenty thousand visas for Indian refugees. My colleagues in Wellington, Canberra, and London have assured me that they also will be offering at least a similar number of visas. These visas will be available both to those currently residing and also to those displaced prior to the formal expulsion order.

"This is only a beginning. We must work together to ensure that those who come to Canada as refugees are not only accepted and integrated into our society, but will also thrive as productive citizens. That is perhaps the best way to combat the hatred and bigotry of their current junta government: with welcoming arms."

As the sound of the minister's speech quieted, a silence like a hoar frost settled upon the crowd. Bhumi, like all the people next to her, was drawn into herself as she tried to process what she had heard.

Suddenly a loud whoop emerged from the crowd. People began to embrace each other as tears formed in their eyes.

"Papers!" Bhumi heard someone yell. "No more waiting!"

A wiry man with salt-and-pepper hair, turned to the woman in front of Bhumi. "My cousins are in Australia. Maybe I can join them!"

Bhumi saw how the crowd surged with the joy of the fantasy. The exhaustion of their daily grind was now cut through with the dreams of a new life, of a new place, of a country where papers could come easy, where they wouldn't live under the knife of a possible deportation.

Bhumi felt a curious mixture of joy and dread.

She would stay. California had never been her choice, but here there was a life: Vikram, Professor Lifschitz, possibilities around the corner. Her asylum hearing hadn't been scheduled, but the professor kept mentioning that she would help find a way for her to apply to college.

No. She would go. California had never been her choice, and here there was only chance and kindness: a seed can cross an ocean looking for the right piece of land to take root—washing ashore didn't mean finding a place to finally thrive. It was better to wait, better to have the tide carry it out again past the breakers, where it could leave to look for the right place to call home.

The crowd slowly formed into a line to make joyous calls. A few people carried the telephone and the table back into the store. Jagdish hovered outside, his neon-green nylon windbreaker standing out like a highlighter in the crowd.

"Five minutes maximum per call," he announced to the crowd as he rubbed the hair on his chin. He had a smile as big as a whale.

An hour and a half passed, and the light, diffused by the clouds in the sky, began to darken. In the parking lot, the orange streetlights turned on and cast long shadows between the cars. Each person in line made their phone call and walked out of the store not with the meek stature of the beaten-down, but with the confidence of one who had a new future tucked underneath their arm like a newspaper.

Soon it was Bhumi's turn to make a call. She noted down her start time on the pad of paper, its reserve of pages running low from the volume of calls. No one seemed to be having issues making calls today. Maybe the bad lines had been a cruel trick played by the General on them all. She picked up the receiver and dialed her home's telephone number—

"Hello? Jaipal? Listen, I can only talk for five minutes," Bhumi replied, impatient to share the good news. "Did you hear the news from the Canadian minister?"

"Bhumi," he replied, sounding tired. "Something happened to Papa."

"What?" Bhumi asked. She felt her pulse quicken and each breath shorten.

"He—he," Jaipal stammered. "He died the night the General announced the expulsion."

She wasn't sure of what she had heard—the static on the call must have scrambled his words, she thought.

"He had an attack, after the General made the announcement about the expulsion order."

She felt dizzy, stuck in a telescopic view zooming away from the sound of her brother's voice.

"I'm sorry, Bhumi. We should have told you, you should have known. He hadn't been doing good since you left. And then, this was all so sudden."

Bhumi, stunned into silence, said nothing.

"It's just, sometimes," Jaipal began, speaking faster and faster, "it feels like for us, all of us, it's easier to not say anything, instead of worrying each other."

"It's true," Bhumi said, wishing she were next to her brother, feeling a tenderness she hadn't ever felt. The clock continued to go down. She only had a few more minutes. "It's not your fault. It's who we are."

"We can be more now," Jaipal said in a faint voice, the statement sounding more like a question built of his unsteady resolve.

Bhumi nodded, forgetting her silent agreement couldn't be telegraphed across the wires to her brother.

"Is it true?" she asked. "Is he gone?"

"He's gone," Jaipal said quietly.

Bhumi was crying softly now. In her rose no feelings of sadness, no deep remorse; instead, she could breathe. "Why did he always . . . ," she said, her question drifting off.

"I don't know, Bhumi. I don't know."

"It was like he always had fun with it. Like he needed to hate me." She couldn't summon the strength to speak with confidence; everything came out like a prayer sent into the night.

"It's what he did. Same with me. Always. I don't know why." It was like they were back at the water's edge, convincing each other that everything was fine, that everything wasn't a negotiation between someone's hatred and someone's plotting.

"We always had the coconut man," Jaipal said. Bhumi could see him behind his cart, splitting coconuts into two with his machete.

"And the chickens."

"And the sea turtle, in the water that turned blue."

"The water that turned blue. I can't believe we swam in the night. It was so dark," she said, tears drying up. She dabbed her eyes with her fingertips and took in a deep breath through her mouth. "You'll be here soon. You'll be safe."

"And you'll be there?" Jaipal asked.

"I'll be at the airport to meet you," she replied, purposefully vague, a feeling in the pit of her stomach that there were no more right answers.

"Something happened a couple months ago," Jaipal said. "Like what happened to you. They fucking took Maqbool. I don't know where they took him. We had this thing at the hotel. They know about me," he said, the words pouring out.

"Oh, Jaipal," Bhumi said. Her brother had never told her anything about this part of his life, but she had always known. She could follow his gaze, see where it landed, no matter the person. She had never pushed him to tell her anything. Theirs was the closeness of presence, of unspoken secrets kept that way—the agreement between two siblings to protect what was hidden from the rest. They didn't have much time left on their call. Even so, she didn't want to rush him.

"Is this all our fault?" he asked. "If Papa wasn't Papa. And if Ma wasn't Ma. And if they loved us and we loved them, would this still have happened? You've always been able to figure everything out. Tell me."

"This isn't our fault. None of this is," Bhumi said.

"You believe that?"

"Of course I do. Are you safe? Is everything okay?" she asked, genuinely feeling afraid for her brother.

"It's fine. I'm going to Vilimaji soon. I wish it was to visit you," he said.

Her time was up. They said their goodbyes, and the line went dead. Bhumi sat there for a brief moment, breathing softly, the world spinning all around her.

THAT NIGHT, SHE DID NOT EAT. SHE TOLD VIKRAM SHE WASN'T FEEL-ing well. Raj and Farida somehow had already found out about her father. They let her sleep in their bed that night. In the dark she couldn't tell whether she was lying still or moving.

He is dead.

This death lacked the sorrow, the rage, the dramatic action, of Aarti's death. It felt right. The past was shrinking to where it belonged.

Still, it had a strange ring to it. *He is dead*. For so long, he had been completely of the realm of *he is*. He is angry. He is drunk. He is slapping her across the face. He is taking a ceramic bowl of Bhumi's mother's cooking and throwing it across the room. He is laughing as Bhumi's mother picks up the pieces of her bowl and mops up her cooking. Later, he is fucking, loudly, grunting while her mother never makes a sound. He is, he is, he is: He is dead. He was.

Was she supposed to feel sad? Angry? Relieved?

She felt none of those things. All she felt was the visual trick: was she moving backward or standing still?

Her scar felt hot as she ran her finger up and down its ridges, its glossy smoothness feeling out of place next to unharmed skin. She had lived. She had gone to SPU. She had left the country. She is her mother's daughter. Her mother is her father's wife. Her father is dead.

She fell asleep as she circled around these words and simple sentences like water whirling into a drain.

It was a heavy and dark sleep, filled with half-formed and blurry images that disappeared as soon as Bhumi woke up and her eyes squinted against the light outside the window. The bitter passion of a lifetime spent alongside that man had turned itself into a night fever, sending her heart dancing against her chest. The bed was wet with her sweat. The dreadful weight remained.

She had recently read about the spikemoss *Selaginella lepidophylla*. It was a small plant, native to the deserts of Mexico. It was nothing more than a bit of green that stuck to the desert floor, no more than a foot or two across, with small fernlike leaves. What made it special was that the *Selaginella lepidophylla* was one of the few known resurrection plants.

In times of drought, its leaves dried down to crispy brown bits, before it curled itself into a tight ball. In the blinding heat and light of the desert, the plant looked dead to all but the keen botanist. Its secret was that it concentrated its sucrose into those dead-looking leaves, causing it to enter a state of near suspended animation. When exposed to just the smallest bit of water, it would revive, by reopening and dramatically bursting back into a living and green thing once more. It had such an intense reanimation that the Spanish missionaries used it to explain the concept of being born again.

Ever since she had quit her first job, she had been feeding her spikemoss drip by drip. Her roots took it greedily and her leaves stretched out with the morning sun. The dead past was slowly falling away and the future that would grow from this decay was filled with choices she wasn't ready to make.

31

WHEN JAIPAL'S FATHER died in the middle of the night, he and his mother left the body in the bed. Everything, by order of the General, was closed during off hours. A new truth: His father was no longer his father. He was a body lying in his mother's room. The fact entered his thoughts as if someone had punched him in the head, stunning him, warping his vision.

Jaipal had called his uncle, the cane farmer, who came over almost immediately. Ashwin Mama and Jaipal's mother sat underneath the house, where his father used to sit, and Jaipal could hear his low chatter and her cries filter up through the floorboards, their sounds filling the house like ghosts eager to take residence.

He was surprised at how much she was crying. He wondered whether it was because her husband was dead or that she had lost the project that had defined every day of the past few months.

He shook his head at the audacity of his own thought. He had become cruel without realizing it.

He couldn't sleep. That night, he tried to keep his eyes from the hallway, though they kept being drawn to look toward the open door in anticipation of some sound's emerging from that silenced space. A list of tasks now sprawled out in front of him, and Jaipal drank cup after cup of chai to try to find the energy to keep himself up. Indians were lining up before dawn for same-day visa interviews in the capital. Unlike them, he had to call the funeral service. The car came rather quickly and they picked up the body. He called the temple, scheduled the last rites.

It was a testament to the normalcy of death that the funeral was so easy to arrange, even as everything rushed to fall apart.

Even so, there was supposed to be a rhythm to mourning and this had been taken away from him. Friends and family were supposed to come, bring food, sit with him and his mother, cry with them. Others were supposed to help plan for the funeral rites. A death was a way to bring everyone together. And it did, for a moment.

Soon, there was no one left to come.

Word moved quickly. The phone calls came in, one after another. "I'm sorry," they said. They would share a memory—"I remember," they would begin.

Jaipal had forgotten these parts of his father. There were other versions of that man, and the one he was at home wasn't the one the rest of the world saw. He was good to those outside the family, sweet as a jalebi. To them, he had a dry sense of humor, an interest in those around him, a belief in education. To his credit, even if he had hated Jaipal's sister, he had never once hesitated with fees or costs or anything associated with his or Bhumi's schooling.

Giving, giving, giving, and then something in him broke, and that drove him out to drink and fuck. He came home to give his family his worst.

After the announcement from the Canadian minister, the phone calls always ended with an apology. All hell had broken loose across the island. Indians were leaving their homes and getting to Vilimaji as quickly as they could. They had to get their papers: passports to be used once and never again, visas from the High Commissions for the United Kingdom, New Zealand, Australia, and Canada. It all meant that no one could come over. They had to tend to their own, to go figure out whatever came next.

Jaipal and his mother were the only two present for the funeral rites at the temple. The front of the mandir was a three-story trapezoidal tower striated with stone carvings of miniature columns painted in a kaleidoscope of pastel colors. Behind the tower was a large open court-yard, with several small buildings to house the individual murtis. At nine in the morning, the sun cast long shadows from these buildings across the courtyard. Jaipal had spent so many hours under the center canopy for countless pujas, but today they were under an entirely separate section at the far end of the courtyard. Death was kept in its tidy corner.

The pandit, shirtless with his rolls of fat spilling over the top of his saffron dhoti, said what he needed to say in a language Jaipal couldn't understand. The pandit's holiness was brought down to earth by a tic: every few minutes, he would scratch a hairy mole the size of a fifty-cent piece on his shoulder.

Jaipal's father's body was wrapped in a shroud. Sometimes, Jaipal was told to walk around, to place rice on the body, to tie a red string on a toe. He completed these commands like a sleepwalker, not fully aware of what was going on, unable to be shaken awake.

From the temple, the funeral service took the body in their black van (hand-painted with the name of the service on the side; every-thing was a chance to advertise) to the crematorium. The crematorium was only a half block away from the temple—the only people who cremated bodies were the island's Hindus.

Jaipal thought it strange that they still had to drive the body for two minutes. The staff at the crematorium was down to one, the operator, an old Indian man hunched over in his age, his hair wisps at the temples. He took the body. It was gone, out of their sight.

Jaipal and his mother returned to the temple. The priest said more things in Sanskrit. Then finally came the time when it was all over, and it was time to pray. His mother seemed to know what to do. She kneeled down in front of Ram and Sita. He watched her fold her hands and place them on her forehead. Even from a distance, he could see how the concrete underneath her darkened with pea-size splotches. She had been crying, on and off, through the morning.

They hadn't talked at all in the past day.

Jaipal stopped in front of Krishna. He'd always had a fondness for him. He probably knew what Jaipal felt: it was never only him and Radha. There were always the gopis—even the divine knew the possibilities of attention from others.

The murti was seated, shirtless, legs crossed under a saffron dhoti with a red border. He wore a garland of flowers, carried his flute.

Jaipal stared into his eyes before closing his own. He didn't kneel down to pray. It felt like the words were slipping away from him, emptiness where feeling should have sat. The sentences began to string together, disparate words without links. Strength, tired, money, don't know, fear, have to do it alone.

Jaipal's world seemed to sit on an edge that he was supposed to jump off, blindly. He wanted someone to at least let him know how far the height, but this was a luxury. He had to take that next step, that flying leap.

He felt his mother's hand on his shoulder.

At the crematorium, he was handed a small wooden box—it was all that was left of the figure that had towered above his life. They walked through the street, which was eerily empty, most of the stores not only closed but with shutters down or padlocks and chains placed across their doors.

The General had finally lifted the mandatory open-close requirements to let the Indians get their papers. Even this he had laced with cruelty. The military was guarding the lines around the embassies and the high commissioners' offices, but they left the highways empty. Over the past day had come news of gangs waiting near the sides of the road. If they saw someone driving alone or with one other person, they dragged them out of the car. They stole the gold off the women, the wallets off the men.

For now, Jaipal and his mother walked east, toward the highlands, the sun hanging over the thicket that lined their hills. They walked toward the river Majivu, where the first Indians had chosen to place the remains of their dead, and where the waters would take his father's ashes to the sea.

The grass stopped at the small ledge that separated the bank from the river. At this time of the year, the river was swollen with rainwater, the current moving swiftly. He hopped down to the muddy shore while his mother waited, and kneeled close to the flow of the hazy gray-green water. His knees sank into the softness of the clay. Further away, he could hear the snorts of the wild pigs digging through the trash carried by the river—plastic bottles, empty chip wrappers, packs of cigarettes.

He opened the box and was surprised to find that his father looked nothing like the fluttering remains of wood ash, but was instead clumped together like coarse gray sand flecked with white.

He poured the remains into the water, which rippled out from the disturbance. He remembered what Maqbool had told him: bodies have power.

There was nothing left. His father had gone from being a flesh-and-blood terror to being nothing more than a whisper, and finally to being nothing at all. His petty hatred, his disgusting desires, his last request, Jaipal's lie in response—none of it mattered anymore. He was floating away, gone forever from the river and into the ocean. In these last moments, a flash of resolve: his father was wrong. There was nothing left of him to hold Jaipal back.

He turned, leaving the small box by the waters, to be taken or left as trash. When it was all over he felt hollow and tired, so tired. There was still more to be done.

THAT NIGHT, HE AND HIS MOTHER SAT AND SWIRLED THEIR TORN-off bits of roti into the curry left for them by one of his mother's cousins, a quick gift before they left for the capital. Neither of them were hungry. Still, they had to sit, they had to figure something out. They needed to receive an official visa from the Canadian High Commission to leave the country. Jaipal would leave the next day in a caravan of coaches bound for the capital.

Caravans were an effective answer to the highway violence, but they weren't foolproof. All passengers had to carry a knife or a cricket bat. If a gang took over the bus, there at least would be a fight. Jaipal had heard a rumor that the military had come to break up one such fight and in the ensuing melee shot two people in the back as they fled.

Jaipal had packed an overnight bag: his passport, his mother's passport, some cash, a kitchen knife wrapped in a tea towel, and a few T-shirts. He would leave before dawn, hopefully come back in a few days.

His mother was looking at him, glancing upward from her meal with a nervous fear—the worry lines creasing across her forehead, emanating from the corners of her eyes. She dipped her roti and set it down, only to pick it up again, and then, finally, eat it with a half-hearted bite, a nibble on a broken corner.

The house was quiet, deadened, and in this silence, he could feel what his mother felt with a blaring clarity. Every look said the same thing: *I've lost my daughter, I've lost my husband, and now, my firstborn leaves.*

He reached across the table and touched her hand, holding her delicate fingers. He couldn't remember the last time he had held his mother's hand—surely it hadn't been since his childhood?

He watched as she began to cry, little tears joining together into rivulets down her cheeks.

Even without a complete knowledge of each other, he and his mother had been brought together in this life by some magic of chance, and this occasional presence, one for the other, was perhaps enough. It was enough feeling to get him talking.

"Do you remember the day Bhumi was bit by that dog?"

"Of course, how could I forget it?" she replied, slowly drawing her hand back toward her cold food.

Jaipal took in a little breath for sustenance. "Papa wasn't at the shop. You weren't at home. Why did you—" He caught the lump in his throat and swallowed it down. "Did you forget about me?"

He saw such a brokenhearted look on her face that he could feel her strength breaking down with the realization that her son had nursed this sadness for most of his life.

"No, of course not," she said, a little too quickly. She turned away, looking through the doors to the balcony.

"I was here," Jaipal said quietly, his voice as tentative as the little boy left alone. "By myself."

His mother didn't take her eyes off the doors. "I didn't know your father wasn't going to come home. He left the hospital without even coming into Bhumi's room."

"I waited for someone to come. No one did."

"It was nighttime. I wanted to wait until Bhumi had gone to sleep, and once she did, I rushed home to check on you. You were asleep in your bed. I was surprised—such a young boy had come home and put himself to sleep! I knew then that you were different, that you could keep on your own. Your sister always needed someone to look after her."

Jaipal opened his mouth to say something, to say that she was wrong, to say that he couldn't keep on his own, to say that he didn't put himself to sleep. But she was right. On the other side of his fear and desperation was self-sufficiency—he had done all those things. There was still something more.

"Someone did come home though. I heard him. I heard the key in the lock and heard someone walking around. I hid in my closet. I was so scared, Ma."

"We gave a key to Raj Uncle and Farida Aunty. Was it one of them?" she said in an offhand way.

"No, I don't think so," he said. The answer had always been there, waiting for him to remember. The sound of drunken footfalls, his father coming home to check in on him in the only way he could, a toxic kind of love mixed up with that gaunt anger that always sat under the surface. He changed the subject. "I'm scared, Ma."

"I know, beta. I am too."

"What if something happens to me?"

His mother took in a deep breath. "I believe in you. You can handle anything they might do to you."

Amid all that could go wrong, Jaipal realized, now was the time to stop hiding. He could use this brief togetherness to make a full accounting of what he was.

"I want to tell you about what happened to Maqbool. I don't know what you heard. I want to tell you the truth now."

A look crossed his mother's face, a brief look of pain. Jaipal felt it say, *No more.* He paid it no mind, pressed on in his confession, his olive branch.

"He was selling cigarettes and chimbi that he got from the soldiers." His mother raised her eyebrows when he mentioned the drugs. "And he gave them to me, and I sold them at the store."

"Oh, beta," she said with a sigh. She smiled and reached out and held his hand. "What choice did you have? I'm sure your father didn't leave everything in the store. And what else is there to do now? We have to make what we can. I'm glad nothing happened to you."

"He took some money from them," Jaipal continued. "He didn't pay them right one time. And then, they found out, and they arrested him."

"Did they do anything to you?" she asked, squeezing the top of his hand slightly.

"They came to the store. They told me what happened. They took away the cigarettes and the chimbi. The bruise—it was them."

"God is good, God is good. They could have done more. Hai Ram," she said, shaking her head back and forth.

Jaipal pushed on further. "They did," he said.

She looked at him with confusion. "Did what?"

"Maqbool and I would go to this hotel, this empty hotel, together. And there would be other men, and we would be together," Jaipal said in a quiet voice. The thought crossed his mind to mention his father: how he knew, how he had been the first to tell him of the hotel. But he said nothing of it.

His mother shot up and walked to the doors leading to the balcony. She opened them with a jerk of her hands, the cool air of the night coming into the house, blowing the fringes of the tablecloth back and forth. She stood facing the night while Jaipal looked at her back, his heart sinking slowly down.

He joined her outside. The cacophony of summer's insects made their way through the dark. When he looked out at the streetlamp, he could see them cloud around its light.

"And the soldiers went to the hotel," Jaipal continued, forceful in his resolve. "They took Maqbool, and they took everyone there. Arjun, he was there. They took him too."

His mother began to shake her head, and he knew it wasn't a sign of relief at his safety. He touched her lightly on the shoulder. She recoiled. She turned around—she was crying, her eyes streaking red and becoming puffy, her cheeks not yet wet. And just like that, his love began to burn away like the black smoke from a ghee-soaked batti.

"I'll take you to Canada. I'll wait for Bhumi. I won't stay with you." Jaipal took a hard swallow and stared again at the activity in the orange glow.

"Of course people said things," she said distractedly, like she hadn't heard what he had just told her. "I thought those were rumors. My son would never do that. Why would he?"

"I have to look after myself now," Jaipal said, channeling Maqbool's resolve. "Papa is gone. At least he gave me work. I'll make sure you and Bhumi are safe, and then I'm going."

"Where will you go? You've never lived away from this house." Her words sounded accusing.

"London," he finally said through gritted teeth, his temper rising.

"How? Everything is set for Canada. Now you want to change to London?"

"I'll figure it out myself!" he shouted, and his words echoed throughout the neighborhood. The only reply was the continued buzzing, the occasional moth that flew toward them.

The stillness between them felt final, an end-stop to a rambling sentence. The quiet the two of them had shared at the dinner table hadn't been of understanding or comfort: it had simply been a prelude to this.

His home had been filled with secrets and silence, and the anguish created when these two mixed together. His father had turned to rage, his mother had turned to anxiety, Bhumi had turned to single-minded ambition, and it was Jaipal's turn now to take that anguish and hammer it into something new.

32

BHUMI HAD BEEN dreading this moment, but there was no getting around it. She had to tell Vikram. They were hiking through Garin Regional Park, which was just beyond Mission Boulevard. At points, the path was so muddy in the shade that it almost swallowed her shoe into the soft clay. Today, the day was clear, and the menthol from the groves of eucalyptus filled her nose like the salves her mother put on weary muscles. The hills had turned from their summer brown to a bright and lush green.

At a ridgeline, surrounded by the orange bells of hundreds of poppies growing among the lichen-covered outcroppings of limestone, she kissed him. "There's something I need to tell you."

He had that look of dread on his face that could only accompany words as banal and serious as *There's something I need to tell you.* "Yeah?" he asked with a forced smile.

"Back home, they're kicking us all out. Forcibly removing everyone. No Indian can stay."

"Holy fuck. Really? That's insane," he said, growing agitated and talking with his hands. "Is your family okay? Is anyone okay? How they fuck can they do that?"

"They're fine, I think," she said, avoiding mentioning her father. "All the Indians have to go *somewhere*, you know? So a few countries are offering us official refugee visas. Canada's one of them. My family's going up to Vancouver."

"I see," he said. He swallowed hard. He paused for a beat, nodding his head, clearly making the connection. "Does that mean you're going too?"

"I don't know, I really don't know. I want to go," she said, and she saw how his face fell. "I want to stay too."

"When do you need to make a decision by?"

"Soon. I think I'm going to apply for the visa, just in case, you know?"

"Yeah, of course, just in case, it can't hurt," he said quickly. "You should ask Professor Lifschitz. You should get a second opinion."

"Professor Lifschitz? Why?"

"She's helped so much so far, you know? Maybe she can give you advice about this."

They continued on with their hike. Something had been taken away from it, as if the moisture and the heat between them had been replaced by dry air.

"YOU'LL HAVE TO MAKE A CHOICE," PROFESSOR LIFSCHITZ SAID. Winston panted softly under her desk. "If you stay here, there's no timeline for when you'll finally get a hearing, right?"

"No, nothing yet. I think the expulsion finally got the INS's attention. The family I'm living with heard back this week, and a few others have heard back in the last day." The community was beginning to cleave: some were leaving, some had decided to stay. Bhumi had watched as Raj moved from driving to dispatch, though this now meant he worked the graveyard shift. The dream of buying a car and a taxi medallion felt closer than ever, and he wasn't ready to give that up and start again somewhere else.

"If you go to Canada, you'll have proper status and everything? They'll let you apply to university?"

"I think so. We won't be citizens, but it's something more official than what we have here."

"To me, the decision's made then. You can go there and start your studies over again. Vancouver is a wonderful city. I've been to a few conferences at UBC and UVic. Absolutely gorgeous area. Skiing right next to the water. And really, Canada is doing so much better than the U.S. when it comes to foreign policy. I think you'll do great."

Maybe it was being told what to do, but something about Professor Lifschitz's confidence pricked at Bhumi, brought up an inclination to be contrary. "If I stay here, I already have a position in your lab, and I'm already taking courses. If I leave, I'd have to start over."

"Bhumi," Dr. Lifschitz said, leaning her elbows onto her desk. "What does this all add up to? These are little pieces of scraps. You're being given a chance at something, and frankly, at something great. You can live in a beautiful place and have a shot at a world-class university. Your family will be there too. Of course I'll miss having you here, but I'm sure our paths will cross again. I don't see any downside to the opportunity being given to you."

"I wish I could stay," Bhumi said from the other side of the desk. The words surprised her—she had never been one to turn away from her own ambition, and yet, the previous months had taught her to slow down, to savor the small victories given to her.

The professor seemed to see right through her. "No you don't, Bhumi. This isn't what you wanted."

Her words were like sunlight. Bhumi's affection stretched out toward her, as far as it could go. "You're right. I just can't stop thinking about a few things." She bit her bottom lip and tapped her foot, the movements of her leg hidden under her desk. She wanted to be honest with her.

"My life has been divided into a before and an after," Bhumi continued. "The place where I grew up is gone, and now I'm stuck with everything I left behind. My accent. My way of standing and walking is different from everyone here. So is the way that I think, the way I see the world. I'm here now.

"Maybe you're right. Maybe it's time to start over again with something that gets me back to what I want."

Professor Lifschitz nodded, beaming with pride. "Just remember one thing. You belong in that classroom. You have a right to be in a lab. When I started studying, women weren't in the lab. And you know what? They'll always second-guess you. They'll question your sound conclusions. They'll explain posters you've presented back to you. They'll always confuse you with someone else, someone they can boss around. Remember, you belong there, Bhumi. I wish you luck. It's been a pleasure having you here for the past few months."

"Thank you," Bhumi said. She shook Professor Lifschitz's hand. "It really has been."

WHEN SHE RETURNED TO ISLAND CASH AND CURRY, THE ATMOSPHERE seemed more and more like a party—everyone needing something or somewhere to go—and at the center of it were Jagdish and his telephone system. People were coming in and out at all hours, placing calls and grabbing a bite to eat.

The scene was equally chaotic two doors down at the lawyer's storefront. He had filled the space with long folding tables and chairs. He knew next to nothing about the immigration laws of Canada, Australia, New Zealand, or the United Kingdom, but he did know the rules for navigating bureaucracy and filling out paperwork. He turned his office into a study hall, and he would wander the room with his hands folded behind his back, taking slow steps between groups of people, leaning over to answer any questions. For this, he was only charging $200—postage included—for all visa applications. She had only paid off her debt to him a few weeks ago.

The lawyer pulled Bhumi aside as she filled out her application.

"I've been doing some reading," the lawyer said in his slow and calculated voice, leaning over her shoulder as she wrote. "I think your application will be fast-tracked."

"Why?" Bhumi asked.

"I think those who have legal proof of employment are streamlined into the higher-tier visa. You might be the only one I've helped who has that."

Those sitting around her heard what the lawyer had to say, and even though they smiled and nodded, Bhumi felt separated from the others. For them, this was like how it had been a hundred years ago, when their foremothers had sat in a depot in India. They sang songs to pass the time with their new sisters and brothers as they waited for white officials to read over their contracts to labor in parts unknown. Even if she preferred to stand alone, there was a loneliness to her position, a feeling that her experiences kept her apart from everyone around her.

SHE WAS AMAZED WHEN IN THREE WEEKS, HER VISA APPLICATION had been processed and approved. They had affixed the visa to the empty pages of her passport. She had travel papers that granted her the ability to move outside a country that would never take her back. At Vancouver International Airport, there would be a bus shuttle service that would take her to the Refugee Arrival Center. Like all the other people with higher-tier R-star visas, she could stay at the Arrival Center until she found it necessary to leave.

When she had applied for this visa, she had included a note explaining that she "would like to resume her studies in botany, as they were interrupted." On the bottom of her letter, some faceless bureaucrat had written by hand: "Check out UBC and Simon Fraser." It was a jarring bit of humanity in what she had thought was going to be an automated process.

Receiving the letter left her with a strange mix of joy and dread. She met up with Vikram at his apartment. He sat quietly in the half light, his face divided into shadow by the room's sole floor lamp. He wore his anxiety in a way that couldn't be ignored, eyes downcast, his eyebrows knit into sorrow.

"What's wrong?" Bhumi asked, knowing the answer to her own question. She had always been the one lost to her anxieties. Now she wanted to hear him speak, to have a chance to lighten his burden.

"I don't want you to leave," he said with a deep breath. He closed his eyes and looked so small and slumped over. Bhumi kissed him, slowly, and she could feel how his lips were searching, a need made fierce.

"I—I," Vikram stammered. "I want to say this before you go. I think I'm falling in love with you."

Bhumi was stunned. She hadn't thought that Americans were actually like how they were in the movies: quick to say I love you without recognizing the ferocity and the sacrifice—the pain—that love entailed. An old line of poetry her mother had picked up from a magazine: "Ek aag ka dariya hai, aur doob ke jana hain." *Love is a river of fire, and you have to dive through it.*

She kissed him again. "We're going out tonight," Bhumi said as she pulled away. She couldn't bear the thought of staying in tonight, of being stuck in an atmosphere of love and mourning. "No one is dying. No one is leaving right now. Let's just go do something." She walked to his front door. As she did, she straightened her back just a little bit to reveal a confidence and swagger, a performance of happiness, for him.

"Going where?"

"Out. Let's get a drink. My palms were itching today. Good news is around the corner for us," Bhumi said with a smile, thinking of her mother. "Let's just go to the Puzzle. Keep it simple."

"I don't feel like it," Vikram began to say. "Maybe you should just go without me."

"Do it for me?" she asked with a smile.

"Are you sure?"

"Let's go," she said, motioning to the door. "You'll feel better."

She saw Vikram hesitate before he got up slowly. "Okay," he said.

They walked out of the apartment. The late winter sun had already set. She looked over at Vikram. Even in shadow, she could see that he still had a shifty-eyed look of nervousness on his face. Bhumi knew better than to try to coax him into conversation. Not yet, at least.

Prince played in the background at the Puzzle. Bhumi walked up to the bar and bought herself a Budweiser Light and him a Corona. "Let's sit in a booth," she said, leading them to an empty one opposite the bar. Vikram sank into the vinyl, his shoulders looking so tight.

Bhumi leaned across the table and placed her hand into Vikram's palm. He folded his hand around hers and, in that moment of relaxation, began to cry. Bhumi kept her hand outstretched until Vikram's tears dimmed to a sniffle. Once she was sure that the feeling had passed, Bhumi leaned back into her seat and took a sip of her beer.

Vikram let out a sigh and wiped his face with a bar napkin. "Sorry. Crying in public. It's not like me. I'm just so nervous. What if I never see you again?"

Bhumi saw him begin to tighten up again. She looked over her shoulder, then around the bar. "Do you want to dance?" she asked.

"Now?"

"I want to dance with you. I don't know what tomorrow will bring. I don't know if I'm staying or going. I want to be with you right now, and I want to feel you when we dance," Bhumi said firmly.

"I don't know."

"Listen," Bhumi said, leaning into the conversation with her forearms resting against the table. "All I want to do is be who I am right now, and be that way as much as I can. I spent so many years reading and studying. I thought my work could give me strength. It was like I could only be successful if I cut myself off from everything and focused on my studies. And that worked back home. Everything is backward here. I can't just rely on myself. I have to be part of the world."

Bhumi took a long sip of her beer. Her leg was furiously bouncing up and down under the table. "I don't know if any of that makes sense. It's just what I think. Do you want to dance?"

Vikram bit his bottom lip, face knit into focus. "No, no, it makes sense. I think." He moved to get up. "Let's dance?"

"Set," Bhumi said.

The Psychedelic Furs' "Pretty in Pink" played from a record. No one else joined them on the dance floor, but no one bothered them either. They danced for a few songs, had another drink, and went back to Vikram's, all the while Bhumi feeling the self-satisfaction of taking him out of a funk, if only for a night.

It felt like years had passed since Aarti had come into her room and announced that they were going out. She had lost so much since then, but she had also gained what she admired most about Aarti: that sense she could grab hold of a moment and make a decision, just for herself. It was a beautiful balancing act of greed and generosity: an optical illusion where it seemed as if she were bending the world to her whim, when in actuality it was just heliotropism. Bhumi had learned to move with it all, bending herself out of the shadow and sending her shoots straight into the light.

33

DAWN CRACKED THROUGH the morning sky at the bus station, the light already hazy from the humidity. Jaipal's mother had been nowhere to be seen, though she had left a note in the kitchen that she was staying with her brother for the night.

The coaches filling the station were divided into those going empty to Indian towns and cities along the coast and those filling up with Indians headed to the capital, mostly husbands and sons brave enough to weather the four-hour journey along the coast.

Native-borns were ready to make money from the chaos. A few enterprising women had set up tables on the footpath near the station to sell banana cakes, soft drinks, tea, and Milo. Jaipal bought a piece of foil-wrapped banana cake and a Styrofoam cup of tea as he waited in line. Finally, he climbed into a stainless-steel bus painted with coral-pink stripes. He took a seat near the middle of the cabin, the back already filled with passengers. As soon as Jaipal sat down, another sat down next to him. His name was Shiu, and he was a cane farmer in the Caroni plain, down past the airport. They exchanged handshakes. Shiu recognized him from the shop.

"Where you gonna try?" Shiu asked.

"Canada," Jaipal sad. "You?"

"New Zealand," he said. "My wife's sister's son is there. Smart guy. Getting a master's and everything."

"Is that enough for an R-star?"

"I think so. What about you? R-one or R-star?"

"R-star, I think."

"Eh, good luck, brother, we'll see, we'll see!" he said with the air of suspicion of a man who had seen one too many promises erased.

Apparently, visas were being handed out with an efficiency never before seen. The bureaucrats who were once the vanguard of keeping these former colonials out of the white nations had now been instructed to let them in. Gone was Rakesh Travel Agency's calculus of asylum-seeking and refugee status, of which country would be best. Gone too was Rakesh—he had been seen in the line at the UK High Commission.

There were two visas: R-one and R-star. R-one visas had to stay in a refugee arrival center and could only leave when some community or religious group took enough pity on them to sponsor them. R-stars had enough cash, or family members in their country, so they could leave the refugee arrival center whenever they wanted.

Jaipal looked out the window and saw the placid waters of the Pacific lit only by indirect light, the sun still hiding behind the highlands. He had never before been to the capital, and any excitement he could have had was tempered by the fear, the anxiety, the unknown of the road as they traversed it. The route was eerily empty, with no cars going the other way. Jaipal couldn't see in front of or behind the coach to count the other coaches that made up their caravan. Inside the coach were the occasional bits of small talk, the chatter and noise to ease frayed nerves, but otherwise, it was more or less silent.

They crossed the Cevaira town line, the furthest from home Jaipal had ever gone. After they passed the town, nothing more than a few sheet-metal shacks clustered between the road and the water, something in the coach began to shift.

Jaipal heard someone clear his throat in a way that could only mean preparation for a song. What came out was an old folk ballad, one that was sung out on the fields, one that everyone had heard since they were kids, hummed on the lips of old-timers. Someone kept the beat with a shrill rap of a ring against the window, another few tapped their feet, while still others clapped their hands.

Aao! Aur katha suno!
Adham log kahte the—
(Kya? Kya?)
Yeh desh hai swarg bhu par—
Aur kya mein kahta hoon?
(Kya? Kya?)
Swarg? To kahan narak?
Ey! Pairon ke neeche!

The song had never before fit present circumstances so perfectly— *Come! Listen to my story! Evil ones said that this country is heaven on earth. And what do I say? Heaven? So where's hell? Under your feet!* They sang and they sang and they sang, and someone had brought a small bottle of Resolution Rum, and someone else had as well, and they passed around the bottles, every one of them taking a nip for strength.

It all began to make sense to Jaipal—for a fleeting second. It could have been a song sung straight from Maqbool's lips to Jaipal's ears: they had hated this country from the very beginning and only had tricked themselves into believing it could be home.

The coach couldn't pull into the central station—there were too many arriving in the city. The driver parked along the street, and from his seat, Jaipal could see the crush of people moving on the footpath.

His sister had invited him to visit four, five, six times. Every time he had said, *Sure, sometime later,* always intending to see his sister's life at the university, but something had always held him back.

Jaipal and his seatmate stood, necks craned as they waited to merge into the aisle. Shiu shook Jaipal's hand as they waited. "Where are you going first?"

"Canadian High Commission," Jaipal said.

"No passport office?"

"I already have mine."

"Lucky, lucky," Shiu said as he slung his bag onto his shoulder. "You know they're charging four times as much for passports now. These chutiyas will keep stealing from us until the day we leave. Probably after too." Shiu looked at his watch. He reached up to pat Jaipal on the shoulder. "Good luck, brother."

"Good luck," Jaipal said, pausing before he added, "brother."

Jaipal started off. He didn't know where the Canadian High Commission was, but he asked around and found a young man with a shaved head and a goatee who said he was going there, too. Everything in the city seemed to be in perpetual shadow, especially when he walked under the single building that towered above all the rest.

As he reached the hill's crest, he saw how the city opened up into a wide street near the ocean. Facing the waters were grand buildings with long driveways and lush green lawns. Flying on top of them were flags of various countries, and the long driveways were crisscrossed with concrete barriers, dotted with armed guards.

In the middle, the grandest home of them all: white colonnade and lush green lawn. From its roof flew the flag of the Empire—a flag that had featured so prominently in every schoolbook he had ever used. Further down the road, he saw the one he was looking for, one that made him laugh every time he saw it: a red maple leaf. Who had thought it a good idea to put a leaf on a flag?

The smirk on his face left as he saw the line. It stretched from the middle of the driveway all the way down the block, working its way up the hill upon which he was standing. He walked down and tapped someone on the shoulder. "Canada?"

"New Zealand."

"Canada?" he asked another.

The person simply nodded.

He stood behind him and waited. Thirty minutes later, he hadn't moved at all.

Long hours in the store had prepared him for this, but now, he could comfortably sit down. From his shoulder bag he took out a small olive-green shawl of his mother's. He placed it on the ground and sat. It seemed hotter near the ground, the asphalt radiating heat and humidity right back at him. He felt the sweat pooling underneath his arms.

Although the line didn't move, the atmosphere around him pulsed with activity. The soldiers, armed with their rifles and bulletproof vests, took every opportunity to sneer at the Indians, to yell obscenities and insults. They also kept the peace. He wished he could talk to Maqbool about what he thought the top brass had probably said: keep it orderly and win a prize.

This all should have been Maqbool's celebration. They could have found their life together, even though Jaipal knew that Maqbool's lot would have left him to slog through the R-one process. Jaipal knew Maqbool could have hustled his way to some cash wherever he ended up.

Behind him was a man, stout and short, who smelled faintly of fish. He told Jaipal he worked at the cannery on the southern coast, in the city of Siwava. He was an R-one—no family, no friends, no one he could call a relation in Canada. Jaipal wanted to know why he had chosen that country.

He shrugged. "During the war, my papa was a mechanic who worked on army cars, mainly from Amreekan army," he said, using the Hindi pronunciation for the country. "My boy tells me Kan-adah is next to Amreeka."

It felt to him so strange that simple choices—some random, others made years ago—were driving all of them to every corner of the earth.

As night fell in a cloud cover's slow transition to darkness, he had moved about a half kilometer down the road. Jaipal paid a native woman three dollars to keep his spot for a half hour. As he walked away, he wondered whether, if the woman decided to leave, the man he had been talking to would keep his spot, or whether he would ignore him, sending him to the back of the line.

He walked toward the water. The sky had clouded over, and the air felt full. The wind picked up a bit and the temperature seemed to be dropping, making it feel like rain was on the way. He bought a roti parcel from a street vendor and ventured to the footpath that ran parallel to the ocean. He leaned over the railing and ate his parcel, listening to the splash of the water hitting the retaining wall, and further out, the waves crashing against the breakers.

He wondered what it felt like to try to cross an ocean in the dead of night, the same waters upon which his grandparents and great-grandparents had traveled. His answer wouldn't be to that question, but to another: *What does the island look like from an airplane?*

He returned to the queue. It had moved a few meters since he had left.

The rain started to pitter-patter on the street. He hadn't brought an umbrella, but he felt no need for one. The cool rain against his face was a welcome change from the wet heat that had blanketed the day. After a few minutes came someone walking down the line.

"Here you go," Jaipal heard him say with a native accent, a soft, kind voice, as he moved from person to person. "I'm with the High

Commission, here you go. Yes, we're processing for another four hours, and we open again at six in the morning tomorrow."

The first thing Jaipal noticed was his legs—strong, muscular things, hips pressing against the fabric of his dress trousers. He wore a white shirt stiff with starch, no tie, shirtsleeves rolled up so he could see his forearms—oh, how Jaipal could wrap his hands around them. Even though he wore large and bulky glasses, Jaipal could see the lines of comfort emerge from the corners of his eyes, a smile that radiated through every part of his face.

He walked up to Jaipal with a small parcel—a plastic poncho. For a beat, the two stared at each other, and Jaipal knew this look well. The breath escaped from their mouths open just so, and they didn't say a word. Jaipal saw the crack of a smile emerge from the corner of his lips.

"This is for you," he said, reaching into the canvas bag that hung from his shoulder. "To help keep you dry. I know it's not much. We're trying to process applications as quickly as possible."

He held out his hand. Jaipal looked down and took the poncho. Before he did, he let his fingers slide over the top of the man's hand—no roughness, smooth, kept clean. It was Jaipal's turn to stifle a smile.

The man let out a small wink, almost indistinguishable from a blink or a raindrop caught in an eyelash. Jaipal's heart fluttered to the tap-tap of the rain on the pavement. And then came the guilt, to desire another body so soon after one had been lost to him forever. To feel a single emotion constantly and cleanly was a luxury in this world. Life here meant moving from one emotion to the next with a whiplash suddenness.

As the night passed ten, the High Commission closed its doors and the line stopped moving. Jaipal wasn't used to sleeping out-of-doors (rolled-up shirt wrapped in his poncho as a pillow, a shawl as a blanket). The night was filled with sounds—the shrieks of a bat or the cackles of a nighttime bird, coughs and snores and hacking spits and sneezes and grunts and far-off conversations from others, the rumble of traffic and trucks—and he woke what felt like every few minutes. And when he couldn't sleep, the thoughts of that fleeting attraction kept him company (the kindness of his eyes, the strength of his legs, those arms ready to receive him).

He woke by five, and by six, the line began to move again. Jaipal paid a dollar to the first barefoot native child he saw to watch his spot in line. He bought two samosas for breakfast from a Punjabi restaurant on a street away from the water. He ate them so fast, he couldn't remember what they tasted like after he swallowed. It was well after noon when Jaipal reached the end of the line and finally entered the drab government lobby.

"R-star or R-one?" the man asked with a familiar tone of voice: the same kindness now as when he had handed out the ponchos.

"R-star," Jaipal said with a confidence born from hope.

"This way," he said, placing his hand on the small of Jaipal's back as he guided him down the hallway to a room with an open door.

Inside, behind an oak desk with a large beige computer terminal, was a paunchy overworked bureaucrat, though Jaipal was surprised to see that he, like the man at the door, was native.

He asked his questions at a rapid clip: who he was applying for, whether he had identification, and finally what qualified him for an R-star. He watched as the bureaucrat held the passports and punched a few words into the keyboard. Jaipal had never seen a computer before and watched with curiosity as the man squinted at the screen, looking from the passports back to the keyboard.

"Looks fine." He handed Jaipal back the passports before he took out two sheets of paper, scribbled a few signatures, and pressed a large stamp onto an open ink pad. He quickly stamped both sheets with large thuds.

"Take this to the window in room B-seven. Someone at the desk will issue your visa."

"That's it?"

"Yes, that's it. You're lucky. When you submitted your previous application, you submitted your notarized bank statements. Sometimes, people sit in that chair for hours. I have to double-check their statements, to see if they're telling the truth. Then I have to send them back to get the proper papers from their bank. Sometimes they don't have anything, but they tell me they deserve R-star. Three hours later, I send them down the hall for an R-one interview. R-stars like yours, easy-easy," he said with a casual air. "And of course, we thank you for your donation."

Donation? Of course, the seven thousand sent to Rakesh. Even with these visas, the world still turned on bribes.

Jaipal returned back down the hallway he had come from and stood in another queue. This one moved swiftly, and soon Jaipal was called to a Plexiglas window.

He slid the passports and sheets of paper under the glass. The native-born woman, plump from middle age, took the documents and opened the passports, stamping them again and jotting a few things down before filing the signed paper into a folder.

She folded a piece of paper into one of the passports before sliding them both back to Jaipal. "You will be notified by telephone of when your charter will depart. I placed more information about the chartered flights in one of the passports. When you arrive in Vancouver, you will be taken to the processing and arrival center. R-star visas may leave the center at any time, but we recommend you stay for the orientation and welcome to Canada."

"That's it?" Jaipal said, opening the passport and seeing the stamp on the visas page. "That's everything?"

"Yes, that's it. Do you have any questions?"

Jaipal stood, dumbfounded. He had slept on the pavement, crossed the island in fear of his life, and had a rubber stamp in a booklet of paper to show for it.

"Do you have any questions?" the woman repeated.

Jaipal shook his head, and he left the room. He was done.

The man was outside. He smiled at Jaipal. "Michael," he said, holding out his hand.

"Jaipal," he replied, feeling the softness of Michael's hand as he shook it. As the two kept their hands clasped, Michael looked around for a brief moment before he leaned in. "The Five Points Hotel, seven, tonight."

In the lobby of a High Commission, marbled tile underfoot, the beams of the day's light coming through the shutters, hundreds of Indians waiting outside, he became again that version of himself that had always lived within.

Jaipal said nothing—old rules. He let out a small smile, grasping his hand a bit harder in the handshake before he let go. He walked out. He didn't look back, not even once.

HE HAD INITIALLY PLANNED ON GOING HOME AFTER THE APPOINT-ment at the High Commission, but now he had four hours to kill until seven. Without a clear idea of what to do, he started to walk, going up a hill toward a suburban area. The late afternoon sun beat against his back. In a half hour he found himself in front of the gates to the South Pacific University. They were locked shut. He peered through the bars and saw nothing on the inside save a few koels in the trees, a cane toad or two bouncing along the grass, and the empty pathways leading to buildings.

He felt an intense nostalgia for his sister: for the trill of her laugh, for the intensity of her smile, for everything about her that was lost, now to be found again. He tried to imagine her walking among crowded paths to her classes, but every time he tried to think of anything, he saw the face of the man at the High Commission, felt the flutter of the chance at someone waiting for him.

All at once came the feeling of possibility, a nervous excitement. He had never once even looked at a native man before, but had one ever looked at him? The soldiers had looked at him like the mongoose did the cane toad. Most of them in Sugar City had ignored him or seen him as part of a background, something to be ignored. Perhaps it was because everyone was leaving that the veil of quotidian hatreds finally lifted—Jaipal could see something in a native when there were no stakes left.

Maybe there was something about living in a city. Maybe there was something about being crammed together that meant that bodies could lose everything that had bound them to the petty, low things, and instead they could come together, find each other as they were meant to. Maybe that's what waited for him in London.

A military lorry rumbled in the street behind him.

Don't be stupid, Jaipal thought. This is where it all began. The General in the fucking Parliament. The man burned alive in his shop. Bhumi getting in some deep shit. The soldiers who took Maqbool, they were probably trained at the base here. Everything that was fucked came from this place.

He finally asked someone for directions to the Five Points Hotel. He had been walking in the wrong direction the whole time. He doubled back toward downtown and turned right onto the Paria Bay Road.

People—mostly natives—walked in and out of businesses, laughing, talking, like nothing at all was happening. He'd see an Indian every now and then, the same pained look of exasperation on his face. There were shops he had never seen before—Le Pain de Miel French Bakery, Tokyo Fish, Seoul Barbecue—and he felt himself making a mental tally of what kinds of stores to go to in London. Halfway down Five Points' street, he saw a strange flag in the distance, red with a white cross running through it. As he approached he saw that the flag was hanging from a pole on a small lawn in front of the Five Points Hotel.

Inside, he was amazed by the soft lighting, the dark wood panel-
ing on the walls. This hotel, so unlike the ones in Sugar City, seemed
to have been made by and for money that didn't waste its time on
beaches. Near the entrance, behind a temporary folding table, sat a
woman, short and blond. She smiled widely, as if she were Arjun expecting him at the Sunshine. "Are you here for the Danish consulate?"
she asked.

"I'm looking for the Five Points Hotel," Jaipal said.

"Right behind me," she said. "The Danish consulate has its office
here too," she added, pointing to a door next to her.

Jaipal looked at his watch and decided to linger. It had been months
since he'd had a casual conversation with a foreigner, and he enjoyed
how the dimples appeared in her cheeks when she smiled. "Where is
Danish?" he asked.

"Denmark," she said, getting up from her chair and moving out to
meet Jaipal. He let out a sheepish smile. She didn't miss a beat: "Denmark is in Europe, between Germany and Sweden, on the Baltic and
the North Sea."

None of that made any difference to Jaipal, but he nodded regardless. She seemed to have green eyes. "Is that close to London?"

"The United Kingdom is across the North Sea. I suppose you
might consider it close coming from an island where the nearest nation is a thousand miles across open ocean."

It was close enough for Jaipal. "So are you giving out visas too?"

"The Danish Refugee Council has agreed to help resettle a limited number of displaced Indians."

"Every crab finds its hole," Jaipal said with a little smile. "How
many do they have for us?"

"Approximately two hundred," she replied.

"And how many have applied?"

"Seventy-five."

"I was approved for an R-star visa for Canada today," Jaipal said.

"That's great!" she said, her dimples appearing again with her smile. "We're limiting applications to R-star candidates only."

"The chartered flights to Canada leave soon. How would I know if I had a visa approved for Denmark?"

"Do you know where in Canada you will be going?"

"Vancouver."

"We can make a note on your application that you will contact the consulate in Vancouver for your visa status after the flights begin. You would be responsible for arranging travel between Canada and Denmark. The consulate in Vancouver can help you to plan your arrival and find a sponsoring organization."

He smiled vacantly. She seemed to expect something from him, but all he wanted was to look at her, listen to her strange accent, and notice small things, like how she leaned forward onto the toes of her shoes when she wanted to make a point.

He looked at his watch. Six thirty. He smiled.

"Would you like to apply?" she asked.

"I'll think about it."

She didn't seem to mind his rejection and kept on smiling, though he could feel her eyes as he crossed the lobby and found the bar outside on the covered patio. Surprisingly, the bar was still open. Not a soul sat in the wicker chairs in the dining area, and no one was on the stools near the service area. There was a single native woman standing behind the bar, looking bored as she polished glasses with a white cloth.

"Island Bitter," he said as he sat down. "Bottle."

She slid a coaster across the glass countertop of the bar. Her nails were painted an electric blue. Jaipal, for a moment, felt in a dream, a place where the coup had never happened, where life somehow continued on as usual.

The bartender had no interest in talking to him and disappeared through a door that led back into the lobby. Outside, the sun had gone down, leaving the patio in a bluish haze before the lights went on, and in the distance, he heard the azan from a nearby masjid competing with the din of traffic.

Seven passed. Seven thirty. He took out a cigarette and began to smoke. He could think of a hundred ways Michael could have become lost to him. Maybe the High Commission had kept him for the night—he was the best one for dealing with the Indians, with his kind eyes and soft voice. Or maybe the look, the touch, the quick flirtation was meant to be simply that—something to never follow through upon, a hook-up that couldn't cross race after all. It was all the same. He wasn't here, and Jaipal had to go home.

Jaipal wasn't mad. Michael had reminded him of the thrill of seeing and being seen. It had been a couple months since the hotel had been raided, but there would always be the magic of a first touch, a heartbeat running away from his breath. He was a reminder that there would be others who wanted him as much as he wanted them.

Over the past day, he had eaten what amounted to no more than street snacks. He felt his single beer going straight to his head with a lightheaded twirl. The decision came to him quickly, not the type of act that would come to a mind well rested and sober. He had seen it less than forty-eight hours ago: the life that awaited him in Vancouver was the same fenced-in life as Sugar City. Late nights with his mother, the attention lavished on Bhumi as she found her way through the world.

He had the strength to find himself in this world. One city had shown him a possibility. What did the others offer?

He left his cash on the bar and walked through the lobby.

"You're back!" the woman said, smiling brightly again.

He had one question. "Could you tell me more about the application?"

34

BHUMI CALLED HER family for the last time a few days before they were scheduled to leave. As always, Jaipal picked up the phone.

"How do you feel?" she asked.

"There's been something on my mind ever since I went to Vilimaji," he said, sounding both excited and apprehensive to talk to her. "Everything you've done—leaving home, leaving the country—it must have been so hard. This sounds weird. I've always looked up to you. It should be the other way, but you know me. I'm not like you."

"You've always been like that, putting yourself down. We're just different."

The conversation paused for a moment. "Do you ever miss Vilimaji?" he finally asked.

"I miss my life," she said. "I miss Aarti. I don't miss a lot."

"It's really that easy to leave?"

"Easier than you think," she said, feeling again the confidence of hearing the compliments showered upon her.

"Bhumi, listen, there was something else. I don't know if it's happening, but I want you to know. Before they took Maqbool, he was going to go to London. He told me to go with him and I was going to. I wanted that chance."

Bhumi had never heard her brother talk like this. She had always assumed being with his mother was what he wanted most. The country had taken that from him.

"I can make my life somewhere, Bhumi. I can be a little like you. There was a visa option for Denmark. Maybe I'll go to London from there."

She didn't say anything in reply. She felt a strange mixture of pride and sadness—the brother who wouldn't ever come to Vilimaji was now the brother who would find a place on his own.

To Bhumi, it felt like everything was turning upon itself. They were like passengers in separate trains that, for a brief moment, ran on parallel tracks. As the trains moved side by side, they could gaze through their windows at the life of another. The tracks would eventually turn away from each other, the trains would no longer be side by side. "So it's set?" she asked.

"No, nothing is. I don't know. I need to know whether I can do this or not. Did you feel like this when you were taking the exams for SPU?"

"I was so nervous. I didn't think I was going to pass. I thought I was going to fail and be stuck in Sugar City forever."

"You never believed you could do anything, even if when you did, you did it better than anyone else."

She felt a little sting from the honesty of his assessment. "And you never tried, not because you couldn't. You thought you couldn't."

She could hear his slow, measured breaths through the call. "And now," he said, sounding hesitant, "I'm trying, Bhumi. Do you remember why we stopped going to the water?" He felt his foot tapping underneath him with excitement, with anticipation.

Bhumi couldn't remember. "We got older? You went into the store. I went to the library."

"Don't you remember? When you started at Sugar City Secondary. Ma would take you and sit you down at the table. You would read and study and she would watch you. And when I wanted to be with you, she stopped me. She told me to stop bothering you."

"I don't remember it like that," she said. She couldn't remember it at all.

"I had nothing else to do, so I spent more time at the shop, started playing more football. It wasn't much, it passed the time. Then all these years went by."

"Why are you telling me this?"

"I miss you, Bhumi. There's so much we lost because of them. Before London or Denmark or whatever, I'll see you. We have so much to talk about. We have so much to do. There's so much more. It'll just be us three now. That's it. You should talk to Ma, she's in the other room. Probably listening to me. I don't know. Be safe, Bhumi. I will see you soon."

"Be safe, Jaipal," Bhumi said. Meager words, but her wish for him was all she could give now.

"I'll see you when we're all in Canada. Here, talk to Ma."

"Ma, are you okay?"

"We're fine. God willing we'll stay that way. I'll see you soon, right?"

"How will I know when you've arrived in Canada?" Bhumi asked her mother.

"We will leave a message with this shop owner. I'm not sure if we will be able to call you when we arrive. Jaipal will find us a place to live. When will you join us?"

Bhumi was still flip-flopping through her decision. "Soon," she said, feeling the awkwardness of a lie. "The lawyer says that if I leave the United States, my status here will be revoked. I don't think I'll be able to come back for a long time. I'll leave here forever."

"Do you want to stay?" her mother asked with a weary voice.

"In some ways it's like home," Bhumi began, sidestepping the question. "People divide themselves in different ways, but they're still divided. Simple things are hard for no reason and everyone says that's how it's supposed to be. People are scared of strangers.

"It's beautiful, though. Some of them can be so open and trusting. All they want to do is help, even if they have no idea what to do.

"The government set aside land just because it's beautiful. Can you imagine? It's not far from the cities either. Next to the city is forest and open land, given to people like a gift. I'm happy to have seen it, even if it may be for a short time."

"You, you've left so many times. It's so hard to keep moving, to do what you're doing. I don't know how you do it, Bhumi."

Bhumi smiled, feeling none of that sickly feeling she had once felt during these comparisons. She felt, for the first time, how her fore-mothers' blood ran through her, how their struggle made her stronger. "I know a little bit of what Nani went through now. She was so strong. You don't think about yourself enough. I get by because I have you," she said.

"You always will," her mother replied. "Listen, I left you some-thing. Go into your suitcase. I sewed my gold jewelry into the suitcase lining. Open it. You'll find it there."

"What? Really?"

"I sewed it in there the night before you left."

"You didn't tell me?"

"I didn't want to worry you."

"How much of your jewelry?"

"All of my wedding gold. Take it with you to Canada. Or keep it in America," she added in a low voice, as if she could sense Bhumi's dithering. "The money from it is for emergencies. I gave it to you just in case. I didn't know what they were going to do here."

"You always think of everything," Bhumi said with relief. She looked at the clock. "I have to go."

"Jeeti raho, beti," her mother said.

"I'll see you soon," she replied. "Be safe in your journey. I'll be there for you when you arrive. We'll figure it all out together."

THAT NIGHT, AS RAJ AND FARIDA WERE OUT DISCUSSING THEIR asylum case with the lawyer, Bhumi opened her suitcase and tore open the lining from a carefully sewn seam near the top. If she squinted, she could see a thin thread from a new stitch. I can't believe it, she thought. She did this while I slept. They were locked in a dance that somehow worked, even though neither could decide who led and who followed. Mixed in with this wonder was a sense of annoyance: if she had been told earlier, she could have avoided nannying, avoided the panic of needing to pay back the lawyer. Then, without that need, there may have been no Vikram, no Professor Lifschitz.

Part of Bhumi feared that if she left for Canada, she would find the two of them changed to the point where the dance would be over, the next song left unsung.

Inside the suitcase lining was a lime-green paisley dupatta. Bhumi took it out and unwrapped it. Out came gleaming bangles, earrings, a nose ring, a maang tikka, and a kamarband, as well as silver anklets and toe rings. Each of the gold pieces was at least twenty-two karat and still gleamed with newness, catching the dull light of her room and reflecting it back with the shine of the setting sun.

How had this not been caught by the officials at the airport? Bhumi asked herself. Had they seen it and ignored it? Had they missed it? Had they looked through the suitcase and found nothing?

She picked up each piece and let it fall through her hands, feeling all at once the filigree, the ornamentation, the memories locked into them from her mother's marriage to a man now dead. It terrified her to think that she had been carrying something so valuable without knowing it.

Bhumi thought it improper to put the gold back into the torn lining of her suitcase. She looked around for something to store it in and saw her small rosewood box with the cane root, still in the suitcase.

She took a moment to run her fingers over the smooth red velvet that lined its interior. She tried to fit the jewelry, the root, and the drawing in the box, but it would not latch. It was only when she took out the root that the jewelry fit.

Even in its little plastic bag, the root began to crumble into dust.

"I don't care for history," Aarti had once said, her voice dancing through her pronouncement. "Just show me something else. Let me build something new." They had been talking about which elective to take during their third year, the year that never came to pass. The memory brought tears to her eyes. Of course Aarti would say something like that, with her flair for the dramatic. She hadn't thought much about what her friend had meant then.

The past had reared its head in a moment of danger—a history of empire, land, labor, mutual distrust, and hatred. Bhumi had wanted nothing to do with this gnarled mess. Her grandmother had left, cutting through fear and the possibility of death, to find refuge in a place so far from home. And her daughter, raised with the idea of departure as a birthright, passed to her own daughter the strength to know when to cut away men and their shackles, and also to know when to invite them near. The ghosts of generations gone were to be found in her solid presence, blood that didn't return to one heart, but instead pulsed between bodies both here and gone, back and forth, never beginning, never ending.

She owed Vikram an answer. She would tell him soon. First, there was one last piece of the past to deal with. The sky darkened, and a late-winter's rain began to tap on her window like a forlorn lover. She could hear steps in the apartment above her, the floorboards creaking out a tired sigh from the weight of others.

Quietly, as if she did not want to wake the resting spirits within her, she stood, holding the drawing and root in her left hand. She walked out of the apartment into the rain. She was wearing home clothes—an old T-shirt over a new pair of red plaid cotton pajama pants—and the chill from the cold rain caused her to shiver. She walked barefoot from the door to a small patch of grass between the apartment complex's walkway and parking lot, the only green near the building.

The grass yielded underfoot like a wet sponge and between her toes she could feel the slimy mud. She opened the bag and turned it over, watching the root fall like a feather until it lay like a dead thing upon wet grass. She ripped the drawing in two, then in four, and onward until she held the past like confetti, which she let slide from her hands until it covered the grass like snow, the drumbeat of rain already sinking the pieces into the mud.

The future was hers now. She knew what she was going to tell him. She turned around, her shirt and pants and hair wet from the incessant drumming of the rain, and walked back through the open door into her apartment, where the warmth of the heater's air grabbed her like a hug and settled the last of her lonely shivers.

35

THOSE WHO LEFT first salted their fields; set fire to their shops and homes; poured sugar water into the gasoline tanks of their buses, taxis, and personal vehicles; and left an inheritance of bedlam for those waiting to usurp. The prize would be tarnished and cracked upon receipt.

The military did not take kindly to this wave of destruction. To make an example, they caught two cane farmers ruining their farms and summarily shot them on the spot. Everything was finally balancing again: there were no more disappearances or helicopters over the ocean. Every life ended in a body.

Jaipal shuddered as he imagined the farmers singing the songs of girmit on the coach to Vilimaji, sleeping as he had on the streets as they awaited their visa paperwork. Now there were two R-one visas for New Zealand that would never be used.

From then on, acts of resistance became sly and hidden. Some would punch holes in their walls and drop dead fish into the voids. Others would fill their cupboards with dog excrement or pour bottles of bleach across teak tables and linen curtains. No one would be able to take something left whole.

They were leaving, and yet there was nothing to do. The information given to Jaipal from the High Commission said that they were limited to one suitcase and one small bag each. All they had room for was clothes, a few trinkets, nothing more.

And then, the wait. The weather had turned damp and sticky, stiflingly hot, as if there were steam rising from the earth, condensing on his skin as sweat the moment he walked out of the house. It had been unseasonably dry lately. It was fitting weather. Everything felt like expectation, like humidity waiting to break with a lick of lightning and a resounding clap of thunder.

Every time he walked outside, he remembered that late winter awaited him on the other side. The information said to pack sweaters and scarves, that the temperature was much colder than anything here. It baffled him to think that when he boarded that plane, he would leave behind both country and season.

Closer to the end came the time to close up the shop. The instructions from the General to all shop owners were easy: leave the front door unlocked. He rolled up the shutters one last time. When he walked in, the place smelled faintly like an onion had gone off in some forgotten corner. He stopped himself from going to find it. It wasn't his problem anymore.

A feeling, like a small bomb, went off inside of him. He wished he could burn the place to the ground, destroy every last shelf, take the ashes, throw them into the sea. How much time he had wasted in this store; how many times had his father berated and beaten him! He felt himself on the verge of crying. Instead, he simply walked out the door.

"IT'S TIME TO GO," HE TOLD HIS MOTHER. SHE HAD PREPARED TWO BOWLS of yogurt and jaggery for them. She took hers to eat on the balcony.

Where was his safe place in this house? If he could have taken the bowl and somehow folded himself up into his own mind, he would have eaten it there.

He walked from room to room. Everything remained in its right place. He had tried to channel Maqbool and sell some of their possessions, but there was no market for used furniture. All of the kaamchor knew it would be free for the taking the moment a family left a home behind.

He finished the bowl, imagining himself throwing it against the wall in his room, a white splotch on the poster of the 1982 football team, a splatter of yogurt across brown faces. He took the bowl to the sink in the kitchen and filled it with water. Whoever entered the house could clean it, could take it as their own.

There was a feeling in his chest, as if his heart were hardening into a stone, pushing up against his ribs. He began to walk from room to room to room. In his own, a final glance at every poster on his wall, a room that had never made the transition away from the life of a child. And then to his sister's room, bare and empty, all that which had once been important taken to new places. His parents' room, where no one had slept since his father died. His mother had slept on the sofa in the sitting room or spent some nights with her siblings, most of whom were headed to Australia or New Zealand as R-ones.

None of this was his anymore: no one to forget him, no one to make him feel smaller than the dust that would soon coat the house.

His mother was waiting for him by the gate now. She had taken the small bags, he would take the large. He walked to the front door and ran his hand along its wood.

"Lock the door," she said. "Take the key." She was crying. Every tear said, *This is ours, this will never again be for us, but it's ours, lock the door, only we can open it again.*

When the bolt slipped into the lock one last time, the sound was deafening.

They left the Minor in the driveway. He had let the air out of the tires the night before—his only act of defiance. The Canadian High Commission knew which families were leaving and on which days. As a gift, they had sent a lorry to pick them up. They sat in the open-air back like cane being taken to the refinery.

They meandered through the back roads of the city, a goodbye tour of all the little houses and some of the tin-shack shanties, until the lorry was about half full. It was completely empty of all human sound. No one, not even the children, had anything to say on that ride from the city to the airport. Only the rumble of the engine competed with the whooshing of air as they picked up speed.

The sky was filled with big, dark clouds, a sheet looking to suffocate the earth below. It was still hot and humid, but the air ruffled his hair as a cooling breeze when they drove down the road to the airport. A sad and nostalgic smile came to him as they passed the hotels. Maqbool would have been proud if he could see him. The money was the first step. All the others were his to take.

A few drops of rain began to fall on his head.

Soon, they reached the tarmac and the Air Canada 747 was ready to take their bags. Everyone was wet, yelling. *Bags here! Get in! Come on!* The airplane drowned them all out: its idling engine grumbled with the wind and the rain.

It was all going so fast now. He couldn't hear anything over the din of the moment, and the rain began to stream down from his hair into his eyes.

He placed their bags near the back of the airplane, where all the other bags were sitting, leather splotched with dark spots from the water. His mother was waiting for him at the base of the stairs that would take them up into the cabin. He joined her, letting her go up first.

It was truly like a big coach. He took a seat next to a window and looked outside as the rain streaked against the pane. He watched the workers throw their bags into the hold without care or concern for what was inside.

The door closed and he learned how to buckle his seat belt, what to do if it all came crashing down. Soon, the engine began to really roar. They gained speed, faster faster faster, faster still. And then, a moment of lightness. They were leaving the earth. His eyes widened.

She had asked him, and he had asked Maqbool: *What does the island look like from an airplane?*

The rock kissed the water. The answer was all around him.